A Son of War

A Son of War

MELVYN BRAGG

SCEPTRE

First published in 2001 by Hodder and Stoughton
A division of Hodder Headline
A Sceptre book

A CIP catalogue record for this title is available from the British Library.

ISBN 0 340 81865 4
ISBN 0 340 73415 9

Typeset by Hewer Text Ltd, Edinburgh
Printed and bound by Clays Ltd, St Ives plc

Hodder and Stoughton
A division of Hodder Headline
338 Euston Road
London NW1 3BH

To Marie-Elsa, Alice and Tom with love.

—⌇—

PART ONE
WINTERING: 1947

—⌇—

CHAPTER ONE

'You can hit as hard as you like and it won't hurt.' Sam whispered the rehearsal as he laid out the big boxing gloves like a bouquet on the table. The words would be addressed to his son but they were aimed at his wife.

The training gloves, blood red, almost new, glistening in the weak white gas-light of late winter afternoon, were nuzzled close, the four knuckle to puffy knuckle, as if waiting for the bell.

Sam stood back to admire them. Nothing in the room compared. Even the thickly berried holly, which Ellen had refused to take down on Twelfth Night with the other decorations, was eclipsed. The berries might be 'red as any blood' but the boxing gloves were redder and bloodier and spoke for a power beyond the holly, as Sam knew. He stoked the fire and settled the kettle on it, took the *News Chronicle* and lit a dog end. But he could not keep his eyes off the snuggling of the large glistening gloves, almost alive as the faintly hissing light played over them; reminded him of new pups. He hummed as he waited – 'Give me five minutes more'. He wanted to extend the time for himself alone with this magnificent present. 'Only five minutes more in your arms'. Blackie air-lifted into his lap so lightly it was almost an embrace, and when Sam stroked her under the chin she purred to match the quiet murmur of the kettle. Sounds full of peace: he felt his mind untense in this quietness that screened no threats.

Joe crashed in first, his face rose-glazed from the raw weather. To Sam's delight he noticed the gloves instantly, a glance of disbelief at his father, and sprang on them. By the time Ellen had taken off her scarf, put down the shopping basket, slipped off her coat and focused, the cavernous gloves were on Joe's seven-year-old paws. He stood there, not much higher than the table, the gloves like gaudy footballs fantastically stuck on the cuffs of his navy blue mac.

'How are you going to get your coat off?'

Joe grinned at his mother and shook his hands. Despite the laces tightly pulled, the gloves dropped to the floor. He unbuttoned, unbelted, flung off his coat in seconds and went down on his knees to cram his hands once more into the hugely padded marvels, which he could not believe were to be his.

'You can hit as hard as you like but it won't hurt – not with those.'

'Ding ding. Seconds out!' said Joe, as he took swipes at an imaginary opponent, taking care to clutch hard to the glove on the inside so that it did not fly off.

'I thought boxers were meant to hurt each other,' Ellen replied.

'Special training gloves. Look at the size of them! From Belgium.'

Sam seemed transfixed by Joe's childish flailing. He wanted to kneel down and coach him but first there was Ellen.

'It'll help him learn to look after himself without causing damage.'

'You're the one who wants those gloves, Samuel Richardson.'

He looked at her directly and her laughter set off his own. Her eyes were lustrous in the light of the small room. He could see that she was taking him on.

'Charlie Turnbull,' he confessed, and held up a hand to ward off the flak.

'When was Charlie Turnbull in Belgium or anywhere else? He was always up to no good.'

'There's nothing on the fiddle.'

Ellen shook her head but held off. The unusual high humour between Sam and Joe was too good to spoil. She picked up the two remaining gloves from the table, pretending to be alarmed by Joe's self-absorbed punching the air. She pressed them gently to her cheeks.

'They are soft,' she conceded. 'I like the smell . . .' She inhaled deeply, her eyes closing.

Sam stirred towards her and then checked himself. 'I buffed them up.'

She opened her eyes and held out the gloves, two succulent globes pressed together, stretching the shiny leather tight. She offered them to him. 'Put them on,' she said, and smiled down at Joe. 'You can't wait, can you?'

'Come on then, Joe.' He knelt down.

The boy sailed in and Sam let the pneumatic blows rain on him. Then he pushed his son away.

'Joe Louis wouldn't do that,' he said. 'Straight left then make a move. Remember?'

The boy skipped around a father in rare indulgent mood.

'One-two,' said Sam. 'This is a one-two.'

Ellen caught his eye deliberately and held it for a message. Fair enough, the look said, but you will not have it all your own way. He winked. And she laughed but maybe because Joe had used the unguarded moment to land a blow directly on Sam's nose.

'Hey-up!' He rubbed his nose with the fat cigar thumb of the glove.

'What was it?' Ellen said, as she swung the kettle off the hob. 'You can hit as hard as you like but it doesn't hurt?'

Sam smiled and Ellen was moved by the intimacy such a simple reaction could reveal. Then his attention switched. 'I've got a real little warrior on my hands.'

Joe felt himself swell with giddy confidence. 'Come on, Daddy,' he said, squaring up. 'Fight me.'

Ellen wanted to calm his all but feverish excitement, but that would douse feelings she saw surging so warmly between the two who had often clashed since Sam's return. Now Sam was smiling approval. Joe was almost dancing, fists raised, suddenly and blissfully – with the gloves on – unafraid of his father.

'Fight me now.'

She put a small piece of holly on the fire and listened. The flames leaped at it but she judged that the sound would not disturb Sam who lay in the bed a few feet away, spreadeagled in early sleep for the six o'clock shift at the factory. She had checked upstairs and stood over Joe, his head nesting on the great gloves, his small face above the blanket, pale in the pillowed red plush frame. He too was sound.

Sam's present had got to the heart of something deep in their son, she thought. It pleased her that there should be that under-standing and firmly she pushed back the shadow that threatened to spoil it. For the six years of the war Joe had been hers alone: she had to let Sam find his place now. A boy needs a father, she said to herself sternly, as she had repeated endlessly since that almost miraculous moment when Sam had jumped from the train that would have taken him alone on the first leg of his passage to Australia and come back along the platform, hand in hand with Joe, come back to her. To her. Even now, after a few months, the memory of it made her hold her breath.

She had not fully absorbed it. It was like a present, almost too good to open and, when opened, too good to use. It was a second chance and better for it. They had just made love in something of the old way, though the necessary silence constrained them with Joe just above them – sleeping?

She missed the pliable umbilical presence of the child who had slept with her into boyhood. And although Sam had subdued his son's cries to retain the shared bed he had enjoyed until the return of the father he had been schooled to love, Ellen knew that Joe's longing was scarcely abated, that the severance was a wound. She observed the boy struggle with the burden of expected love for the stranger who had come back to redeem his fatherless condition. She saw the bewilderment, the hurt, the anger that this father to whom he must kow-tow and wanted to, must love and wanted to, be grateful to and was, should displace him so conclusively, overrule, oust him.

Awake as the father and son slept, feeding the fire with the richly ruby-berried holly, which she had found in an overgrown lane less than two miles out of the town, Ellen let herself drowse. The fire burned, lightly, on her face and as she leaned forward her loosened hair swung down, swaying sensuously, an indulgence secretly cultivated – swaying languorously as she moved her head to the rhythm of the song she hummed low, like a lullaby. She could picture the small town all about her in the cold bleak January dark, its yards, alleys, runnels, streets, people, all so familiar she could sketch them in her mind without effort, all ready to be conjured out of the midwinter blackness, swaddling her in this cradle of her life. The town was her captive dream. It was so comfortingly easy for her to call it up but she

7

resisted that temptation, as she had fended off the shadow provoked by Sam's fighting gift of the gloves.

Sam and Joe. She let their names surf on 'The Bells of St Mary's', which surged gently through her mind. Joe and Sam. Ebb and flow. Her face now glowed from the fire thrown up by the holly and glowed too from the scent on her, the recent weight of his body on hers, the nearness of that complete loss in pleasure. The leaf, the berry and the thorn. Aware of herself alone. And Sam. And the sight of Joe – his face in that halter of bulging red leather, his copper hair outshone, splayed on his back in perfect sleep.

Ellen frowned at the realisation that this luck was so little appreciated by her. What was here was world enough. Their one-up, one-down house absorbed all the town and fields and land and country around it. The place was in her and the three of them were safe.

She hugged herself as the last of the holly fed the dying fire, hugged herself tightly, digging her fingers into her shoulder-blades, holding it in.

CHAPTER TWO

The girl stopped him in his tracks. Joe had hurried through the narrow alley, but found the lavatory occupied. There was a growl from Kettler, who would often settle in there for the duration. Joe clenched his buttocks against the pressure that had finally forced him out of his besotted immersion in the latest Water Street kickabout, and decided to go into the house where in an emergency there was a potty. A risk. He might be kept in. He wanted straight back to the football in the softening twilight of the cold day when strained breath came out visibly and the dusk changed and charmed the game. But there she stood, in front of the house she had just moved into, and she stopped him in his tracks. She might have fallen down from the moon.

Her hair was black, short, a pudding-basin cut. Despite the weather she wore no coat but the bottle-green cardigan came below her waist and the black pleated skirt was like a frill below its severity. Her socks were also green, her pretty brass-studded clogs bright red. Joe took that in and much more that he could not consciously map or describe: the incitement about her eyes; the wraith wisp of a smile on the serious round face; the exciting angle of the body as she leaned back against the window-sill; just the fact, the presence of her there, near, now, waiting. He had to speak but there was a strong sweet nausea in his stomach that made him nervous about opening his mouth. His legs weakened with a watery sensation and he clenched hard to avert another accident. His throat thickened.

'I'm next door,' she said.

Joe nodded and experienced a waterfall of gratitude for this good fortune. He wanted to yell but could not even whisper.

'Are you seven?'

Joe nodded again.

'Mam said you would be. I'm just six.'

'That's my cat.'

He smiled at the triumph of speech. Blackie allowed herself to be picked up and handed over. The miraculous girl dived her face into the thick glossiness and murmured baby sounds.

'You can hold her any time you want.'

She did not respond. In the fading light there was no seam between the girl's jet hair and the black fur.

'You can keep her all night if you want to.'

Joe's recklessness came without a qualm. Still she ignored him. She imitated the purring.

Kettler came out of the lavatory at a drunken stagger and tacked towards his hovel without a glance at the children. Joe felt the pain of the pressure in his bum but he endured it. Besides, he hated going in after Kettler for the stink and the mess. He always asked his mammy to clean it up first. But it was hard not to go. The pain tightened – a strange pain that had some pleasure in it. That confused sensation mingled with this new pressure of the girl.

He had to go. Yet how could he leave her? She might disappear.

'Mam won't have cats,' she said.

Tenderly she placed Blackie on the ground.

'Can you do this?'

Mary turned to the house, took a step or so back, a skip forward, dipped onto her hands and swung her legs up against the wall, swung them it seemed to the mesmerised Joe through the most perfect arc, the legs lazily tracking each other into the air, and with a grace that winded him. He stared at the two small shiny red clogs neatly nailed on the grimy brick and saw the bare legs with the skirt now dangling towards the ground.

A year or so before, before the move to Water Street, when he had been a full member of the Market Hill gang, the rather older Harrison girls, twins, who led it, had sometimes teased the boys by being bad. Joe had been left frustrated and pining for days after these rare encounters with the incomprehensible. Now he had the same hot feeling of wanting to do something urgently but what it was he did not know.

The Harrison girls had also done handstands against a wall. But they had tucked their skirts into their knickers.

That brief snap of memory was frazzled by this posed, erect figure, polished red clogs gleaming side by side, bare legs, green knickers, the skirt all but covering her upside-down face. And she stayed like that. For more than a second or two. Joe was helpless, dizzy with awe. It was beyond him yet it possessed him.

He could hold it no longer. Unmistakable. The hot clart of it on his cold thigh. Yet still he stood there. Then she reversed the action and the feet nudged lightly against the wall, the legs swung down, just as gracefully, and she stood and turned and smiled at him and saw her applause in his face.

He nodded and swallowed the saliva that had gathered in the well of his mouth. He had to take on trust that she would not vanish from the earth as he hobbled as fast as he could to the messy stinkhole just vacated by boozy Kettler to try to sort out his own mess.

How could he get her to do that handstand against the wall again?

—⟨⟨⟩⟩—

Speed was a hero and sometimes a friend. His advantage in age was almost three full years. One of Joe's multitude of ambitions was to be as old as Speed, to be ten, to be as brave as Speed, to be as bad and as dangerous as Speed. To have Speed in him. He envied his slight squint and tried to copy it.

Speed ate scrunts. He even ate the stalks. He chewed candlewax for gum. Speed drove cattle down Water Street and New Street to the pens at the station. Speed smoked dog ends when he found them in his scourings of the gutter. Most grown-ups shouted at him and Speed shouted back and then ran. Speed led the Water Street younger gang in stone fights and raids on other streets. He would go to the tip and always come back with something good that just needed holding under the tap. Speed swore and then crossed himself. Nobody, said Speed, was better than the Pope. Speed's daddy was in hospital because of the war but if anybody referred to it Speed hit them. Some days, market days, he just did not go to school. Speed boasted that his big brother Alistair would be lucky not to go to Borstal before he got called up. Joe's daddy called Speed 'a little warrior' and always seemed to be smiling at him. Speed said things to Sam that Joe would never dare.

'Put them on.'

Speed was reluctant. The gloves looked too expensive. But Mr Richardson was an idol outpointed only by his brother Alistair. He pulled on the glossy gloves and felt his fist disappear as Sam tugged the laces tight across his thin wrist.

'Now remember you're bigger, and remember you're older.'

Speed nodded. The gloves were unwieldy and unnecessary. His fist felt imprisoned.

'Just some gentle sparring,' said Sam. 'OK?' He looked over to Joe who was experiencing an unexpected sense of calm. Perhaps because Sam had just sprung this on them and he had had no time to work up a funk. And he could see that Speed was uncomfortable in the gloves. And Sam was there.

'Seconds out. Ding!'

The boys came towards each other cautiously, Joe adopting some semblance of the classic English stance – left foot forward, head tucked behind his right glove, left glove feinting for an opening. Speed was hopeless. In a fight he just flailed away until it was over. He could not play at it.

Joe saw that Mary had come out into the yard. She leaned against the window-ledge as she had the other day. Joe danced, just a touch, on the balls of his feet and waved his left glove more emphatically. He tried a punch. Speed let it land on his shoulder. Joe glanced at Mary and shot out a straight left.

'Good lad!'

Joe burrowed his head further into the protecting right glove and found that he was advancing. Speed was waving his arms, almost as if he were trying to shake off the bulbous impediments. Joe jabbed out the left once or twice, did not connect, looked good. Mary had not moved.

Speed swung his left hand in a looping swipe that landed on Joe's glove and rocked him. But instead of alarm, he felt fired up. He could tell that Speed was not going to hurt him. He had seen it in the pleading look his hero had cast to Sam.

Joe skipped a little more then flung his right hand forward. Speed caught it between his two gloves, as if it were a ball, and when Joe tried to free it, his hand slipped out and Speed stood there holding the empty glove like a trophy.

'First time I've seen that!' Sam laughed and Joe hoped it was not he who was being laughed at.

'Can I stop now, Mr Richardson?' said Speed.

'You're hardly warmed up.'

'But I don't want to fight him, Mr Richardson.'

Joe was much relieved. The stoppage had jolted him into the realisation that he was pushing his luck. But, for Mary's sake, he tried to look keen.

'This is boxing,' said Sam.

Speed shook his head. You had a fight because you meant it. You could mean it so badly that you thought you wanted to murder somebody. Sometimes it was hard to stop when it was over. This with the gloves was just no good.

'He can hit me and I won't hit back.'

Joe gave a little jig to show willing.

Sam ruffled Speed's cropped hair. 'You're a real 'un,' he said, and unlaced the boy's gloves. Joe looked on carefully. He remembered Speed saying, 'I wish thy father was my father,' and it had made him proud.

Liberated, Speed muttered a lie of excuse and fled.

'You'll have to make do with me again,' said Sam, and he coaxed and coached Joe for a respectable ten minutes before taking the gloves into the house.

At last Joe could go across to Mary. He had a light sweat, a sheen against the cold, and it gave him a swagger.

'Bella wants to see Blackie,' said Mary.

Bella had not been seen since before Christmas, much to Joe's relief. The big over-clumsy girl whom Kettler scorned as 'backward' and 'mental' had ceased to worry him after he had come into possession of the kitten Blackie. Bella was besotted by Blackie and a promise that she could hold her never failed to check the mauling play with which she had unsettled the much smaller Joe. He was still nervous of her.

'Mammy says she's very badly.' Joe lowered his voice, as his mother did when she spoke of illness. She had referred to it in oblique and embarrassed snatches so that Joe came to the conclusion that Bella was a leper – he had heard a forceful sermon on lepers – and if he so much as touched her or let her breathe at him he would be covered in boils and sores and die.

Part of Ellen's reluctance to tell the boy the truth – aside from her ineradicable conviction that a host of adult truths, especially on personal matters, were not to be shared with or imposed on children – was that she feared she would reveal her anger.

It was criminal, Ellen thought, and said as much to Sam, that Bella's mother Madge should insist that she house and nurse her sister riddled with TB when everyone with any sense knew that the disease fed on such intense crowding in a small damp space. She had read the doctor in the *Cumberland News* who was agitated that so many people turned their back on the obvious ways of alleviating the current Wigton rampage of tuberculosis. But Madge did not take the *Cumberland News* and Ellen could not engineer a discussion without giving offence.

Influenced by the social rigidities of a childhood with an aspiring aunt, Ellen had no truck with unannounced neighbourliness. You were friendly but not familiar, not dropping in without knocking, not sticking your nose into private business, not giving advice unasked for. But it said clearly in the paper that the sanatorium only ten miles away was prepared to take patients and there would be no charge. Ellen had seen the doctor visit the stricken house next door and surely he would have made the point. But what if he had overlooked it? Or if Madge had been too fussed to take it in? Or had misunderstood it? There was no mistaking what was written in the paper.

Even so she would have held back but the sound of suppressed coughing which reached through the thin wall in the night – suppressed, she felt, because Madge's sister and Bella did not want to intrude with their illness – disturbed Ellen and challenged her neutrality. What if Madge did take the hump, what if she flew up, what did that matter besides something being done for that poor wasted sister and for Bella, so docile in her obedience to a mother confining her in a room of death? Finally Ellen could bear the struggle no longer. She scissored out the relevant newspaper report and pushed it through the letterbox.

Madge knew where it had come from. She said nothing. Relations cooled. Ellen's usual offers of 'doing some shopping while she was upstreet anyway' were frozen out. Bella was banned from playing with Blackie. Greetings were not returned. Ellen felt crushed.

Mary, with the clean passport of the newcomer and the apparent reliability of childhood, had already been allowed to play with Bella. Despite Joe's efforts to distance himself from the worrying attentions of Bella, he was a little put out that Mary already was such a friend as to be a messenger.

He went to find Blackie.

'Mammy says I can't go in Bella's house.'

It had taken Ellen some effort to give him that instruction. She did not want him to be rebuffed by an offended Madge Hartley, that was true. But the greater truth, and one which in the driven fairness of her spirit she felt ashamed of, was that she feared that Joe might pick up TB. She reasoned that a few minutes would be neither here nor there but the image of that condemned room infested by coughed-up infection was too much for her. Poor sad Bella. Ellen felt that she was walking by on the other side.

Joe handed Blackie over to Mary.

As usual, she battened her face into the long fur and Joe stood by respectfully while she breathed her fill.

Bella's face appeared at the window. Joe had spotted her a few times over the weeks but given her no more than the briefest nod as he sped about his business. Now he looked a little more carefully and even he saw a difference. She was not the same, he reported to Ellen, out of which she had to draw that Bella was paler, thinner, altogether subdued. But there she was at the window, her eyes full of hope.

Joe waved, properly. He pointed, indicating the cat she could not touch. She remained all but motionless, afraid that any movement would trigger a summons from her mother to leave the window.

When Mary came up for air, he indicated Bella's presence and they went and stood in front of the window. As soon as she saw Blackie, Bella's eyes shone, a smile came to her large sickly face, softening and sweetening it. She gazed intently on the object of her adoration, gazed as if she were feeding on it, feeding deeply and urgently to store it up for revisiting in barren hours.

Joe picked up a touch of her passion, remembering it from the past, and he took the cat from Mary and brought it closer to the glass, and closer still until its fur rubbed against the pane. Now Bella did move. She leaned towards it as if, for a moment, believing she might be able to hold it, the transparent barrier between them melt away. Joe saw into the room. Mrs Hartley's sister lying on the bed. Mrs Hartley herself at the sink until Bella's excitement alerted her and she turned and called the girl off and, with such reluctance, Bella slowly pulled away and stepped back and bit her lower lip.

—⟋⟋⟍—

'He's still in the army,' said Ellen, of their new neighbour, 'in Germany. As soon as he gets a house they're off to join him.'

Sam smiled at her. He was nursing his second cup of tea. He liked the two-to-ten shift, giving him the long mornings and this quiet intimacy deep into the night. It was the best time to be easy with each other.

'Joe told me,' Ellen said. 'He seems to have got it out of that Mary.'

'She's a quaint little article, isn't she? Old-fashioned. They're real country people. Down from the hills. Innocent people.'

Ellen did not reply.

'She seems to have latched on to Joe,' he went on. 'Poor lad! She won't let him alone.'

Again Ellen held her tongue. It was perfectly obvious that it was Joe who was the infatuated one. Disturbingly so, Ellen thought.

'He loves those boxing gloves.' Sam smiled again. He was tickled pink that the present had been received with such rapture. Even the painted wooden train he had brought back from Burma had not met with such a reaction. 'And it'll do him no harm, you know.'

Ellen knew that she was being challenged to answer and she rose to it, knowing that silence would indicate disapproval. 'He would wear them to school if he could.'

'He would! I went up last night and he had a pair of them on. Fast asleep!'

Ellen enjoyed Sam's pleasure. It was a short moment and a small matter perhaps but it was at times like these that she could sense that he was beginning to find a way out of the war, which still shot through his mind in nightmare and anger.

'So you'll pop in and tell Leonard about the house in the morning?'

'Yes.' She hoped it sounded casual.

Ellen had given up her ambition to move into the large run-down romantic town house, a house she had dreamed of having. In fairness, she conceded, Sam was right about the amount that needed doing to it, the cost, the debt that would be around their necks, the decorating and heating and furnishing of such a place. In that scheme of things her own longing to be fortressed in the centre of the small town she loved so much had to be weighed carefully. She gave in partly because she believed she owed him a debt for not leaving them behind, not striking off alone to Australia.

'I think I got a bit carried away,' she said, to reassure him because she knew he did not like to see her disappointed. 'Even though the council owns it now. It would have been too posh for us.' Saying it aloud helped her to believe it.

'And you really want our names down for a new council house?'

'Oh, yes.'

Sam picked up the urgency in those two syllables. She wanted out. He knew how hemmed in she often felt in this tiny one-up, one-down, the small yard, the shared tap, the lavatory she had to clean, daily, the feeling of being immured. To him, it was a perfectly acceptable first nest in a married life. There was scarcely any damp. It was a warm little place.

'Council houses are nice and new,' she said, loyally.

He finished his tea and shovelled a few more lumps of coal on to the fire. Almost midnight and all was well. Ellen began to get undressed.

'I'll let you warm the bed up,' he said.

'When do you imagine they might be going to Germany?' she asked. 'Next door.'

'A month. Two? I'll just pop upstairs and see him.'

'It's those gloves you want to see,' said Ellen.

'They can't hurt. Take my word.'

He took the torch and, in stockinged feet, stepped silently up the twisting little staircase.

Ellen was drawn to the window by a line of light that had appeared in the crack between the curtains. She looked out. The sky had cleared. By stooping down and craning her neck she could see the moon, full, gleaming, fixed. The small well of the yard was so light you could have read a book. The moonlight lent quaintness to the crush of damp hovels. Ellen imagined the town asleep under the moon, and the country around, from the sea to the mountains, basking in its radiance.

She could see only one star, and although she knew there would be others, it was still legitimate, just about, to make a wish. As a girl, after the death of her mother, her uncle Leonard had tried to nurse her grief by telling her that her mother had turned into a star and she had gazed at the night sky earnestly again and again, hoping somehow to identify her mother's star. A single star brought out a wish that her mother was happy. Later, as a young woman, she had found, with some distress, that she began to wish to see the father who had left them so soon after her birth. A father about whom to this day she had been told so little.

This night, she wished that Sam would find himself. There were good days here and there but he was still too often out of her reach. The war, years of growing apart, early intimacy ruptured, so much between them that was not to do with the two of them together. Perhaps Joe would help.

She remembered, ruefully, what her uncle Leonard had said when Sam turned back from emigrating to Australia: 'I would have put a bet on it,' he said. 'He could never leave the boy.'

CHAPTER THREE

The letter came with the second post just before the afternoon shift. Even though it was air-mail it felt like a wad. Sam put it in his kitbag. He visualised it there many times throughout the shifts which seemed to drag on. Back home there was supper and talk with Ellen. He saw it through as patiently as he could but Ellen needed no signposting and they opened up the sofa-bed earlier than usual. Only then did he mention that he had received a letter and would stay up for a while to read it. 'From Alex,' he said. Proudly, Ellen thought and felt a brush of unease as she watched Sam dip into the kitbag and bring out the letter with an expression that reminded her of Joe hoping he had struck gold at the lucky dip.

This first letter from Alex, the educated, the schoolteacher, who had yet been one of the private soldiers under Corporal Richardson in Burma, ought to be welcomed. Sam had told her enough for her to appreciate that it was Alex who had unlocked Sam's paralysis, literally pushed him off the train, denied himself the companion to Australia, yet the letter unsettled her.

She undressed rapidly, pulled on her nightdress, took the *Woman's Illustrated* and whipped into the cold sofa-bed, propped up on an elbow, facing the space Sam would occupy soon.

He read the back. 'Alex Metcalfe. Bradfield Park. Sydney. Australia.' So he had taken to 'Alex' in public: it had always been Alexander. Selecting the smaller blade in his pocket knife, he slit the blue paper.

Dear Sam,

Here in the Boondocks, a man could go round the bend like poor old Jackie. So please excuse the scrawl and if I'm just droning on you can always skip. I'm trying to keep cool in a dusty corrugated-iron hut on stilts out here on the edge of the Bush with the sun melting the tarmac and a pack of wild Irish kids outside playing hell or some other game. And you can soon lose your affection for screeching cockatoos. I've just re-read this. I'm in a foul temper. I'll stop.

Later

It's cooler now and so am I! Coming to Australia and not being able to cope with the heat is rather bad planning. Don't you agree?

Sam could hear Alex asking that question. He had loved the feeling of engagement in his mind when Alex rather daintily flicked his cigarette, looked into the mid-distance and began to talk in a way that Sam ached to learn.

In the north of England we rush out and worship each measly ray of sunshine as if, secretly, we were Aztecs. It's always seemed to me that civilisations which worshipped the sun were eminently sensible, even though it provoked them to barbarities. But we in the sunless north of Europe could hand out lessons in barbarities, couldn't we? In Wigton, the sun was

24

rarer than a miracle – bound to happen once or twice a year, but no one knew when. No respecter of bank holidays or school holidays or even summer. Here the sun just pours down every day. It glazes the sky. On my way to the train I see men in white singlets working on their own houses and they are so tanned that the skin has a purple sheen on it. It's like Josie's chip shop out here: 'Frying Tonight'. Perhaps it will warm through our rather cold manner.

Something has to. They don't like the Poms here. Even Poms of a few years' residence seem to feel free to despise new Poms. You have to stand up to it. I suppose they see us as imperialists and colonists, which is quite funny considering that almost everyone on the ship out here was one of those who have every right to consider themselves ground under the heel of the ruling imperialists back in England. Imperialism is first learned at home – don't you agree?

Sam put the letter aside and lit up a cigarette. Alex's voice was so clear. He could see them together in Burma: in a clearing on a safe night, or at a time stolen from the war. Alex would always come up with those questions. Did he agree? What did he think? What was his view? And Sam, feeling inferior to his friend in knowledge and the manipulation of knowledge, would attempt to take him on. 'Imperialism is first learned at home.' Is it?

He recalled that some of the Labour Party lads on the ship from India had given lectures and talks and some of what had been said must be relevant to this. He scratched behind the screens of his memory but he could not reassemble it with enough conviction. It was not difficult to understand what Alex meant: it rarely was. The problem was to find enough evidence for himself. You could not call the Royal Family imperialists. Or the forces – he knew that; and Sam was reluctant to apply the word to the Houses of Parliament. Besides, in his dictionary, it was not a bad word. Yet these Australians, according to Alex, the very men whose matiness and sense of equality had attracted him to them, were throwing it at the English as an accusation. Why was that? He concentrated but he could not enlist any further thoughts. He read on and smiled. Alex had addressed his own question.

You could of course say that there's not much wrong with imperialism. Our sort, anyway. Not as bad as the other 'isms' that have caused such mayhem over the last few decades. Think of them. All disastrous. Most systems are strictly for the birds. How can any system take account of variety and individuals? It's bound to repress all that. At least we're stuck with the least worst system. Did Churchill say that about democracy after the last election? Anyway. Imperialism may have had its day but it's a bit rich to use it as a curse, say I.

You would have enjoyed the trip out. To tell you the truth, old man, I missed you a bit. I didn't seem to click with anybody. Pleasant enough bunch. I met two lads who had been in Burma but none of us wanted to talk about it – except for the weather! One of them was still obsessed by the Burmese girls who sold the cigars. Nobody I really fancied, though. Ships can be suffocating. I used the ship's library as a get-out. Talking about imperialism, I rediscovered Kipling. He is fantastic! I really got stuck into the old boy. I'll look out for a selection of his poems and send it over. An imperial gift! I would have enjoyed having you there. I enjoyed our talks a lot. Out there, I relied on them more than I realised.

Sam wished Alex had not written that. A sense of loss hit his solar plexus. He lit another cigarette from the stub of the one he was smoking. His hands were steady: it was his mind that was trembling. What if he had made the wrong decision? What if his reasons and his painstaking progress to the train that would have taken him on the first leg to Australia, to a new start . . . Why had Alex urged, even pushed him off? Why had he let him?

He sucked deeply on the strong cigarette.

It had been a good decision, he told himself. His return from the war had been like an order. The second time, however close a shave, was of his own will. He had come back, and finally, to Ellen and Joe.

But the doubt he had repressed so successfully now oozed its poison. Was that the real truth of it? Did he not want to be out there, in the purpling sun, with Alex, starting a life freed from the ball and chain of his past? What was there for him in Wigton but to do this and this and no more? To know his place, his limits, his limitations, his predestined mediocrity, his inevitable failure to be at the full stretch of himself. Those cramping chains, he believed, would have melted away under the sun. And he had turned back and turned his back on it. Ellen and Joe could always have followed. They would have followed. Surely.

The force of this loss (this mistake?), which came like an instant onrush of retrospective insight and regret and pain, rattled him and but for the demand of the rest of the letter he would have gone outside, cold though it was, to shake it off.

He inhaled even more deeply so that the smoke swelled out his lungs. He glanced around at Ellen. The magazine had fallen out of her hands. She was dead to the world.

He had taken a path and he had to stick to it, he told himself. No retreat. Regrets were weak. You got stuck in.

It can be both unnerving and exhilarating to know that most of us are stranded here every bit as much as the early convicts. They could not return until their sentence was up. We are here until that unimaginable day when we'll have saved enough to pay the full passage back. By which time we'll all be good Aussies saying 'Beaut' and 'See you this arvo' and we'll look down on the next shipload of Poms.

One thing that happened on the ship – I just want to tell you. None of us will forget the children the Japs had bayoneted and tied to trees with barbed wire. You made us bury them. Even though we should have pressed on. I never admired you more – even the time you saved my stupid life. You never referred to it.

That scene come back to haunt me. There were dozens of children on the ship. Some of the men rigged up a sort of gym-playground with ropes and you would see them hanging there – semi-naked like the little Burmese kids. I had nightmares for days.

The source of one of Sam's own most violent and deeply planted nightmares found a perfectly matching echo on the thin blue paper. He felt a bond closer than kinship fly from the room over oceans and continents to Alex in his lonely dusty lodgings many thousand miles away. Alex was right. He never had referred to it, not to Alex, not to Ellen. Like so much else in the year since his return, his only defence against his past had been to use all his might to force the war out of his mind. It was some time before he could read on.

But in the very next sentence Alex switched mood, just like that, just as he always had done.

The refresher course for teachers is well organised and I'll be in harness soon enough. Meanwhile I am studying the inhabitants – out of interest and for survival. The deadly spiders I have seen so far include the redback, a tiny little devil said to wait in ambush everywhere; then there's the trapdoor spider and the funnel web spider which is reported to scare the business out of you. There's the famous hairy tarantula but I can't say we've been introduced yet. As serum is not readily available, you are advised to cut a cross on the skin with your knife or a razor blade and suck and spit like the boyos at the Wigton Fountain. You want snakes, Sam? Only carpet snakes and vipers so far. The rules are worse than the army. Never put on shoes or socks or anything without shaking; never put hands in crevices or under surfaces; yell and make a noise at all snakes. You, we were told in a ship's lecture, are bigger than they are, which is not a great deal of help!

Despite this, I'm thinking of becoming a naturalist. Honestly. I've been into the bush a couple of times – perhaps I got a taste for that in Burma – and found a river and camped there, eaten in the open, felt the magic and the moods of the place. I was never very good at feelings about dear old Cumberland. No romance. Though I have to confess that when I got hold of the last weekly edition of the *Manchester Guardian* and saw a photograph of a dry-stone wall on the front page (in Yorkshire but no matter) I did – for the first and I trust the only time – feel homesick. But the Aborigines have their own Dreamworlds – there's a lot to find out – and, in the bush, I hope to begin to understand the Dreamworlds.

The strangeness and newness out here, Sam! The lyre birds with their amazing tails, even the kookaburras, although they

are ugly little beggars, and the scent of the frangipani –
something like a philadelphus – in the evenings. The bottle
brush, as it sounds, and huge gum trees, giving out great
golden globules of resin when you nick them with a knife, and
the colossal distances that make you think – I don't know why
this should be – that everything is possible.

There were a few more sentences, best wishes to Ellen and Joe and to
poor Jackie and the others from the section if he ever bumped into
them but the phrase 'everything is possible' all but clouded them out.
And the final nail. 'You'd have loved it, Sam. All the best. Yours truly,
Alex. P.S. I wish I'd brought the bush hat.'

Sam read it again, rapidly this time, then folded it with care. It
would take some answering.

Perhaps he could send Alex his own bush hat.

He smoked a final cigarette out in the yard. The red tip was all the
light. There was a spatter of hail. The wireless reported practically
Arctic conditions everywhere else in the country. So far the North-
west had been lucky but it was still bitter. Sam let the cold seize him
and numb him.

He had told Ellen she could read the letter. She took her time and
waited until he was down at the factory.

Like Sam she read it thoughtfully, stopping now and then to
reflect or dream a little. Like Sam, she read it twice. Like Sam, she
brooded on it, fully realising for the first time the narrowness of the
victory and the strength of the enemy.

CHAPTER FOUR

Ellen walked up King Street, head bent into the punishing wind, one gloved hand clutching the collar of her coat to keep it closed around her throat. They were told on the wireless their part of the country was getting off lightly.

It was past midday and the girls had come out of the clothing factory in which Ellen herself had worked before her marriage. They scattered into the web of lanes and yards, sucked from the streets for their dinner-break. There were few men other than the dole brigade, propping up the Vic and the Vaults, congregated at the mouth of Meeting House Lane, leaning against the railings of the George Moore Memorial Monument, better known as the Fountain, from where they chronicled the daily history of their town in pedagogic detail. Everybody knew Ellen. Most greeted her, no hello, how do? how are you? just plain, even gruff, 'Ellen' and a nod. Her name chimed her up the street.

There was a queue outside the Co-op and normally she would have enquired and almost certainly joined it but time was tight between the morning cleaning job and the afternoon work in the chemist's shop and she had a mission.

She forced herself not to glance into the cobbled yard where the house of her dreams stood, still empty and for ever out of her reach. It was just too bad. That was that. 'Ellen', 'Ellen', 'Ellen' as she ran the gauntlet between the Fountain and the King's Arms. She wondered they had not turned to stone, the men, in the deep cold of the day. Every single one, she smiled, had their hands in their pockets. Not one pair of gloves between the lot of them. 'Ellen'. 'Ellen'. She liked their knowing her that well.

Ellen had always admired West Street. There was something grand about it – the pillars outside the Mechanics' Institute and the columned doorways of the houses opposite. And just beyond, the sandstone simplicity of the Quaker Meeting House. Ellen had been at school with some of the Quakers and, privately, when she took a view of the religious sects in the town – the Roman Catholics with their nunnery at St Cuthbert's down the East End, the Primitive Methodists in New Street next to the police station, the Salvation Mission between the factory and Ivinson's stables in Station Road, the Congregationalists in Water Street beside the pig auction, the Methodists in Southend next to the girls' grammar school, the Salvation Army in Meeting House Lane right down at the bottom, the Plymouth Brethren in George Street up some steps, the Adventists next to the river Wiza, in Union Street, and beside the ancient market-place, still used seven hundred years on, the centrepiece, her own church St Mary's, C. of E., where she had sent Joe to be in the choir in response to a call for trebles – when she considered all these competing houses of God, interpreting His word to the Wigton five thousand in so many different ways, not only dominating Sunday but colonising every day of the week with morning communions and evening youth clubs, seasonal rummage sales, whist drives, dances, outings, choirs, football teams, flower arrangements, Bible classes – when everything was accounted for, Ellen secretly plumped for the Quakers. She had been in the building once only when Noreen

Morrison had broken her arm and they were stuck for someone to clean. Mrs Johnston, whose house she did twice a week, was a Quaker and asked Ellen for a favour.

She walked past it swiftly, on her way west, past the high wall of Wigton Hall, a place beyond dreams, no more than a peep over a wall, but the memory of the Quaker Meeting House stayed with her. Something about the recollection was tender. As she went down the hill from Wigton Hall, past Ma Powell's field, which was the short-cut they used to take (but only when feeling bold) to get to the park, she visualised that Quaker cleaning. Such a silence in the room. As if it had been worked up, over the years, Ellen thought, and preserved, sealed in this place, its own private quiet. But no altar. She had looked everywhere – even opened cupboards. No altar. No cross. Just chairs. Not even hassocks to kneel on or cushions to soften the hard wood. Plain chairs. Books, a few books. There was little to clean.

Noreen had come in, for company, arm heavily strapped in a white sling. She explained that at a Quaker meeting people simply sat there and spoke 'when the spirit moved them'. She told Ellen a little about their history and what an important part Cumberland had played in it and referred to Philadelphia and Pacifism and Quaker porridge oats, but it was 'when the spirit moved them' that had captured Ellen's imagination.

There were fields which acted like a moat, between Wigton Hall and the next cluster of houses known as Western Bank. The old town had ended. Ellen passed the Famous Copper Beech at the bottom of Ma Powell's field, which she had looked up to every time she sped by on her way to the park. The park had been the daily destination in school holidays and the Show Fields across the way presented the lure of the circus that came every autumn and then camped down for a couple of months – all familiar, familiar as the Fountain and just as

33

'Wigton', yet Ellen felt outside the walls of her town. As a girl she would scurry back up the hill from the park in the evenings as if afraid invisible gates would be closed against her.

The wind grew fiercer. On Western Bank she arrived at the settlement of houses built before the war. Sam and herself could have had one for ten pounds down and a just affordable rent but they had opted for rooms that had been dreadful. Yet it turned out for the best. When Sam joined up, Ellen had moved back into her aunt and uncle's large semi-guesthouse where she had spent most of her childhood – a house in the heart of the old town. She had been happy there. And safe, with Joe.

Now on the last lap of her mission, the exposed part of her face cemented in cold, she went past unattainable detached houses: the Miss Moffats', one of whom had taught her at school and was now teaching Joe; Mr Farrell's – he who owned the sawmill and had taken a fancy to Sam before the war, offered him a job she wished he had taken because there was no shift work; Glen Ritson's newly-built house – he was her age, the solicitor's son who had been sent away to public school and spent four years in a prisoner-of-war camp after having been shot down in a bombing raid, a fine big man, Ellen thought, always pleasant; and on past houses less grand but no less desirable to Ellen, until she came to a gate.

She looked through it at the field. In the foreground, a small herd of Jerseys clustered around some recently dumped hay. In the distance, machinery, a hut and a scattering of men indicated that work was starting up. This would be the next big council estate. Brindlefield, up Southend, which had already taken some of the irredeemably overcrowded Water Street residents, was already spoken for; the lists for Kirkland, to the east of the town, were reported to be full although her uncle Leonard, with his clerking and council contacts, had hinted that it was still a possibility; but this, to the west, was a clean start.

Ellen stared at it. She wanted to be attracted to it. She wanted something to happen as she looked at that field. Something which said, 'Come and live here: it'll be fine. It's almost a mile from the town but the walk is one you like and you've done it hundreds of times. You can always bike it. Put a basket on the front. There'll be other young families here. You'll still go to the same shops up in Wigton, see the same faces, be part of the same town.' But as the wind buffeted her and she felt the cold gripping her feet, she could not shake off, however hard she tried, a persistent fear that the burrowing, intense, common, close life and stories and net of the town would no longer quite belong to her. Even in prospect she already missed them.

Ellen shook her head in exasperation. After all that Sam had been through – and millions of others – how could she be so feeble? This bond to the old town had already put her marriage at risk, a risk of which Alex's letter had again made her aware.

She stamped warmth back into her feet and made up her mind for this wintry field. They would live at the very edge of the town. She would beat down the childish fear. It had almost been a curse.

She turned and hurried away. The wind was behind her now and suddenly she laughed aloud as it pushed into her back and almost made her stumble. She had been thinking 'as the spirit moved her'.

The new estate would be called Greenacres.

CHAPTER FIVE

'I know where there's some turnips,' said Speed.

There were two others and Joe, by a good margin the youngest. The boys stood shivering in the middle of Water Street, cow and horse dung frozen on the ground, nothing moving in the auctions mid-Saturday afternoon.

'They're under a sheet,' he continued. 'Easy to swipe.'

Speed was poorly dressed for the day. Ill-fitting hand-me-downs – vest, shirt, patched pullover, patched short trousers, short socks, old plimsolls. The two other boys were quite well wrapped up. Ellen had layered Joe like a mummy. Even a coat. Joe was vaguely uneasy because he wanted to be hard like Speed. But no one made fun of him.

They set off at a trot, past the burnt-out tannery, past the lemonade factory and down a slit in a wall that led over a narrow early medieval bridge. Into the Lonnings where they cantered, like ponies, alongside the black iron railings that had fenced in the once great Highmoor Estate, along past the tip, taking care – Speed's order – to hide their faces from any pigeon men on the go, until they were in real country and on the wrong side of the hedge of the targeted turnips.

Along the way, Speed had freely given out intelligence about what

37

they were up against: the farmer who had a stick as thick as a drainpipe and a dog as mad as a bat; the policeman who every now and then would take his bike along that particular path on the lookout; passers-by and other snoopers. Joe swallowed every word.

The canter had put a sweat on him and, while Speed surveyed the territory, the sweating continued as he comprehended, fully, what was about to happen. This was stealing. His mammy would kill him for stealing. His daddy would beat the living daylights out of him. According to church he would go into hell-fire. His hands moistened inside the gloves: his whole body dampened with fear under the well-belted navy raincoat. He wished he had not come. But he was in Speed's gang.

'You're the lookout,' Speed said to Joe. 'You see anybody – whistle.'

Joe nodded and swallowed. He liked whistling. He whistled a lot these days. But what sort of a whistle was this? Would 'Bobby Shaftoe' do?

'We can get in here.'

Speed had found a gap in the bare hawthorn hedge and he led the other two through it.

They were away for so very long that Joe feared they had gone home by another way and left him. He looked from left to right constantly, left, right, then swiftly left again, then an even quicker flash back to the right, then right again just to fool them, then a bit longer left while the hairs crawled on his neck for fear of what was happening on the right but nothing was up on the right so he could go back to the left again and stare it out until he was fully satisfied that nobody was there and nobody was still there on the right and a slow panic began to burn low in his stomach and he sensed he might want the lavatory but how could he do it when nobody was around but somebody might come and it was hard to hide cacked pants although his mother never mentioned it, they must have taken off, or been captured and hauled into the police station, into the cells, back to the left, right, left, no farmer, no dog, no policeman . . . and right, left again . . .

Then, relief, even joy, as about half a dozen turnips flew over the hedge and he had to dodge them. Speed and the others crashed through the hedge and they scooped them up and hared back the way they had come. Speed stopped them before the tip.

'Hide them,' he ordered.

The boys stuffed the turnips up their jackets or jumpers and scuttled pregnantly past the unseen pigeon men on the tip.

Speed pointed to a straggle of pine trees, last of a handsome plantation on the estate.

They settled in the middle of the bare copse.

'Who's got a knife?'

Joe hurried to oblige but as he wriggled his hand under his coat and his jacket and into his trouser pocket he felt the familiar clag of his number two sticking to the inside of his pants. They weren't his best pants or his school pants. They were his worst, two years' ago school pants, the pants he only played in. But he knew that he was still supposed to keep them clean and he was ashamed.

Speed opened the bigger blade after wiping the dirt off the turnip with the sleeve he wiped his nose on. He peeled it, clumsily but well enough. Then he hacked off four chunks. They ate, biting hard.

'Better than goodies,' Speed said, whose ration of sweets was rarely cashed in.

He ate from hunger.

The other two munched away.

To Joe, every bite was a complication. He loved being part of the gang. Now it was done and the farmer had not come and the dog had not savaged him and the policeman had not arrested him and told his mammy and daddy, he felt proud of himself. It had been a real raid. He himself had not done the stealing. Keeping lookout was different. He tried to keep up with Speed's turnip consumption and pushed his right eye into a squint.

By the fourth turnip they were beaten.

Speed looked at those uneaten.

'Bury them.'

He got on his knees and tried to dig into the ground. No yield. No chance. He stood up and hacked with his feet, but the worn-out plimsolls were useless. The other three looked on, colder now after their seated feast, though not as cold as Speed whose bluing hands and taut chilled face looked painful.

'We can't leave them like this,' he said, 'they'll be swiped.'

He walked slowly towards the edge of the copse, stopped and raised his hand. The gang arrived, with the turnips. There was a dent in the ground. The turnips just about fitted in and Speed covered them with grass.

'We can have another feed tomorrow,' he said.

Sunday! Joe thought. He would not be let out in his playing things on a Sunday, and besides, eating stolen turnips on a Sunday would be even worse. But he said nothing. They cantered back into the town, rather more slowly, stomachs tight.

As the evening drew on, Joe's stomach began to hurt. He merely pecked at his tea. He would not have a slice of bread and jam before he went to bed. He tried not to groan.

Yet he insisted on going upstairs alone – which Sam had encouraged him to do although Ellen had no conscience about going up with him when, as tonight, Sam was not in the house. But he needed to take off his pants carefully and fold them so that his mammy would not see. He had scrubbed and scrubbed them in the lavatory with the squares of paper from the *News Chronicle* but there was still a noticeable stain, a thin veneer, hardening. He did not want to be called 'cacky pants'. He was sure she knew but was just not saying, just as she knew about the turnips. 'Have you been eating anything else?' she said. And when he said no, 'What have you been eating?' she said. Nothing. So he lied as well. Joe believed that his mother had X-ray eyes when it came to him. But he was grateful that she said nothing more. He had sworn to himself he would never do it again. His stomach felt almost detached from the rest of him, a tight little fist inside there, a swelling football, trapped in there. His sleep was uneasy. They were after him.

A few days later, the tale of the raid trickled back to Sam and Ellen. One of the other boys had been sick and the evidence on the lino had been unmistakable. Sam was amused, even pleased, and the fact that it brought him out of himself for a while encouraged Ellen to let it pass, although stealing of whatever kind was a slippery slope and the wrong gang could get you into bad trouble. Joe was growing bolder, less careful, she thought, to seek his father's approval and it coarsened the nature she alone had nurtured for almost seven years.

—ɱ—

Miss Snaith opened the door in the side alley that led off High Street and took them into the house behind the shop. Miss Snaith was in the shop itself. Ellen and a scrubbed, subdued Joe were pointed upstairs to Miss Snaith's piano room.

Ellen was not the only one in the town to find particular satisfaction in the three Misses Snaith. Wigton was rather proud of them. One of them had the business head and ran the clock and jewellery shop established by their father, another kept house and sang beautifully in the choir and was often called on for solos at social gatherings, and the oldest, to whose domain Ellen and Joe ascended on thick carpet – Ellen hushed by the glimpse of paintings on walls and good furniture, Joe fearing the worst after the cleansing and combing he had been subjected to – was the piano teacher.

'Come in.'

Ellen's knock had been on a half-open door. The first Miss Snaith had said, 'Go right in, Ellen, she's expecting you.' Ellen was compelled to knock.

The piano teacher, like her sisters, was short and thin with a briskness that belied a lifelong asthmatic condition. Her face was pale but not sickly. Her hair bandaged her head in a thick grey plait. Spectacles swung across her chest, hanging on some sort of cord Ellen had never seen before. She wore a heavy tweed skirt and a big cardigan even though one bar of the electric fire was on. Like her sisters, she had faded blue eyes and a smile that made you smile back.

'I've seen him in church,' she said. 'Do you like the choir?'

'Yes, miss.'

'The choir is a good grounding.'

She noticed that Joe was glancing at the large model ship that filled the broad marble mantelpiece. 'All boys want to know about the ship,' she said to Ellen. 'Father made it. Every bit of it. He could make anything. He was such a wonderful man. We do miss him so.'

Ellen was almost winded by the force of passion that came so unexpectedly from the dry-looking little body before her.

'It's HMS *Cumberland*,' she said to Joe. 'Father worked from photographs but every detail is just so. And you can lift out the upper deck. See. All those little rooms and the furniture. We helped him with the furniture. And these hammocks. All from linen handkerchiefs.

42

There was nothing he couldn't do. He was in the choir just like you. What a beautiful light tenor voice. People commented. Such a sweet sound. I've never heard a man's voice as sweet.'

It was so personal, the way she talked, such private feelings that Ellen almost blushed to hear it, so directly from the heart.

'Sit over there, Ellen.' She pointed to a *chaise-longue* laden with elaborately embroidered cushions. 'And you sit here, Joe. On this piano stool.'

Joe hoisted himself on to it, his feet, annoyingly, not reaching the floor. He wished he were as tall as Speed. He would not tell Speed about this.

'What can you see directly in front of you?'

'A book, miss.'

'What sort of book?'

'A music book, miss?'

'Do you know what those things are called?'

'Yes, miss.' He looked at her. Go on, said her expression. 'Minims, crotchets, quavers . . .'

'You see what I mean about the choir,' said Miss Snaith to Ellen, who sat uncomfortably on the edge of the *chaise-longue*, not wanting to disturb the display of cushions. 'Now look down, Joe. You find the letter C stuck on one of the white keys. Put your right thumb on it. No. Harder. Make a sound. Good. That is called middle C, Joe, and that's where everything starts from. Again. Good. What is it?'

'Middle C, miss.'

'Put the next finger on the next note. That is D. And the next. Harder. That one is E. The next one? F. Now. Here's a peculiar thing. You push your thumb under those two fingers to get to that F. It seems a little bit silly now but it has a purpose. Watch me. Now you try. Just push it underneath. That's it. Now you see you have all four fingers left to take you to the top of the ladder. To top C. Up you go. But you go by way of A and B. They didn't think about children when they invented the piano, did they, Joe? Let's try again. These are called scales. You'll do a lot of scales. You should do them every day. Like your teeth. Now I'll do it alongside you, down here . . .'

One and threepence a lesson was affordable, Ellen thought. The clincher had come when her aunt Grace had said that Joe could practise on the piano in her drawing room. It would be good for the piano, to be used, she said. It would be good to see Joe again on a regular basis, too, she confessed. Both Leonard and herself and Mr Kneale missed him, for though Ellen popped in and out – giving her aunt a day's cleaning a week and doing the washing for both of them on the Monday, Joe's visits had dried up since his increasing involvement with the Water Street gang and the other gangs he was building up at school and the choir.

Ellen had the one and three ready in the corner of her handkerchief.

When the lesson was over, she unwrapped it.

'No, no, Ellen. I never charge for the first lesson. This is just a little try-out for both of us. Joe must think it over for himself.' She smiled. 'I think he has the makings.' She picked up a jar of boiled sweets from a side table and held it out to Ellen, who refused, and then to Joe, who checked with his mother and took one.

'Thank you, miss.'

'You're welcome, Joe.'

They went to the door and across the small landing Ellen saw Iris Miller's girl sitting on a bare chair, a brown music bag neat across her school skirt. So school wear was permitted, it need not be the Sunday suit, and she would have to find a music case.

Downstairs, Miss Snaith was waiting for them. She wore a plum-coloured overcoat, a scarf and a hat. 'I expect you would like to see inside a grandfather clock. Boys like seeing the workings,' she said to Joe, and took him into the shop. Ellen followed. She had only twice been in the shop – when she took to be mended and later collected a fine brooch-watch belonging to her uncle Leonard's mother and given to her aunt Grace.

The room chirruped with the individual tickings of a dozen clocks. They made a lovely tantalising sound, Ellen thought, a tune of their own.

'This was Father's best,' said Miss Snaith, as she opened the beautifully polished oak door on a long-case clock. 'He even painted the face. He could do anything at all. But clockmaking – that was his pride and joy. Mr Telford said he was the best pupil ever he had and Mr Telford was a great clockmaker in his day. Wigton is very famous for its clocks, I'm sure *you* know that, Ellen. Father called it the Tick-Tock Town – wasn't that marvellous? Wigton made clocks for hundreds of years, Joe. Here's a clock by Mr Sanderson of Wigton – you see his name on the brass face, that's what it says with the S as an F. Seventeen hundred and twenty. Father said this was "beauty in simplicity". Those were his words. You can't beat it, he said. He was going to write about the Wigton clocks. And what a book it would have been, wouldn't it, Joe?'

Joe gaped at the weights and was allowed to touch their cold pocked lead: Miss Snaith held his hand to a chain and he wound up a Simpson thirty-hour clock. She pointed out a Peet clock with a sportsman on the face whose gun went up and down with the ticking and tocking and he admired the phases of the moon on a Sill clock – all made and painted and carved and engineered by Wigton men over the centuries, said Miss Snaith, probably 'culminating in Father' whose prize contribution in that shop display was a small graceful wall clock, unequivocally admired by Ellen, low down Joe's list. The big clocks were for him.

'Your uncle Leonard as a young man was quite a favourite with Father,' Miss Snaith said, 'because of the council connection. That's why we've always kept a special eye on you, Ellen.'

Ellen felt rather blessed. She had always been warmly greeted by the sisters when they passed her on their walks in the town. But 'special eye' . . . She was touched.

Miss Snaith took advantage of Joe's being on the other side of the shop and out of hearing. 'Did Fanny say the boy "had the makings"?' she whispered, her pale eyes staring.

'Yes,' Ellen whispered in echo voice. 'That's what she said.'

'Then he'll do,' said Miss Snaith. 'Fanny's never wrong. Father always swore she had the ear.'

Ellen was unexpectedly pierced by this final 'Father'. The word had been given such warmth and passion by both sisters. To have had such a father, she thought. To have had a father. It rarely got to her. She turned and pinched her nose to check the prickling behind her eyes.

'Would you like to learn the piano, then?' Ellen asked the question as soon as they got back on to High Street.

She had made up her mind even before the 'test' but she followed what Miss Snaith had said about Joe thinking it over for himself. Joe was fully aware of what he had to do and, besides, he had liked the sounds of the notes that played when he pressed the keys. So he nodded and Ellen squeezed his hand as they hurried back along the midwinter streets acknowledging everyone they met.

'So,' said Sam later, as all three sat around the fire, Joe reading his comic, Ellen knitting mittens for Speed at Joe's pleading, Sam staring at the flames, 'so we're going to learn the pi-a-no, are we?'

Joe glanced up, alert. Looked from one to the other. Saw them looking steadily at each other. But they were not angry. He always knew when they were angry. So. It was all right.

'He starts on Tuesday,' said Ellen.

CHAPTER SIX

Sam all but marched Joe down the street. Partly to beat the weather. Partly, though, because he liked to push the boy now and then and enjoyed the child's determination to meet the challenge. After trying to match the length of his father's step, Joe had fallen into unsatisfactory syncopation. But he squared his shoulders and mimicked his father's bearing. One or two people noticed and remarked, 'Like his dad, now,' and Joe felt proud. Already around the town he was called 'Sam's lad' by the older men, although grown-up women still called him 'Ellen's boy'.

Sam's copper hair was still army short with a touch of Brylcreem to keep every follicle in formation. Joe's copper was beginning to lose the deep hue and was becoming merely ginger, even rather brown in places. But the blue eyes were father and son.

'Fine lad,' said Henry Allen, the bookmaker, who came across the street to walk with them. Sam took the compliment. Joe pretended to ignore it but felt a tickle of pleasure shimmer through him.

'What brings you out?'

'Good business practice, Sam. Something that has to be learned.'

Henry's sallow face was blank white with cold save for the redness of his nose. He was wrapped up for a Russian winter.

'These landlords, you see, Sam, they do me a favour when racing's on. Collect the bets. Or let Tommy' – his runner – 'come in and collect them. All definitely illegal, Sam. Outside the law and an offence. You can come to the bookmaker's office but the bookmaker's office can't come to you. Sorry business, Sam. Law made to be broken. So when the racing's off, I make a point of going into the pub, buying a round or two. Good business practice.'

He coughed, a dry scratchy cough that felt sore just to listen to it.

'Stomach bad enough. Ulcers forewarned. Chest joining in,' he said, and they had to stop while he coughed it out.

They were near Market Hill, early Saturday afternoon, enough people for it to be embarrassing. Henry walked to the front of the big house owned by the manager of the Lion and Lamb and coughed into the wall. Sam and Joe waited.

He came back, watery-eyed. 'Terrible thing,' he said, 'bad health.' He diverted matters to Joe. 'You look after your health. What's he going to be, Sam?'

'Tell him.'

'World champion,' said Joe, 'or,' and this came, new, from nowhere, 'have a band.'

Both men laughed at the innocent unreality of it and Joe knew he had pleased his father. He had to. And in that moment he believed what he said.

'What they come out with,' said Harry. He excavated the layers of his clothing, finally found his money pocket and fingered through the change until he found a sixpence. 'Don't spend it all at once.'

'Thank you, Mr Allen.'

'See you, Sam. Frost's got all the courses now. Not a horse moving in all the land.'

The bookmaker peeled off to continue his good business practice in the Blackamoor Inn. Sam and Joe swung on to the crest of Market Hill and made for the house in which Ellen and Joe had taken refuge during his war years. Joe still treated it as a home. Sam rarely came to it without remembering the man who was himself, who, less than a year ago, after the eternity of the slow return from Burma, had bounded up the steps on a mild morning to reclaim his wife and child and past.

This time he went in by the back door. Joe had already darted ahead and the door was ajar. Just as Leonard and Grace had been as parents to Ellen, so they had been as grandparents to Joe and he took all the leeway they gave him.

Sam had picked the time carefully so that he could have a quiet talk with Leonard, who was as near as he got to a confidant in Wigton.

Grace had made them a pot of tea. She had softened towards Sam since his second return but Sam knew that it was because she thought he was weak for not going to Australia. She had been looking forward to having Ellen back in her house, skivvying (as Sam had cruelly put it to Ellen's distress), and Joe as the plaything. But the piano had brought Joe back and Ellen was grateful once again to the magnificently coiffed, deep-bosomed Grace, lady of this castle of a house on the hill. Now, superior in resolution to a man she had always rather feared, Grace felt well compensated. Sam tried to block it out. Of those few who had joshed him about that damned turning back at Carlisle station, only Grace had got under his skin. He was extra polite to her. She spotted that, and she enjoyed that, too.

Leonard opened with the offer of a cigarette. Both of them were on Capstan Full Strength. The semi-basement kitchen was an uncomfortable place for confidences but it was the best that could be found outside the luck of an empty snug in one of the pubs. And you could not always afford to drink. Grace was upstairs planted in her overseer's chair in the window, chronicling the town as closely as the lads around the Fountain, relishing the sight of Joe, at the piano, doing his scales, getting on.

Leonard wanted to talk politics. Over the past couple of months, he said, he had realised that although Mr Attlee was a gentleman and although there were one or two other gentlemen in the Cabinet – Mr Stafford Cripps came to mind – they were turning out to be no better than a bunch of Communists. He had woken up to the fact, he said, when all that 'nationalise' this and 'nationalise' that sank in. The big question nobody asked was – who was going to pay for it all? The answer was 'Joe Soap', at which point he would direct his right index finger towards his chest. It was a recipe for crippling the country, he said. If people got something for nothing, they would do nothing for it. That was the first law of nature.

Sam enjoyed Leonard in full spate. He argued with him for the sake of it as much as for any difference of view. Joe would sometimes come in to listen when their voices rose and Grace would then declare that talking politics always led to trouble. Leonard was particularly inflamed this day by the continuing dock strike.

'There's food on those ships,' said Leonard. 'Rotting. People crying out for food. Kiddies starving. And they go on strike! Where's all this "pulling together"? It's needed just as much as in the war, Sam. These are selfish men. Brothers my backside! They're holding the country to ransom. And we're supposed to admire them because they are "the workers". We're all workers, Sam. Get the troops in.'

'Shoot them?'

'Some of them could do with it.'

'Gaol them?'

'Most certainly, the ring-leaders.'

Sam took up the debate but his heart was not in it. There was no space in his mind for it, no energy there to fuel the enthusiasm needed. He went through his paces but still dominating his thoughts was the letter from Alex and the fallout from it. He was possessed by the fear that he had made the wrong decision and an irreversible decision. 'Everything is possible' went through his head like the call of the siren. He could be talking to Alex at this moment, not stuck in this semi-basement ding-dong that hardened and blunted all arguments but engaged in talk that led to unexpected openings and surprising advances. So as he sparred with the usually detached Leonard, whose poise was always attempting to be that of the gentleman, rather above it all, immune from it all, Sam bit on that letter like a fox in a trap gnawing at its leg.

There seemed nothing he could do against the pull from the letter, from Alex, from that continent of possibilities in the southern hemisphere. It was an undercurrent, growing in strength, taking him out to sea however hard he tried to swim. It was a torment he could not understand and it felt like self-indulgence, which he could not tolerate.

Sensing that Sam had not the heart for it, Leonard tailed off and they talked football. Mr Kneale came in as they were doing so – 'Don't mind me. Don't let me interrupt' – but they knew the schoolmaster had nothing to contribute to football and, politely, they let it peter out. Both of them glanced at the large parcel he had brought in with him but neither offered a comment. Sam preferred to say as little as possible to Mr Kneale these days. The history teacher and widower who had long been Grace's prize 'paying guest' had pestered him about his experiences in Burma once too often.

He had been assembling a book about the experiences of ordinary soldiers there, but although superficially willing, his sources – like Sam – soon dried up. It was just too hard. Sam had tried to make this clear without giving offence. To his relief, Mr Kneale had finally taken the hint.

So Mr Kneale had begun to shift his centre of interest from the one campaign to the next war, the Third World War that all the signs told him was inevitable. It had the makings of an obsession. Sam had already seen Joe wide-eyed as this mild man who had been in paternal residence while Sam was in the army, and had become at the very least a mentor, had spoken of destruction, mass extinction, certain doom. Joe had been fearfully convinced.

Sam had tried to laugh it away to protect his son and to exercise his own authority, but he could see the lad's eyes flinch when Mr Kneale went into detail about the atom bomb. He described its 'mushroom cloud' – 'It was studying it as a photographer that turned the argument for me,' he said, proud that his beloved hobby should play such a part. 'That cloud, Joe, that cloud could be carried by the wind anywhere in the world and fall on our heads and give us the most hideous death. Hideous beyond understanding. And there will be more of these A-bombs as they call them – more and more and don't think the communists won't manufacture them and then how long will the Cold War so called stay cold? We can blow ourselves to smithereens and if we can, you take the word of a historian, we will. Men always use the weapons they invent. Sooner or later, the moment arrives and BANG!'

Joe would dream about that.

'I was glad of that bomb,' Sam said. 'If it hadn't been for that bomb the odds are we'd be out there yet, pushing the Japs back inch by inch with more killed than were ever destroyed by that one bomb. I was glad of it.'

'Would you have wanted it to be dropped if you'd known it was so destructive?'

'We talked about that.' Alex, of course. 'Maybe.' Defiantly. 'Very likely, yes.'

'And if there had not been a bomb?'

'We'd have slogged on, I suppose. For as long as it took.'

Mr Kneale sensed the aggression and changed the subject to his friend the Reverend Rex Malden who was leaving St Mary's to take up a living in Northumberland.

'It was the Reverend Malden who brought proper standards of photography to Wigton,' he said. 'We were just amateurs before Rex. There's not a photographer in Wigton doesn't owe his skills to Rex Malden.'

Leonard and Sam had no answer to that. The silence was a good cue. The scales upstairs had stopped some time ago.

He stood up. So did Mr Kneale, his almost unlined moon face set in an expression of kindliness.

'This,' he said, handing over the parcel well wrapped up in brown sugar paper, 'is for you. For Joe, that is. Don't open it,' he said, though Sam had made no move to do so. 'It's a music case, that's all. It belonged to my sister – in Chester – I knew she would have no more use for it. My only anxiety was that she might have given it to the church rummage sale. But here it is – rather worn but extremely good leather and so I hope it will serve. It's a pleasure to hear that piano played. Especially sitting where I am, at the top of the house. Distant music.' He smiled, and handed over the parcel.

'That's very kind.' Why did he hate getting such a present – needed, generous – from Mr Kneale – friendly, kind? What did that make him?

'I believe you'll find that Joe's slipped out to play with his old friends,' said Mr Kneale. 'They were a good little team. It's pleasant to see them together again after his piano practice. Just like the old days.'

A jet of resentment soured Sam's mood. He forced it back. Mr Kneale was well-meaning but Sam could not shake off his jealousy of the schoolteacher's closeness to Ellen and Joe during the years he had been away.

'My sister played the piano beautifully,' said Mr Kneale. 'And then – a complete loss of interest. No rhyme or reason. None at all. We mustn't let that happen to Joe.' His benign, Pickwickian features furrowed anxiously.

'I'll be going then.' Sam tucked the parcel under his arm. 'Thanks again.'

'Think nothing of it, Sam. A bright-eyed and bushy-tailed laddie like that deserves all the help we can muster.'

Joe was nowhere to be seen on Market Hill. Sam hurried up the street with the brown parcel as if he were carrying something he was ashamed of.

'You get fourpence for every time you go and sixpence is knocked off every time you miss.' Joe was explaining the payment of choir boys to Speed in order to lure him in. It would be a great thing to do another favour for Speed – the mittens had been well appreciated. Speed had said very little but Joe could tell, even though Speed had already lost one of them.

'So,' the smaller boy repeated carefully, as they stood outside the lavatory door which Joe had been using as a punch-bag for his boxing gloves, 'fourpence for Thursday choir practice, fourpence for Sunday morning, fourpence for Sunday night, that's a shilling a week and you get your pay every three months so that's thirteen bob if you keep at it. *And*,' Joe's monstrous fists biffed each other to emphasise the next point, '*and* there's special pay for weddings *and* there's a summer trip,' Joe paused, tried to sound offhand and looked somewhere beyond Speed, 'and you wear a black cassock – from your chin to your toes.' Covers your clothes, the message smuggled through. 'Thirteen bob.'

Speed was inclined to believe him. 'All that lolly? Just for singing?'

'Just for singing. It's easy,' said his young acolyte. 'You'll know the hymns anyway.'

Speed thought about it. Once a month his mother, Annie, marched her three sons down to St Cuthbert's. She would have gone more often but the embarrassment about the poor state of their clothes was too hard to bear. She had to go sometimes to pray properly for her husband Jackie, still in hospital. The priest taxed her with this meagre attendance and listed the punishments in store but Annie was obstinate. She made the two older boys promise to go to confession every Saturday as she herself did when she thought the church would be empty. There was not a sign of religion in their painfully bare house and, unlike many of their fellow Roman Catholics in the overwhelmingly Protestant town, Annie rarely if ever referred to Blessed Mary or the Saints and sought no comfort from them.

'I'll have to ask,' said Speed, and went home to wait for the right moment.

Joe bashed the lavatory door a few more times, feeling rather lordly. To be able to do favours for Speed! Before choir practice two weeks ago he had been invited to a birthday party by Alan, another choirboy, who lived in the house over his father's shop. There had been hundreds of sandwiches, Spam, jam, egg, sugar, fish paste! Six jelly babies each. And a slice of a Mars bar. Speed would have eaten more than anybody. He would have beaten the lot of them. They played blow football and pass-the-parcel and tiddlywinks. He could just see Speed at a party like that. He laid into the door one last time and went back into the yard and there she was.

She needed no telling now. In truth, though he could not articulate this, Joe wished that Mary was not quite so open about it. He gave a shifty look around.

In the dark bolted lavatory he took off his boxing gloves and by the time he had done that and found a safe place for them on the floor, Mary had taken up the opening position, bent over the toilet seat, skirt up, knickers down. Joe, almost shaking from the fear that someone would need to go right now, and as always baffled as to what he should or could actually do, stared and touched and smelled as tentatively as if he were an aesthete savouring a rose at dawn.

They were not struck dead.

When they were once again in the yard and Mary had done two full stand-ups, she announced, 'We're going away to live with my dad next Saturday.'

Joe had a faint inkling of a terrible loss but next Saturday was far away.

They played until his mammy came back and summoned him in for his tea. When he told her about Mary going away to live with her dad she said, 'That'll be nice for her, won't it?'

He went out after tea, in the twilight, to hear Jack McGee and his Mission Band at the end of Water Street singing hymns and calling on all sinners to repent and give up the sin of drink. Joe loved the music, especially the cornet and the big drum.

Speed arrived and delivered the verdict on the choir at St Mary's Anglican Church. 'Mammy said God'd murder us if I joined your lot.'

Joe was disappointed, but he nodded, as if he understood.

Along the gas-lit streets they followed the Mission Band back to its home down Station Road, Speed shouting out, 'Jack McGee, Jack McGee, he sold his wife for a cup of tea,' as the deep winter darkness blanketed the town and people concentrated on keeping warm.

CHAPTER SEVEN

After another week, Sam was fit to be tied. He was so restless in his own skin that there were moments when Ellen thought he was battling with the delayed emergence of some virulent disease caught in Burma. His temper was foul and the small downstairs room became a bear pit. Whatever Ellen and Joe said or did seemed to provoke him. He pushed away their most innocent overtures as if they had gone for his throat. Sam knew that he was behaving unfairly and badly and yet he was gripped by what he could neither overcome nor resist. He tried to stay out as much as he could but the weather was growing daily more dour and just too cold while pubs, with their obligation of public conversation, were intolerable.

Joe felt that the anger streaming from his father was directed specifically at him. He scarcely dared move about the confined space, and crept like someone chained in a cell, cowed under the impenetrable burden of what he had done wrong, flinching in anticipation of the blow.

Ellen bore it as long as she could. He had been uncomplaining since giving up his dream of Australia. It must have been hard for him. But Alex's letter had detonated something he could not control. She watched it and at first she pitied him. In his eyes she saw the dumb torment of a beaten dog and this was not her Sam and yet it was.

Go then, she thought she should say, just go, as you wanted to. We held you back. I thought it was me at first, more likely it was Joe. He made you turn. So, go.

'Why don't you go?'

It was late. He had been sleeping less, going to bed later. This night she had decided to stay up with him. He was eating less, too, and in the gas-light he looked gaunt, pale skin tight on the cheekbones, lines chiselled down to the mouth, the eyes when he looked up from his dream in the fire feverish with questions he could neither ask nor answer.

'We could save up again,' she said.

He shook his head, to dismiss her talk. She was being loving and helpful and yet she was just stirring her finger in the open sore. He could bear no reference to himself.

'It's no good,' he said, eventually, bent forward in the chair, crouched in front of the embers as if yearning for a last lick of warmth.

She had not seen him so low.

He took a bus to Carlisle after the Saturday morning shift and made for the Tullie House library.

He remembered that Alex had told him about schemes for recruiting teachers. One of the librarians brought him the 1944 pamphlet. He took it into the Reading Room inhabited by five old men – all wearing cloth caps and buttoned overcoats and scarves and one wearing gloves, all validated by their news-papers.

There was a slight but undeniable lift of hope. He had once confessed to Alex that his ambition would have been to teach in a village school, given the opportunity. It had long been a shy dream, only the once confessed, but it was a true ambition.

The pamphlet opened with the list of 'Information to be

obtained regarding candidates: a. School or schools attended with dates and examinations passed.'

From that opening sentence there arose immediate obstacles. Examinations passed? Two: one for the grammar school, another for a public school – a scholarship available only to Church of England village schools in Cumberland and Westmorland. His father had stamped out both. No money for uniforms and all the rest. Even when there was help on offer for one of the scholarships, he was adamant. There would be a catch in it and, besides, Sam was the eldest, the sooner he got out working the more help he would be. But those were not the examinations these people wanted. They wanted Higher certificates and college degrees. He knew that and he had always known it.

'e. Information as to teaching work undertaken in a civil capacity either professionally or voluntarily, or any other activity with young people.'

Leading a section in the Forgotten Army? An activity with young people?

There seemed a second chance in the next part.

'In respect of candidates who are or have been in one of the Services during the War.'

Particulars of service – information about aptitude – that should be OK. But the 'do not walk on the grass' sign came up again.

'i. Particulars of any course of education followed while in the Services with, if possible, reports on the candidate's work.

'j. Information about any work carried out while in the Services as an Instructor or Teacher.'

Nevertheless he read on until he hit the buffers. As he had anticipated.

'We therefore recommend that the following should be accepted for interview.

'a. Candidates who have passed an examination hitherto recognised for admission to a Training College.

'b. Other candidates whose records as a whole furnish evidence of suitability, e.g. continued education, work as a leader or instructor in the forces or in civil life . . .'

Would corporal in the Border Regiment in Burma be counted as 'work of a leader'?

He read the whole pamphlet so that he could always tell himself that he had done so.

There was nothing in it for him.

He sat back and took out a cigarette, struck a match.

'No smoking allowed.'

One of the old men. He looked frightened. As if it were he who would be kicked out.

Sam returned the pamphlet, left the library and lit up on Castle Street. The castle itself looked every bit as a castle should, Sam thought, under the lowering dark grey sky, and his mind flicked back to the day of the reunion. It brought a smile to his face. How many of them had been arrested afterwards for disorderly behaviour? Just a bit of fun. Twenty shillings fine! A badge of honour, Alex had said, although he himself had been out of it.

After the reunion they had walked back past the cathedral as he was doing now and Alex had gone in to look at some feature, though which one Sam had forgotten. Staring about him, checking that no one from Wigton was there to report back, he bent his head and turned into the close and went into the cathedral for the first time in his life.

It was a place full of greatness, he thought, but his affliction was that he did not have the means to discern why. He wandered around, tentatively, not knowing the worth or history of what he was looking at – he had not noticed the little table of guidebooks tucked behind the door. He wondered what Alex had wanted to see. The ceiling? That was magnificent, and he came across a mirror, half-way up the central aisle: when you looked in it you could see a close-up of the detailed ceiling work. The big window was probably a talking point, he thought, but it looked flat in the dull winter light. Alex would have explained it. He liked the choir stalls and when he sneaked close to them he saw the goblin and demon carving underneath the raised seats and admired that carving and the zest of it more than anything else in the cathedral.

He was soon out. His visit had lasted no more than a few minutes. He felt that he had been dipped in something that ought to have done him good and refined him – but he had not been able to understand enough of it to feel that he had been altered as he ought to have been.

He walked through the Lanes to the bus station. The Lanes reminded him of Water Street. He had become fond of what its detractors called 'the gutter of Wigton', because of the excrement left by the cattle and sheep and horses driven down the street from the auction to the railway station, but carrying another unmistakable meaning . . .

It was a little village to itself, Water Street, shops and skills to call on, tinkers at one end – and squatters now – the fine Congregational church at the other end. Carlisle's Lanes had the same kick about them. He felt more uplifted after walking through that ancient, run-down, notorious common crotch of Carlisle than he had in its crown, the cathedral. The absence of awe was a bonus for Sam. He began to relax.

Annie was on the bus and Sam sat beside her. She would have been on her weekly visit to see Jackie in Garlands, the mental hospital a few miles the other side of Carlisle – two bus journeys for Annie and a weekly challenge to her resources that she never failed to meet. She nodded but wanted a moment or two more in her own company. He lit up and waited. There was not only Jackie to worry her: the three boys were growing wilder without their father and though Sam kept a fairly close eye on Speed and would go out of his way for the other two, Alistair, the eldest, had started to get himself into serious trouble. 'Just once more and it's Borstal,' Annie had told him the previous week when he had gone to see her in her damp semi-basement ruin, the barest accommodation. There was little doubt that Alistair would 'disturb the peace' just once more. A big-boned fifteen-year-old, he was angry at all the world. Sam, when talking him down the once or twice he had been opportunely on hand, had picked up the indiscriminate and terrible fury that was just as likely to turn on Sam himself. It would not be constrained.

And Jackie?

'He's looking better, I'll give them that. He gets better feed than I could manage.'

The bus was taking them out of the city now, on the winding road between the fields that led the eleven miles to Wigton. Annie looked out of the window, and though the bus was almost empty, she spoke softly. 'He wants to come out, Sam. He keeps saying he wants to come out and I ask the nurse but she says it's too early.' She lowered her voice further. 'It breaks my heart, though, Sam, him asking me to get him out and when there's nothing you can do where are you?'

Her grief was reined-in but Sam knew her well and it got to him. He never failed to be impressed by Annie. With her plainest of looks, squat figure, lank hair held with a cheap clip, broad, tired, unmade-up face, borrowed coat, socks, and legs blue with cold, she was forever ignored and overlooked and that had been her lot. But she tried so hard to keep things together. Enduring. Suddenly Sam remembered Ian, his close friend in the war, who had sacrificed his own life for the sake of others including Sam himself. When he had told Ian's father of the true circumstances of Ian's violent, drawn-out, agonising death, the older man had been shaken but stood firm. Let it make its wound in him but he would endure it.

When they reached Wigton it was dark and he walked her up the street, quite busy despite the razoring east wind. At the top of the steps leading down to her house he said, 'Wait a minute, Annie.'

He had manoeuvred a pound note out of his wallet while on the bus.

'For something for Jackie.'

'No, Sam. You're always giving us.'

'And the boys.'

She looked at him and tightened her lips until they all but disappeared. He put the note in her hand.

'Believe me,' he said, hoping his earnestness would tell of his admiration for her stoicism, 'believe me, Annie, you've done me a favour today. Never mind how.'

Her expression was her thanks and she went down the steep steps slowly.

When Sam opened the door of his own house he saw that both Ellen and Joe cringed and fell silent. He had seen that on previous days and resented it. It had further twisted and inflamed him. He had regretted it but the regret had been overwhelmed by the lava of anger erupting inside him.

Now the regret predominated. He felt weak with it. How could he make them react like that? Cringe, be so much less than themselves, withdraw? What did you say to redeem that? The greetings were stiff and subdued. Joe went back to his comic. The boxing gloves were behind him on the chair. Sam noticed this with relief. They were still in favour.

'I'll make some tea.'

'I've been to Carlisle.'

'See anybody?'

'No. Yes. Annie. On the way back.'

'She has her work cut out.'

'I've got a lot of time for Annie,' said Sam, over-fiercely but with a warmth that Ellen noted. She looked at him again. Perhaps he was beginning to come out of himself.

'Your sister came. She brought some scones.'

'Any news?'

'Not much. I think Ruth would like to move into Wigton but your dad seems stuck in that cottage. She said that Miss Jennings is having a very bad do with bronchitis.'

'I suppose Ruth's been enrolled to look after her on top of everything else.'

'She didn't complain.'

So it went. Picking their way very carefully. Putting their story together again through short familiar sentences. He still felt un-certain.

'Six times eight,' Sam shot at Joe, knowing how the boy liked this.

'Forty-eight.'

'Nine times nine.'

Again Joe heard the regular morning chant of tables in his head and skimmed down to 'Eighty-one.' A few more and then Joe said to Ellen, 'You set them, see who wins.'

'Eleven times seven.'

'Seventy-seven,' said Joe.

'Nine times eight.'

'Seventy-two.' Joe looked triumphantly at his father. 'Two–nil.' Sam won the next two.

'First to five,' said Ellen.

When Joe had won, Sam said to Ellen, 'Do you think that he'll make a teacher?'

'Funny,' Ellen replied. 'Miss Moffat said something on those lines when I met her in the street the other day.'

'Miss Moffat, eh?' Sam nodded. 'They're all still there, aren't they?'

Not only Miss Moffat, but Miss Ivinson, Miss Bell, Miss Steele, Miss Bennet, Miss Tate, a long-serving regiment of teachers – spinsters of the parish, admired, devoted, in their own way uncounted casualties of the First World War.

'I still want to be a boxer.' Joe, so soon charmed by his father's warmth, presented a known pleaser.

'He's coming on,' Sam said, weightily, 'there's no doubt he's coming on with the gloves.'

'What's the capital of America?' Joe asked, cockily hoping to catch out his mother.

'Washington,' said Ellen. 'We were going round to the baths for the last hour.'

'It's freezing out there.'

'We'll wrap up. Won't we, Joe?'

'I'll come with you,' said Sam. 'I haven't had a swim for months.'

'It'll probably be empty,' said Ellen, concealing her warmth of reaction. 'Just the three of us.'

'I'll race you,' said Joe. 'I can do a breadth now. But I should have a start.'

Sam wanted to pluck him from the ground and hug him but he held back and felt the weaker for it.

CHAPTER EIGHT

Ellen was so happy she did not know what to do with herself. The room had never felt so good. She tidied it unnecessarily yet again. She checked the time, needlessly rearranged the plates on the table, and calculated precisely where Sam would be on his walk up from the factory – past Harry Moore's garage by now, surely, and the Blue Bell, across to Johnston's the shoe shop, into Water Street. He opened the door only a few moments before her mind had mapped him home.

She smiled as she had rarely smiled over the past months. For Ellen, any wholly unguarded expression of the deepest feeling was laying yourself too open. Even alone with Sam she could feel under examination as she had so often felt since the desertion of her father and the death of her mother when she was still a child. She had been schooled to feel grateful, bred into a repressed world, and learned for herself that the value of restraint was high. Ellen aimed at anonymity and although her prettiness, her energy and the bubbling quiet confidence pulled hard against it, anonymity was the goal, anonymity was a prized virtue and she thought she had achieved it.

Yet so much about her provoked the attention she sought to evade. Had she realised how highly she was thought of by so many in the town that meant so much to her – how idealised by the girls she taught the dancing for the carnivals and by the older generation whose family histories she knew in flattering detail – she would have concluded that she must unknowingly have become a show-off.

Showing-off was unforgivable. Show-offs should not be given the time of day. Show-offs got above themselves and who had the right to do that? Showing-off was so bad it made you blush for those who did it. In the confused constrictions of her childhood this had bitten deep, bitten into her character and bitten into her behaviour, seized the heart of her feelings and held them suffocatingly tight however often and deeply she would long to be free.

But today, in the afternoon room already darkening under the gathering clouds of the long promised snow that had been laying siege to the rest of the country and now threatened to capture the last redoubt of the white-free North-west, on this gloomy dull winter day, she was as open as a wild rose in high summer. Her gaiety – expressed in every move she made – infected Sam instantly. He had to smile. His spirits were lifted by the lightness, the zest, the unconcealed happiness that poured out of her.

He did not ask. Biding your time for good news was a nice rare pleasure. She would tell him when she was ready. But for a few minutes she was truly lost for words. So with Ellen bursting to talk, it was Sam who chatted away, factory talk, town talk, who was doing what, like the river, always the same, always different.

How easy he can be, Ellen thought, how easy he is. Not much of a tea after a day's hard physical work. Powdered eggs. Two small slices of poor bacon; fried bread to make up for it – always more or less like this, never a complaint. Often as not he would thank her and declare how good it was even though she knew it was average fare. She did not appreciate him enough, she knew that, in this full alertness, this shock of happiness.

'Sam,' she began, but so dry-throated. She sipped the strong tea. 'I don't know how to start.' She appealed for help but what could he say? Silence was his best contribution.

'It's all a bit sudden.' She shook her head, dispelling the dizziness that had confused it. 'Colin's down with Leonard and Grace. He just turned up. This morning. He just announced himself. Colin,' she said, and she drew in a full breath, 'is my half-brother.'

There was triumph in her voice, there was the tremble of loss, there was unsustainable excitement.

Sam waited. So this radiance, this burnished Ellen, was not on his account, not connected to him in any way at all. He realised that he had taken it as a personal tribute and rued his mistake, which was unfair on Ellen and so he waited for more with a determined air of enthusiasm. How stupid of him to have broken the ancient rule – not counting your chickens.

Ellen was fighting hard.

'Dad,' she began, and stumbled on the word but held herself and even repeated it to show resolution. She could not say 'Daddy' as Joe did. She could not say 'Father' like the Snaith sisters. 'Dad, when he went away, just after I was born, met somebody else. Then he got married.' She paused. 'After Mam died, but Colin was born before that.' She flushed at the implication but it was out now. 'He died, Dad, just over a year ago Colin said, and then Colin's mother went south with somebody else and Colin said Dad had always wanted him to meet up with Grace and Leonard – they're his aunty and uncle as well as mine – and so he's come up for a visit.'

There was something passionate and child-like in this account – in the gestures as well as the words – that irked Sam. It was not true to her real character, he thought. It was new.

He took a grip on himself. She had every right.

73

'What do you make of him?'

Ellen shook her head in slow motion. It was the question that had saturated her thoughts over the last few hours.

'I want you to judge for yourself,' she said, eventually. 'I want to know what you think about him.'

'We'll go down now. Joe'll find us,' he said.

'Yes.' On her feet, darting to scoop away the plates and wash them and wipe down and tidy and get herself ready and all with that sure light rapidity which elated him. 'Joe'll be going there anyway,' she said, 'for his piano practice.'

She looked moon-struck, Sam thought, altogether out of herself.

Grace sat in her usual chair in the bay window inside the large drawing room made solid by the bulky furniture she had inherited from Leonard's parents. With the upswept splendour of her bodkin-fixed helmet of hair and the vast bosom secured under an unyielding black blouse, she was a true descendant of Queen Victoria, whose public attitudes she still stood by, almost fifty years on. This was how Sam had first seen her, this was how she liked to be seen and, as a girl, Ellen had been in no doubt that her scurrying and helping were executed in homage to this majesty. To be exploited by Grace was to be brought into civilisation. Sam had resented Grace's grip on Ellen. After Ellen herself had rebelled against her overseer by marrying such a common man as himself, he had tested Grace to agitation by his refusal to moderate what he knew she despised as his coarse manners. She had noted that the war had improved him, but the old battle lines had not been eroded. Leonard, whose inheritance had hoisted his wife to the imperial state, had become Sam's subversive ally, but their defiance of the crown took place well away from home, in snug bars and Henry Allen's betting shop and now and then in a billiard room. Within her realm, Grace, whom Ellen still dared call nothing but Aunty Grace in her presence, within the gleaming heavy furniture of her domain, Grace was sovereign.

But a troubled one, Sam thought, as he entered the room, and it was the first thing he noticed. Everything outward was as it had ever been. But Grace was disturbed. Not with the high giddy confused love and loss and excitement of Ellen. Darker anxieties possessed her, although, Sam noted admiringly, she was putting a good face on it.

'Colin,' said Ellen with shy pride, 'this is Sam.'

Sam put his best foot forward and shook hands and offered a cigarette, accepted, took one himself, sat in the chair next to the younger man – and contrived to fall silent while Colin and Grace and Ellen steered a precipitous course as if just learning to ride the new bicycle of conversation.

Ellen, it was painful to see, was mesmerised by him. It was as if he were conducting her, so minutely and adhesively did she follow every nuance. When Colin said something even remotely clever or witty, she appreciated him disproportionately, Sam thought: when he listened to Grace, she listened with him. When he looked a little worried, her brow creased, smiled, she smiled with him, glanced at Sam, she too glanced at Sam, reassured, she was reassured, spoken to, spoke back in a manner that would please, seeing him pleased, was herself pleased. Sam had never seen her like this. Not anything like this.

Grace's reaction was much more concealed. Sam was not certain he was judging it rightly, but he would have bet on it – Grace was unnerved. He could see that the eruption of Colin, son of her disgraced brother, into a court beyond all reproach could be catastrophic. As if a rebellious subject had marched on her, gained access and, worst of all, claimed legitimate authority. What would Wigton make of her when it knew about him? Sam could have smiled as he intuited that anxiety but he set his face steadily to the attentive.

Sam fought hard to be fair. There was a distinct look of Ellen about the young man, although his face was rather narrower than her heart-shaped face, the skin much poorer, even sallow, the nose a weak little thing, but the eyes, the whole formation and structure of his face around the eyes – these were the clear kinship. His black hair was almost glued to his skull and the quiff perched on top of his forehead looked unstable.

What was it he did not like? The fawning repetition of 'Aunty Grace', said in a plangent Lancastrian accent, but said too often, ingratiating and, Sam could see, uncomfortably intimate for its recipient. But that was unfair. The new man had to walk carefully. He had no clue what reception he would get. It paid to be over-polite. Sam made himself accept that Colin could be too easily dismissed for seeking to make a treaty with Grace.

His attitude to Ellen, though, was not as easy to excuse and yet what was the lad doing that was wrong? He seemed too amused at Ellen's earnest curiosity and too careless of her doting. When she screwed up the courage to ask a question about their father – where he had worked, what he had done with himself, stiff little questions, all of them transparent excuses for the big questions – What was he like? Did he ever refer to, talk about my mother, about me? – he would dole out a meagre portion or say, 'Wouldn't you like to know?' and laugh, showing his bad teeth, and Ellen, helpless and tormented, would laugh along with him. Still, Sam reasoned, keeping calm, these were early days, allow the lad more rope. He was probably every bit as dislocated as the two women.

Save that he was basking in it. He was like a seal being fed fish. Up he leaped and every time more indulgences would be given. Ellen kept his cup full. Grace had brought out a valuable fruit loaf. The sandwiches were soaked in syrup. His every remark was weighed.

When Sam entered the stumbling conversation, Colin drew himself up in his chair rather as a boy would have stiffened his back as the teacher addressed him. A certain wariness. A certain preening. No, he had not been in the army or anywhere else for his National Service. Weak chest – Ellen looked alarmed. Failed the medical. Tried three times. Failed three times. Trouble holding down a job. Get a start. Do well. In line for early promotion. Chest played up. Out on his ear. What he needed was a job that did not get to his chest and a boss who would give him a real chance.

Sam sympathised. Rotten luck. His attitude softened. Without irony, he offered another cigarette. Accepted. Tucked behind his ear for later.

It was when Joe came in that Sam switched to full alert.

'This,' said Ellen, unwrapping the biggest present of all, 'is your uncle Colin.'

Joe just looked. It would mean no piano practice and that was a relief, although he did not mind the piano. He liked the praise it could bring.

'Colin.' The young man leaned forward, arms outstretched. 'None of this "Uncle". You just call me Colin.'

Joe looked to Ellen, who did not shake her head. He moved towards the waiting cage of embrace. Calling a grown-up by his first name! And a new uncle! He allowed himself to be hugged, rather winded by it.

'What a great lad! Here.' He fished in the pocket of the shiny navy blue suit. 'This is for you.' It was a shilling. Again Joe looked to Ellen and again she did not shake her head.

'Thank you, Uncle . . . sorry, thank you . . .'.

'Colin, say Colin.'

'. . . Colin.' Joe stalled for a moment at the strangeness of it.

'Can you do this?'

Colin winked with his left eye, then his right, then his left eye again and again the right, slow to start and then quickening the pace. Ellen laughed aloud.

Joe could only wink with his right eye.

'I'll teach you,' said Colin. 'And what about this?' He stuck out his tongue and touched the tip of his nose with it. Again Ellen laughed, though not so warmly, but Joe was delighted.

'I'll have to teach you that an' all,' Colin said, when Joe's best efforts failed. 'What you going to be, then?'

Joe weighed up the form.

'A boxer,' he said, but quietly.

'Good lad!' Colin raised his voice and raised his arms in the classic English pose. 'Straight left – bang, bang! On the nose! That's the one – bang, bang! I could have been a boxer. This chest.' He hawked and swallowed. It was not a welcome sound.

He looked around for the applause he had so quickly got used to but the smile of Ellen was not as full and the stillness of Grace was plain disapproval.

'Daddy told me about the straight left,' said Joe.

'Always know your left from your right and right from wrong, that's what my daddy said to me, Joe.'

'Did he?' Ellen's question was so eager.

'One of the things. This is the sixty-four-thousand-dollar question, Joe. Will Freddie Mills ever win a world title?'

'Yes,' said Joe, loyal to the British champion.

'No is the answer.' Colin reached out, grabbed Joe's arm and hauled him to within inches so that their faces almost touched. 'Always respect your mammy and daddy now. Won't you? I want you to promise.'

Joe attempted to look for support but Colin had him in a grip. 'Promise,' he said.

'Good lad.' Colin let him go. Joe smiled at his mother as if he had given her a present with the promise and she looked so happy he knew that he had.

'We'd better be off,' said Sam.

'Joe hasn't done his practice,' said Grace, swiftly.

'He plays the piano,' Ellen explained to Colin, trying to neutralise her tone. 'Well, he's starting to.'

'A musician in the family!' Colin looked amazed.

'I can play three scales and two tunes,' said Joe, flustered with the excitement of it all. The moment the boast left his lips he was aware of the ice blast from Ellen.

'Give us a listen then.'

With a glance of what he hoped was sufficient apology to his mother – but she would not satisfy him with a forgiving look – he went to the piano and performed the scale of C major with both hands.

'That's terrific!' said Colin. 'No flannel. Can you do another?'

Sam went out. They would think he had gone to the lavatory. They could think what they wanted. Two more minutes of Colin and he would have hit the ceiling.

In the cobbled yard he leaned against a wall opposite the row of run-down cottages from each of which came a glow of gas-light intimating a luxuriance of cosiness. He took his time over a cigarette and damped down that sudden flare of intense dislike. The man would go soon enough, he reassured himself. A visit was a visit. He would just have to shut his eyes and his ears and block out the effect the man had on Ellen and Joe. Sam shook his head to rid himself of the images of his wife and son, the one clinging admiringly to this worthless man, the other straining himself to please.

He ground the butt into the cobbles with an over-emphatic twist of his heel. He could drag it out no longer.

Only Grace was in the room, in the same seat, forlorn, her subjects all deserted her.

'Colin wanted a walk up the street,' she explained.

Sam felt a rare sympathy for her.

'So what did you make of him, Grace?' The boldness of tone and question caused no offence. She was deep in the well of her past.

'He is my nephew,' she said, separating one word from the other with a pronounced gap that made them sound like a forced confession. 'He is my only brother's son. Whatever I make of him.'

'What did you think of his father?' It was a question that Sam had wanted to ask in his first weeks with Ellen. Not then. Not since. But now.

'I thought the world of him.'

Her voice was low and it vibrated with sorrow. Her head was bent and she seemed to be talking more to herself than to Sam. And that proud imperial figure lowered her head.

'I always understood,' said Sam, after a pause that indicated she would say no more unprompted, 'that he was a bit of a black sheep, Grace. Word was you were glad to get rid of him.'

'He was a black sheep.' She nodded grim assent. 'But I would have done anything to stop him running away.'

'Why did he?'

'Because he was weak!' She was abrupt. Her head lifted. 'He couldn't face up to the consequences of what he'd done.'

She breathed in deeply and he knew that there was only this opportunity.

'What had he done?'

She looked square at him again but now the beseeching had faded. Yet there was a sense that having gone this far it was only fair . . .

'There was a history to it.' Grace was regaining her caution. 'Father was bad with him. And he couldn't handle drink. There were a couple of scrapes. Leonard managed them but it couldn't go on. He should never have married her. A pleasant little body, from the Newcastle side, sent over here to live with some aunt up in the hills. She was a very good-looking lass – you couldn't deny that. And there was something about her – quiet, but she had Ellen's smile about her. He fell hook, line and sinker, of course, and he could charm the birds off the trees when he wanted to. Leonard thought she would be the making of him because he did adore her at first and there was such a lot that was good in him.' Her head tilted back, just slightly, as if she were swallowing imminent tears. She looked at Sam as if he were an inquisitor. 'I'll tell you no more. Leonard tried his best. But he ran away. A card now and then at Christmas and that was it.' She looked out of the window but by now her poise was recovered. 'I never even knew he'd passed over until that Colin of his marched in. He's very like. Very like.' She paused for a while and by straining Sam heard the music from a wireless in one of the guest rooms – a sound that barely rippled in the silence. Finally she looked directly at Sam, her eyes glazed with unshed tears, and added, 'But I fear he hasn't his father's . . . good heart. No mind that he was weak.'

The words were murmured and Sam pursued it no further. He stayed on just for a while, as if he were visiting a patient in hospital and wanted to make sure that everything was settled before he left.

The cold outside caught him by the throat and a few flakes of snow twisted and swirled in the bitter wind. He clutched his jacket collar around his neck and bowed his head into the weather.

CHAPTER NINE

'They sent me a through ticket,' said Mrs Baxter. 'It means I have to set off from Wigton station.'

'Sam'll carry your cases down.' Ellen guessed that this was the reason for Mrs Baxter's uncharacteristic visit and the expression of relief confirmed it.

'If he wouldn't mind.'

'No, no.' Ellen discouraged gratitude. 'More tea?'

'No, thank you. That was lovely, thank you.'

'How long will it take?'

'Nearly three days. By the time I've changed from one thing to the other. There's people to meet you at London and on to the boat. I wish it was over with.'

'I'm sure they'll have it organised. Mary tells me she's looking forward to it.' Ellen smiled at the little girl, who was sitting deep in an armchair, her short legs just jutting over the edge of the cushion, her concentration fully trained on the farmyard she was crayoning in. Joe, thankfully, was at choir practice.

'I wish I could say the same.' Mrs Baxter blinked away the emotion that threatened and hid her face behind the cup, searching for a last sip of tea. 'But there we are,' she said, when she re-emerged.

'It's what he wants. You have to go where they go. What else can you do?' Ellen felt chill. She leaned forward to poke the fire. 'He says they give you nice houses. And there's a school for Mary. But for all that Germany's a funny place to be going, isn't it? When you think.'

'I'm sure it'll work out,' was the best Ellen could manage.

'We were calling them everything not so long ago.' Clearly Mrs Baxter wanted to talk.

'People change,' said Ellen, as dampeningly as she could.

'But what they did!'

'Sure you won't have another cup?'

'No.' The hint was taken. 'We'd best be getting back.'

'You don't have to rush off.' Ellen knew that her guilt was painted on her face.

'It's time to go.' Mrs Baxter pursed her lips. 'And if Sam can't do it . . .'

'He will.' Ellen's interruption was over-loud. She repeated it quietly. 'He will.'

When they had gone, Ellen went into a wholly unnecessary bout of cleaning.

The two suitcases were obese and Sam had to keep half a pace behind Mrs Baxter on the narrow pavements. Mary and Joe trailed along, saying nothing, both bulked out in winter layers, twin dumplings. Mary was wearing the maroon scarf Ellen had given her that morning.

They were the only ones in the waiting room, so they could stand right next to the stove.

'Can we go out and play?'

'Not on that bridge,' said Sam. To Mrs Baxter, 'He once scared his mother half to death by monkeying along the ledge of that bridge. Not today. It's too cold. There'll be no grip.'

Joe had to accept this. But the urge to get out of the waiting room overwhelmed any exhibitionist disappointment and he led Mary around to the back. There was a narrow space between the black railings and the sandstone building and Mary squeezed in first.

'She'll miss him,' said Mrs Baxter. 'They played well together.'

'They soon make new friends.' Sam was impatient for the train. His manner became more distant. Where was the train? He broke the silence when he realised it had become embarrassing. 'What is it you'll miss most then?'

'I've thought a lot about that. And do you know?' Mrs Baxter smiled rather coyly and Sam saw that she was an attractive woman, the smile transformed her utterly. 'It's the whist drives in the parish rooms. Maybe because they let the kiddies come. Silly, isn't it?'

'They'll have whist drives in Germany. And housey-housey – it'll be just the job. Is that the train?'

Joe had heard it first and he and Mary were standing on the platform, demurely apart.

'One last thing,' said Mrs Baxter, after Sam had swung the suitcases into an empty compartment and swung Mary in after them. She lowered her voice and looked at the ground. 'What do I give porters for tips?'

Sam, whose impatience had been accelerating, almost burst out laughing. 'Threepence at Carlisle. Sixpence in London. But only if you feel like it because they're getting paid anyway.'

'Thank you.'

'Well then.' Sam put out his hand. 'The very best of luck to you. And you, Mary. You'll look after your mother, won't you?'

Mary nodded and then, as bidden, said bye-bye to Joe, who

solemnly returned the message. Sam wanted to leave immediately but Mary leaned out of the window and waved and Joe stayed rooted until the small figure withdrew.

Joe looked up at his father and for a moment or two, as their eyes met, it was as if they could not see each other, did not quite recognise each other. Thoughts too deep for their words were stirred by the fading rhythm of the train as it ploughed through the white fields and eventually disappeared, leaving only a wave of smoke in the air as a last farewell.

'Race you over the bridge.'

Sam's challenge was half-hearted, but Joe wrenched himself into a response and made an unenthusiastic dash for the steps.

Later that afternoon the pain that had been sending out signals for a few days suddenly intensified. It seemed to explode in his jaw into his ear, into his brain, and within an hour or so it was difficult for Sam to remember a time when he had not had toothache. It was too late for the dentist.

'I'll go across to Alf's and get some arrowroot,' said Sadie.

'Let Joe do it. It's just across the street.' Ellen did not like the way Joe had been moping all afternoon. 'Go to the back door,' she said, and handed him a shilling.

His exit was rather lethargic.

'Hurry up!' Ellen was sharp. 'Your dad's not well!'

'That should fettle it up,' said Sadie. 'You just bite on it.'

Sadie had come to go to the pub and then the dance. Rather unusually, it was Ellen who had decided that she wanted to go out for the evening. She had mentioned this to Sadie who had promptly invited herself to go with them. Ellen was glad of it. Sadie had been her best friend for so long that she would have felt a touch lost on any outing without her. There was a little flattery in it. Sadie had always been devoted to Ellen and ever grateful that such a well-liked, well-known, respectable person, with Sam for a husband, should pick out someone like her. Sadie had no illusions. Her lean and gypsy looks bred unsavoury rumours; her husband's occasional drunken batterings made her a woman of bad luck, better avoided; her menial existence allowed almost anyone in the town to feel superior if they chose. But she knew that Ellen really liked her.

'You could rub Vaseline on your gums. And put something cold on your cheek. That can numb it.'

'I'll go and stand in the yard for a minute or two.'

'It said in the paper it's going to get very bad. We've had the best of it up here so far.' Sadie loved the feeling of privilege this transient and freakish singularity had brought to the area. 'It says down south they have no electric for five hours a day.'

'That would finish us off, then.' Sadie missed Sam's sarcasm.

'There's trains buried in snow, down south. Just think of that. Buried. And seventy-eight women was trapped by snow in Hull.' The drama consumed her. Sam enjoyed the performance. 'Coal ships is stuck in ice out at Newcastle. Stuck! Millions of factories can't work.'

Sam attempted no tease here. The paper-making factory that employed him as a slitter was on a continuous process and the managers were now letting the process run out until the material in circulation was exhausted. Then the factory would be closed down for maintenance work, usually done in the summer fortnight. They would be glad of Ellen's wages. That irked him.

He shifted in his seat as if that would help reduce the toothache. Curiously, for a moment or two, it did. 'How long is he going to be?'

'Alf'll probably have to ratch around for it.' Sadie always took Joe's side.

'There's ice in Water Street. In that horse trough,' said Ellen. 'I could wrap it up in a flour bag. You can hold it to your face.'

She took the poker and pulled on her coat as she went through the door.

'She's gone to look for Joe.' Sam smiled, a smile that turned into a wince. 'She clucks over him all day.'

'Who better to cluck over?' Sadie's indignation was high and instant. 'He's a super-dooper little lad. He sang "Yes, We Have No Bananas" for me last Wednesday after his piano practice when he came round with Colin. He's very friendly, isn't he, that Colin? Full of beans considering his condition. "Roll on the snow," he says, "me and Joe's going to make the biggest snowman in Wigton!"'

'Any chance of a fresh pot, Sadie?'

Sam turned on the wireless and found some big band music. 'I wish they wouldn't try to go for the Glenn Miller sound,' said Sadie – they were playing 'String of Pearls'. 'Glenn's the only one who could do it.'

Still, as she drew out the simple act of making tea, her feet picked up the rhythm and in tiny steps she danced on the lino in front of the sink. 'There'll be more of this at the dance tonight.' She sounded grim. Music mattered to Sadie. She hated Wigton's failure to keep up with the fashion, indeed to seem to glory in lagging years behind it. 'Billy Bowman and his blooming borin' band again.' She brought him the cup. 'I've put the milk in for you.'

'Thank you.' He left it to cool. Gingerly he fingered the aching tooth and rubbed at the gum, which seemed to help. Then he fastened a grip on it and yanked firmly. It yielded nothing save further pain that flooded into his skull.

Sadie was now wholly absorbed in the music, dancing dainty half-steps on the prodded rug, turning and swirling with her imaginary partner while holding her cup ship's-compass steady. 'Come on, Sam. It'll take your mind off it.'

He got up. Held her correctly, politely. They turned the cramped space into a dance-floor. When Ellen and Joe came in they were well into it, Sadie's cup still in hand. Ellen immediately partnered Joe, who jumped about in time to the music. She did not try to teach him.

'It always ends when it's getting going.' A cultured voice had replaced the band. Sam switched it off.

'No arrowroot,' said Ellen, her eyes sparkling, and Joe's even brighter. 'I've left the ice outside the door.'

'We met Colin,' said Joe. Ellen still had to stop herself from saying 'Uncle Colin' although that correction lit up in her mind every time Joe used the name, but the child was so pleased to be able to call a grown-up by his Christian name. 'And he said,' Ellen's warning glance was too late, 'that when he got the money together he would buy me a train set. A real one. He would put it up in the room upstairs. Railway lines, signal boxes, passenger trains and goods trains and I would sit in the middle and just make them all whizz around.'

'He has to get the money together first,' said Ellen, uneasy now at Joe's over-excitement. 'That could take him a long time.'

'That would be fantastic, though, wouldn't it?' Sadie appealed to them all. 'Would you let me have a play with it, Joe? He's more like a brother than an uncle,' she observed to Sam.

'He sent his best.' Ellen spoke placatingly to Sam. 'He couldn't come in because he was meeting somebody in the Half Moon.'

'Is he going to the dance?' Sadie asked.

'Yes.'

'I bet he's a good dancer. I'll get him up. They always have a Ladies' Choice late on.'

'Maybe he'll get you up first.' Ellen felt flustered. 'I'll get the ice.'

While she was making the pack, Sadie took Joe down to Grace's house where he would spend the night.

Sam held the pack against his face until the numbness set in. The diminution of pain was dramatic enough to release him first to the pub where a couple of whiskies helped, then to the dance and back home to pick up more of the ice, and spend another half-hour nursing his jaw.

But in the early hours of the morning the pain returned and violently. He should have had them all out on the ship on the way back like some of the others. They said the salt air hardened your gums faster than anything else could and by the time you were back in Blighty the false teeth had settled in and you were set up for life – no more trouble. It had been Alex's expression when he had raised the idea: that expression, nothing said, had stopped him.

He had written back to Alex and he tried to remember the letter word for word to take his mind off this wearying pain. Only the faintest glow came from the fire. He had banked it up with slack for the night. The silence outside was so complete it was eerie. It must be the snow. It had started while they were in the dance hall. Colin had thrown snowballs at them as they walked down King Street. Nothing much wrong with a chest that could take in drink, dancing – and he had proved a good dancer, delighting Sadie by asking her for the first quickstep – and now snow. But Sam turned those thoughts away.

The letter was very awkward. He wanted to ask questions and ask for more about Kipling. Instead it was a catalogue of Wigton gossip to which Alex was never particularly addicted, and news headlines – the Big Freeze, Palestine, more rationing – he would know all that anyway.

He doubted Alex would reply. Probably well into teaching and being a naturalist and getting on with his new life.

The relentless pain was tiring and Sam managed only to surf on the crest of sleep. How was it that such a small pain could be harder to bear than the much bigger injuries of war? They had talked about mind over matter after seeing the fire-walking in India. And the lying on a bed of nails. But he had seen British soldiers, ordinary lads, put up with the most terrible pain – amputations without any anaesthetic, he'd seen that, holding on with both hands to spilled-out entrails as if they were a child to be cradled, Sam had seen that, and the terrible protracted death of Ian, his best friend before Alex, in such pain and yet lucid, able to talk gamely – how did they do that when a titchy toothache threatened to split his skull? Alex would have had a line on it all. Maybe the answer was to fill his mouth with snow and numb it all and when the snow melted do it again. What was it he had read that Australians ate on Christmas Day on Bondi beach? More like a brother? Going back soon. Just here on a visit. Maybe it was not pain at all. Maybe he could think it was something else. 'String of Pearls.' Was this a good life?

In the morning when he opened the door, the snow in the yard was over two feet deep and the large flakes fell in graceful unending profusion, silently, attractively, suffocating the town.

CHAPTER TEN

They sledged on Pasce Egg Hill. They pronounced it 'Pace'. As the snow deepened to a glorious fastness and the obliging ice gripped it ever harder, the town became a white ecstasy for the bolder boys and Joe – thanks to Speed – was now just about in that enviable circle. Only a few of the children knew what Ellen had told Joe – that when she was a girl, they would go down to the Show Fields after the Easter Monday service and in the third field cross the river to the steepness of Pasce Egg Hill and roll their dyed extra-hard-boiled eggs down the lower slopes. That was the Easter treat. Ellen was eager for Joe to know that. She wanted him to know that she had gone before him in the town for her pleasure too and in the self-same place and out of that came the name Pasce Egg Hill, meaning Easter Hill if you knew about church. It was not something Joe passed on.

Snow made the house better. It was so burrowed and snug, its smallness a bonus now, the fire never allowed to die. Paradise began after breakfast. Into the yard down the new white alley cut out by his daddy, snow walls either side, his full height, through the squatters' yard, into Scott's yard, into Water Street for the first snowball fight of the day, mittens caked white and soaked in pleasure, but nevertheless by five to nine imprisoned as usual in the neat new red-brick primary school, Miss Moffat calling the register.

Playtimes were dreamtimes, snowballs slapped into quick shape, stacked up in ready pyramids of ammunition by the smaller boys and the gamer girls and full-scale wars between the forms. Joe found himself leading a gang and yelling, 'Charge,' with snowballs clutched to the chest, chapped hands, chapped thighs, face stiff with the freezing and pumped up with blood and battle and the soft violence of snow. Shoving snowballs down the necks of scaredy-cat boys or simple screaming girls and the older ones said to stuff snowballs all the way up the bigger girls' skirts, even into their knickers. Splatting hard snowballs against a target on the lavatory wall. Failing to build an igloo. The schoolroom in those weeks only a place of refuge and recuperation, drying out between the white dramas of snow.

Snow made life better. Snow did not hurt. Snow beat everything. Snow was for boys. Snow made you happy. Just to look at it. You could suck snow for a drink. Snow made your hands red and the big vein on the back of the right hand swelled up but that was OK because it was snow that did it. Snow changed everything and made everything look better. Wigton was like a picture with snow on. His mammy said that. But most of all, snow meant the bolder boys could sledge from the top of Pasce Egg Hill.

You could get a bit in after school before it got dark but the hill was a good walk and a short time was not the same. Saturday was the day.

Colin had asked him to come to finish that monster snowman. Joe turned up right on nine. He was badly torn. He wanted to get it over with so that he could go sledging. But Colin was Colin – see the way his mammy liked him – and so better than sledging, surely?

'He's in his bed,' Grace told the child. 'But he said send you up. Don't stay long.'

He was in the bed that Joe had shared with Ellen while Sam had been in the war. Two pillows were puffed up behind him. There was evidence of a largely consumed breakfast on a tray. He was reading *Tit Bits*.

'Thought it might be Aunty Grace,' he said, and opened his hand to reveal a just-nipped stump. 'She says smoking makes it worse.' He rolled his eyes and lit up. 'I'll have to spin them out.' Talking and inhaling together caught his throat and he coughed so violently it was like retching. Even two floors down in the basement, Grace could hear it and frowned at this clear evidence of the weak chest, even though he had not helped it by larking around in the snow and getting himself soaked the night before with Joe when he had finally got round to building the promised snowman. It stood next to the pens at the bottom of the hill, a huge trunk, a lower dent indicating legs, but without arms, a neck or a head. The night had frozen it hard.

'Fancy a game of pontoon?' Colin's deck was snappily new: a belated Christmas present from Grace. 'I'll divide up the matches.'

Joe had enjoyed being taught the game but now? With the snow, and sledging, the sun bright, which could melt the snow. He took his share of the matches.

'Use your loaf,' Colin grumbled, after Joe revealed a hand on which he ought not to have twisted. 'It's no fun if you don't.'

There was a vague hope in Joe's mind that the sooner he lost all his matches, the sooner the game would be over, but Colin merely pencilled the number of victories in the margins of *Tit Bits* and began again.

As the sun sparkled the snow on the rooftops he could see out of the window, Joe could not conceal his decreasing relish for pontoon.

'How about Hangman?'

The boy nodded. Colin found space in the magazine and pencilled in nine short dashes – an interrupted line.

'A,' said Joe, dutifully.

'No.' Colin drew the base of the gibbet.

'E.'

He marked the E.

Then, abruptly, and roughly, he grabbed Joe under the arms and held him aloft, squeezing him quite fiercely.

'Who's down in the dumps today?'

'Nobody is.'

'I know somebody who is.'

Joe wriggled. The grip hurt but Colin was smiling so it must be all right. The pressure tightened.

'Who does he like best, then?'

He wished Colin would not ask that. He really wished he would not make him answer that.

'Next to your mammy.'

And Daddy, Joe felt he ought to say.

'Colin, isn't it?'

The boy was near breathless now. It hurt.

'Isn't it?'

The threat was unspecific but clear.

'Yes. Colin. Yes.'

'Put the boy down!'

Joe landed on the bed and rolled off it immediately.

'He'll get what you've got,' said Grace.

'Sorry, Aunty Grace.'

'Sorry, Aunty Grace,' Joe echoed.

'Off you go,' to Joe. 'And you.' Colin waited for his sentence: she sniffed, twice. 'Just don't let me catch you smoking a cigarette.'

'Did I smoke, Joe, tell her?'

Joe panicked. But he had to fill the pause. He looked down and muttered and blushed. Grace was not deceived but Joe was not her target. Yet Colin's expression was of one exonerated. A flick of her head sent Joe out, down the stairs, up the street, into the yard, grab the sledge, trail it behind him on the road to polish the runners his daddy had found down in Vinegar Hill, where he used to live as a boy and where he remembered his own first sledging winter but never snow like this.

As he trotted down the gashed black road between hedges of mottled white Joe weighed up the Wigton sledging map. The slopes beyond Howrigg were long but not steep enough; around the baths they were too short and there was no run at the bottom before the fence. Station Hill was unexplored but no great reports came back. Old Carlisle was lumpy and twisty because of the Roman ruins under the ground so you could not motor. Some of the Show Fields slopes were good for learning on but – and here Joe warmed with pride – nowhere and nothing compared with getting to the third Show Field, inching across the frozen river Wiza, finding a gap in hawthorn hedges, winter blossoming in nets of frost, dipping through the fence and then, rising up, Pasce Egg Hill, the king of all Wigton's sledging hills, steep, glassy, long and short runs, easy and hard runs and, toughest of all in the middle of the hill, a huge bump which lifted you clear off the ground so that you sailed, just sailed, it made you scream with pleasure.

His thighs were already chapped in the short pants, the mittens were freezing soggy, his fingers were already nipping, his wool-framed face was iced cold on the periscope window of skin unmasked by the balaclava, but his clogs had held against the weather and as he tugged the Daddy-made sledge up the hill he would not have changed places with any other soul on the planet.

The only girls were from the tinkers down at Vinegar Hill, a few Water Street girls and others, ex-Water Street, now rehoused on airy Brindlefield. He noticed Lizzie who had once lived in the next yard and tried to catch her eye to show that he was one of the bigger boys now, but she was screaming for a go on a tray. Her gang had only a couple of sledges between them and those who could not pile on to the high child-stacked vehicles that teetered and wobbled into reluctant service would stick a tin tray or a cake-tin top under their bottoms, lift up their legs, use their hands like short urgent oars to build up acceleration and then, when they hit the run, roar and yell and spread out their arms like a tightrope-walker's pole as they hurtled towards the Wiza river, frozen for days in its serpentine wendings.

Speed had a tray. Joe waved and gratifyingly the wave was returned. Then Joe – one of the smallest – took his place among the boys in the queue at the very top. If you had the jitters you sat on the sledge so that falling off was easy. If you used your loaf then lying belly down flat on the wooden slats was far more thrilling and manageable although more dangerous. Your face practically shaved the snow – now sledged and runnered to packed ice. Your feet could dig in and slow down and steer, but not on the bits that mattered and slowing down was not the point. The point was sensation.

Joe, braver now because of the boxing gloves, pushed the sledge in front of him – the runners glazed from that trail through the streets and a quick professional rub with snow – and ran, hunched over it, hurled himself on to it, his chest thwacking the wood, gathering momentum, urging it on, the surface snow surfing his bare legs, the world reduced to white, the big bump not soon enough, too soon, here we go and that freedom of leap, that soar of gut soul happiness, the lifting off and for a split second he was in the air, free, flying until jolt, crump, judder, back on earth, on track, the whistle of the descent like a high note, the finest note, the only note you every wanted to hear. Just sledging for ever and ever, sledging and being lost to everything except what was most important of all – being in that moment and nothing else, nothing at all else mattered. Now the final flat slowdown before the fence, digging in the toe of the right clog to swerve left because he had almost got to the fence, which was one of the aims but not quite yet, swerving left and luxuriating in that beat, that searing emptiness before re-entering the world as it usually was and immediately, though a little dazed, tugging the sledge back up the steep ascent of Pasce Egg Hill, whistling, his heart high as the sun.

Speed joined him and they went down together, Speed on the bottom, Joe lying on top of him, double-layered over the big bump and crashing down but not damaging the sledge at all. Speed took a massive run at it the next time and it was all Joe could do to keep up and hurl himself on top of his imperious friend who scraped the ground with his fingers for more pace even as they hit the steepest stretch, more and more pace and Joe on the wire body of Speed, so very happy that the world and all about it could have comprised nothing else but this, his, their, sledging.

Malcolm, one of Joe's new friends from the choir, came to ask for a go. Speed was adamant, and it was Joe who backed off and let the friend take his place on the back of Speed, but it was not a success. The boy was frightened of Speed. Word at home and at school had taught him to be frightened of Water Street, Roman Catholics, too much poverty, violence in the family and Speed's family in particular. He was not a coward, the boy, but Speed's ferocity, which was by now part of Joe's bloodstream idolatry, unnerved him and he slunk away, aware that he was not brave. Joe was confused by it. He wanted his friends to like each other. He felt, obscurely, that he was to blame but for what? He also felt pumped up that he was the unafraid friend of the mad Speed who by now had been singled out as the hero of the hill and took his next turn, alone, standing upright on the sledge, holding the rope with one hand, with the other performing lasso movements, war-whooping as it careered towards the bump and threw him spectacularly, but he was up instantly and seven-league strides down the hill in his soaked plimsolls, leaping through the off-the-run snow to capture the runaway sledge and dare to do it again.

Word went out it was dinner-time and the congregation filed away to their homes, hurrying through the fields, Joe running until he got home to bolt a meal and see his gloves and short trousers dry and warm on the lowered pulley beside the fire, shivering to get back as soon as humanly possible to the total life of sledging.

Diddler stood a respectful couple of yards from the front door. He had refused the invitation to come in for a cup of tea. 'Not dressed for the job, Sam,' he said.

The big Irish tinker was chief of the scavenging settlement called Vinegar Hill, the poorest part of the town. Diddler was kerchiefed around the neck, a horse trader and general dealer, a rogue rover, and the leader of a pack bypassed by history, outside the mechanisms of society, harking back to days before the town itself was settled.

'They want us to shovel the snow, Sam,' he said, 'in the manky little places.'

Diddler grinned – it split his large, slightly Mongolian-looking face and revealed within the fine sculpted skull a cavern of gum. The teeth only went in for occasions.

'It beats the dole.'

'I'll get my coat.'

The bell had just gone for early Communion. Ellen rapidly packed Sam some bait, which he stuffed into the deep pockets of his army greatcoat.

Kettler joined them from across the yard. He was badly hung-over but despite his professional skiving he was known to be a good man with a spade and he never missed out when Diddler, his cousin, called on him. There would always be something more to it, there would always be a bonus somewhere, and a story.

'Surprising what you get to see in these out-of-the-way country places. My old da made me wise to that,' Diddler said to Sam as he clicked his tongue, flicked the reins and kept the strong pony at a trot. There were four of them on the cart, Diddler's younger brother making up the gang. 'They'll be grateful to us, you know, for shifting this snow, and you'll get let into houses that wouldn't even answer your knock another day. The things that's lying around and tucked away in those little places, you know, about those old farmyards, in the old byres and barns – they don't know the value – it's a rare chance for a good look-see, Sam. And all on the council!'

'The money's good,' Sam agreed.

'Beats your dole,' he repeated, and spat a jet on to the verge. 'Don't let them get you on to that, Sam. They'll have your number then, so they will.'

Sam only nodded. He did not want to open his mouth more than necessary for a day or two. The infected molar had left a crater which his tongue probed regularly. How could anything so badly rotten at the roots – the dentist had shown him the evidence with pride – have been so violently difficult to pull out?

The job was to meet the parish council's responsibilities by clearing the smaller tracks and lanes that netted the farms into the town. Throughout the day they were never beyond sight of the town – the tall incongruous Italianate tower of Highmoor was always there and often they could see a portion of the impacted cramped huddle that still housed most of the five thousand inhabitants.

Yet even by the separation of a few fields they felt cut off, well outside the place and, in Sam's case, free of it, well free of it.

The weather had closed the factory. With no money coming in, the cash deal that Diddler made with the council – he had the monopoly on exceptional and dirty jobs – was a godsend. The work was hard but Sam had never been afraid of that and over the following weeks he grew to love it.

Maybe it was the gang of them – all things discounted, it was a bit like the section of eight or nine men he had been part of then led in Burma. The patter of cynicism. The plague that was on all. The work was basic, shovelling. You couldn't hide. Now and then Diddler would stroll off to bargain or ferret around or mark down and they would all enjoy his knack of returning with loot just as certain men in the section had fine light fingers, much appreciated by their immediate comrades. There were echoes of war, echoes of the better bits.

The root of his love of this uncomplicated labour, however, was more likely planted in his life before the war. When he was a boy in the small, ramshackle, teetering, runnelled, storeyed maze of Vinegar Hill, moated by aborted fields though plumb in the middle of town, he had been aware, made aware, that he and his kind were the bottom of the heap. As a soldier he had served in the East, India as well as Burma, and seen untouchables and mutilated child beggars, and now he knew how deep the heap was; but as a boy in Wigton he was the lowest, which was why Grace had been so resentful of his courtship of Ellen.

Now he was back where he had started. With a shovel. Men like him. The pay of the day. Work casually given, almost contemptuously terminated. He knew where he was. And he felt not liberated, not revolutionary, certainly not resentful: he felt secure. Here he was. Bottom dog. Just like in the army. Pushing the Japs back from Imphala to Rangoon. The Borders smack in the front line. They were the front line. His section. There's the wood. Bunkered Japs, dug in Japs. Japs! Best warriors as good as any on earth. You. Go in. No questions.

And they went in that time and in that wood against that enemy, and they lost seven men dead and eleven wounded and slaughtered a hundred and thirty-nine of Japan's deeply prepared élite troops. The joy of it survived, Sam knew, to be concealed throughout his life, but that was a fact. He was there. How did you get back from that?

It was not proportionate at all to bring Burma to Wigton – he knew that – but sometimes comparisons were like that, he thought, completely out of kilter, unmatching, but an excuse for linking wildly different parts of life that craved kinship.

To see the four of them, himself included, shovelling snow, was to feel he was thousands of miles away. Like the section he had led, they just set to and did the job, There was no hourly rate about it, no time to be filled up. They were below all that. They bent their backs to do the job as effectively as possible and then they took a view and sought out the spoils.

Sam liked to observe Diddler with his prey. He would praise people never praised and flatter people to whom flattery was a foreign language. He would scrounge a cup of tea and a scone or two in such a way it became a favour, and then he would notice something and barter for it and not get it and tell them they were the ones, they had the nose and then suggest that this or that trifle might be dispensable and so it was and deals were struck and because of the favours Diddler granted – shift the snow off that barn roof, no extra payment, mister, who do you think I am? – gifts would come and easy access to what seemed obsolete to the farmer but Diddler knew for a bargain.

Flattery, aped sincerity, serious hard work, favours, sleight-of-hand, the pre-agricultural arts of scavenging, and never a complaint from the fleeced – Sam had seen such reivers in Burma, the Borderers cleaning opportunity to the bone, and the cart that went back to Wigton, relieved of the grit and salt, would be laden with loot, as from a raid, loot partially concealed under the old sacks brought on purpose, and sometimes so heavily laden that the four of them had to walk as the pony hauled the spoils of victory back to Vinegar Hill.

The days of shovelling cleared a lot of snow and the shifted snow seemed to unblock his mind. He was no scholar nor would he be. That chance had gone if it had ever been there. He would always have the streak of wonder and the dreaminess of a life the other side of under-education but that was best put aside. Alex was gone now. These lads, the roughest lads, these were where he came from and if he kept to them he would be all right. Stray too far, in the Wigton he had returned to twice now, and he would dither and upset himself and everybody else. By the time the job was finished, his resolve was set.

CHAPTER ELEVEN

On the Saturday, Sam went out to see that his father and his sister, Ruth, were still in the clear. He had battled his way through after the first heavy falls of snow and spent a day with the old man carving tunnels of communication between his father's cottage, the big house he worked for and the lane that another parish council was responsible for, but the further falls had worried him.

There was something else. His father, now approaching seventy, a veteran of the Western Front of the First World War and the perilous coal mines in West Cumbria, had laboured alongside him to clear the snow. Sam had not worked with him since he had been a boy and forced to be his father's unpaid apprentice – he was then a farm labourer – after school. The old man could still shift work. The raw heft of it still gave him a command, which he turned on his son, unspeakably bringing up those earlier times of domination, authority, beating. Sam resented it and admired it and gave up.

This was the man who had wrecked his chances of a scholarship. Twice. This was the man who had, once, thrown a book of his into the fire. This was the man who had told him that books were no use. Yet now, side by side in the snow, father and son, the old man scooping and slinging the white spadefuls with relentless application, Sam realised that he was as near to him as ever he had been or would be. This was his father. Together in the remote and profoundly silent countryside, while they cut the packed snow, Sam observed him closely. I am this man's son. However much harm he did me. He is in me. Together, we are making a path through the snow.

Ellen tried not to show that she was pleased that he had gone to see his father but she was. She would never have admitted it to anyone – she scarcely admitted it to herself – but days without Sam meant days when she could concentrate on Colin.

She had been lucky at the shops the previous evening. She had an unusual surplus of coupons left in the ration books and she had found the Co-op and Walter Wilson's better stocked than usual. By dividing her custom between the two, though this was an embarrassment to which she would not normally have exposed herself, she managed quite legally to secure an extra tin of sliced pears, a second large tin of condensed milk, which Colin especially liked, and two bars of milk chocolate – one for Colin. And ten Players Full Strength. She was not being greedy, she told herself, because stocks were almost plentiful, she had the coupons to cover the goods and, anyway, Colin was not well and her half-brother and every visit to him was like taking a birthday party to him.

The fact that the streets were white banked under the few working lights, the road itself a black canal, the shops lit by paraffin lamps and candles, made the whole experience, to Ellen, one of magic. Wigton became a fantasy. The drifts of snow, the alleys dark between the white, sky so clear every star hard cut, shadows shuffling in yellow flickering light that made shops seem like Ali Baba caves, and the people, cold, perhaps even fearful some of them, but actors in this frozen exotic scene as they stepped out of unlit yards and followed the directions delivered by the tyrannising snow. Wigton had never been so wonderfully isolated and independent of all others and so loved by her.

She gave Sam an hour or so start, as if, guiltily, she were making sure she would not be caught out if he returned. She did not examine the guilt.

She went down the street with the provisions in a basket, her heart lifting at the prospect of seeing Colin. Grace understood and sympathised. It was almost heartbreaking for her to watch the care, the love, the zeal that Ellen brought to the straightforward task of preparing a tray to take up to her brother. Grace herself was still shaken by his arrival.

'Did you get any fags?'

'Let me put the tray down first.'

He glanced at what was a feast of treats but they could wait. 'I'm gaspin'.'

'You shouldn't smoke so much. Not with that chest.'

'It helps my chest – what do you know? It eases it up.'

'There!'

'Only ten!'

Ellen tightened her lips. 'I brought ten yesterday.'

'Ten doesn't last long.' He was almost gobbling the cigarette. 'Not when you're as badly as I am.'

His dip into pathos touched her. 'I'm sorry,' she said. 'I'll bring some more tomorrow morning.'

Now he was smoking. He lugged the smoke into his lungs in heaves of addicted pleasure.

'I can contribute,' he said, cautiously.

'No, no.'

She looked at the tray, hoping for a comment. He took his time. Then he stubbed out the half-smoked cigarette. 'Better be safe than sorry,' he said, reproachfully, and stuck the stump behind his ear.

'You like condensed milk on fruit, don't you?'

'Generally,' said the young man. He took the brimful bowl and slurped a few spoonfuls of the sweet milk before attacking the tinned pears.

'Very tasty,' he pronounced, and Ellen beamed.

'I knew you'd like them.'

'Dad,' he said, and paused, and licked the spoon, and paused again. 'Our dad, sis, he used to love tinned fruit.'

'Did he?' The elation was plain on her face and Colin smiled.

'You went to the flicks in Carlisle again yesterday with Sadie, didn't you?' His tone was not quite accusing. 'What was it this time?'

'*Rebecca*.'

'What happens?'

Ellen told him the story succinctly but he was soon bored.

'There's Jane Russell coming on next week, it says in the *Cumberland News. The Outlaw.* I hope I'll be better enough to go to that! There's all this talk about her cleavage. Apparently it has to be seen.'

'George Formby's on as well.'

'Damn George Formby.'

'I thought you might like him. He comes from your part of the world.'

'That means I can see through him. Ukuleles!'

Ellen produced the chocolate which he accepted quite civilly but deferred eating it and lit up the stump of cigarette.

'I'm clapped out, sis,' he said. 'Just in my twenties and clapped out.' He spluttered through the cigarette and banged his chest. 'Your health,' he said, 'you're nothing without your health.' He felt so genuinely and deeply sorry for himself that he was generous. 'Dad used to say you were nothing without your health. That's what he would say about you. When he told me. "As long as she has her health," he said, "I'll be satisfied." '

So he had talked about her – Colin had alluded to it and, she was well aware, fibbed now and then, fibbed to please, which was forgivable. But this sounded true. So he had thought about her. She choked down the feeling that welled in her throat.

'Am I like him at all?' she asked, finally summoning up the courage.

'I've been thinking that over and over, sis,' said Colin, snapping off two squares of chocolate. 'I'm coming to conclusions and when I get there I'll tell you but one thing: we've both got his eyes. And his hair. Both of us have the same hair.'

He rolled back on the pillows, talk done for the moment. Ellen knew, even after their short experiences together, that to press him would be of no use.

He had fed well. He seemed to doze. She took the ravaged tray downstairs and went over what mattered. Same eyes. Same hair. Sam had always liked her hair.

He *had* talked about her.

By the time the thaw came she and Sam were deep in love. Better than before, she thought. Better than the snatched times, better than the honeymoon, better than the first year, better than they could have imagined. Shift work, Sam said, was not so bad after all, it gave them the freedom of the afternoon when Joe was at school.

It was a time of their lives. It was them, it was sex, it was relief, it was freedom for her – partly because of Colin – and the discovery of a father, it was the abandonment of Alex, it was fatalism for Sam, but a fierce accepting even joyous fatalism, and for Ellen it was the discovered way to have and to hold, to conquer and to keep. It was the time when all that was curled up and enfolded in the expectation of life uncurled, unfolded, undid the disciplined and oppressive instincts of years, and in that house in that small condemned yard in that thawing, bleak town, they knew that they loved each other and could do this, could do this, could do this.

CHAPTER TWELVE

Ellen and Sam had been to the second house of the pictures and mingled in the street with the last to leave the pubs. Now they were alone. Joe had spent the afternoon with Colin and he needed no urging to stay the night at Grace's house. Sam had already taken off his slush-soaked shoes and was holding them in front of the fire.

Finally Ellen just came out with it. The winding tactful way seemed almost deceitful. She had nothing to be ashamed or afraid of and yet her colour rose and she felt a pulse of trembling. But she would not be silent about her feelings for her brother.

'Colin's going back,' she began, and rushed on as she saw Sam's expression gladden. 'He's going back to get all his things and then he's coming to live here. In Wigton.'

'But he's no good, Ellen.'

It was like spit in her face.

She did not hesitate for long.

'Samuel Richardson that's a terrible thing to say about my brother.'

'He's a dead loss, Ellen.'

'Don't say that! You can't say that! Joe loves him.'

'That's another worry.'

She had aimed to wound but only steeled him.

'What are you talking about?'

'I think he's a bad influence.'

'And I suppose you're such a good influence egging him on to fight?'

'He has to learn.'

'Colin plays with him. That's what Joe really likes.'

'I didn't think you had it in you, Ellen.'

'What's that?'

'Spite.'

That winded her. That and the knowledge that she, too, had noted flaws, though not as ruthlessly as Sam. But they should never be admitted or brought into the equation and they counted as nothing, insubstantial passing shadows, compared with the dazzling light he had brought into her life. Colin was a new life – for what he had brought and what he was; that he was weak made it all the more necessary to defend and help him. That he could be a bit demanding at times was undeniable but understandable. There were darker areas which she would not and could not address.

'I think you're jealous of him,' she said. 'Because of Joe.'

'Jealous? Of that drip?'

'Because of Joe.'

Sam put the shoes on the floor, sat back and folded his arms to get a grip. His hands covered the muscles on his biceps, muzzled them. So far he had been as patient as he knew how.

'And don't look at me like that,' she said.

'Like what?'

'You know.' She lashed out, blinded by her wound and his intolerable rightness. 'At least Colin doesn't hit him.'

Sam's throat constricted and dried and he locked his arms

together. 'It's no more than a cuff,' he said, looking intently at his empty shoes. 'Somebody has to keep him right. You'd ruin him.'

'He wasn't ruined when you were away.'

'Pity I came back then.'

His tone was soft, even regretful, and where mere anger would have fired Ellen up, this unexpected sadness stopped her.

In the silence the accusations they had made to each other hooped around their minds and both realised how near the brink they were. Neither would say sorry. Ellen wanted to go out of the door, come in and start again. Spite? No good? Sam kept his eyes away from her. Jealous? And he scarcely touched Joe.

'Where'll he live?' It was flatly asked and the answer came just as empty of feeling.

'With Aunty Grace. Until he gets a job. Until he gets settled in.'

'He might not find it easy.' He hesitated, then, 'His chest,' he added, to be perfectly clear and offer an olive branch.

It was grasped.

'He'll get something. He's very clever, you know. The head-master begged him to stay on at school but he wanted to earn his own living – even though *Dad* begged him as well. Would you believe that?'

You did, Sam thought and said nothing.

'You know a lot of people,' she said, eagerly, the wound almost miraculously healed now that Sam appeared to be onside.

'No doubt I'll see what I can do,' said Sam, knowing there was no one he could trust the man with.

'I told him you'd give him a hand,' she said and she smiled, the smile that usually warmed his heart but there was a chill on it now, knowing that it was for Colin she smiled.

'Bed?'

'A cup of tea first,' she said. To unwind. To pretend nothing had happened.

'A cup of tea,' Sam repeated. To put off making love. To keep him at a distance. To pretend nothing had happened.

———∭———

Curly was one of the old men who chopped kindling at the workhouse and brought it down to Johnny Holdsworth's barber's shop in Station Road where Johnny gave them twopence a bundle, which he sold on for fourpence.

Curly always wore the same brown flat cap to conceal his baldness, a brown three-piece suit and brown boots with long shoe-laces that flopped on either side like spaniel's ears. He wore neither collar nor tie but his shirt was still fastened at the neck by a brass stud, which humped a protuberant Adam's apple. His face was unwrinkled, almost baby-skinned, and his eyes were watery blue. His front teeth had gone, top and bottom, but the remainder, seen when he grinned, which was often, were long and yellow. Mostly he had his hands in his pockets, playing with himself, vigorously.

After he had delivered his sticks, he went up to Blue Bell corner to grin at the world going by. Everyone who passed got a nod or a word and, save for a few Puritans, the greeting was returned. They all knew about Curly. When he saw Speed and the lads approaching, a strange gurgling sound came from deep in his throat. Speed was a beloved old enemy.

There were five of them, including Joe, who was on his way to Cubs and awkward in his uniform, the cap, the woggle, the badge-spattered green jersey. Speed came close up to Curly, much closer than Joe would have dared.

'How about it then, Curly?'

The gurgling grew and became throttled laughter. He shook his fist at the boy but it was a helpless gesture. The boy had him fixed.

'Down there.' Speed pointed to a yard that led off from Station Road to the back entrance of the Vaults, an unfrequented yard at this time, the pubs not yet open.

Curly shifted from one foot to another, a sort of war dance, his eyes swirling up and down the street. Who was watching? Did he dare?

'No. Nooo,' he said, and the laughter spluttered out, some spittle dribbled on to his chin. But the laughter was becoming a panting sound and Joe could feel the tension as Speed tugged on the line, tugged on it hard, drew it in.

'Come on, Curly. I'll give you a tanner.'

He produced the sixpence and held it out. Curly stomped again and then, with an expression of wicked sly mischief, he made for the yard, trotting like a fat little pony, and cackling now, loud and delighted.

Joe had no idea what was going on. But he followed. It was twilight. That was a comfort.

In the yard, the boys spread out. Speed somehow organised that. Curly stood against a wall, the top half of which supported the only billboard in Wigton – 'Guinness Is Good For You'. He was trapped. He made as if to challenge the semi-circle and dart through it but the boys were now set on their prey.

'Come on, Curly!' Speed urged, in a coaxing voice. 'Show us it, Curly. Show us it.' Speed had not taken his eyes off the man and he feinted with his left arm as he coaxed, like a boxer, like a lion tamer.

The old man looked around wildly as excitement possessed him and then, pulling his hands out of his pockets, his head swivelling about on the lookout, his face wild with panicked pleasure, he undid his flies and there was his large erect member pointing straight at them. The boys cheered and pointed back and yelled. Curly laughed louder and did little jumps so that it bounced.

The boys cheered again, then jeered, but the man did not register their change of mood. He laughed even more and jumped even more and his mouth was flung open in gap-toothed delight and he waved to them to come closer and, goggle-eyed, he held the bared penis in his right fist proudly waving his free hand.

'Dirty old bugger!' Speed yelled. 'You dirty old bugger!' Curly honked now and tugged at himself. The boys made untranslatable animal noises, louder and louder. Suddenly fearing the attraction of the noise they were making, Speed ordered, 'Run!'

They ran, Joe so confused that he was breathless. Curly howled. Howled at their treachery. Howled to be abandoned. Howled in fear of the policeman or that the superintendent at the workhouse would punish him and not let him bring kindling down the town to Johnny Holdsworth's ever again.

The boys raced across King Street and up Water Street into the Straits. The size of it! What about the sixpence? The size of Curly's thing! On to the Waste behind the wash-houses. Curly would not find them there.

They stayed on the Waste and went over the adventure many times, exaggerating and embroidering and hysterical until they had laughed it out. Then they tried to make a fire but they could not find enough dry bits of wood.

All the others drifted off, but Speed went back to the wash-houses, squatted on his haunches and leaned against the wall, 'smoking' a twig. Joe ought to have made for the parish rooms and the Cubs but he was trembling too much, too disorientated to want to leave Speed. He squatted beside him, although his rather plump legs were not as moulded for squatting as Speed's skinny shanks. Some silent moments passed.

'What's that?'

Speed's right index finger jabbed Joe's arm, not gently, in the bull's eye of one of the three badges on his thick Cubs jersey.

'That's for tracking.' Speed squinted down at him and Joe already felt inadequate, even before he began the explanation. 'You go to the park and they go in front, the ones you're after, and they cut special signs in trees or they get bits of wood and make arrows on the ground so that you can follow them.' Each sentence was slower than the last as Speed's incomprehension at this activity alchemised into unmistakable contempt.

'You don't need tracks in the park. You can find anybody,' he said. 'They always land up behind the bowling hut.'

'But you have to know the signs,' said Joe, feeling stupid though he did not know why.

'Anybody that needs signs in the park is blind.'

'But,' Joe lunged, 'it gets you better ready for wars.'

'What if there's no trees?'

Joe looked around, in alarm. No trees?

'Indians listen like this.' Nimbly Speed dropped into a kneeling position and from there pressed his ear to the ground. 'They can hear horses coming from miles away. Does the Cubs do that?'

Joe was forced to shake his head.

Speed lost interest. Joe raced off to Cubs, late, already fearful of the inevitable rebuke.

The following week he took his Lighting a Fire test for a new badge. First you had to Make the Fire and then you had to Light it with One Match. A parent had to supervise this.

Ellen chose a Saturday morning when Sam was at the just

117

re-opened factory, doing overtime, part of the Government's demand to step up productivity.

'From the beginning,' Ellen said, rather severely. She had been in the Guides and still helped them out now and then and she had been taught to take these tests seriously.

Joe had seen his mother and sometimes his father set up the fire often enough and sometimes he had helped and he could have done it sleepwalking, but now the responsibility was totally his and he felt panicky. Still, he riddled the grate and took out the ashes without too much mess on the floor, although he himself was well smudged.

He was still in his blue and white striped pyjamas which were suffering. He had put on his green Cubs cap to validate the occasion.

He looked to Ellen but she shook her head.

He took out the clinker and put it to one side. Then he unfolded the *News Chronicle* and, taking care, tore it up, scrunching up each ripped fragment and placing them in the grate, soon too full of newspaper.

With sticks the lesson was a mantra. Cross your sticks. Make a deck. Criss-cross, and so he did, with the kindling that Ellen bought at Johnny's barber shop in Station Road. It looked OK now, over-full but it looked like a real fire.

The coals were in the scuttle and there was a small indoor shovel to dig them out. Perhaps he put on too many coals and was unlucky that most of the pieces were big and heavy and still rather damp.

Ellen handed him the Captain Webb matchbox. Captain Webb, the first man to swim the English Channel, eccentrically fronted the fire-sticks in a one-piece bathing costume. Joe took out a stout red-tipped match and again looked at Ellen. She nodded. He took a deep breath, as if he were preparing to blow out a cake of candles, and struck.

Hurriedly, he dabbed it at the corners of newspaper which, insufficiently, peeped up through the weight of coal and kindling. He managed to get three points going and then his over-hastiness fluttered the match-flame and it went out. As did one of his lighted corners. He willed and stared at the other two but the flames were sickly and after a brief fight, they too gave up.

Joe began to push the box open again but his mother leaned down and took the matches from him.

'Next time,' she said.

'Why can't I try again now?'

'Because it wouldn't be right.'

'But I can have one match again.'

'That would be two matches. Even if the fire's not lit the first time. It would still be two matches.' She paused. 'Like this,' she said, and struck a match and tapped the paper with the flame, here and there and there again, at the back, the sides, the front, touching it like a fairy wand and soon there was that crackle, that little moan, the fire had taken hold.

Alex's latest letter was much shorter but there was the promised book, a scuffed and thumbed copy of Rudyard Kipling's poetry.

For the next few days it became Sam's secret vice. He had often heard the Barrack Room Ballads chanted out by the lads and 'Fuzzy Wuzzy', 'The Sons of Martha' and 'Gunga Din'. He recognised lines that had slid into his mind as if out of the wind. It was familiar, which made it friendly. Reading it surreptitiously, he was back in Burma. He saw action again and knew that the poet was on the side of the ordinary Tommy and he felt proud of that – of the poet and of himself. In Mandalay. Reopening the Indies. He saw Denny Deever swing in the mornin' and was moved though he did not know why when he read the hero's charter 'If'. That was what you tried for. That sort of honour, that sort of stoic greatness. He knew McAndrew as a brother and sympathised entirely with that Scottish engineer. Of course it was the poor sod who slaved below the water line who kept the ship afloat, who got ignored or patronised for his skills and guts. Join the army! When he had finished it he hid it in his kitbag. The book lifted his spirits.

It also helped begin to wean him from Alex. Certainly his return letter to Australia was much shorter than before and when he slid it through the big cold mouth of the main post-box he sensed then that already the correspondence was dying and soon it would fade away until a Christmas card would be all, cramming a year into a few sentences, cooled embers of their former shared time breathed into a little life by an annual celebration neither he nor Alex believed in.

The library was in the council yard just off Station Road. Up a short flight of stone steps and into a muffled mantled gloom. Willie Carrick, Town Clerk, Town Historian, Town Librarian, opened the place up twice a week for two hours in the evening.

Sam was there smack on six, calculating that he would have a few minutes alone with Willie, who greeted him with ill-concealed surprise and open pleasure.

'Do you want any help, Sam?'

Willie Carrick's face was broad, brown from his all-weather walking, eyes that missed nothing, long thin lips, white hair neat around the tonsure of baldness, as reliable a face as you could want, Sam thought, and because Willie was friendly, he hurdled his embarrassment. 'To be honest, Willie, I do.'

'Westerns? Very popular with one or two of the regular men.'

'I see enough of them at the flicks.'

'Detectives? They can take you out of yourself. There's different varieties.'

'No.'

'Adventure type? Man against the odds sort of thing.'

'Had enough of that.' It was a useful excuse. Anything that helped to get him to the destination he was blind to.

'You won't want romance.'

Sam shook his head. 'I seem to be hard to please, Willie.'

'Not a bit of it.' The response was a little forced and Sam noticed.

'What are you on at present? Reading-wise?'

'Rudyard Kipling.'

'A bit kiddies' stuff,' said Willie, and Sam could not bring himself to reveal that it was the poetry so he nodded, as if agreeing, betraying the passion of the last week.

'There's always the classics,' the librarian waved a hand towards the darkest part of the room, 'over there. Charles Dickens, William Makepeace Thackeray, Robert Louis Stevenson – we've got them all on parade. There's J. B. Priestley, Somerset Maugham. More up-to-date type of thing.'

'I'll try him.'

'I should give you a Thomas Hardy as well. Just to keep the balance.'

Sam did not ask what Willie meant by that.

'And,' concluded the librarian, seeing a potential disciple and treading carefully, 'I'll throw in a bit of a kiddies' book by P. G. Wodehouse. You like cricket?'

Sam laughed.

'*Mike*, it's called. There's amusing parts in it. Now. I'll need your particulars.'

In his beautiful copperplate handwriting, Willie filled in Sam's library card and told him the rules, emphasising the fines, and even had time to give him a brisk tour of the shelves.

Sam took Joe along to the library the next time although by now the boy much preferred to go on his own. Ellen had taken him with her for a year or so. She liked to have a romance on the go and Mr Carrick fed the boy unhurriedly from the small but adequate selection of his 'kiddies'' books, one of which was *Mike.*

CHAPTER THIRTEEN

It was on the Saturday that Ellen had gone to Carlisle with Joe and Colin to see *Great Expectations*.

Annie came to their house, her first visit, and when Sam opened the door, she said, 'He's gone on the tramp, Sam.'

Speed and his two brothers stood some distance away, across the yard, next to the cold-water tap.

Annie had delivered her news, and now she waited.

'When did he go?'

'Yesterday morning. They didn't miss him till night.'

'Who said he'd gone on the tramp?'

'Me, Sam. He's been saying he would. But . . .' She had kept it to herself, another fear suppressed, another burden carried alone. Her face, rarely relieved by much colour, was lard pale, her eyes expressed misery, her sturdy shoulders slumped, hands in pockets, the cheap headscarf no protection against the rain.

'We'll find him.' Sam tried to sound optimistic.

He left a note for Ellen.

'Best if you stay at home,' he said to Annie. 'As likely as not, that's where he'll be heading. I'll go and talk to them at the hospital.'

Speed had edged forward. 'Can I come with you, Mr Richardson?'

The boy was forlorn, his hand-me-down raincoat soaked. Sam nodded.

'If he goes, I go,' Alistair declared. 'I'm oldest.' Alistair, as always, looking for trouble. Even now.

'That's why you should stay with your mother.'

Sam's instant and rather flattering reply deflected the violent young man's temper. But still, he pointed to the third brother.

'He can do that.'

'Your mother would be better off if you stayed.'

'He can't afford the bus fares to take the lot of you,' said Annie conclusively.

Speed wanted to go upstairs and sit at the front. Sam let him have his way, knowing that for the boy this bus journey was, confusingly, an outing.

Somebody at the hospital had heard Jackie talk about a liking for 'the Scottish side'. A doctor offered to run them over to Longtown, near the Border. They had to wait until he had finished his duties and in the waiting time Sam saw Speed's growing consternation at the distressing evidence of incapacity around him. Is my dad (Sam could almost hear the boy saying this to himself) like him? Like him? Him? Sam had once told Speed his father was a hero. What sort of a hero landed up in a place like this?

By the time they got to Longtown the pubs were open and Sam went into three of them. Speed was not allowed in and stood outside, on his guard. There were always tramps passing through was the gist of it. Maybe one or two that morning? A fumbled, more willing than convincing consensus. But maybe.

Sam brought Speed a packet of crisps and a bottle of dandelion and burdock out of the last pub.

They stood at the central crossroads of the ill-reputed brawling

124

Border town, outside the Graham Arms Hotel, scanning the broad streets. Sam checked the timetable. There was a bus up to Gretna Green in twenty minutes. If Jackie was sticking to the main roads – and Sam suspected he would in the early days – then even by hard walking he could not have got much further.

They found the fish and chip shop and stoked up.

On the road to Gretna Green the darkness began to gather. 'You take that side, I'll take this,' Sam said to the boy, who then glued his face to the window. This time they had to travel downstairs and Speed understood why.

When he saw the stone 'Welcome to Scotland', the boy cheered. He was still nursing the bottle of dandelion and burdock.

Gretna Green was dark and empty. This time Sam ignored the pubs and searched out the police station.

Speed stood in a state of full readiness as Sam, after no little persistence, extracted from the duty desk that there were two or three tramps in the area all heading north. The young policeman on the duty desk had no further details beyond their being tramps. He had no idea where they might be sleeping. There was one in a cell.

Speed slid along with them and looked blankly at the heap of multi-coated, ragged, greasy hair tangled, bearded, sack-strewn stinking man. It was not his father. But, Sam thought and feared that the boy thought, he could have been.

It was too late and too dark to do more. They caught the next bus back to Carlisle and by a whisker the late Saturday-night bus back to Wigton. Speed slumped asleep on Sam's shoulder. Sam put his arm around the boy to keep him steady.

He got up at five on the Sunday morning and went down to Grace's for his bike. The rain was merely a drizzle and he had an old but effective cycling cape which he had bought before the war. Ellen had made up sandwiches and a flask that fitted in his saddlebag.

He was well into Scotland by mid-morning and now and then people coming out of church tried to be helpful. In the early afternoon he caught up with him. Jackie was sat leaning against a gate and when Sam slewed across the road to him, he said, 'You old bugger. I knew it would be you.'

Sam squatted down beside him and brought out the sandwiches. He had asked Ellen to cater for two. Jackie stuffed his face.

'I'll miss that feed,' he said. 'Three times a day. Top calibre.'

'You could go back.'

'No, Sam.' He accepted the cigarette. They lit up. 'They'd marked me down for the duration, see. I heard a doctor. "He's here for the duration." Well, Sam,' he sucked in so hard that his cheeks hollowed, 'that's when I had to get out. See my drift?'

'They told me they thought you were on the mend.'

'That's what they tell you, Sam. They tell that to every poor bugger.'

'What about Annie?'

Jackie paused. When he spoke the almost staccato nervousness was absent. The pitch of his voice dropped.

'Isn't she great, eh, Sam? Isn't she?' He stopped, but it was not a pause. He had no more words.

'I'll tell her you said that.'

Jackie nodded and stubbed out the cigarette, put it behind his ear. 'People can be decent,' he said. 'A cup of water, a bit of bread. I got a fresh scone this morning.'

Sam smiled at Jackie's perkiness. He had come to draw the war-shot man back into a world still in touch with his old life. Yet Jackie's new life had an attraction and for a few moments Sam could sense the pull of it. He sensed that it might be Jackie's only way to live a life he could respect himself for. Yet for all that he had to try to prise him out of it.

'It'll be rough, Jackie.'

'You talk about rough after what we went through with them Japs?'

'We had to do that. That was a war.'

'I can't be in that spot for the duration, Sam. Anyway, the Japs was coming into the ward at night.'

'They can help you in there.'

'You have to keep moving, Sam. That was it: keep moving or the Japs'll have you for breakfast. Tojo's way. The little buggers are still after me, Sam.' He grinned, suddenly reassuring Sam. 'Daft, isn't it? That's why they locked us up.'

'Where you headed?'

'Loch Lomond,' said Jackie, promptly. 'I've always fancied Loch Lomond. "You take the high road and I'll take the low road." Loch Lomond. I'll be all right when I get myself there. I can make do on very little, Sam. Bred to it.' And again, there was the utterly sane, almost boyish grin. He could only be in his early thirties, Sam thought.

'The boys?' Sam felt it was a dirty trick but it came out all the same.

Jackie simply shook his head. But the question prompted him to retrieve the butt from behind his ear and lean over for a light.

'What do I say to Annie?'

'Tell her. Tell her I'll manage, Sam. And tell her I'll get word to her, when I can.'

'You won't come back with me?'

'You know the answer to that, Sam.' He drew deeply on the stub.

Sam saw Jackie and thousands like him, squatted against a tree or a rock in their sweat-starched uniforms, swept up in the flood of war, walking into lead and fire, kill or be killed, almighty confusion about cause and purpose reduced to the single act of smoking a cigarette before the next order, which could be the last order. In that moment, he was amazed not that Jackie was doing this but that many more of those thousands were not with him, walking without order, walking neither into fire nor lead, but going back beyond civilised war to the scavenging of times past.

They talked for a while longer and then Jackie declared that he would be on his way. Sam gave him the rest of the sandwiches and the cigarettes and the two pounds he had brought for an emergency. Jackie accepted it all with uncluttered gratitude.

For a few minutes, Sam watched the slight figure walk away. Rather jaunty, a pack over his right shoulder, the coat still respectable enough, almost like a normal man it seemed to Sam, out for a stroll in the country on this cheerless late winter day, almost free.

Jackie did not look back.

Sam cycled home at a steady pace, dying for a cigarette, already dreading the meetings with Annie and Speed.

CHAPTER FOURTEEN

Soon after Alistair had been sent to Borstal, Speed, at Joe's urging, went down to Greenacres. A few days earlier Joe and his parents had taken advantage of a fine dry spring evening to go and look over the property.

The first dozen houses were well begun, including theirs. Joe had looked at the piles of sand, the scaffolding and the barrows lying about and saw it as a great playground. Speed had to be introduced to this. He had exaggerated its attractions quite a lot. Speed was bored in minutes. They wandered across the empty distant fields on which people of Wigton would be resettled, taking the great majority out of the bounds of the town in which its inhabitants had been secure for centuries. When they came to the railway line they encountered a gang from Western Bank. They had a big mongrel dog, which was unwearyingly chasing sticks.

At first Joe feared there might be a fight, partly because of Speed's moods these days. His daddy had muttered something about Speed going through the mill but Joe had not really understood. He did appreciate Speed's temper, though. But the moment passed and they set about conquering a particularly big and difficult beech tree. Joe was soon stuck about a third the way up. By then, Speed was making for the crow's nest.

One of the boys had stayed on the ground and threw sticks for the dog, threw one on to the lines even though he could see the train coming around the corner under the little bridge. He yelled, which alerted the other boys but not the dog, which dashed alongside the track and went for its stick, saw the train on him and sank flat, snaked out into a stretch. The boys shouted at the driver and he waved back. He had not seen the dog. When the train had gone past, the dog stood up, bit on to the stick and trotted back with it.

'I could do that,' Speed said, and saw that they doubted him.

One of the boys climbed up on to the bridge on the lookout for a train. Joe felt electric with fear and excitement because – unlike the others who doubted – he knew that Speed would do this.

When, finally, the boy signalled that a train was on its way, Speed went to the spot he had chosen, nearer the bridge than the dog had been so that there would be no chance of the driver spotting him and stopping the train.

Joe trailed behind him. One of the gang held the dog by the collar. The others were ready to run.

When the noise was loud and the train certain, Speed slid himself between the rails and stretched like the dog, put his arms flat out, pressed his face down between two sleepers. When the train came near and nearer and then went over him, Joe was so bottled up with his frenzy of alarm and thrill that he swayed on his feet, his stomach churning to the beat from the track, stared at the big wheels piston forward, squinted to see Speed and tensed his thighs hard. The steam flowed back like a heroic plume, the wheels outcharioted those vehicles of war, the carriages drew by in superior splendour and there were kindly passengers who waved at the little boy so intently watching the train go by.

Speed waited, to be sure, and then he got up and walked back towards them, hands hanging by his side, white fists fiercely clenched.

'See?' he said, and walked on and when Joe joined him – walking proudly behind him, squire to the knight – he knew absolutely that Speed might still be a sort of friend to him and would always be a hero, but it would never be the same. Something else had happened, something unmistakable. He knew and felt but could not explain it. Speed had passed over into legend.

—⚏—

There were times when Ellen felt an all but unendurable revulsion in cleaning the common lavatory in their yard and this was one of them. She had volunteered for the job soon after their arrival, volunteered without telling anyone but the message was soon out and the others left her to it.

One reason for doing it in the first weeks after they had moved in was to assuage the guilt that came from her deep dislike of the run-down, poverty-struck, dead end little yard. Other people had to put up with it, what was so special about her?, and at least it was a house, one-up, one-down never mind, it was their house, many couples were still in rooms or with their family, Sam was pleased enough, Joe never complained, it must be a terrible sort of snobbery on her part, lady of the manor after living in Grace's mansion, a sort of showing-off, the lavatory would be the punishment.

By now, after several months, she longed for somebody else to take a turn, just now and then would do, to untie her from the daily obligation, the bracing of the stomach muscles, the attempt to minimise breathing, the bad thoughts provoked by the bad smells and sights and the whole doing of it, just the doing of it. Her life.

There she was, Ellen Richardson, cleaning up other people's sh——. She could not bear the word.

And this was one of the worst days. The heavy rain had driven in under the door, somebody had left the paper on the floor and it was sodden, Kettler had too obviously been . . . Ellen wanted to be sick and stepped outside to breathe the less ripe air in the well of the claustrophobic yard. Bella at the window, a tender tearful wave, she looked ghostly now. Kettler's broken window still stuffed with brown paper after weeks. Her own home, in truth, a woeful little thing, bare accommodation. The sooner the new house in Greenacres was built the better. She breathed as deeply as she could but the pain in her stomach did not ease. It felt as though she herself had to go.

She walked, unsteadily, across the yard to get paper for lining the seat. Another shower began and the rain was welcome: she held up her face to it for a moment or two as if seeking a sign, a help – until, conscious that it might seem a pose, she hurried on.

She bolted herself into what Kettler called the Winston Churchill. She felt better at first but something was not right. It was dragging out of her. It was thick gouts of darkest blood.

The miscarriage extended over four days. It was not difficult to hide it from Sam. She told him she was ill and he enquired no further and was solicitous. Her severe paleness and her unusual tearfulness worried him, but she would say nothing.

He had been so violently against having another child when she had suggested it, just after the war. It all went back to Burma, she thought, and Alex's letter has confirmed that. Ellen knew, beyond any doubt, that the war marched on and on inside his skull, on many a night and in the full daylight too. So she never told him about the miscarriage. She told no one. But she remembered the date of it. She would not let that pass. And she dreamed, sometimes, about the child who never formed.

—~~—

Joe ran everywhere. To school, to choir practice, even to church in his Sunday suit, to the Cubs, to Vinegar Hill, to the baths, to his piano lessons. He ran to the Show Fields, to the park, to Market Hill, to the shops, to the library, to his friends, sometimes humming, sometimes agitated, set up games after school, chasing games in and out the labyrinth of alleyways, got into fights and was caned more at school, but Miss Snaith told Ellen that she was entering him for an examination. Sam smiled at the domestic wildness of the boy and encouraged more exploits with the gloves on, while Ellen waited patiently and the boy flew like a shuttle between these two strong people, warp and woof, male and female, parents, power, fear, love, and Colin who paraded and teased him until the boy was all but maddened by it. 'Sam's lad.' 'Ellen's boy.' 'What's your hurry?' the men would say, those who leaned against the Fountain and chronicled the town. 'Where's the fire?' He ignored them all.

He ran.

PART TWO
GREENACRES: 1948

CHAPTER FIFTEEN

They had been there just five months and already it was more than half furnished. Ellen was quite pleased. Their bedroom and Joe's were done. The third bedroom was useful for storage and earned its keep that way. The sitting room still waited for its three-piece suite but the old sofa bed and the chairs, a side table from Grace and another table and chair bought in the weekly auction in the market hall made it presentable. The kitchen was basic, there was too much lino wherever you looked, the walls were bare, the stair-carpet was a poor thing, the curtains could not disguise what they were – quickly run up stop-gaps made from cheap recycled material. But it was on its way, Ellen thought, and when Sam left for work and later Joe for school, she enjoyed the eerie sense of newness as she cleaned the big council house, which stood at the end of the first row built on the rawly excavated Greenacres. Throughout the day there was the noise of building. At night, if she listened intently, she could hear the lonely call of the trains passing by.

The house included an indoor bathroom and lavatory. In the early days Ellen, when securely alone in the house, was drawn to that room as if under the compulsion of hypnosis. She folded her arms, stood in the middle of the small room, hummed to herself and devoured its cleanliness, its purity, its blessed hygiene. Now and then, feeling foolish, she would pull the chain just for the sake of it and listen with intense pleasure to the whoosh of scentless, effortless water. The satisfaction was visceral. It was silly to have any qualms at all about a move that had so conclusively ended what had become a miserable burden.

Nevertheless, she was always eager to go back into the town.

Sam had dug up the short front garden to make a lawn for the look of the thing. On the back garden he had less frivolous designs and a good two thirds were already spaded into an allotment. Ellen had to argue hard to preserve an apron of peaceful grass for the washing line against his ranks of thrusting vegetables. Poultry, to Sam's annoyance, were not permitted. He thought of keeping a pig, just to test them.

Although it was a bright June morning, the wind was up and the fine hail of sand and grit that plagued the site whipped against the newly white window-frames, splattered the shiny blue door, penetrated into the house itself, a relentless enemy provoking equally relentless counter-attacks. She could not imagine that soon, even down to the railway line, the fields would yield up more than two hundred houses, but so they had been told. Without shops, without pubs, without banks, or schools, without any of the old gods of the town, it would be an encampment a mile to the west, a brick and mortar settlement as external to the ancient and traditional commerce of Wigton as the even more ancient Roman camp, an equal mile to the south.

Sam had taken a fancy to walking to the factory by way of the park and then the river, following its smooth wending through the couple of fields, looking for trout, basking for a few moments in the slow seasonal inchings of each morning change now that he had settled for the day shift, recovering some of the best of that lost young time before the war. It was a glimpse of liberty before he punched his card into the clock at the factory gate and accepted incarceration for a weekly wage.

Ellen could have biked into the town, often did, but on fine days it suited her better to walk. To gaze rather ungratefully, she would have admitted, on the large detached private homes and bungalows along the West Road, with their wooded gardens and wrought-iron gates with names, every one, not a number in sight. This for her was a dreamtime and as the river took Sam back to those flickering jewelled-framed pleasures snatched from the past, so Ellen's houses gently buffed forbidden fantasies of the future.

Joe had a pass for the service bus for which a new stop had been instituted at the entrance to Greenacres. The bus took him to Market Hill where there might be time for a biscuit and a perfunctory look at Blackie, now lodged permanently with Grace after several unsuccessful attempts to settle her on the new estate. She was a town cat, Leonard said.

Colin had promised to buy Joe a bike for his birthday, or for Christmas, when he would have got the money together, because it had to be a brand new bike. The boy was now in Miss Bennett's – the class above Miss Moffat's – and very nearly at the end of his fourth year in the bright red brick building, nearly in the top class now and so nearer to the time when his gang could take on all comers and he himself would be expected to challenge for cock of the school. Miss Bennett, who also took the music lessons, had told Joe he would be singing 'When Johnnie Comes Marching Home' at the concert in front of everybody. This panicked him but he did not let it show. The flattery of it buoyed him up.

Ellen arrived at the new canteens just before ten. They had been completed at Easter and provided dinners – in shifts – for the junior

139

school, the national school, and the boys and girls' grammar schools. The gleaming white new secondary modern had its own canteen. The Catholics down at St Cuthbert's stayed with the nuns. Ellen felt lucky to have secured the job. She had not enjoyed work as much since she had been in the factory as a girl. The pleasure came from being with so many of those with whom she had spun the sewing-machines before the war. Like Ellen, those who had married had been shown the leaving gift. Like Ellen, most of them had children. Like Ellen, all of them had grabbed at the new job, so perfectly bracketed inside the day. The bonus was each other.

It was back at school, it was in the clothing factory, it was the dances, it was the snatches of song and the socials and on the bus for the treat to Carlisle, it was the old faces, the old names, the old references, the detailed knowledge of personal histories, and there was always a laugh. It was the old town still thriving and well knit in that still young company of married women making and serving decent meals to feed the town's next generation.

Ellen had given up all her other jobs save the unpaid work she did for Grace. That was a lifetime's obligation, a sort of vassalage. And now, another bonus, Colin was there and, also Joe who went to Grace's house from school every day to meet up with her and the piano, and to set off for Cubs or choir practice. It all fitted in, kept her in with the town, her base, unimpaired.

Luck piled on luck because Sam had begun to do some work for Henry Allen. It had started when Henry's usual runner from the factory had given notice and Sam had volunteered, collecting the bets at the dinner break and walking up into the town right past the police station. Henry had asked him to do a little more and then more and the extra money had decided Sam to leave shift work and take the less well paid day-work.

Sam liked being part of the betting trade. He had always liked a gamble. He liked talking to the other men about the form, the going, the jockeys, the trainers, the tipsters, unjust losses, narrow wins, missed opportunities, the quality and breed of the horses. He liked the numbers, the mathematics of each ways and doubles and trebles and accumulators, the wonderful and multiple combinations of bets that a man could squeeze out of a shilling. He liked the role of transparent secret agent slipping through police lines with the coppers and the tanners and the bobs and the occasional florins and half-crowns deep in deep pockets. The illegality of this innocent bet-reaping heightened the day. And on these summer nights he liked going off to the hound trails in the countryside with the perpetually ailing Henry, chalking the odds on the board, handing out the tickets, keeping the books, being close to the nudge and rumour, racing certainties, philosophical losers, gambling men.

The luck for Ellen was that this kept Sam happily in the town most evenings until at least seven so that she could delay going back to Greenacres to make their supper. As often as not, Joe would eat with Colin and Grace. It was good for Joe too, Ellen maintained, rather stoutly, to herself. There were very few of his age on the new estate yet and in town he could keep up with his old pals. Sometimes it seemed Joe did little more than sleep over at Greenacres, and there were nights when he did not even do that, when Grace or Colin claimed him and Ellen yielded, happy enough to share her fortune.

More than any other song she could think of for years, Ellen loved 'Galway Bay', which was all over the wireless. Bing Crosby's crooning sorcery seeped into Ellen's mind like a lullaby, a soothing sealing song of hope realised, down among the anonymous, those 'scorned just for being what we are', a song of simple powers and pleasures – the sun setting, the moon rising, and all that could be discovered plain there before you, you only had to reach out, could even catch a penny candle on a star. In those first months at Greenacres, it became her signature tune and when she hummed it she felt the world was good, and luck was on her side.

CHAPTER SIXTEEN

'Still no new P. G. Wodehouse?'

'Still no new P. G. Wodehouse.'

'Popular fella,' said Sam, gloomily.

'Surprisingly,' Willie Carrick admitted as he signed Sam off on a collection of short stories by Guy de Maupassant, recommended by the librarian as the French answer to Somerset Maugham.

'He just makes me laugh,' Sam explained, apologetically. He had read the P. G. Wodehouse books at least twice on the first borrowing and occasionally reborrowed them a few months later. They had become a happy addiction. That alternative universe, with its constellations of brilliant butlers and great houses, barmy aunts, true lovers, common-touch eccentric aristos and amiable brainless wonders had ensnared him and there were sentences he wanted to read aloud. They delivered so many shades of pleasure, laughter was often the least of it. He had pressed Willie to call in reinforcements from Central Stack but Central Stack so far had not responded to the call.

'Short stories,' said Willie, pushing the Maupassant across the table, 'rather leave me cold. Except the dialect, but that has another interest in it. You've just got into them and then they finish, type of thing.'

'Useful when you're busy.'

'A man can be too busy,' said Willie – whose days carried not an ounce of fat. 'I have noticed you've been coming in less lately. Both ends of the candle, Sam.'

He met Leonard in the back room of the Hare and Hounds at seven thirty. This way they could avoid Colin. Sam had helped Henry to clear up before he had gone to the library and Leonard had taken his usual hour for tea after the Friday clerking in the solicitor's office. Friday was always a day that dragged for Leonard. There was rarely any necessary work to do. A morning would log the rents he had collected on the Thursday. No business would be undertaken after midday on Friday. It was largely a matter of sharpening pencils, looking out on the sunny street, trying not to watch the clock and thinking about Grace's special Friday tea.

There was a courting couple in the snug, undisguisedly glum at the entrance of the two men. They left noisily, bad losers.

Sam seized the moment. 'Henry's suggesting I might think of going in with him.'

'Is he now?' Leonard enjoyed his opinion being sought out. He took a stiff pull of his pint of mild and porter and offered Sam a cigarette.

'Thanks. His ailments don't get any better.' They lit up and a small drift of smoke set off to recce the brownly varnished room.

'Never a well man,' said Leonard. 'Got it from his mother.'

'Now the hound trails are back in full force. You can do very nicely at the evening meetings. But it gets too much for Henry.'

'Could be nerves.'

'I could take most of that off his hands.'

'What happens when the hounds are out of season?'

'There's scope to build it up in the town.'

'Henry takes enough from me as it is.' Leonard was on a poor run.

'I think he's waiting for me to make a move.'

Leonard's nod marked the shift from Sam to himself.

'You have a steady job down at the factory, Sam.'

'It's boring, Leonard. You've no idea.'

'Henry's offer has to carry some guarantees to beat it.'

'He mentioned a six-month try-out.'

'That'll nicely see him through the hound trailing.'

'Then?'

Leonard tapped off a droop of ash, using the gesture for dramatic effect, hung in a pause.

'Not a sausage.'

Sam waited for more. Leonard took his time. Took a thoughtful pull on the cigarette. 'I know Henry,' he said. 'He's tried this once before. Built a fellow up – I'll keep the name to myself – business slackened, dropped him flat.'

'We get on well enough.'

'That's what the other poor beggar said.' He waited a while but Sam said nothing. 'A half?'

Sam nodded. He would appreciate a few moments alone. He was winded. He had anticipated encouragement. Leonard went out for the drinks.

As he walked home west towards a flagrant scarlet sunset, he sensed that he would turn down Henry's offer. Leonard's certainty had blown away the froth of expectation and already he was picking up threads – phrases, even glances, the moods of the man – which drew to a conclusion similar to that reached by Leonard. He discovered that he was not surprised.

There were even the beginnings of relief. He had escaped something. Leonard was right. He needed more than a promise and a prayer. Part-time was all there was. Boring would have to do at the factory. At work, boring was your lot. However many card schools and running gags, however much sport talk and companionable grousing and ingenious gambling, such work was and would remain for ever and ever boring. It was meant to be.

He whistled his way through the back door, after the evening patrol of the vegetable plot.

'It's a bit dry,' she said, taking his plate out of the oven. 'I didn't know when you'd be back.'

'It all comes out the same way.'

'Sam!'

His good humour lifted even higher at that authentic flash of censorious indignation. How she preserved it he did not know, but she did and, unfathomably, it made him smile with a sudden stab of love, as if she had eloquently declared unbridled passion.

'And you can't grin your way out of it either, Samuel Richardson.'

He went up to see Joe, who was lying foetally on his side, reading a comic. The only strong colour in the room came from the boxing gloves, worse for wear now, but still carrying the reminder of raw meat as they crouched in a white corner.

'Only three weeks, Joe.'

'A man said it'll be "the fight of the century".' The notion, the phrase and the prospect were awesome to Joe and there was some of that in his voice.

'Still fancy Joe Louis?'

To the boy it was simply not in the universal plan that Joe Louis could lose the heavyweight championship of the world, not even to wily old Jersey Joe Walcott.

'I'll take Walcott,' said Sam. 'Just to add to the interest. Straight bet. Evens.'

Joe did not rush in. Sometimes he won, most times, but when he lost his daddy made him pay up. 'Threepence.'

'You're on. I needn't give you a ticket. Gentlemen's agreement?'

Joe nodded, solemnly.

There was a mirror above the empty fireplace in the sitting room. It was oval, bevelled round the rim, the first adornment to the walls.

'What did it cost?'

'What do you think of it?'

Sam had no opinion at all about a mirror. Ellen waited in vain.

'More than ten bob?'

'Yes. There was a sale.'

'There always is.'

She did not tell him that to afford it she had to pass up the opportunity of buying in the first clothing sale – half price, half coupons – since before the war, an event buzzing around the canteen kitchens all week, and on this Friday, threatening to become even feverish in its northern fashion.

Ellen had slipped into the market hall on her way back because the fag end of the Friday sales often threw up a bargain. The mirror had to be bought. There was also a carpet that she knew could banish the barren feel of the sitting room, but she was outbid. The mirror had decided her against squandering money on clothes. Just because there was a clothing sale, she told herself sturdily, did not mean you had to rush out and buy. But she would still have to go and look – no harm in that. She had saved a lot of coupons after all.

Sam was happy with his new-fashioned biro – a gift from Henry – transferring the bookie's scrappy entries into proper columns in a hefty new account book bought for the purpose. His writing was clear and neat. The numbers were graphically elegant. It was a simple copying and culling task and he hummed intermittently as he brought order out of mess.

Ellen was rifling through the newspapers of the last few days.

'I see the King insisted on morning dress for the Derby,' she said, both intrigued at the idea of glamorous high-society people wandering around a muddy racecourse in broad daylight as if they were at one of those posh dances in the films and also, by this sporting reference, throwing out a grappling iron to haul in Sam to conversation.

'Showing the flag', Henry called it. 'Good business practice'. He did not look up.

'I wonder what it would be like to be there.'

'Next year.' Sam did not interrupt his copying. 'If I hadn't been working for Henry I'd have put twice as much on "My Love". There's something about the job makes you hold back when you're on a cert because you don't want to take it out of your own kitty. I bet less now. I could use a cuppa.'

From the foot of the stairs she called up to Joe to turn off the light and go to sleep. When the kettle boiled she opened the new packet of digestive biscuits. She wished Sam would not dunk them in his tea but at least no one else was watching. It was enough to have stopped him slurping from the saucer.

As she brought in the tea she was conscious of the silence and isolation of Greenacres. Years ago it would have counted as a different place, a neighbouring village, not Wigton at all. She glanced at the mirror. Things were coming together. Joe would be asleep. Sam dunked the biscuit. It was not a house she would care to spend the night in alone. The town was no longer around her. The surrounding silence was not peopled.

—ᕈᕈᕈ—

'Tap dancing?' His tone was intended to bury her suggestion.

'Why not?'

They whispered in bed. Even though they knew Joe was deep asleep in the next room, they could not escape the pitch of those who had lived early and long in intense cohabitation where searching out a place for urgent and secret talk was a trial of ingenuity. Intimacies were whispered by their nature, but whispering was not confined to sentimental conspiracies: even in safe places whispering was imperative for all matters of privacy.

'Rita Irving,' Ellen explained, lying relaxed after their coupling. Sam's silence proved his ignorance of her fame. 'She's very well thought of in Carlisle. She does ballroom dancing, competitions, and tap dancing. It's been a big success. She's opening up in Wigton tomorrow in that place at the bottom of Union Street. You read the paper. It was in the paper.'

'You'll turn him into a lass if you're not careful.'

'What about Fred Astaire?'

She knew how much he liked Fred Astaire and her retort scored a pause.

'He's a film star.'

'It makes no difference.'

Oh, yes, Sam thought, something in what I have said holds a whole world of difference. 'Isn't it a bit showy?' he asked, striking, accurately, at her fear.

'I know of more than a dozen others taking them.' And all, she did not need to add, normal, ordinary, unshowy Wigton.

'All lasses.'

'At least two other lads.'

But why mine? Sam thought, yet in the drowse of contentment unwilling to strike. 'The piano's enough, isn't it? Surely to God.'

Joe had passed his first piano exam at Easter and the ornate, authoritative certificate had gone some way to dispelling Sam's doubts.

'Tap dancing!'

'Good night.' Ellen's tone was amiable. She turned on to her side and let sleep come.

Their talk had touched on a sore. Sam was uneasy that Joe was still too much in the magnetic field of his mother. He could see how much she wanted for him and that was good, but there was an element of dreaming, he thought, of opening up paths that simply could not be pursued, making promises that would inevitably be broken, confusing the boy. He knew she was doing it for the best and who could criticise her for that? But it would leave the boy stranded. Of that he was certain.

Ellen was asleep but he wanted to say, kindly and not in one of those moods of fury that could still pick him up like a leaf: let the boy be. Let him learn that his life will be like mine, and much like my father's, a life of closed doors and poor jobs you have to make the best of. For all the pianos and tap dancing in the land, Joe will leave school too early, get work he knows is basic, be aware that he is bright enough to aim higher but that won't be possible, and what he needs to be taught early and hard is to endure – to make the best of it, even get something out of it, but mostly he needs to know how to endure. Enduring is what our lot have learned about for centuries, Sam

150

thought. We became experts at it. We recognise it in ourselves and salute it in others. That is how we manage. Stray from the creed of enduring and you are in danger.

Sam believed that. To be able to look after yourself and to be made fit to practise endurance: these were the lessons. You could not have what you wanted.

CHAPTER SEVENTEEN

When Joe heard that *Snow White and the Seven Dwarfs* was returning to Wigton 'By Special Request' he felt panic. What if he were not allowed to go? He had seen it first time round and been drunk on it, clutching at the melodies, jigsawing the words together with Sadie's help, lusting after the raven-haired, peach-skinned Snow White, returning again and again to the ideal brotherhood of the Seven Dwarfs, loathing the Wicked Stepmother, 'Who is the fairest of them all?'

There were to be five performances. The first and second were on Friday and Saturday and, uniquely, the children's Saturday matinée was to be switched to an afternoon performance to draw in some adults at adult prices. Snow White would oust Kit Carson, the Three Stooges, even Zorro.

Joe could not bear to wait for the Saturday afternoon matinée.

'It's the same price on Friday night first house.'

'You'll want to go to the matinée as well,' Ellen said.

'I won't. I promise. I won't! Please.' A deep breath. 'Please.'

His face was red with the urgency of it.

'What does your daddy say?'

Sam was in what now looked like an allotment. The light

northern nights were lengthening deep into the big hours. He could do his evening work for Henry and, if there was no hound trail, spend a couple of hours in the garden in the steel evening light, sufficiently alone, a cigarette. He had a yen for a pigeon loft, partly because it might have teased Joe in. He was too impatient a gardener himself to be much good at drawing the boy into the allotment, hard, over-hard as he sometimes tried. So far, the council had set its face against pigeon lofts on the estate.

'Mammy says I have to ask you.'

'What's the rush?'

Every reason. Every disaster and tragedy the boy could think of. None of which he could articulate. But the longing to go had by now, this Thursday, Joe having raced back from choir practice with the one aim burning his mind, been transformed into a physical ache.

'If you say I can go, she'll say I can go.' It was a stab.

'Did she say that?'

Joe made a noise that was not a word but undoubtedly signified yes.

'It's the same price as the matinée.'

'You'll still want to go to the matinée.'

'I won't!' His sincerity was emphatic. 'Please.'

Sam was a touch disquieted at the child's vehemence. But it was not a big deal. 'Toss you for it,' he said.

Joe nodded, not trusting himself to speak. His throat suddenly constricted.

'Your call.'

'Tails.'

Tails always luckier. Tails always better. Tails always.

The sixpence flew from Sam's thumb and spun in the air, landing on his palm, he glanced. Heads. He slapped it over on to the back of his hand. 'You win,' he said, and handed over the sixpence.

By eight o'clock on the Friday evening when the first house was let out and filed down Meeting House Lane past the queue for the second house, Joe knew all the songs by heart and the film had possessed him. He went down to his aunt Grace's house singing 'Heigh-ho, heigh-ho' at the top of his voice and entertained them with three of the songs before climbing on to the pillion of Ellen's bicycle and holding on to her waist as she swooped down Western Bank to Greenacres. 'I'm wishing,' he sang, as he splashed in his Friday bath before bed and from the bed itself Sam and Ellen heard the umpteenth reprise of 'Heigh-ho, heigh-ho, It's off to work we go'. Such force of happiness.

'Sixpence well spent,' said Sam.

Ellen smiled. She did not want to talk. She wanted to listen to Joe's singing, as chirruping as any bird in a gilded cage, she thought.

The next day after tap dancing he sought out Colin in the stables up Court Yard. Joe saw the afternoon performance large and compelling before him and the need to go had grown on him from the moment he woke up.

Colin was harnessing a ginger pony to a small neat trap. One of his better 'bit-jobs' (Leonard's phrase) was delivering bread and cakes for Grainger's on Saturdays. Joe loved the treat of it, the frisky little pony, Colin teaching him how to click his tongue and give a light toss of the reins at the same time. Colin was good with animals: even Blackie would sit on Colin's lap where she would spurn others. It proved that there was something about him, Grace maintained to a disillusioned Leonard, who saw an irredeemable sponger, a menace.

'They tell me somebody was singing his head off last night at Aunty Grace's.'

Joe flushed. Colin always caught him on the hop.

'Come on then. Give us a sample.'

The words fled. The music was stoppered. Outside the nicely stinking stable in the old cobbled yard with other doors half open to the poking heads of town horses, there seemed no space for *Snow White*.

He tried. He wanted to please Colin. Colin demanded to be pleased. He did not know whether pleasing Colin pleased him or it was the fear of displeasing that was stronger. Colin could get angry. Colin could hook him and play him and pull him in and throw him back. But it was all right because his mammy thought the world of Colin. Colin told him that many times over.

'Whistle it then.'

Joe had a very poor shot at whistling 'Heigh-ho' and dried up before half-way.

'Give me a cowboy picture,' said Colin, 'any day of the week.'

He hoisted Joe into the seat, gave him the reins and led the pony down the street. He liked that. It was giving Joe a treat, it was showing what a generous fellow he was, it was sharing in Joe, the town's deep knowledge of Joe, Sam's lad, Ellen's boy, it was an eye-catcher, Colin glowed.

They put the neatly white-bagged orders in the back and set off for Station Hill, down King Street, into Station Road, trotting on the level stretch beside Sam's factory, which belched out the rank chemical fumes that gave Wigton its distinctive smell, under the railway bridge, past the stone bust called Belted Will the Luck of Wigton, which was bedded into the high sandstone wall, and up to the superior, grand houses cresting Station Hill, factory managers, solicitors, substantial, looking loftily over the roofed huddle of the town to the serene mountainous skyline of the Lake District.

Colin stopped. Joe took the package. Trotted up the path. Knocked on the door. Handed it over. That was the routine. On such a June morning, the mildest of west winds, clouds high and light and scurrying almost apologetically under the summer canopy of blue, the few people in sight seemed to have all the time in the world. It was so very different from the crushed certainty of the town or the bare building on the estates. Joe looked forward to it as if he were going to the seaside. The boy had picked up its particular atmosphere at other times, but this morning was dominated, dominated increasingly as time ran out, by the transferred matinée and the date he was not allowed to keep with Snow White. He had asked at breakfast if he could go again but there was no yield at all.

The best part came when the deliveries were finished and Colin steered the pony round on the very top road where houses stood in their own grounds. He handed the reins to Joe. He had taught him carefully over the weeks but Joe still felt the slight shiver of nervousness, still saw runaway covered wagons, still failed to achieve the ease of full control. He would never have admitted it but he was a little frightened of Ginger, much as he liked to nuzzle against him and stroke his long blond mane. He had seen the pony flare up once or twice when Colin had been putting the harness on him and the sudden high temper had alarmed him.

On this morning, though, it was as good as it got and as he clicked his tongue and flicked the reins and urged the fine pony into a spirited trot along the dappled country road, he liked the way he must have looked – though no one but Colin was looking – and even Snow White, who looped and looped again inside his mind, faded just a little.

'That's the boy. We'll have you in the Kentucky Derby before they know it. Bring him to a walk now. Careful. Not so hard. Good lad. And turn him round, to the right, that's it. We'll have another couple of laps.'

The manoeuvres were completed well enough. They turned to see coming towards them a young woman high on a fine grey mare.

'Walk,' Colin commanded.

The woman stopped. Colin took the reins and halted alongside.

She was in her early twenties, in full bloom, flushed cheeks, long blonde hair falling down from her jet hat, jodhpurs taut over slim high-booted legs, sports jacket open to lush soft breasts ill-concealed under a thin cotton shirt.

'How are we today, Colin?'

'Well enough, Miss Tomlinson.' Colin looked up at her almost beseechingly.

'And Joe?'

'Joe's well as well, aren't you, Joe?'

Joe nodded, unaware of his own attraction towards Miss Tomlinson, but a touch conscious of Colin's doggy lust.

'He's got the hang of it now,' she said, and Joe rather cringed at the compliment because it was not quite true.

'We're taking him over to America for the Kentucky Derby.'

'Smart little pony,' said the goddess as she waved her crop, tapped her heels and walked on.

Colin set Ginger in motion then handed the reins back to Joe, who began to click the pony into a trot.

'Walk!' Colin's tone was curt and Joe knew better than to contradict him.

The fun drained out of it.

At a signal from Colin, he turned the pony and trap and faced the direction taken by the young horsewoman. She had gone.

'I call her Miss Tomlinson,' Colin brooded. 'Miss, see. She calls me dirt. That's how they get you. Snobs, Joe. I'm not good enough. Flaunting her knockers. I know what I would like to do to her. *And* she'd like it; *and* she'd like it.'

Joe dared not look at him. The tone was savage. He had no idea what had brought it on, nor could he decipher any of Colin's complaint, but he said nothing. Colin's sulk lasted until they went under the railway bridge and passed by the factory.

'I bet she wears Passion Killers,' he said, and he cheered up as if a problem had been solved. 'Her sort does. You can trot this bit, Joe, up to Harry Stamper's.'

He took the reins from the boy as they came up Station Hill and Joe instantly and deeply plunged into images of *Snow White*, letting 'Some Day My Prince Will Come' sing unheard in his mind.

'What about the football then?' as they turned into King Street. 'Score again?'

'Just one,' Joe muttered.

'Just one! You'll have to do better than that if I'm going to get you that trial for Carlisle United.'

Joe did not elaborate as sometimes he felt compelled to do under the pressure of Colin's interest. It was the pressure, perhaps, that had caused him to lie in the first place. They did not play football every Friday afternoon at the primary school. They kicked a bald tennis ball about in the playtimes but there was no formal game. No game, no goals, no glory. He had lied to please, to impress, to live up to Colin's steep expectations. It had been thrown off, just a little fib, just an inconsequential untruth. Colin had seized on it. Joe dreaded the questions. He flinched inside as he spun the lies that grew heavier by the week. He would certainly go to hell. He was terrified that Colin might come to the school one Friday afternoon to see this invented game. He even kept the game going out of season so afraid had he become of crossing Colin. 'Some Day My Prince Will Come' pulsed weakly as the shame of the lie rippled through him.

Ginger was stabled and they walked down the sun-shining High Street, canopies shading the bare window displays in the line of small shops, alleys gapping the formation every few yards, neither car nor horse in sight, only three cyclists and the eddy of midday late shoppers stocking up before closing time. Colin led the way around into the narrow funnel of Duke Street, underneath rooms that had been flung across the upper space, suspended like bridges. It always gave Joe a thrill, that walk under people's floors.

They went through the open door of the bakery and although the ovens were cooled down by this late hour, the smell of bread was powerful. Joe sucked his lungs full, let the dense warm breadiness line his mouth, felt he was eating the air itself.

There were a few butterfly cakes scattered on the central table. Colin could see that they were rejects. In proprietorial fashion he took one, bit off half and passed the other half to Joe, who gobbled it, hiding the evidence. Near the cakes were two pennies, unguarded. At the matinée there were wooden seats downstairs at the front which cost fourpence. Half-way. Colin noted the longing glance.

'Look at that spider on the ceiling,' he said.

Joe looked up.

When he looked back, the two pence were gone.

Colin winked.

'Finders keepers,' he whispered and he held out a closed fist. 'I've always told him not to keep that back door open. No telling?'

'No telling.' The words just made it through Joe's parched lips.

'Cross your heart.' Joe did so.

The clenched fist hovered over his outstretched palm for a moment.

'Hope to die?'

Joe nodded, trembling at the wrongness of it.

'Say it.'

'Cross my heart and hope to die,' whispered, croaked, through a strangled throat.

The two pennies dropped heavily into his palm.

Now he had to get the other two pennies.

He could not ask Colin, nor could he ask his aunty Grace or uncle Leonard with whom he had dinner because they would ask what it was for and then his daddy would get to know and Joe knew that he would not like that at all.

He had to get the other twopence by two o'clock.

He had an hour and a half. He trawled the gutters outside the shops in King Street and High Street. Speed was sometimes lucky there. He was not. He could have gone to Henry Allen's front room, which doubled as an office, and offer to run a message but his daddy would be there. He went into the Co-op, to the counter in the back of the shop where Isaac Pape worked. Mr Pape had been at school with his mammy and was always very friendly. He compelled himself to go through with it.

'What can I do for you, young man? Be sharp. We're closing in a few minutes.'

'Do you? I want. Can I run a message?'

'I don't have a message.'

Joe felt oppressed. What did he do now?

'Sorry, Mr Pape.'

'Hasn't your mammy got a message for you to run?'

Joe nodded and scuttled away, not hearing Mr Pape's 'Joe!' as it dawned.

The boy was panicking badly now.

He went to the Fountain where the men stood in the sun, backs against the railings, smoking, spitting, passing the occasional remark, hands in pockets weighing coins that would take them to the King's Arms, the Lion and Lamb or more than a dozen other pubs for the one careful midday drink.

'Can I have a penny, mister?'

'What for?'

Joe shook his head and moved around the square of railings that guarded the memorial monument.

'Have you got a penny, mister?'

The panic seemed to turn to tears inside his head, making it heavy so he had to bow it and it was a great effort to look up.

'Have you got a penny, mister?'

By now there was an awful turmoil inside him. He could not be seen crying. But he badly wanted to cry. *Snow White* would start – soon – there – he stood and looked down Meeting House Lane. There was already a small queue. People with enough money. If it had been Christmas he could have sung carols and got a few pennies but you could not sing to a queue outside of Christmas. There was his uncle Leonard. He would be going to the betting shop. Joe turned away. He had told Colin he was going back to Greenacres.

'Have you got a penny, mister?'

He stood outside the Crown.

Then he remembered that Speed had said sometimes if you went to the back of pubs they would have left out crates of empty lemonade bottles. You could nick them and take them back to other pubs to claim the penny on the bottle.

Nothing behind the Crown: could not get behind the Kildare or the Half Moon: nothing behind the Lion and Lamb and no empty crates behind the Hare and Hounds, the Royal Oak or the King's Arms. He passed the post-office clock. Ten to two. By now he was badly upset; panic began to possess him.

'Have you got a penny, Mr Diddler? Please.'

'What does Sam's lad want with a penny now, tell me that?'

Joe had to risk everything.

'I want to go to *Snow White*,' he said. 'And I haven't enough.'

'If I give you twopence can we both go?'

Joe looked up in agony. He did not understand the joke and the face he saw was unpromising, bleared by midday booze and sun.

'Here.' Diddler flushed out a penny. '*Snow White* it is,' he said, and lurched on.

The queue was beginning to move down Meeting House Lane. At the bottom of the lane was the Salvation Army Hall where you could go on Wednesdays even if you were not a member and play all sorts of games, see slide shows, listen to the band. In the yard next to it was the Salvation Army man who ran the club. Joe liked him. He hurtled past the moving queue and into the yard and knocked on the door.

Eventually a girl appeared. She was little older than Joe but an adult seriousness was already established on her slim, solemn face.

'Is the Captain in?'

'I'm sorry, no.'

No? It could not be no. He had to be in. He would help. Joe knew.

'Where is he?'

'He's with the band in Maryport.'

Joe was adrift now.

'He won't be back before two o'clock, will he?'

163

The solemn face swung from side to side and the door slowly closed.

Joe came out of the yard and began to climb the steep hill up the lane, lurching, tacking a little, not unlike Diddler.

He stopped at the picture house and watched until the last person went in. The tiny foyer was empty. Drawn by a line from which he had no means to unhook himself, he went in.

Mrs Hurst was cooped in a ticket office inadequate for her bulk, which may have been one of the causes of her permanent irascibility. The counter was just above Joe's head but when he stood on tiptoe he could see in.

'I've only got threepence, missis. Sorry.'

'So am I.'

'Can't I go in for just a bit of it?'

'Fourpence.'

You were not allowed to cry.

'I'll bring the extra penny next Saturday.'

'Away with you.'

'I promise, missis, I really do promise. I really promise, missis.'

The opening bars of music came through the cheap swing doors. Joe was helpless. It had started. *Snow White* was there.

'Away with you.'

He turned his back to the box office and slid down on to the floor.

'What's this?' Mr Cusack, the owner, who knew Sam and Ellen well.

'He's only got threepence.'

'You were in last night, weren't you?'

Joe nodded. He was too tired to speak. Besides, if they were all quiet he could get a bit of a free listen.

'So you like it, eh?'

Joe looked at the man uncomprehendingly.

'Take his threepence.'

'If I give him a ticket it won't add up.'

'Take his threepence – no ticket – and I'll pop him in.'

Joe did not believe it until he was on the hard wooden seat a few yards from the screen and only then did energy fill the drought of him and he was taken over again and every bit as intensely by the songs, the forest, the dwarfs, the wicked witch and he was the Prince and there was Snow White the fairest of them all, only it should have gone on for ever.

———

Sam came in about seven and Ellen immediately scented danger. But he said nothing for a while, just glanced at Joe now and then with a hard look that Ellen recognised. She braced herself. She was lengthening the hem of the new skirt she had just had to get in the sales.

Joe was quieter and more tired than usual. But he had been singing those songs again and now he was playing with the rather depleted Meccano set handed on to him by his uncle Leonard. He was on his knees trying to build a bridge. The slender green metal lengths, the screws and bits lay untidily about him. Tiredness was making him fumble.

'Where did you get the money to go to the pictures this afternoon?'

The question rifled out. Joe was startled.

'Come on!'

Joe looked at his mother.

'Did you give it to him?'

Ellen shook her head. She must protect Joe. There would be a simple answer.

'Aunty Grace,' she said. 'Or Uncle Leonard.'

'I asked them.'

'Or Colin?'

'I asked him as well. He said he had no idea.'

Cross your heart. Hope to die.

Joe blushed deeply.

'There's a guilty look.'

'Guilty of what?'

'Where did you get the money?'

Hope to die. Colin had no idea.

'Where *did* you get it, Joe?'

Her gentleness was no better. Prickling behind the eyes. No crying.

'I'll count to three.' Sam stood up and the height of him made the kneeling Joe seem horribly vulnerable.

'Don't shout at him!'

'One!'

'You're scaring the daylights out of him!'

'Two!'

'Joe.' Ellen went over and knelt down beside him, dropped her voice. 'Where did you get it?'

'He pinched it,' Sam said, bitterly. 'He pinched it most likely from Grace's house.'

'Did you take it, Joe, did you take it?'

Ellen's alarm was not hidden by the soft tone.

'He pinched it.'

'You didn't. Did you, Joe? You didn't pinch it? Did you, Joe? Say you didn't.'

The boy looked from one to the other, panting now with fear, hope to die, his daddy who could always terrify him now tall as a tree and set-faced with anger, cross my heart, his mammy talking in that funny voice as if she might start to cry, she never cried.

'Just tell us,' said Sam, trying hard to be calm, but with no great success.

'I didn't pinch it,' he heard himself speak. It helped to speak. 'I didn't pinch it, Mammy, I didn't pinch it.'

'Tell us where you got it!' Sam's voice rose again. 'Just *tell* us!'

'I didn't pinch it. I didn't. I didn't pinch it. I didn't.'

Ellen reached out to put an arm around his shoulders but Joe evaded her and stood up and backed over the Meccano, trampling on it, noticing, could not do anything to mend it, backing away, hope to die.

'You must have got it somewhere!'

Sam moved towards the boy and Ellen was on her feet between them. Joe was now babbling into a scream.

'I didn't pinch it. I promise. I promise. I didn't pinch it.'

'Why won't he answer?'

'Why won't you tell us, Joe?'

The boy was now against the wall.

Sam suddenly stepped past Ellen, picked him up high and shook him.

'Where – did – you – get – that – bloody – money?'

'Sam!'

'I didn't pinch it, Daddy. I didn't. Daddy! I didn't. I didn't pinch it! Cross my heart! Hope to die! Hope to die! Cross my heart!'

The words were screamed.

'Sam!'

167

Joe broke into terrible sobs. Held high. His body shaking.

Slowly, Sam lowered him to the ground.

He nodded to Ellen, who came over and hugged the child now buckled with grief.

Sam went back to his chair and waited for it to stop. Ellen took Joe into the kitchen for a cup of water. When after a little time she brought him back she was holding his hand tightly. The boy was still not quite over the sobbing.

'I believe him,' said Sam, rather hoarsely, staring at Ellen as if not seeing her. 'I don't know how he came by it. But I believe him. I believe you, Joe. You didn't pinch it.'

Joe looked through the blur of water, his face simply aching for approval. Sam took a deep breath. 'It'll be your secret, then, Joe. Everybody can have secrets.'

Tears came again, but unconvulsive now, tears that the storm had passed.

And then a magnificent thing happened. Something which Joe would cherish throughout his life. Something which he could never have imagined or dared to dream of. A greatness.

'Tell you what,' said Sam. 'You give your face a wash. Better use cold water. And clear this Meccano up. And we'll all three go and see the second house. How about that? Upstairs. Posh seats. OK?'

And that is what they did.

—⟋⟍—

In the cinema, Joe sat between them, erect and attentive as a soldier on guard. Now and then Sam glanced at him and saw that every word was being mouthed noiselessly. Once, Joe returned the glance with a look of such gratitude that Sam remembered another look, long ago now, when he had returned from Burma and given the boy the painted wooden train with three carriages.

He carried him most of the way home. A few minutes along the road, through the lines of the old town, Joe had just gone. The soft weight of him. Bringing him back.

CHAPTER EIGHTEEN

On a cold Saturday afternoon in June, the orphans came to the park as they did most Saturday afternoons. The boys had cropped hair. The girls' cut was matchingly severe. There was a cheapness and uniformity about the drab clothes that further distanced them and they tended not to mix. After the first flush of arrival they moved in rather a desultory, dutiful fashion between the banana slide, the swings, the roundabout and the long plank of the American swing. They were always under the supervision of two nuns who escorted the crestfallen crocodile through the town, one leading, one following.

On a Saturday afternoon in June, even a cold one, the serious bowling men were out for a league game in full white force on the lovingly mown green and the two tennis courts, again sporting white, boasted their usual patient Saturday queue. The putting green had just been established. It was not a great draw. Few wanted to waste their money on it. The orphans had no money.

Over the summer weeks, Joe had struck up a friendship with two of the orphans. Both were older than he was. Xavier was as tall as Speed, black-haired, gaunt, big-knuckled; Billy was more Joe's height but broader, very white-faced, a gap between his front teeth. Both were passionate in their friendship for Joe who was deeply attuned to them, to the unimaginable idea of being orphaned, to the longing for escape and normality.

Since his grandfather and his aunt Ruth had moved into Wigton a few months earlier – following the death of their employer, Miss Jennings, and their subsequent eviction from the tied cottage – Joe had acquired status. His grandfather was employed part time in the park and he was given part payment in a minute but rent-free cottage a few yards from the main park gates, a cottage left over from humbler days before the road to the park had become lined with the detached villas of the town's top drawer. Ruth, to her relief, had been helped by Ellen to find cleaning jobs, including two in Park Road itself. She also went in for lemonade at weekends. This base made the park – which lay perfectly placed between Greenacres and the town – more than just a playground for Joe. It was owned.

He had taken the orphans to meet his aunty Ruth and they had shared a free bottle of dandelion and burdock and a dainty cake each. Joe had felt royal.

The best thing of all was to commandeer the long plank American swing. Settle one of the three of them alone in the middle and have the other boys at each end push it so high that it bucked and the boy sitting had to duck deep to avoid crushing his skull against a crossbar. Unfortunately the swing was near the neat beehive-shaped shelter from which the nuns ran the operation and at the first sign of high bucking one of them would stand up and windscreen-wiper wave and they would have to slow down immediately. The next best thing was to skin the banana slide with candle grease and dare each other to zip down: if you did not jump off with fine judgement you would certainly overshoot and land splat on tarmac. That depended on candles for the greasing and although Billy usually managed to nick a stump of candle, being an altar boy, he had failed to strike lucky on this day. So they settled for spinning the roundabout as fast as they possibly could and jumping on and off it when it was at the highest speed they could manage.

It had limited appeal.

They went into the long grass near the river, looking for sweet dockings to eat. Finding a few of the elephant-eared leaves, the three boys sat on the riverbank and chewed contentedly.

'This is our last Saturday,' said Xavier, casually.

'The boys are being shifted,' Billy explained. 'The girls are staying put.'

'We're being sent to Lancashire. All fathers. No nuns.'

'So you won't be here again?'

Billy shook his head and continued to disturb the surface of the water with the small stones he always seemed to have in his pockets.

'Maybe it'll be better,' said Xavier. 'Without the nuns.'

Neither boy showed emotion but Joe felt the looming loss.

'Come to our house for your tea,' he suggested, out of nowhere.

'What'll your mammy say?'

'She knows,' he lied. 'I said. Come on.'

Obediently, his two friends stood up.

It was a simple matter to drift past the nuns in the shelter and then run across the two fields that took them to the new estate.

No one was in.

'They'll be upstreet,' Joe said.

Ellen had done the usual Saturday morning baking for the week and there were a dozen teacakes. The boys limited themselves to two each but they did use up all the jam. Neither Xavier nor Billy was keen on scones but the thinly layered currant squares went down well, the whole tray. They took only one slice each of the plate cake. Perhaps

Joe ought not to have cut it with the short blade of his pocket knife. He offered to put the kettle on but Xavier sensed the probable consequences and they settled for diluted orange, finishing off the half-bottle which with reasonable economy would have seen Joe through another week.

They ate on the hoof. Neither the gaunt Xavier nor the ivory-faced Billy could get enough of walking up and down the stairs and, best of all, going into Joe's room, sitting on the bed, just looking around at the bare walls and then bouncing up and down and then jumping up and down on the bed.

The boxing gloves were greeted with delighted disbelief and Xavier's proposal that each of them should wear one and they should all fight each other on the bed while they were finishing the juicy slices of rhubarb plate cake was adopted enthusiastically. Billy suggested they did war-whoops at the same time.

This was how Ellen found them.

Silence came down like the Iron Curtain.

'Are these the friends you told me about?'

'Yes.' The three of them were in a line in the kitchen stoically awaiting execution.

'I'm pleased to meet you,' said Ellen.

Joe, after a moment to let it register, beamed proudly. Xavier and Billy looked at the ground. The iron fist would surely follow.

'Have you had enough to eat?'

'Yes, thank you, missis, thank you,' said Xavier, without a compass in this new sea.

'I got some sweets with the last of the coupons. Joe won't mind, will you, Joe?'

He shook his head as his mother produced the white bag full of aniseed balls. When Xavier and Billy were encouraged to take two each and Joe saw them light up, it was almost true that he did not mind.

'We'll have to go,' said Xavier, 'they'll have set off by now.'

'We'll get belted,' said Billy.

'I'll come with you,' said Ellen, touched by the awful loneliness of the boys. The terrible ease with which a little common generosity could provoke such a longing of trust in their expression.

'Doesn't matter, missis, who comes back with us. Father Doyle'll belt us for going off.'

'He belts Xavier all the time,' said Billy. 'He hates Xavier.'

'We're going into Lancashire,' the older one said. 'It'll be better down there.'

'I'm sure Father Doyle,' whom Ellen saw in the street, a dumpy cheery man of God, much respected and not only by the Catholics, 'doesn't hate you.'

'He likes to belt me,' said Xavier bleakly, and Ellen pulled back from what she did not want to know.

Joe ran back to the park with them but the rest of the orphans had already marched off. They went up through Ma Powell's field and fled down the street but no sign. They had been well and truly left behind.

Outside St Cuthbert's, in the East End of the town, into which Joe strayed very little, the three of them paused for a moment, the briefest moment.

Perhaps the boys wanted to say, 'Thanks,' or express their envy of such a house or their deeper envy of such a mother, or just hold, for a few seconds more, hold the freedom of that short time, when they had been for tea in a normal home with a boy they had met in the park, not even a Catholic. And Joe wanted to say, 'Goodbye,' and also some sort of thanks for the unexpected and raw company of boys without parents for the intensity of the friendship.

But words failed them all and after the smallest acknowledgement, Xavier and Billy walked steadily through the black gates towards their certain beating.

CHAPTER NINETEEN

Ellen decided that the socials in the room under the Congregational church were ideal for teaching Joe to dance. It was a good floor. The socials were well attended but not crowded. The music was only Johnnie King on the accordion and Tom Pattinson on the drums but they kept strict time. Not many men turned up. Other children learned there too. It was friendly.

On this Wednesday of the factory-holiday week the committee branched out and announced that the social would be preceded by a Pea and Pie Supper (bring your own knife and fork). Joe's first lesson would be coupled with a treat. Ellen had hoped that in the holiday week they might have taken 'days' – the schools and so the canteen were on holiday too – but Sam had been willingly commandeered by Henry Allen to help him out at Carlisle racecourse where he always rented a pitch for Race Week. There had been a successful visit of all three to the John Patrick Supreme Equestrian Circus on the sands at Carlisle one evening and the two of them had taken a Carlisle Bus Service Mystery Tour to Silloth and Allonby, but the coast had been stormy. There was nothing else planned.

Colin and Sadie came along, which made it more of a party. Sam said he would join them later, if he could.

As soon as the trestle tables were cleared away, the band put out their cigarettes and struck up for a St Bernard's waltz. Sadie grimaced at the carthorse plod of the music but partnered by Colin she made a fluent graceful routine out of the simple step and twirl rules of St Bernard.

Although Joe was markedly smaller, Ellen made him hold her like the man so that he would be used to it from the start. She had seen him jumping around to music from the wireless. He could follow rhythm. Singing in the choir helped. He had done well in the piano exam. He had got the hang of swimming quickly enough. She had hopes.

The tap dancing had been a disappointment. Ellen was not to know that an encounter with the earthquake force of Speed's scorn had finally ripped the heart out of Joe's rather modest commitment to an activity that could be bettered in several ways on a Saturday morning, including singing for a wedding (which he had been forced to miss) at the inflated fee. Ellen could not persuade him to keep it up, little helped by Sam's poorly disguised pleasure in the boy's obstinacy. Seeking consolation she could be relieved that she had only hired the tap shoes. But even the few lessons with Rita Irving, she thought, should have rubbed off an idea of it.

'You're as stiff as a board,' she said, though she smiled.

'To the left,' she said, as two other mothers were also saying, 'three steps. Here we go. One. Two. Three. Bum. Bum. (Stamp your feet.) Two steps forward for you. Now two steps back for me. Now I turn around under your arm. Then one-two-three, one-two-three, one-two-three. And, stop again. One. Two. Three. Stamp. Stamp. Two steps forward for you. Two steps forward for me . . .'

Stiff as a board.

Joe felt that he was being scrutinised by every eye in the room.

The blush did not leave his face. He could not listen to the music for concentrating on his mother's words. He was too small when she turned around under his arm. In the final 'one-two-three, one-two-three' bit, his feet always collided with his mother's and he did not quite know what 'one-two-three, one-two-three' meant.

'Here we go again. Just relax. To the left. One. Two. Three. Bum. Bum. That was better.'

If it were possible for him to stiffen further as the waltz continued its numbered torture, he did. Externally in a state approaching cramp, internally practically liquefied with humiliation.

'There we are,' said Ellen when it finished. 'Bow to your partner. That's me. Take her back to her chair. We'll sit over there next to Colin. That was fine,' she said valiantly but instantly qualified the lie, 'for a first time. For somebody your age.'

'Very good for a first time out,' said Sadie, unprompted.

'Fred Astaire,' said Colin, 'started like that. That's what your mammy wants.'

The band struck up a quickstep.

'Well,' said Sadie, nipping her cigarette, 'it isn't boogie-woogie but it's all we've got.' Colin slid into her arms and they criss-crossed the floor with scissor steps, neatly swerving around equally expert couples who turned the dingy, underlit, barely furnished, brown and cream peeling-painted basement into a dazzle of dancing, precise, exhilarated, their imaginations transforming the meagre music of Johnnie King and Tom Pattinson into Glenn Miller or Tommy Dorsey, spinning the basement of the Congregational church into a ballroom in Manhattan.

The older ladies, some with their coats on, danced with each other, just as nimbly, just as neatly, but with less obvious ambition. No children were up, which was a relief for Ellen. Joe had been much less able than she had expected. She bought him a bottle of cherryade.

The Dashing White Sergeant, the Three Drops of Brandy and other country communal dances that Sadie executed in a sardonic spirit, unloosed a whooping wildness in Colin and one or two of the others, and the skipping and swinging easiness got Joe into it much less self-consciously.

She tried him with the military two-step then let him play with other children until the interval.

While the adults restored themselves on tea and biscuits, the play of the children became wilder. There was another boy, about Joe's age, and several girls older than them. The emptied floor became their playground. They launched themselves at it and managed to skid quite effectively. They rapidly fabricated an interior version of chasey, which roamed even on to the stage itself until someone called them down. An old cap appeared and served as a ball which the girls flicked between themselves, denying it to the two boys who dashed about in an uncoordinated frenzy. Joe was like a will-of-the-wisp, an imp, quite enthralled, flushed with excitement at the play, the girls, the baiting. Colin's longing to be part of it had made him increasingly agitated and when the cap flew in his direction, he grabbed it and sailed into the game, announcing, 'The boys is outnumbered!'

The play became more violent.

Ellen maintained the calm level of gossip with Sadie and other friends, despite Colin.

Joe did not know if he was proud that a grown-up was so involved in their game and especially proud that it was Colin. There was a streak of that feeling but there was also something else, tugging it down, an embarrassment.

Colin's greater height, reach, speed and even commitment made him the star. He taunted the little girls to 'Come and get it,' holding out the cap at tempting length and at the last minute snatching back his hand or passing it, generally, to Joe.

The girls began to lose interest and abandon the game. Colin's enthusiasm frothed higher. The band, Ellen noticed and was thankful, began the trudge back to their instruments. She finished her tea.

When she looked around, both Joe and Colin were gone.

Johnnie King announced, 'Take your partners, please, for a valeta.'

The valeta was another easy one. Ellen got off her seat and peered around the room. A faint but persistent high but weak pitch of screaming galvanised her and she was at the door and up the short flight of stairs into the small cloakroom where she saw Joe on the floor, his face feverish, red, disordered, his body kicking convulsively, helpless piping screams and feeble pleas of No! No! No, as Colin knelt over him and tickled him, savagely, gleefully.

'Stop it!'

Colin appeared not to hear but kept kneading at the boy's tummy. 'This is what you like! This is what you like! This is what you like!'

Ellen caught a glimpse of Joe's eyes – pleading, frantic – his tongue rolled out, his head twisting side to side but with no rhythm, just trying to evade.

Ellen took hold of Colin's shoulder and pulled him away. His upturned look was almost a snarl of disappointment.

Joe trembled still and for a few moments he thrashed like a landed fish. 'There we are,' Ellen said, kneeling beside him, putting her arm under his head. 'There we are. It's all right. It's all right.'

The panting began to subside, the shivering lessened.

'He likes being tickled,' said Colin, now on his feet and defiant.

Ellen ignored him. Colin could not bear that. 'I wasn't hurting him! He likes it.'

'There we are. It's all right now. It's all right.'

Joe sat upright and looked around as if quite suddenly called out of a profound sleep.

'He won't do it again,' said Ellen, very clearly, talking to Joe. 'He'll never, ever, never do it again. Will you, Colin? It's all right now. We'll see you back inside, Colin. I'm sure Sadie wants another dance.'

'It was just a game, Ellen.'

She did not look round.

Joe was a little groggy when he got to his feet and still occasionally sucking in a deep breath which seemed to pain him. His clothes were in extreme disarray and Ellen helped tranquillise both of them by spending time carefully reassembling them.

It was not an option to leave immediately. The rebuke to Colin and the gossip that would flow would help no one. She took a much subdued Joe back into the hall where the floor was mercifully full with a robust military two-step. Ellen steered Joe across to the refreshments corner and coaxed half a cup of lukewarm tea into him and a cream biscuit was found.

She nursed him through the next couple of dances and if anyone asked she said, 'A bit tired.' Sadie came, saw, and went, with tact, taking a subdued and furtive Colin with her.

'By special request,' said Johnnie. 'Take your partners for the St Bernard's waltz.'

Sadie, Ellen concluded, rightly.

'Think you can do it this time?'

Joe nodded. The close and loving attention of a rare and concentrated quality had made him dreamy, soft-boned, suggestible. Perhaps because of that, he was 'Great. Different again,' Sadie pronounced, after the waltz was over. He swung into it, the three steps to the side, two forward, two back, even the twirling of his mother: only the actual waltz eluded him but even here he looked better because Ellen allowed herself to cheat and held him an inch or so from the floor so that he floated 'one-two-three, one-two-three'. He would make a dancer.

They left soon after that, which was acceptable.

'I'll give him lessons,' said Sadie, linking the boy's arm as they walked down Water Street. '"Yes, We Have No Bananas", Joe?'

Sadie led, Joe joined in. They marched to their song. Ellen and Colin walked behind them, both silent.

They found Mr Kneale and Leonard in the kitchen, which boasted three tables – the biggest for the family, the middle-sized for the two regular lodgers, the smallest one in case an overnight arrived.

In a surprise move, Mr Kneale had begun to take some of his evening meals downstairs. Breakfast was still commanded in the heights of the two-roomed eyrie he occupied in a state now tacitly accepted as permanent. He showed no inclination to re-marry: one wife, he had confided to Leonard, though very pleasant, had been sufficient. And there was a certain sentiment clinging to the status 'widower' of which the senior history teacher was not unaware. Breakfast, delivered up by Ellen's replacement, was another satisfying distinction. In the evenings, though, he had begun to come down, if not for meals, then after the meals, drawn by the company of Leonard.

Each of them had an overriding preoccupation. The ultimate nuclear war for Mr Kneale, the evil of socialism for Leonard. Neither of them, for corresponding reasons – reticence, politic position in the town, bone-bred caution – was given to public argument. Yet their preoccupations would not be denied. The gentleman factor came into it. Mr Kneale's membership of that caste, in Wigton and undoubtedly in wider worlds, was not to be questioned. Leonard, though without the developed education, was a fair match for wealth (and, after all, Mr Kneale lodged in his house), dressed with equal care especially in the matter of clean collars and burnished shoes, and had that detached air about him, as unmistakable as a Masonic handshake. He was, also, a mason.

Grace would sit like an umpire though never called on to make a decision. They were more encounters than conversations. Each would listen politely enough to the other's spiel and take only slight exception because to take too much time would delay the presentation of his own case. But it had its own vigour: it was becoming addictive. They had to try quite hard to pretend that they welcomed the intrusion of Ellen and Colin and Sadie and Joe. Sam arrived soon afterwards and took a cup of tea.

Immediately he noticed a coolness between Colin and Ellen. He also saw that Joe was beat, though gamely trying to disguise it to squeeze every extra moment from this holiday treat. And Sadie was supporting not only Joe but Colin, equally, puzzling to Sam who sipped and entertained Leonard at least with gossip and news of the winners at Carlisle Races. He touched on the latter with delicacy: it was not acknowledged by Grace that Leonard gambled.

Sam conveyed the information Leonard wanted inside a general description of the race meeting. Leonard sipped at his tea thoughtfully after calculating that it had been a poor day.

'We should all go to Carlisle pictures,' said Sadie.

'I see Margaret Lockwood is appearing,' said Mr Kneale, wistfully, of the actress celebrated for her 'quiet English beauty'. 'She has rather a look of the late Mrs Kneale. About the eyes.'

'Give me the Yanks.' Sadie's loud voice jarred with Grace. 'There's Ava Gardner and Jane Russell, both of them's in Carlisle as well. They knock spots off Margaret Lockwood.'

'That cleavage,' said Colin of Jane Russell, shaking his head.

'I want to see it.' Sadie grinned and her new false teeth shone in the bright electric light. 'I want to make sure it isn't falsies.'

'Ava Gardner for me,' said Ellen, and Sam was pleased. He too liked the idea of Ava Gardner. The Hollywood legend of the savage girl from the poverty of remote mountains whose female force had burst her chains had captured his imagination too.

'We should organise a trip,' said Mr Kneale. 'A picture-trip. Rather unusual.' He was pleased with his suggestion and his fine plump little hands conducted his words and paused for a response from the players before him.

'Great!' Sadie was in first. 'Jane Russell for me. And for you, Colin.' She wanted to save him the hypocrisy.

'Margaret Lockwood!' said Mr Kneale, all but putting his hand up.

'Seconded,' said Leonard, who looked at Grace. 'By both.'

'I'm not going to Ava Gardner on my own.' Ellen looked at Sam.

The outing would have to be on the Saturday. The last day of the Races. Henry had already told him that many of the bookies stayed on, found a pub, treated all round, money flowed, said Henry, and it was 'bookmaker talk, bookmaker talk, bookmaker talk wherever you looked'. He always attended and by now they were used to his tonic waters. Attendance, he gave Sam to understand, was a responsibility, 'good business practice'. Sam had been looking forward to the company of the rather eccentric, loud-spoken bookies with whom he had shared a plot of legalised gambling land for the week of Carlisle Races.

'I can come if it's late afternoon,' he said, wanting to please Ellen.

'Late afternoon is perfect,' said Mr Kneale.

'Joe can come with me and Sadie,' said Colin. 'Can't you, Joe?' He turned to the room, crossed the index and middle finger of his right hand and held it in the air. 'We're like that, me and Joe, aren't we, Joe?'

Sam noticed that Joe's reluctance to reply was far from his usual anxious jump to comply with Colin's rather bullying demands. 'I think he won't be much bothered either way,' he said. 'How about coming to the Races with me? You can do bits of jobs, then we'll go and meet your mammy and see Ava Gardner.'

Joe nodded, privileged and unaware that in Ava Gardner an icon of obscurely understood sexual fascination was about to beam into his life from the screen of the City Cinema in Carlisle. Ellen looked relieved.

'We can all assemble for afternoon tea,' said Mr Kneale. 'I'll be guided by Ellen where we take that – and then we can arrange a suitable meeting point for later on, probably the bus station, even though might you take the car, Leonard?'

'Tell them what SHAZAM means,' Colin demanded, abruptly. 'He can just rattle it off. What it stands for. Can't you, Joe? Tell them what it means.'

But a newly discovered splinter of resistance made Joe hesitate and he looked to Ellen.

'He's tired, Colin. We'd best go now.'

She was not cold but Colin could not bear any abatement of her warmth.

'He tells Colin! Tell them about the football matches at school, Joe. Tell them about the goals!'

Grace and Ellen exchanged looks of muted anguish but there it was. Mr Kneale was a little perplexed and Leonard, as often happened when Colin was in a loud mood in the evening, found it was time for bed. At the mention of goals, Joe's head had sunk to his chest like the head of a bird dropping to sleep. By this ploy he hoped to avoid Sam's glance.

'I'll teach him to dance,' said Sadie, standing up. 'He could be as good as Colin.' Ellen was grateful for the rescue. 'You can stand on my feet, Joe – that's how you learn to waltz, stand on my feet and we go "one-two-three, one-two-three",' and Sadie twirled around the kitchen, cheap in her clothes, worn in appearance, barren in so many hopes, dancing like a movie star, healing the room, dancing as lightly as a drifting leaf.

It was near midsummer's night and though it was ten o'clock, the pubs' last call time, the chip shops preparing for the final rush of the day, it was still as light as many a winter afternoon.

Sam had hoisted Joe on to the crossbar of his bicycle but he walked it up King Street and Ellen did the same. There was an unspoken agreed unwinding. A few men trickled out of the pubs and no one was passed by without a word.

Ellen took advantage of being away from Colin and Sadie and Grace to sink into her own rather disturbing reflections. Sam let her alone and asked Joe, 'What about those goals – Colin's football matches and the goals?'

Joe looked frightened and Sam was there in one.

'We used to have a kickabout at school as well,' he said. 'Sometimes we could get hold of an old tennis ball that Miss Keys

– she was the headmaster's daughter – she used to give us when it was no good for tennis. What about you?'

'Yes,' said Joe, trying to speak while holding his breath. 'A tennis ball.'

'A stone would do,' said Sam. 'Anything we could kick.'

He pulled a yard or so ahead of Ellen as they passed the Fountain – at this time of a weekday, ungarlanded with the guardians of the town's daily history. 'You know what happens to boys who tell lies? Even lies they don't mean to tell? Lies that are harmless?' He neither looked at Joe nor waited for an answer but put some toughness in his tone although he did not raise his voice. 'They get so they can't tell the truth about anything and then nobody believes a word they say and so nobody'll have anything to do with them. They just get left out.' Like Colin, he wanted to say, but he checked himself to save confusing the boy and to stopper the anger that threatened to possess him whenever he concentrated on Colin.

Still he did not look at the boy, allowing him to collect himself the quicker for being unobserved. They were in West Street now, alongside the splendidly columned front of the Mechanics' Institute, just become the premises of the British Legion; the billiard tables the best for miles around. 'OK?' To Ellen. She nodded. 'Hold the middle of the handlebars.' To Joe.

He swung on to the bike and settled his arms around Joe, who swivelled his body to the front. They pedalled easily, Sam and Ellen, well used to keeping close, good times in the cycling club before the war, well over a hundred miles on many a Sunday, once, a bit of a holiday, six of them into North Wales with two tents and full provisions.

'So that about this SHAZAM, then?' Sam asked.

'It's how Billy turns into Captain Marvel.' Joe grabbed the chance to make amends. He swung round to talk to his father and wobbled on the crossbar.

'Steady.'

'It's a magic word.' When Billy said it, that was. His own attempts had met with no success. 'It's the first letters of names.'

'Go on then.'

The mild wind from the west, from the sea no more than ten miles away, tanged their faces as they cruised past Wigton Hall before the swoop down the hill, over the bridge and then the shallow climb to Greenacres.

'S is for Solomon. He's wisdom. H is for Hercules. He's strength. A is for Atlas. He's . . . stam-ina. Z is for Zeus,' pronounced Zus. 'He's power. A is for Achilles,' Archieless. 'He's courage. M is for Mercury. He's speed. See? SHAZAM's all of them put together.'

'Do you know any of those fellows, then?'

He had not only been let off. He was being appreciated for showing-off with something he had learned by heart merely because the names sounded so gaudy and grand.

'Solomon's in the Bible. He says he'll split up the baby. But he doesn't because the real mammy says he can't.'

'That's right.' They were gliding down the hill, two bikes, the three of them, no effort, no pedalling, the spokes disappearing in the speed, the illusion of no weight, borne aloft, the drag of the body all gone in those moments, no weight in the world.

'Race Mammy,' said Joe, as they crossed the bridge.

'C'mon then.'

Sam did not have to allow much. He had the weight of Joe and Ellen had never been far behind him as a cyclist. They launched the black bicycles up the long slope towards the estate, Joe's cry shrill as a corncrake in the otherwise silent light-skied midsummer evening, almost becoming a single four-wheeled vehicle so close they were as they swerved into Greenacres and pulled up at their gate.

'We won!' said Joe. 'We won.'

'Your mammy eased off,' said Sam, and he felt a sudden flow of happiness at this wife, this son, this life.

CHAPTER TWENTY

'Where have you been?'

'Nowhere.'

'Who did you see?'

'Nobody.'

There could be some truth in that, Ellen thought. She herself had made no close friends in Greenacres. Half of the families had been brought in from villages round about the town. She knew the others but not well. People were friendly enough and probably thought her rather standoffish because she did not drop in or encourage others to drop in and spent so much time up in the town, but there was nothing she was prepared to do about rectifying that.

'The man told you not to play in the new houses.'

'I didn't,' said Joe, which just about scraped home as true because they had swung on the scaffolding all morning and that was not 'inside the new houses'. But he was vulnerable and he moved on fast. 'I went to see Grandad and Aunty Ruth,' he said, and this was also true.

'How were they?'

Joe went blank. Now and then adult questions came up that were wholly impossible to answer.

'Grandad wanted me to help him with the flower-beds again but I said I had to come back.'

Which is why you are early, Ellen did not say and let the smile stay inside her head. 'Get washed,' she said. 'We're going as soon as we've finished dinner. I've made the sandwiches.'

At his aunt Grace's house, Colin helped them catch Blackie and stuff her into a very battered bookie's bag, which Sam had borrowed for the occasion and lined heavily with brown paper. Colin's attempt to insinuate himself into the trip was rebuffed by Ellen with unusual firmness. It would be just the two of them.

Joe got on the bus for Silloth feeling confused. Why was Blackie coming with them, even though it was funny to see her head peeping out of the bag? Freddie Miller the conductor, a friend of his daddy's, said he wouldn't charge for the cat and he snapped his ticket machine loudly and then winked and did not take the proffered money and did not give Ellen and Joe any tickets either, which made Ellen blush and feel the coins clumsily large as she returned them to her purse.

The bus was only half full. Saturday was not the big day for the seaside and although the weather was bright it was not sunny. It did not feel like an outing to the seaside, to Silloth. Silloth was always a destination that kept you excited days in advance. Silloth was the Solway, the sea whose incoming tide was so fast, they said, it could beat a galloping horse. Thousands of English and Scottish soldiers, Joe had also been told, lay dead beneath the ocean bed from the wars. Silloth was the deep sands over the railway line beyond the docks, it was the dunes you could jump from and play around, it was the cold water you had to brave, the ponies going along the hard ripple-ribbed sand, the gallant sandcastles and the pop from the shed. Silloth was the crock of golden time at the end of the bus-ride.

But this time there was a discordance, which Joe sensed but could not fathom. Why was Blackie with them?

Blackie timed her evacuation quite thoughtfully – they were already in Silloth – but the insistent ripe rich stench of cat stink reeked through the bus as Ellen grabbed the bag from the lap of her grimacing, squirming son and hurried to the platform at the back, holding the bag out into the air, masking her mortification as best she could.

'Dirty things is cats,' Freddie said helpfully and amiably: his own cleanliness was not a priority; he rather liked strong smells.

Beside the bus stop were steps that led down to a rather half-hearted playground. Not a patch on Wigton, in Joe's proprietorial opinion. But sometimes when they had caught a later bus home, he would go down to pat the donkeys, which were led there from the green and stood in a docile huddle under a high sandstone wall unresponsive to patting. Ellen went down the steps beckoning Joe to follow. She handed Blackie to him, stripped out the layers of paper, bundled some of them into the bin and waved the open bag in the air before lining it again. The smell would cling.

She carried the bag at the end of a stiff right arm and hurried Joe around to the railway station to wash her hands in the public lavatories. She took the cat in with her. Joe was given a penny and pointed to the name machine.

This was a large bulky object, taller than Joe and three times as wide, pillar-box red, with a silver pointer on its front. This could be aimed at any letter of the alphabet and any number from zero to nine. All thirty-six were inscribed around the rim of the dial like the numbers on a clock. On one side of the machine was a lever. You put in the penny, pointed at a letter, pulled the lever and that letter or number was punched on a strip of metal which tongued out of the machine a foot or so from the ground. Joe considered it carefully. He had attempted it twice before and not got what he wanted. Either he had forgotten to punch in any gaps so that all the words ran into one, or he had run out of his quota (twenty-one, including GAPS) before he had finished.

He had been working on it. First punch the GAP, that was what he had always forgotten. Without a GAP, the J started at the very edge and looked wrong. He concentrated and swung the pointer. GAP. J. GAP. RICHARDSON. GAP. WIGTON. GAP. Exactly twenty-one. He pulled CUT and gazed intently on the strip of metal. It would last for ever.

They crossed over the railway lines that took the goods vans to the docks and walked alongside a corrugated fence for some way before arriving at the village of marram-topped sand dunes that characterised West Silloth. A hardy little golf course threaded its way between the sandy hillocks, following the curve of the sea. There was a brown wooden refreshment hut. And the new sanatorium.

Madge Hartley had sought Ellen out in the street as she was coming back from the canteen. She had made the request with her head averted and in a low scathing drone, reciting rehearsed lines and doing so under pressure. Bella was going crazy to see Blackie and the doctor had said it could make no difference at this stage. The date of the visit was set there and then.

A few of the patients were sitting in deck-chairs, letting the weak sun stroke their upturned faces. A nurse took Ellen and Joe to a little fenced-off area used for parking the small children of visitors. Blackie would be safe there.

The neat sanatorium, single-storeyed, well proportioned, carefully located near sea air, fine, and yet a tomb from which very few would return, brought to Ellen a sense of loneliness and fear. These were dying rooms. And the fear triggered sorrow: that Bella's short, circumscribed, half-buried life in the yard should find such air, such space, such niceness only at its brief ending. Ellen found that her teeth were nipping the inside of her bottom lip as she remembered how little, really, she had done for Bella and how severely she had withdrawn Joe from contact once it was obvious that the TB had its grip on the poor girl.

She smarted at the regrets, which were justified punishment. Her omissions could be found excuses, but she had taken the easier, uncharitable course. Suddenly, as she looked at the marram grass tall in the dunes and the hills beyond across the sword of sea, she experienced a sense of privilege that she was alive and well, that Joe was alive and well, that Sam had come back only with wounds he tried to keep to himself, that she had so much in her life. It made her hot, this waterfall sensation of good fortune, and she glanced around to make sure that she was not being observed because it must be visible, she thought, this great luck in life and to show that off in the sanatorium would be unforgivable.

But Bella, Bella . . . who decided that there should be a life like that? And the sweetness of the girl, the innocence of the girl, so often unappreciated through impatience at her mere slowness, her weak hold on a world too much and too little for her.

When Bella came out, Ellen felt a rush of tears but she forced them back. The girl was so thin, now, spectral. But where, before, there had been clumsy bulk and uncoordinated ugliness, there was now a grace, even a wistful loveliness. Illness had refined her and Ellen found that as moving as the thought of the child's illness was unbearable. She disliked herself for standing – unobtrusively but effectively – between Joe and Bella. To compensate, she gave the girl an uncharacteristic hug.

'Hello, Blackie.' Bella lifted the cat and pressed it to her thin chest. She crooned into its fur and turned away from Joe and Ellen to be alone with the object of her love. Then she walked a little, swaying gently, stopping now and then, a figure at peace with the world, and when she did turn around and smile, the sweetness of the smile cut Ellen to the heart.

'I've brought a picnic,' Ellen said, and began to lay it out.

Bella nodded but she was on her own. Time with Blackie was too precious to share. The darkness was closing in on her and this was the best of the life she was leaving and she turned away once more to be alone with Blackie for those fragile moments.

—⟋∭⟋—

'You're back early.' Colin's greeting managed to sound like a reproach and a question.

'There weren't many about,' said Ellen, which was true but no reason.

'And how's Master Joseph?'

'Tired.' Ellen knew she sounded terse and it was she who was tired, but she knew that Colin was waiting to pounce and she was not up to it. 'I have to wash this.' She indicated the bag and went into the kitchen.

Joe was thoroughly out of sorts. Nothing had been right. Taking Blackie in the bus and the terrible stink of her number two. Bella never speaking to him, hardly looking. Mammy sharp with him afterwards when he had done nothing. The tide far out and going further out so that when he got there, white in his woolly black swimming trunks, the water was shallow for miles, useless for swimming, and hardly anybody around, nobody likely to play with. Sitting beside the open door downstairs on the bus coming back, with Blackie in the luggage hole and his mammy buying return tickets which she dropped into the used ticket box when they got to Wigton, which was a waste of money and made no sense at all. None of it had been right. And on top of all that, Colin was in a funny mood.

'You could go upstairs and do your practice.' Ellen's amiable-sounding suggestion floated through from the kitchen with the effect of a command. The boy slouched across to the stairs and climbed them as slowly as a very old man. Soon the sound of resentful scales stalked the house.

Ellen heard the resentment and smiled. Scrubbing the inside of the bag had already made her feel better. Joe's heavy message topped it up. Perhaps she asked too much, she thought, at times. She knew that she had to stop worrying about Joe but she did and vaguely she realised that she worried much more about Joe these days when she was in Grace's house and, to let the awful truth enter her mind, when Colin was there.

'I know you all want me gone,' he said when she came back into what Grace had begun to call the dining room.

'Where's Aunty Grace?'

'Don't try to change the subject! Leonard took her out for a spin in that old Tin Lizzie of his.'

'*Uncle* Leonard. And I think it's a very nice car.'

'They didn't want me to go with them.'

'I'm sure that wasn't it.'

'What was it, then?'

The scales had now been ousted in favour of a simplified scrap of Mozart. Ellen caught the stumbled melody. It shot through her like a smile.

'There's no need to laugh at me.'

'I wasn't laughing at you.'

'You all want me gone.'

'That's just not true, Colin.'

But it was. Even, in some undeniable way, on her part.

'I can see through you, sis,' he said. 'I can see right through you.'

That was also true. Ellen failed not to blush.

'See?' He was miserably triumphant.

He tugged out a cigarette and coughed as he lit up. Joe was now playing the melody for the third and final time and it almost sounded real, Ellen thought.

'I can't help it if I can't get a full-time job.'

'I know,' Ellen said, helplessly. 'It's not your fault.'

'I've tried to make a fresh start. Haven't I?'

'You have. You have.'

His desperation was unfeigned. Compared with every other man she knew, Colin's feelings, and especially his wounds, were open. Before Ellen, they were naked. And, she knew, beneath the wheedling, the manipulation, the emotional blackmailing and cheating, the wounds were real. She knew that and latterly she had tried to avoid knowing that because it made her his subject. But he would not be denied.

'Nobody'll have tried harder.' He took a deep pull on his cigarette. 'But it's health that's against me. For full-time. Part-time, I can manage. Can't I, Ellen? I can, can't I?'

'Yes,' she almost whispered. Upstairs, Joe was heading for the finishing line with a laboured flourish of arpeggios.

'But you all want me gone. I know what Dad would say.'

'What would he say?' And the feeling of helplessness came on.

'I'm not telling you,' he said. 'You like me, don't you, Joe?'

Joe nodded as he came down the last few stairs. It was a silly question.

'Want to go for a walk upstreet?' Joe held his tongue, appealed to Ellen. 'Walking upstreet,' Colin repeated bitterly. 'The poor man's Saturday night out.'

Joe had planned to track down the Market Hall gang, failing that to seek out Speed, now spindly tall and drifted away from his chief acolyte. He did not want to walk upstreet with Colin and his hesitation revealed that too clearly.

'Not Joe as well?' Colin cried and he turned to Ellen as to a judge.

'You'll go with your uncle Colin,' Ellen said.

'Colin,' Joe corrected her.

'You can't force the lad.' He nicked the cigarette and put it back in the packet. 'I'll go on my own. I've got plenty of friends in Wigton. Not everybody wants me gone.'

The desperation beneath the bravado touched Ellen. She was all he had. He had no one else. No one close. Not even Grace, who seemed to fear him. In his sad-eyed petulance she saw a call for help and she had no alternative. He was her father's son and she had adopted him as her own and would never let him down. She could see the deep well of weakness and maybe her father had been like that.

She got her purse and took out five shillings. She held it out to him but talked to Joe. 'We all want Colin to stay in Wigton, don't we, Joe?'

'Yes,' said the boy, laconically, hoping he did not have to go upstreet.

'I'll let the lad find his old playmates,' said Colin, pocketing the cash, happily bribed to instant contentment. He took up a boxer's stance and jabbed out a left. Joe parried and they shadow-boxed each other for a few moments.

'Freddie Mills is never going to be a world champ!'

'You wait,' Joe said.

'I can't.' Colin's reply was delivered as a stroke of wit. 'I'm off upstreet!'

'Can I go out?'

'Yes,' Ellen said, although she would have given a lot to have had Joe stay, just to be there, as she felt the events of the day lining up to distress her.

—ϻ—

On Sundays, Ellen would see Sam's unmarried sister Ruth. The women appreciated each other more the more they met. Ruth looked so like Sam – the very tone of the copper hair, the blue eyes, quick movements and occasionally a gesture so precisely similar that Ellen would laugh aloud and say, 'Sam does that. Exactly that,' and it brought them even closer.

She went down to the cottage next to the park trailing Joe who had been allowed to change out of his Sunday clothes – no matter the cassock covered all in the choir – into his school clothes, an act of charity enabling him to play in the park without disabling guilt. The park was always a plus for Joe, and his aunty Ruth would produce a cake and most likely a bottle of pop, which his mother would insist on paying for, and Joe would drift out of earshot of their gentle argy-bargy. The minus was that he had to sit in the little front room for at least half an hour before he was set free and there might be nobody in the park he could gang up with and his grandfather tended to commandeer him for a job even on a Sunday.

But his grandfather had gone down into West Cumberland to visit another of his daughters.

'I think he went to look for work,' said Ruth.

They were having tea. Joe was sucking at his pop. He had eaten the bread and jam. He had to wait for the interminable grown-ups to finish theirs before he would be allowed a bit of that icing cake.

'What about this?' Ellen looked in the direction of the park.

'He's frightened it'll go.' Ruth's fine handsome face wore an enigmatic half-smile when she felt obliged to explain her father. 'The council says it's broke. They can't do anything about that death-trap past the bridge beside the Show Fields. They can't put in the phone boxes they promised either. They just had the money to clean the beck beside the factory. Dad's convinced it's him next.'

'Does he have to work?'

Ruth shrugged.

'You can have the cake now,' she said.

'You can take it out with you if you like,' Ellen added, sensing that Ruth wanted a private exchange.

Joe catapulted from the room.

'I'll never be able to convince him that I don't want to put him in the workhouse as he still calls it. Whatever I say. He thinks moving into Wigton is part of a plan of mine. He knows that we had to move. We were lucky to get this place.'

With care and ingenuity Ruth had managed to redeem the old cottage and give it a brief last life.

'There's something else,' Ruth said, later. She had rehearsed it but it made no difference. The strength of this early-middle-aged woman that had kept her father's paranoia from breaking point, the assurance of this loyal daughter who had shared her loneliness and his fears through several thousand nights of intense cohabitation and intense separateness, none of this helped as she stammered: 'There's somebody. There's . . . there's somebody I'm seeing.'

'Ruth!'

Ellen wanted to cheer but knew it would stifle her with

embarrassment. Out of her own suppressed delight she hoped she sounded casual.

'Do I know him?'

'He's from Maryport.'

'Where did you meet him?'

'At the pictures! In Maryport. I was seeing Marjorie and there was time in hand. He sat next to me and we got talking in the interval.'

'Well.' Ellen's sigh was deep in satisfaction. 'I'm really pleased. I'm really pleased. He's a lucky man.'

'I'm the one who's lucky.' Ruth's response was so earnest that it gave Ellen the chance to laugh aloud.

'Is he serious?'

'Yes.' Ruth's expression was surprise, even wonder. 'Although we can't see each other much at present because of his work. He's a salesman.'

'With a car?'

'With a car.'

'Ruth Richardson!'

'But Dad,' she said, fighting off the elation that Ellen's transparent pleasure provoked, 'he's found out and he thinks I'll leave here.'

'You might have to.'

'He could come.'

'What does your – what's he called?'

'Frank.'

'Frank think about that?'

'I haven't raised it.'

'Don't rush it.'

'I keep thinking I should.'

'Not yet . . . I'm so pleased, Ruth.' She emphasised each syllable, heavily. 'I am so pleased.'

The park had been dull. None of Joe's new friends had been let out on the Sunday or at least none had been allowed the pleasure of the park. He had climbed two trees behind the bowling hut: like 'Just William' whose tactics he studied carefully, he believed there were only two sorts of trees – those you could climb and those you could not. The coppice behind the bowling hut was rich in climbables but being alone up a tree palled quite soon after you had worn out being adrift on a raft in the middle of an ocean, looking out for an island from a crow's nest, or pretending to be Tarzan. The usual two old men from the workhouse were in the shelter and they had tried to tease him in for the passionate hugs they traded in, but Joe avoided them. Even the banana slide was a disappointment. An earlier shower had slowed it down.

'We were going to send out a search party,' Ruth said.

'That's such good news,' said Ellen.

'Ssssh. Little pigs.'

'Have big ears.' Joe knew that. What was the secret?

'I'm sure it'll work out,' said Ellen. 'I'm sure it will.'

Sometimes luck happened to the right people, she thought, as they walked back to Greenacres by the fields. Sometimes there was a happy ending that deserved to be a happy ending. Ruth had looked so lovely, transformed. Ellen tried to remember when she had fallen for Sam, but they had both been so young and it had happened over the years and then there was the war. But there must have been a time, a few weeks, when she, like Ruth, had been transformed and that thought made her walk faster than usual, keen to see if Sam had come back home.

It was Colin who was waiting for her. He saw them and ran directly at them, flagging them down with his right arm.

'Aunty Grace had a fall down the kitchen stairs. She's most likely broken her wrist. She was concussed and the doctor said if I hadn't "acted quickly" – "acted quickly" he said – then it could have been quite nasty. They've taken her to Carlisle Infirmary. Uncle Leonard's down there with her. He said I had to come and tell you right away but there was no need to worry. He said I'd done well.'

He looked so happy, Ellen thought, so proud, so happy.

CHAPTER TWENTY-ONE

'It'll only be for the three nights,' Sam said.

'You can't not go,' Ellen replied, straight-faced.

'If I work a double shift on Wednesday and the early shift Thursday, Ted'll do the Friday for me.'

'They won't miss him one day at school. I'll write a note.' She could see that her complaisance rather undermined him.

'We catch the train Thursday afternoon, that gives us all day Friday and Saturday and be back on Sunday. Not too long, you see.'

'I'll stay with Aunty Grace,' said Ellen. 'She's still shaky.'

'That would fit nicely in for you, wouldn't it?'

'Whatever. You go. You both.' She enjoyed the relief undisguised on Sam's face.

'What'll Joe think?'

Ellen simply smiled her response. Joe would be dumbstruck.

The smile punctuated Sam's anxiety and Ellen's undisguised pleasure ruled a line under it.

'I'm sorry you're not included in the invitation.'

'I don't mind.'

'We'll just be watching cricket all day.'

'I would be bored stiff.'

'He only has the two rooms, you see. Two altogether. It can't be done.'

'How did you meet him?'

'In Burma. I was in his section for about three months. What a hard man he was. They offered him a commission if he stayed on but he wanted to come back to his family.' Sam grinned rather bashfully, aware that this high excitement was prodding him into garrulity. 'Like the rest of us.' A wave of warmth broke over Ellen. 'But, from what he told me, it just didn't work out. Anyway, he lives on his own now. He was up in Carlisle and I just happened to bump into him in the County Bar when we were coming back from the Races.'

'That was lucky, then.'

'Henry's a bit huffy about it. He says it's his busiest time of year.'

'Henry Allen was always given his own way as a boy,' said Ellen. 'They had money. That was the trouble.'

'Huffier than he needed to be.' His huffy attitude had nettled Sam, confirmed him of the sense of Leonard's advice, and almost prompted him to walk out. But Henry had sensed that and his instant practised emollience had averted a rupture.

'So I'll tell Joe in the morning.'

It was perfectly clear to Ellen that Sam wanted to run up the stairs, wake up Joe and tell him there and then. It was only about nine o'clock. Still bright daylight.

'He wouldn't sleep if you told him now.'

But, Sam thought, he would know for that bit longer. He would have the extra night to be excited about it. The pleasure would be all the greater for that.

'OK. I'll leave him be.'

'Tea?'

When she went out, Sam got up to walk about the room. It was rarely that he savoured their new place. He had thought it too big at first. The garden had seized his chief interest. But this evening the expanse of it made him feel well off. The neighbours were no trouble. The journey into Wigton was nothing. The distance from the town, for Sam, lent it added value: he did not quite know why but just getting out of that ingrown place, so dear to Ellen, raised his spirits. So he had left Wigton after all, he caught himself thinking, and gone all the way to Greenacres.

Joe tried to take it in at one go the next morning but it was too much. To go to Leeds. To go to a Test match. To see, to actually see, to watch, to be near, Denis Compton, Len Hutton, Cyril Washbrook, Edrich, Evans, Laker – those English cricketers he turned himself into when playing in front of the dustbin wicket – and to be in the presence of the visiting demi-gods from Australia, Don Bradman, Ray Lindwall, Keith Miller – men whose exploits were exaggerated and sanctified in the giddy conversations of awestruck boys – was simply too much to absorb. He needed it to happen.

He saw his best clothes and two clean shirts and socks and spare shoes put into a case with his daddy's clothes. He got on the bus to Carlisle and then took far and away the longest train journey in his life. He leaned out of the window when the train swung across the bare magnificence around the Settle line, saw the curve of the many carriages, the long plume of smoke, scrunched his eyes to avoid specks. He sang a song for the black-faced, white-teethed miners who got on for a couple of stops, and at Leeds mighty station he shook hands with Mr Carter who said, 'Fine lad.' He took the tram and got into a narrow bed in which his father joined him, but later on when Joe was already plumbed into exhausted sleep.

It was when they got into the ground, after queuing from seven thirty, it was when the men in immaculate white walked out on to the immaculate green and he was one of thirty thousand who cheered, it was only then that he began to believe it, but it would for ever retain something of a dream, sitting cross-legged next to the boundary rope, praying for the ball to be hit for a four and come his way. It would always be something of an unattached event, a time of enchantment.

Of so many moments, one. It was on their first day, Friday, the second of the five-day Test. He was sat beside the boundary rope and although never quite certain that he would ever find his daddy again in this, for him, uncountable city of people, he knew that his daddy would find him. He had his score card. He had his pencil. Every ball bowled was noted. Every run. The heaven was in the detail. He saw Bradman bowled and Hasset and he marked it down. He saw the unbelievably glamorous Keith Miller go and he noted it down. He saw the nineteen-year-old Neil Harvey come to the crease and begin to lay about like a crown prince of the game. He noted every run.

His hero above all, though, was the Middlesex and England cricketer, Denis Compton. Although he was honour-bound to support Cumberland and Westmorland in all things, there was space allowed in cricket, because Cumberland and Westmorland could only field a Minor Counties team. So you could support one of the great cricketing counties that rolled off the tongue like the great county regiments, Worcestershire, Gloucestershire, Yorkshire, Lancashire . . . Joe picked Middlesex, for Denis Compton, the cavalier of cricket and an England International footballer, a double of such breathtaking rarity that Joe's natural inclination to hero-worship described a line of growth that took it off the charts. Cricket for England and Football for England: if he had played darts, they said, and darts had been for England, he would have played darts for England. His was the world. There are mists of romance and primitive magic in the hero worship of boyhood, perhaps a precursor of sexual passion, surely a form of idolatry, and a terrible yearning for initiation, and from all these pleasurable afflictions Joe suffered for Denis Compton.

The English crowd appreciated the Aussies, liked them, they knew their cricket, admired them, saw a great side usually cruising at a higher altitude than their own although in this Test the battle was gloriously even. Joe had never been encircled by so many, such a genial unison, such a pacific focus. It uplifted him.

Then the miracle occurred.

With the slightest roll of his wrist, timed to a millisecond, Neil Harvey, golden with youth from golden Pacific beaches, struck a cement-hard ball that travelled towards him at over eighty-five miles an hour. From the narrow blade of willow it bulleted over more than a hundred yards of shaven turf so quickly that the English fieldsmen scarcely had time to stir.

The ball joggled over the boundary rope and came as directly into the lap of Joe Richardson as if it had been directed by divine providence. He clasped it with both hands. For a moment he was crushed with the responsibility and the attention. Everybody would be looking at him. Most of the thirty thousand were applauding. How could he carry out his clear duty? Somehow, after a second or so, he struggled up, watery-kneed, head rather bowed with the responsibility, and held the ball out for the fieldsman who came up at an elegant leisurely pace. It was Denis Compton.

Joe held out the ball as Oliver Twist had held out his bowl.

Denis Compton smiled and spoke. He said: 'Thanks, son.'

And he took the ball and measured the distance and lazily, easily, threw it in a high and perfect arc to land after one bounce in the gloves of the keeper.

When the boy sat down, after the daze cleared and he caught up with his score card from the others, he looked around to see if he could catch the eye of his daddy who had to have seen it because, if not, no one would believe him, not in Wigton, not on earth.

—ɯ—

They had a memorable supper in the back room of a vast fish and chip shop and after several games of draughts in Robert Carter's minute flat, Joe was willingly led to bed and, Sam announced, 'dead to the world before his head hit the pillow'.

Sam had bought half a bottle of whisky, Robert had a few bottles of Guinness under the sink. They waited for the news to hear any comments on the game and read the evening edition of the paper to savour again the details of the game and then they settled down to talk in depth about the game.

Sport had become Sam's ballast. Work at the factory was a slab of time for a slice of money. Ellen and Joe seemed to be stable enough and in so far as he could pursue domesticity he did but it did not claim him. Pre-war friends had not come back and the range of new acquaintances had not replaced them. What the war had damaged was buried as deeply as possible: but sometimes the wounds bled and sport was the staunch.

Sport was bare contest. Men fought, most nakedly in boxing, but also in football and cricket. Men fought men for their name, their honour and the validation of victory – as they always had done and, Sam thought, always had to.

Because you had practised those sports yourself, you knew the skills involved, the toughness, the courage, and you saw yourself idealised and heightened by the professionals. These men were your champions: from the ranks an Achilles took the field, a David went to battle. In such sport, as in war, you saw strong men fold: you saw the less gifted outcraft the chosen: you saw fury canalised, grace realised and character made visible. The guiding mystery of luck was almost palpable, the famous rub of the green, the punch of a lifetime, and all the complexities of confidence and form.

Sport, like war, to Sam, was fundamentally about men: men at full stretch, men pitting their best against the best, surfing luck, testing fortune, and above all things seeming unafraid.

'I like the Aussie lads,' Robert said. 'Did you ever come across any?'

Sam nodded. The unaccustomed convergence of Guinness and whisky had weakened him, but happily so.

'A few of our own fellas wanted to go over there. Some did.'

'I thought about it myself,' Sam replied.

'What stopped you?'

Sam looked for words but they failed him. It was so long ago now and he wanted the sea to close over.

Robert nodded. He was drinking faster than Sam but he looked well enough, sitting on the edge of one of the two deep armchairs, jacket off, sleeves rolled up, forearms giving notice of his strength. He was balding and long, looped, inadequate wisps of fair hair testified to his disappointment at this early defeat.

'Family, I'd bet,' Robert said, unerringly. 'We're all in their hands.'

Sam waited. He was not sure he wanted to talk, the day had tired him so pleasantly, and these gold and black drinks both sated and sapped him.

'Mine had got herself a fancy man,' Robert said. The look of desperation that accompanied the confession was impossible to answer.

211

The silence was protracted but not awkward.

'It's the kids you miss,' he said. 'Two. One of each. Ten and twelve.'

When he went into the bedroom, Sam decided to sleep on the floor. He had woken up in a sweat of nightmare the night before and feared that it could be much worse after such a day and Robert and all that was there, unsaid, reminding them.

He took a cushion from the armchair and the blanket off Joe's bed, leaving him just the sheet. The night was hot.

The boy's light, sweet breathing was like a song, he thought, in his musky near drunkenness, better than a song, the boy's breathing, as he lay on the floor in some way the guard, a good day, looking through the skylight, his mind surging slowly into unwelcome sleep to meet the subject he and Robert had spent the day suppressing.

CHAPTER TWENTY-TWO

Joe had not reckoned on grown-ups other than teachers being there. Perhaps it was that which triggered the feeling of strangeness. Seeing his aunty Sadie with his mammy who just that morning had said she might slip across after the canteen, and other women grown-ups who also stood at the back of the room, destabilised him. Did they know he had to sing?

He liked to sing. If the word had been permissible he would have said that he loved to sing. Especially in the choir where other voices closed around his own and the basses and tenors and contraltos went their own road but always chimed in and made such an harmonious sound at the ending that inside his head he was singing their parts as well as hearing his own voice singing treble.

There was the level almost humming murmur of the psalms and the versicles and responses that quietly flowed into the silence of the church. There were traditional anthems, full of mighty words, vast adoration, absolute promises modestly proposed in calm, and antique chants that reached back thirteen hundred years. There were the hymns, *Ancient and Modern*, from tub-thumping to wistful, hymns you could bellow and march to war on, hymns you whispered in lullaby, love songs to Christ, hymns of triumph and pain and hope, each one drawing from Joe and others in the choir wholehearted identification. And all the words were holy, aimed for the vaults of heaven.

In the choir you were safe. In the choir you could stop for a few moments and no one would really notice especially as the choir-master also played the organ, ambitiously, so he was not quite able to give a hundred per cent attention to the trebles a hundred per cent of the time. Yet you could still hear your own voice clear and there was a sense of well-barricaded solitude in that, a contradiction that gave it mystery.

But singing on your own. In his bed it was fine and he would often lie there humming or picking through the songs of the day neither to stave off sleep nor to encourage it but simply because of the joy of it, in the big dark room in Greenacres, lying on his back, eyes wide open, the music coming out of him. And he would be caught singing or whistling to himself sometimes when he had gone shopping and joined a queue, patiently bored while a shop assistant made an expedition of every item or a conversation developed to which purchasing was secondary. At Christmas, of course, carol singing became an industry and he worked the houses. Sometimes with Alan but mostly alone. It was quicker and you got more money. And in the class in music lessons when he was asked to sing the tune solo he did it because you did what you were told and nobody could hold that against you even if you liked doing it.

But this was different from anything and as the day went on and three fifteen p.m. approached, the difference dug away at his con-fidence. His imagination went on a rampage of fear. He kept repeating the lines of the song. And again. Even when he went to the lavatory. The clock went too quickly. Miss Bennett made him do a rehearsal in the dinner hour and told him to sing up and said he would be all right on the night, which he did not quite understand. Three fifteen was afternoon.

It arrived. It came in a rush and he was not prepared for it. The other classes crowded into Formroom One, which was far bigger than all the rest, and then the grown-ups who stood at the back and the teachers who sat alongside the piano. Miss Steele, who was quite well known locally for her piano playing, gave two pieces with many swoops and trills. Mr Scott, the headmaster, who would give his speech after Joe's song, introduced Miss Moffat who recited two poems. Pauline Douglas from the top class did an exhibition of Scottish dancing, kilted, with Miss Steele back on the piano. Then it was him. His name was announced. He had to leave his seat but it was as if only part of him left the seat, blushing deeply.

Miss Bennett nodded and offered a personal smile of encouragement. He faced up to the audience, standing more or less at attention, sandalled feet anchored together on the shallow platform, socks at half mast, hands helplessly dangling down his sides. He saw those he knew and the room swayed just a touch as the little breakers of panic gathered pace and raced towards his throat. Miss Bennett sounded the brisk overture and then a voice sang:

'When Johnnie comes marching home again
Hurrah! Hurrah!
When Johnnie comes marching home again
Hurrah! Hurrah!
The men will cheer, the boys will shout
The ladies they will all come out . . .'

And the song went out but something else seemed to go too. He heard the song and he was doing it but there was something so very strange, set apart from the voice, which he could not begin to name, as if he were one thing, the voice another, distinct, uncoupled. It touched him with fear and a kind of wondering numbness so that when he saluted at the end and people clapped it was as if he were dizzy and he did not know what to do until Miss Bennett said, 'You can sit down now, Joe.'

—ɯ—

There had been no rise for more than two years and when it came the anticipated threepence an hour had melted down to twopence. There was no union. An *ad hoc* committee was mooted in the ten-minute tea-break and assembled in the twenty-minute dinner-break. Sam was one of the five.

Even by midday the ardour of some of the most belligerent had ebbed. Strikes were foreign to the Wigton factory where a full day's wages was a big consideration. But the committee, sitting in the hut – a corrugated-iron shelter with one cold-water basin – elected three of their number to go immediately to the office of the manager and part-owner, Mr Drummond-Gould. Sam said they should all go, and with no notice-able enthusiasm the two who had been excused accepted their inclusion.

The manager's office was approached through narrow, twisting passages, grudging routes between the shouldering sheds shuddering from the machines that turned out the transparent Cellophane paper. The smell from the chemicals fed into the process could be nauseat-ing. But that smell, the local saying went, was money. The straitness of the route forced the men into Indian file.

The last lap was across a narrow wooden bridge and up a flight of wooden stairs. Sam took them two at a time, reached the office door and looked around. No one had followed. He waited. No mistake. They had all dropped away.

Mr Drummond-Gould's secretary opened the door. 'Can I help?'

Sam took a breath, took a beat, weighed up retreat, regret, a certain angry disappointment, an unexpected amusement at it all, and the imperative of a decision.

'Is the boss in, Susan?'

The door was opened widely enough for him to enter the mean outer office. A door, half frosted glass, was broached by Susan's dimpled knuckles and she answered the growl by opening it a sliver and announcing: 'Sam Richardson to see you, Mr Drummond-Gould.'

'Well now.' Sam thought he heard a rather sarcastic chuckle. 'We mustn't keep Sam waiting, must we?'

'You can go in.'

Sam obeyed, ignoring the clear, worried warning mapped on Susan's open plump face.

He was not asked to sit down.

Mr Drummond-Gould chose this moment to light one of his famous cigars. Two a day, the men were told, one after he had come back from his dinner called lunch. The other after his supper called dinner. The lighting of the cigar was an absorbing job, it seemed, and Sam had time to weigh up his man.

Even sitting behind his desk, in his white shirt that always looked so much whiter and crisper than anyone else's white shirt and the heavy silk tie, the coloured silk handkerchief in his breast pocket, the fine subtly striped suit – not made locally – that announced, literally, a person of a more distinguished cut, Kelvin Drummond-Gould was a big man. The bets were that he was the tallest man in the town, broadly built but not yet gone to fat. His hair was black, wavy, thick, swept back. His face was rather bloodhound large, dark brown eyes, thick lips, a smile that flashed out like a scimitar. His wrist-watch had a heavy gold face. On the little finger of his left hand was a thick gold signet ring bearing markings that gossip related to nobility.

What was respected about the man was that his engineering background and bloody-mindedness had kept a skeleton factory going through the war and managed to kick-start it back into life so that now it employed over three hundred, men and apprentices. What was relished by some and deplored by others was his mistress. He himself lived in solitary state in Wigton Hall, served by a housekeeper, a cook, two maids, a gardener and an under-gardener. His mistress, the outstandingly handsome wife of his senior employee, was still lodged with her oblivious, blind or complaisant husband in a respectable detached house ranked alongside other respectable detached houses on the West Road. There was a son whose looks were copied straight from Drummond-Gould without, it seemed, being brushed by a trait of the mother. The boy had gone early to prep school in another part of the county, but holidays were spent back in the town. Drummond-Gould motored regularly into Scotland, sometimes for two or three weeks, prompting more rumours.

One puzzle was how the senior employee – an educated man also respected in the factory for his engineering skill and hard-headed maturity – managed to stay in the same town or even in the same county. How he managed to allow himself to be sent away on marketing expeditions up and down the British Isles, leaving the coast clear. How he managed.

Finally, the cigar was perfectly serviced.

'Well now, Sam . . . ?'

There was an empty seat to tempt him but he decided not to give Drummond-Gould the satisfaction.

'The lads think twopence is not enough.'

'The lads?'

218

'The men.'

'It's the best I could come up with, Sam. Believe me.'

Sam did not and his expression relayed that.

'There's been no rise for more than two years.'

'That's why I've given one now.'

'The wages are low, Mr Drummond-Gould, when you compare. Around the county,' he added swiftly, to head off the obvious question.

'There's worse.' The manager breathed in the cigar like a sigh. The smoke filled his mouth and induced a dreamy look, then it funnelled out towards Sam, a blue-grey stream that smelt good and strong enough to chew on. 'And there's better. I concede that.'

'We expected the threepence.'

'If I could have afforded it . . .'

'Can't you?'

The edge in Sam's voice interrupted the flow. For the first time the manager looked directly at Sam and saw that the hard blue eyes were measuring him up.

'I'll be the judge of that.'

'We'll be the judges of whether we take your twopence.'

'Who's the "we"?' And, recomposed, Mr Drummond-Gould flashed the scimitar smile.

'Everybody.' Sam's tone was over-emphatic.

Another pull at the cigar was required.

'Not what I hear, Sam. Not what I see before me now, either.'

Hear? Who had spotted the wilt of support and welshed? Sam knew two possibles and following that thought they clicked into certainties.

'I can't see the men putting up with it.'

'Yes, you can, Sam. I can read it in your face. Never go in for a diplomatic career.' Once more the smile, this time with some warmth. 'How many set off with you?'

Sam shook his head.

'Half a dozen? Three or four? They didn't even make it to the steps.'

Sam was beaten but he did not want to surrender. Not yet. Not until he'd got some sort of bat in, struck some sort of blow, something.

'They'll accept it, Sam. I know that. You know that. You're a smart fella. Restless, but they often make out the best.' He paused and once more made deliberate and theatrical play with his cigar which, he openly indicated, had been produced as an entertaining prop, to tease the young man, to taunt him with this contemptuous caricature.

'What would you say if I told you I was considering you as a foreman?'

'I wouldn't welsh for you, mister. Thanks all the same.'

Susan's farewell nod was funereal.

—ⱲⱲ—

Ellen preferred the cold to the heat. Heat flustered her. Her clothes were never right. As a girl she had gone down to the river and felt cool in the grass after a swim but that was a blocked option now. The sun scorched her and although her dark complexion would tan quickly, the intermediate phase of smarting red was uncomfortable. It fussed her and she disliked the obvious weakness of being fussed. So this sudden soar into high summer, serious heat after a bitter July, she publicly welcomed – everyone felt they deserved some sun – but secretly disliked.

It made harder work of her club-round on such a hot Saturday evening. Ellen had taken this over from Mrs Askew. These weekly collections of a few pence, or a shilling or two, were copied into Ellen's book and also into the book of the club member and the money was there, to be spent on the catalogue, whenever occasion struck. Ellen had taken it on as a favour to Mrs Askew who had anticipated no more than two or three weeks' absence, but her husband's slow deterioration and his absolute refusal to go into hospital effectively confined her to her house.

Despite the movement out to the estates, the old town was intact. Ellen still walked in the layered maze of centuries, which she loved. It was a physical pleasure, always, for her to turn into alleyways and lanes one person wide, dark little tunnels from which she was ejected into a cobbled yard of quaint and cosy, though to later eyes poor, damp substandard dwellings, but that did not prevent her always enjoying the old weave of time and people and place.

Grace had been set back by her fall and there was a new frailty – just a shade but visible. Ellen sluiced herself with cold water before making tea and taking it up to the front room, still Grace's headquarters. The east-facing room mantled her in cool relief.

They were alone in the house on this Saturday evening. Joe was away with the Wigton Junior Swimming Team, competing in Whitehaven. Sam was at a hound trail, helping out with Henry's business, less enthusiastic since Leeds. Leonard and Mr Kneale who were becoming 'thick as thieves', Grace said, were taking a stroll around by the baths and up to Lowmoor Road no doubt, said Grace, enjoying themselves 'talking about how everything's going to blow up or go to pot'.

Ellen poured the tea, put in Grace's sugar and milk and stirred it before placing the cup on the convenient side table. It was impossible to do all this without both women feeling awkward.

'Where's Colin?'

'He'll be in one of the pubs.' Grace's attempt to neutralise her tone failed.

'It's not easy to settle into a new place.'

'Not easy.'

Grace could have been referring to the careful passage of the cup from the table to her mouth. She blew on the tea, several steady breaths, and then sipped, held the cup in both hands, did not attempt the journey back until further cooling, more sips.

'He's done well,' said Ellen, defying evidence, determined, even desperate, that her half-brother be shown in the best light. There was no reply, none deserved, she knew that, but still the silence hurt. Why could what she wanted for him not be so? Just come about by wanting it? It was little enough. For him to steady himself, not even get a full-time job, that hope had drained away, but – just to stop being a worry, that would do.

'I wish he could have held on to the delivery job on Saturdays, though,' she added. 'Joe loved going out in that pony and trap. And Colin is good with animals.'

'He is.' Grace nodded and returned the cup. 'He is good with animals. And,' she added, her contribution to dispelling the gloom that threatened to depress the two women whenever they talked about Colin, 'he's been a big help to me since the fall. He's laid fires and done a bit of cleaning and washing up, not what you'd expect from a man but he's more than lent a hand.'

'That's good, isn't it?' Ellen smiled, in that moment happy. 'Like our dad?'

'He's willing enough.' Grace nodded and did not add aloud 'just like his father'. Nor did she confide to her brother's daughter the comparisons and similarities between Colin and their father whom she had loved. She confided them to no one. But at such a moment, caught off-guard by the terrible longing of Ellen to fathom her unknown father though all she had were the blatantly unreliable reports offered by Colin, she was badly tempted to unlock her store.

It would do no good.

'He seems to have made his home here, any road,' Grace said, and smiled with just the merest stiffness in the lips on the right-hand side of her face. The doctor had said the stroke had been minor and she should make a complete recovery.

'Yes.' Ellen greeted this as if it were proof of an achievement. 'He has, hasn't he?'

'He needs a lass. Courting would sort him out.'

'There isn't much sign of it.'

'We'd be the last to know.'

Ellen smiled at the reassurance but she did not believe it. Colin had made no fast friends outside the family. In Wigton it was possible to know that with some certainty.

'Ruth's found herself a man, a salesman from Maryport.'

'I hope he's worth the wait,' said Grace. 'She must have thought she was on the shelf.'

'She's a very nice-looking woman.'

'There's plenty of those . . .' Evidence of the positive kind was offered as a concession. 'I married late,' she said. And, unsaid, would that your father had not married early. Or at all. Some men, Grace had concluded, were simply not born for marriage and he was one.

When Leonard and Mr Kneale came in, Ellen made a fresh pot of tea even though she had been ready to go. She came up the stairs with the tray to serve them in the drawing room just as she had done since childhood.

After a rather lyrical passage from Mr Kneale on the balmy

223

quality of the air and, more importantly, the fascinating quality of the light, which had led him to take five ambitious photographs across the town from the Lowmoor Road, Leonard turned an avuncular face towards Ellen and said: 'Your Sam isn't going in for being a Communist, is he?'

'Leonard!'

'I told Grace I'd bring it up,' Leonard said, pleased with his mischief, always pleased to have a teasingly personal line to Ellen who had been all his unborn children.

Ellen looked from one to the other and held her tongue as she had learned to do.

'The same man tried to start a strike down at the factory,' he announced to Mr Kneale, who had not heard the story.

'It wasn't a strike. It was just for extra pay.' Ellen's face was hot, her words flat and emphatic. Grace's warning frown failed to deter Leonard, who had taken on authority since her fall.

'If that's not a strike then blow me down. What do you think all the other Communists and socialists are doing? Extra pay's always the excuse.'

'We mustn't,' said Mr Kneale, 'confuse socialists and Communists.'

'When it comes to strikes they're all in the same boat.'

'They have different aims,' said Mr Kneale, 'and that is very important. I'm sure that Sam would never dream of being a Communist.'

'That's how they all start,' said Leonard.

'Not Sam. And anyway. None of them went with him.' Ellen had been hurt for Sam when he had confessed to his failure, yet it made her proud of an action she would otherwise have considered unwise.

'All mouth.' Leonard was grim now. 'Like the big cheese Mr Nye

Bevan. "The Tories are lower than vermin," he says. That's a terrible thing for a man to say in this country. Who's lower than Nye Bevan? Nothing but jumped up.'

'Now then!' Grace reached for her old impaired command and did indeed recover enough of it to subdue her husband.

'Nye Bevan,' said Mr Kneale, whose fair-mindedness in all such matters would never be compromised, 'will turn out to be as great a man of peace as Winston Churchill was in the war. "From the cradle to the grave" is a more worthy remark of Bevan's, Leonard. I agree about the vermin, distasteful.' And his moon face pinched with a representation of distaste. 'But for what he is doing for the health and general benefit of the people, there will be monuments, Leonard, and I speak as a Liberal.'

'No more politics,' said Grace, exploiting her unexpected ally skilfully.

Ellen walked back to Greenacres, revelling now in the warm evening, still light, those on the streets softer-mannered because of the warmth, telling each other how warm it was, how good it was to be warm at this time of day, how this was more like the thing.

Sadie spotted her as she was passing the Fountain and broke away from the group she was with. 'We were just walking up and down,' she said. 'No dance tonight. Typical.'

They walked along the West Road and Ellen let Sadie do most of the talking while she watched the last emberings of the red sky. To Ellen a bonus of the walk to the new estate was that she would catch sunsets, plain and huge before her as she came down the hill and looked towards the sea, to Silloth and other resorts where the sunsets were famous. She loved them. When she had gone cycling with Sam before the war they had sought out romantic spots – in the Lake District, along the Roman wall, into Scotland – not only to do their courting but for the beauty of the place, soaking themselves in it.

Sadie walked her back all the way. No one was in. They had a cup of tea and then Ellen set Sadie back down to the bridge. Even by that time, it was still light, deep purplish shade on the small hills lapping the town.

'It said on the wireless it was eighty-eight degrees in Carlisle cemetery today,' Sadie announced. 'Some of them'll think they've been put in the wrong spot!'

'Too hot for me,' Ellen confessed to her trustworthy friend.

'Can't be hot enough for me,' said Sadie, and the sun had more deeply tanned her always brown skin. 'I could live in Africa. Same tomorrow, it said.'

'They're not always right.'

'They will be tomorrow. "Red sky at night: shepherd's delight." I thought you'd have noticed it.'

Ellen watched Sadie begin up the hill and then turned for home.

Speed gathered his gang early. Joe had gone down to the Show Fields as on other holiday mornings to fish for sticklebacks under the bridge but he followed Speed without demur, unafraid. Speed had shot up in height, left Joe far behind, moved into a gang of bigger boys, too big for Joe, but Speed let him join.

The half-dozen of them padded through the long-grassed summer fields upstream alongside the serpentine Wiza river, through one kissing gate, through another until they came to the third Show Field

226

and the object of Speed's purpose. There was a dam built a few score yards downstream from the bridge, almost opposite Pasce Egg Hill. It turned a natural pool into a deep luscious bathing hole, black water until the sheltering alders and willows. Three boys were there adding yet more height to the stoutly constructed barrier.

They pretended to ignore Speed and his gang but it was no help. Joe was in total ignorance of what was about to happen. He was bewildered by the ferocity of the attack. The three boys ran. Speed and the others, Joe belatedly joining in, broke up the dam. They broke it up with dedication. They used the larger stones to batter the patiently patted mud and pebbles and branches that had held the wall. They carried the bigger stones down-river and dumped them in a small deep pool. They destroyed it. 'We need this water,' said Speed, who led them at a gallop chanting, 'We are Kit Carson's men,' back into the first Show Field.

Here was the best place. As the river swayed between the soft sandy banks in this first field, the popular field, the field of circuses and football, it had carved out a deep swathe, a little bay. Here, traditionally, in such hot weather, the big dam was built and those who built it owned it.

By midday it was well founded and they raced to their homes for dinner. Ellen made sandwiches for Joe to take back with him after hearing a bowdlerised version of the building of the dam. She herself had swum there, in years before the war and as she sheltered from the heat of the glowing hot day, she remembered with affection that tang of river water, the coolness of it after lying on the grassy bank, the free amiable anarchy of the boy-made pool.

Word went out. It became a little resort, a spa, an adventure. Speed and some of the bigger boys made a raft. Smaller boys braved the trickle of water on the wrong side of the dam and hopped across stones on the river-bed. One or two of the bigger boys ran hard across the grass and leaped and bombed the water. Joe loved swimming and was developing pace in the front crawl. Here he was reduced to the breast-stroke, more sedate, but more able to look around and avoid being bombed.

There was a girl there, who had just moved into the estate. She had come from a knot of houses in the East End, cottages just one up from mud and wattle, thrown together for weavers in the previous century. Joe had caught her eye more than once in the Easter holidays when they were playing around the half-built houses, chasing games, hiding games, easily converted into the obscure excitement of en-counters. Then she had largely disappeared again, to the Catholic school. Now she was here, with her mother, but her mother was absorbed in conversation with another woman and it seemed to Joe the girl slipped away especially for him and together they played around the raft, a private game of tag, of touch, of splashing each other and showing off (him), switching from chaste to the occasional stun of flirtation (her), she in her red bathing suit covered in little blobs waiting to be popped, he in his over-large black woollen trunks held up by his snake belt, white-skinned both, larky, superficially innocent, making a month out of the long, slow, hot hours of a boon day.

The dispossessed gang came late, after the crowd had moved away, hoping that Speed and his gang had been drawn off with them, but Speed had waited.

The invaders scaled across the river along the fence that spanned the bridge beside the kissing gate. The numbers were about even. Speed and the others picked up as many throwable pebbles as they could find. There was plenty of ammunition.

The raiders fired the first stone. The early volleys were careful. The boys sought protection from the uneven land and squirmed flat between the necessary boldness of leaping up to aim and fire. Most of these were boys of twelve, thirteen, strong enough now to make the stones rifle across the evening tranquil water that lay between them. Joe and Ed, another smaller one, had been dispatched to the wall itself, which gave them more protection but also – Joe reckoned – opened them to the brunt of any frontal attack on the dam.

Speed began to work his way up-river. He was still wearing nothing but the handed-down pair of his father's army underpants that served as a costume. His spurt of growth had made him even leaner. This long-distance battle was getting nowhere, relying on a lucky hit, not frightening enough. He crossed the river.

But they had used his desertion from the main force to begin what Joe dreaded, a move towards the dam and now there were three of them almost there, stones hailing down as if by windmill arms. Joe knew one thing and that was that you did not run away. There was nothing else in his head as the confidence and war whoops of the enemy grew stronger and Speed, out-manoeuvred, found himself stuck behind a tree, attacked steadily and with accuracy by two of the three remaining invaders. The small section of his own forces left on the bank seemed frozen in their posts, held down by the single fire directly opposed to them over the water.

The enemy started hacking at the dam. Speed saw it and stepped out but a stone welted into his shoulder, another hit the slender tree. These were good shots. He stepped back. He needed more ammo. Meant going further back. On to the riverbank.

Ed worked his way along the dam towards the raiders and Joe had to follow him. The other gang were loosening the end of the wall and the water was trying to flow. Ed looked at Joe and nodded and Joe understood that he had to follow Ed. The bigger boy took a breath and then yelled and stood up, as high as the parapet, and scrambled on to it, hurling his pebbles all but indiscriminately, and Joe went after him and then there was a terrible thud on his face. He yelled, as much at the surprise as the hurt, but the yell was loud enough and then too much happened at once.

'They've put his eye out!' Ed yelled in triumph. 'They've got his eye!'

Joe felt his right eye where the thud had been and his hand came away wet. He looked at the blood with disbelief followed by fear. Speed emerged from the trees like a mad thing, hurling himself at the three boys who were off balance, distracted by Joe's cries and his garish wound. Faced by Speed's howling, fearless kamikaze fury, they fled. Speed's forces from the bank now raced down to the water to be in on the action. All the invaders ran away, two of them with head wounds, though nothing as dramatic as the spurting crimson eye of Joe, which to all concerned meant trouble.

Speed grabbed their clothes and led Joe across to the estate.

Ellen was in. She put a cold swab on the wound and told the shivering Joe to press it there hard while with the facecloth she wiped the blood off his body, towelled him gently, took off his bathing trunks and got him into his clothes. Speed, having answered the direct questions unsatisfactorily, left as quickly as possible and went back to rebuild the dam.

On the pillion of her speeding bicycle Joe felt heroic twinges as he held on to his mother with one hand and with the other kept up the pressure of the cold swab.

Another quarter of an inch, the doctor said, even less than that, and it would have been the eye, Mrs Richardson. He's a lucky lad. Joe, he said, you shouldn't get mixed up in stone fights. Two stitches. Almost as many as Gus Lesnevich, he said, in his reassuring Scottish brogue, when Freddie Mills beat him for the Light Heavyweight

Championship of the World. Wasn't that a turn-up? Gus Lesnevich had not cried either. One boiled sweet. The plaster was a long beige scar.

When Sam came in, Joe was in Sam's armchair by the unlit fire, sipping cocoa, a primed invalid, placed there by Ellen as unmistakable proof.

This is what came of fighting.

She told him what the doctor had said about the eye.

Sam asked what had happened just to fulfil his duty to Ellen but he knew he would get nowhere. With her. But it had to be addressed, and not only for Ellen's sake. Such a thing could not be just let pass.

This, she said it aloud now, is what comes of encouraging him to fight. There was no triumph but there was a level accusation and Sam could not begin to explain how even this was better than the boy being soft. Not that this meant he was happy with the pirate's patch down the child's face. Nor with the doctor's remark. Not in the slightest way that would convince Ellen. But this was what happened, sometimes, in fights and better you learned young.

'It wasn't Speed,' Joe said. 'I was in his gang.'

'Good lad.'

Sam skipped the meal and went straight back upstreet. Before all else he wanted one meeting. Speed was winging around the streets on an old bike someone had been scared enough to lend him for a 'go'. He made no attempt to duck Sam but skidded the brakeless machine to an immediate halt.

'Sorry, Mr Richardson.'

'It could've been his eye, Speed.'

'Sorry, Mr Richardson.'

His head was bent down. Sam had to resist the temptation to reach out and ruffle the spiky hair.

'You've got too old for him now, Speed. For that sort of thing. Leave him out now.'

'He wanted to come, Mr Richardson.'

'You won't tell me who did it?' No answer. 'So I won't ask.'

How could he say it? How could he close so many gaps, heal the different wounds? He stabbed at it.

'D'you know what you want to be, Speed? When you leave school?'

The boy looked up, let off, he knew from the change in tone. He shook his head.

'You want to be a soldier. They take them at fifteen – what's that? – just about two or three years on. Boy soldiers. I knew some of them. Fine lads they were. Regular grub. Good pay. You'd like that – what do you think?'

'Yes.' Speed grinned and that, with the faint squint, lit up his thin face with the whoosh of a shooting star. 'That would be great, Mr Richardson.'

'Will you promise me something, then, Speed?'

'What is it, Mr Richardson?'

'Bear it in mind. You tell your mam. And you tell anybody who asks you what you want to do that you're going for a boy soldier and when you're fifteen I'll take you down to Carlisle Castle and see that we get you signed up. Will you tell them that? It means keeping steady till you leave school but you can do that, Speed, the same lad. Is that a deal?'

Still the radiant grin.

'Yes, Mr Richardson.'

Sam held out his hand. 'We'll shake on it, Speed.'

Which they did, there, on King Street, near the Fountain.

Speed went on his charge around the town, imagining the old boneshaker to be a TT motorbike, but now with a rifle slung over his back and real bullets to fire.

Sam went into the nearest pub, the King's Arms.

Not for a drink. A bottle of dandelion and burdock and a packet of crisps for Joe. He had rushed out of the house, he realised, in large part because he could not face Ellen's legitimate accusation. The boy could have lost an eye.

But yet, he thought, still, as he stepped out at a hurried march along the West Road, copper sun glinting on copper hair, smoking, anxious now, inexplicably more anxious than before, the presents bulging his jacket pockets, the boy had not welshed, he had been in a real fight, he had come through.

CHAPTER TWENTY-THREE

'This is the big one,' Sam said, 'the big fight,' and Joe caught the excitement.

Jackie Tempest of Lancaster was the first to walk towards the ring. He punched the air and as he jigged down the aisle the crowd in Carlisle's Covered Market, oiled in the sweat of August heat, gave him a sporting hand. Cheering was reserved for their own, the local light-heavyweight hope, Jackie Moran. Sam knew him and Joe's baying was proportional. It was the main and final bout of the evening.

Sam had picked the back row so that Joe could stand on his seat. They were near enough to the ring.

Everyone agreed with the report in the *Cumberland News* that Moran versus Tempest 'was one of the most terrific fights ever delivered in Covered Market Tournaments'.

Joe could not remember hearing his daddy shout so much, not even at football. 'Come on, Moran!' 'That's the way!' 'Come on, Moran!'

Both men flew into it as if a first-round knockout were the only acceptable result. More like Freddie Mills than Joe Louis, Sam said, as the game pale-skinned northern lads stood up to each other in the middle of the ring and traded punches like bare-knuckle boxers on the scratchline a hundred and fifty years back. Defence was flimsy and all but disregarded. To land the haymaker was the sole purpose. The crowd jelled into a blood growl of contentment, which crested into loud delight when Moran floored Tempest in the second round. 'What a bat!' Sam turned to look up at Joe, his eyes glittering. 'What a bat that was, eh?' Joe nodded, letting his father speak for him, almost stifled with the strange pleasure of seeing Jackie Tempest on his knees, listening to the count, getting up on eight and being allowed to wade into more haymakers from Moran.

The third round was so vicious that the crowd winced, there were moments of intaken breath, a comma of quiet, then the guttural sound swelled up again and Joe was in some deep cave, torchlit, jaws masticating grunt words, fists flailing at the call of the crowd. The clear slap-slap of leather on skin, the pillowed impact crunch of a punch aimed to stun, entwined him in the fight and he swayed and ducked and jabbed and swung with the fighters, who ended the round so exhausted by their aggression that they slumped against each other like Saturday drunks. When the bell went they wandered unevenly to their corners. The crowd applauded, the Covered Market boomed with the sound – like the swimming baths, Joe noticed, the same echoing boom.

The boy had put his hand on Sam's shoulder to steady himself and he kept it there between the rounds.

Like most men watching the bout, Sam lit up while the boxers rested. 'Good fight, Joe!' The statement needed no response.

The warmth and comradeship in those three syllables made Joe feel proudly older, an accomplice in men's matters, men's sport, men's ways.

In the next round, Tempest hurled himself on the Carlisle man from the opening bell and floored him. Moran was hurt. The crowd, his supporters, his well-wishers, rolled in tides of noise as if noise alone, their well-wishing supportive noise, would in itself lift him, unbeach him, raise him up to face again the Lancastrian, now scenting a famous victory, pacing alongside the ropes, ready for the kill.

The noise worked. Moran scraped himself off the floor by the count of seven, somehow muffled the impact of his opponent's charge for victory, steadied himself and then, with the desperation of those who know that glory is such a long shot, that fame is not really for them despite the dreams by day in the bleak pub back-room gym, but with the hope that with one punch, one glint of fortune, a life of bare pickings could change utterly, the local lad called on every available resource. Buoyed up on the ocean of support surging in his ears, sounding all around the darkened Covered Market, he went for his man and put him down, and only the bell saved Tempest and the crowd went berserk.

Joe looked at his father whose grin of intense pleasure mirrored and electrified his own.

In the fifth they were tired but, Sam observed, it was Tempest who looked weaker. Look at how often he's missing with those big punches, Joe, that takes the energy out of him. Joe did not understand that, but it was not the time to ask questions. It's all about getting your strength back. And Moran had to nurse that cut eye. Sam tapped Joe's Elastoplast. Cut eyes were in fashion, he said.

It happened in the sixth.

Moran the local hero was on top, no doubt. Even now. So punished, neither man had much of a defence. But Tempest suddenly hit home with one of his right swinging punches and Moran stopped, stock still, and as his supporters held their breath, Tempest landed what was later described as a 'sledgehammer blow', which caught the local man on the right temple and shuddered his skull, blanked his

237

brain, his body keeled, no brake, slam into the canvas, he did not hear the count, he did not know that even now the crowd, his crowd, tried to lift him, he had to be carried to his corner while a jubilant Tempest, energised by triumph, saluted them.

'Pity,' said Sam, as they moved along the aisle. 'And I'd put a few bob on him. But he was game, eh, Joe?'

The hubbub of excitement followed them out into the balmy summer street, still light. Sam had intended to take Joe round to see Joe Moran in his dressing room but the sight of the poor lad being carried to his corner had made him think again. It would be too humiliating for the man, especially in front of a boy, Sam thought, although, as they sought out the fish and chip shop on the way back to the bus station, he could be mistaken: perhaps poor Moran would be grateful for a friendly face. On the other hand, Sam was not in any way a close friend, just that Moran followed the hound-dogs and would sometimes place a bet on Henry's board at an evening meeting. Henry had not been best pleased when Sam had insisted on taking the evening off for the fight: the hound-trailing season was at its height and you could also chalk up the odds for the evening's horse meetings, bring in more business that way. But since Leonard's warning, Sam found that he tested Henry now and then, always confirming Leonard's words.

'Sam! You old bugger!'

Dougie was leaning against the wall scooping pawfuls of chips from the greasy cone. Joe noted that the swear word was not noticed. Not here.

'This your boy?'

Sam nodded.

'Been in a fight?'

Joe fingered the Elastoplast rather proudly. In this world it was without any doubt a mark of honour. But he looked at his father for the answer.

'Bit of a battle,' Sam said.

'A hard man, your father,' Dougie said, gaping open his mouth, full of half-chewed chips and stumpy discoloured teeth. 'Him and me was in the war, eh, Sam?' The drink ponged at three yards. 'Bloody great times, eh?'

'How's life treating you?'

'Just now and then, Sam. Just now and then.'

The small half-drunk ex-soldier, who had found the truth of his life as a licensed, righteous killer in Burma and since his return found those talents obstructing his admittedly reluctant attempts to lead a peaceful existence, took a last gulp of chips, scrunched up the paper, chucked it in the gutter, slid his hands into his pockets and took aim for the nearest pub. 'Fancy a pint?'

'The boy, Dougie.'

'He could sit on the steps.'

Sam was tempted. Doug lived north of Carlisle in a grim little border town; the odds against seeing him again were high. And here was someone with whom, literally, he had been through the jungle and seen and done things unimaginable to the raw young man he had been at the outset of the war, and in the brief companionship of a drink something would be said that would raise up that unreal violent time of his life.

But one drink would not be enough with Dougie. It never had been. And with Joe there, it was not the time to take on that past. Nor, he realised, did he ever want such a time.

'Another night, Dougie.'

Dougie waved and rolled away.

On the bus, they talked in detail about the fight and brought in

Joe Louis and Freddie Mills. Their talk put the boy in a whirlpool of blows and punches and brave blood.

'Dougie was the real hard man in the section,' Sam confided, as they got off the bus opposite Greenacres and walked across the road to the lighted house. 'Dougie was as hard a little man as I've ever met.'

There was admiration in Sam's tone and Joe understood.

CHAPTER TWENTY-FOUR

Sam wrote to the brewery, without confiding in anyone. By return he received a letter authorising him to look over the premises. He went down there on the Sunday morning well before opening time.

The Blackamoor was just across from Grace's house, facing Market Hill. It was the first pub hit by those walking up from the East End of the town, an area of winter gypsy encampments and weavers' cottages and men, Sam always remembered, described at the time the militia came from Carlisle to put down the riots as men who 'would fight each other just for the love of fighting'. The pub was now sandstone-built, a steep-raked slate roof, but there were photographs of it thatched and stories of it even before that bygone time.

Over the past years, even during the boom drinking war, it had become run down. The old widow who kept the pub had finally been persuaded to give up the tenancy but there were no takers. It took very little time to see why.

The cellars were dark, filthy, and organised on no principle Sam could discern. There were five wooden barrels on the ramps but only two were tapped and lengths of unused black rubber piping curled over the flagged floor in a sludge of neglect. Yet, he noted, they were three good-sized rooms, with a coal-hole as well as the trap-door that opened on to the wide paved front of the pub, making delivery of the beer a simple job.

Four small rooms made up the pub itself. A narrow men-only bar with a long settle as the sole furniture and sawdust on the floor. A Darts Room, a room without a piano nevertheless designated the Singing Room, and the kitchen. The kitchen was both the family kitchen, served by a ship's galley of a pantry, and licensed premises. All the rooms were in a poor decorative state. The furniture was worn or cheap or both. The cost of fittings and 'goodwill' on the handover would be very low.

A wooden gate at the bottom of the stairs marked off the privacy of the flat above. Mrs Hewson puffed asthmatically up the stairs at the top of which was a small landing. The biggest room had recently and brutally been battered into a bathroom and indoor lavatory and the walls still bore the scars. Sam was allowed a quick peep into Mrs Hewson's bedroom. Like every other room, it smelt of stale beer. There were two more, narrow, single, connected by an inner door. Finally there was the parlour, more like a mausoleum, apparently undisturbed since the death of Mr Hewson of 'a seizure' in 1938. There was also a large loft – Mrs Hewson pointed to a trap-door – but she had never been in it. Her late husband had said it was too big and cluttered to do anything with.

At the back there was a small yard, raked, showing the slope of the hill, with lavatories for the men. The women came upstairs and used the bathroom of the house. There were stables in the yard, above which was a good dry loft that Mr Hewson had once thought of turning into a workshop. The back yard was permanently gloomy. A very high wall hid the garden of what had once been the old grammar school, next door, now occupied by two maiden sisters.

After the tour Mrs Hewson offered him a drink and approved

when he asked for a bottle of milk stout. 'I'll join you,' she said. 'It keeps me going.'

They settled on hard chairs at the bare scratched oak table in the kitchen. Mrs Hewson poured the stout slowly and skilfully keeping the glass correctly aslant so that the bottle did not disgorge an unnecessary quantity of froth. She was of a type – a bit like Grace, Sam concluded as he studied her, but older, even more corseted, steeped in virtuous and complacent gloom about the world. She had put on widows' weeds ten years ago and had stuck to them ever since. Her hair was grey, centre-parted and bunned. Her skin was remarkably pale, faintly criss-crossed by telltale red veins. Her hands were steady enough but the depth of the first sip betrayed her need for the stout.

'Ellen won't like it here,' she said. 'The hours are terrible. Eleven thirty to three, five thirty to ten weekdays, twelve to two, seven to ten Sundays. There's no escape. Between times you're clearing up and cleaning up other folks' messes. Christmas Day no exception. Fires to be laid and lit, she'll need help. Mrs Glaister says when I go she goes, she's hung on long enough. Women coming into your kitchen and then gallivanting up into your toilet on Saturday nights – don't tell me women aren't as messy as men.' Mrs Hewson took another pull of stout. 'I only carried on because Mr Hewson passed over. I'd been on at him to give up and get a nine-to-five life for years. I was always on at him for that.' She nodded to herself in approval at the tender memory. 'Ellen will go mad in here. It's no life.'

Sam had to put all that to one side. For perhaps it was true.

And to take issue with Mrs Hewson or others of the matriarchy who wore the moral stays of the town was a waste of breath. On market days you could see them out, the women like Mrs Hewson, heroic, broadly built from neck to hip, dressed invariably in black or deep grey, billowing on the windy streets, their ocean, often sporting bare gums, peering with unhappy appraising look, knotting together every thread of gossip, gone it seemed with desperate inevitability from childbearing to elder with no intermediate breath, the calendar, the chronicle, the keepers of the secret history, the furies of moral certainty taking their revenge on life.

She let him see the account books, which were hopelessly kept but easy to read – turnover small, profit slight. All the beer had to be purchased from the one brewery at Workington, twenty miles away, and for that the tenant got a contract that could be terminated only if the tenant broke the law or by mutual agreement. In brief, provided you bought your beer at the one brewery and kept the law, you were independent, your own boss. You were your own man. Under no authority. Liberated from service.

That, that above all things.

On his way out he offered to pay for the stout.

Mrs Hewson paused, so that the pause was noticed. 'I'll let you have that one, Sam,' she said. 'I've just got a feeling.'

To make up, he asked for twenty cigarettes. 'I'm out,' she said. 'There's a shortage again. That's another thing. Never any warning either.'

The street was like a release from the tomb.

He waited a few nights.

Joe was reading the *Wizard*. Sam also read the comic. His initial pretence had been so that he could talk to Joe about the adventures of the fabulous men in the stories – especially the super-athletic Wilson, at least a hundred and fifty years old, who came out of a deep sleep in a cave in Scotland to boggle at the world and break records wearing

244

black long johns. And Alf Tupper, the Tough of the Track, the ordinary lad, the welder, self-coached, who beat the privileged and then ate fish and chips. In truth he admitted to a mild addiction, as loyal to the *Wizard* and the *Rover* as to many of the story-tellers recommended by Willie Carrick on his less regular visits to the library.

Like Joe, he raced up and down the columns of tight small print, pulled in week after week by the high adverse odds, the apparent certainty of failure, the cunning and the courage of the last minute, the clean-cut honour of the home-grown heroes, the satisfying fiction of another victory of the right and the good. He read the comic after Joe and they would chat over the stories.

He turned on the wireless for *Take It From Here*. Ellen came in from the kitchen to join them. It was still light but the evening hue infiltrated the room, enclosing the three of them, positioned attentively around the brown mahogany cabinet, like 'millions', Ellen had heard, all over the country, millions and millions waiting as they were to be entertained and laugh together and talk it over the next day. Both Ellen and Sam felt an extra lift in the eager laughter of Joe. They joined in: 'Ooh, Ron,' they said, in unison.

The next half hour was cocoa and bed for the boy with Ellen back for her own special programme, *Family Favourites*, which Sam stayed in for, unusually, and laboured through *Hornblower* who was usually a fast read. Another half-hour's break, when Ellen went upstairs to make sure that Joe was asleep and not reading, and then she made them both a cup of tea while Sam waited for his favourite programme, *Much Binding In The Marsh*. Ellen usually drifted out soon after it began.

She came back into the room a few minutes after he had turned the wireless off. What she wanted to say was that the evening had been so like evenings she had hoped for. The tranquillity, the three of them. Sharing the jokes on the wireless. Sam quietly teasing Joe. The three of them quietly doing what she imagined millions of others were quietly doing, no more no less, and joined to them all through the songs, the laughs. Sam in one of his up times, no diving down into himself where she could not reach, not for weeks now, and Joe surely less scared of him, less clinging to her, this big new house becoming their home, even so far out, a place to start afresh. Yet little of this was transmitted in the few commonplaces she offered. The saying of it would have spoiled it, she thought, even if she had the habit of turning such feelings into words.

Sam closed the book.

'I'm going to take the Blackamoor,' he said.

Ellen tilted her head to one side and her black hair swung free and softly across her face. She smiled. There was no sign that the words had registered. He thought – How lovely you look.

'I've thought it through. I could build it up. God knows, there's scope.'

And, still, for another moment or so, it did not dawn.

'Leonard'll be one reference: I've written to Colonel Oliphant for the other. He was a good officer. He should be OK.'

'Take the pub?'

'The Blackamoor.'

'Why are you doing this, Sam?'

Her expression, her postures, her tone, it seemed to her that her entire personality experienced a change.

'I've no future in the factory now.'

'It's steady. Isn't it? We manage.'

'I want to be my own boss, Ellen.' The well-rehearsed explanation was offered as a mutter.

'But I don't like pubs. I've never liked them. I hate men in drink. I don't like drink.'

'I won't drink on my own premises.'

'Not you.' She looked at him in a sort of wonder that he could have engineered such a shock. 'You've settled it, then.'

'It's still to be tied up.' He paused. 'But yes.'

Ellen nodded, repetitively, as if she were bowing again and again to a household altar, distracted, locked in the shock of it. 'It's settled then. That's it?'

'I wanted to talk to you about it before the paperwork.' Sam's lame half-truth sounded more like a non-truth than he would have wished.

'What about all this?' She made a small, sweeping, rather hopeless gesture with her left hand.

'There's plenty of room there.'

'So you've been round the house part as well?'

'Mrs Hewson says you're welcome any time.'

'Who else knows about it?'

'Leonard. I told him after work. He'll have told Grace.'

'And who'll Mrs Hewson not have told?'

'It's not settled, Ellen. It's really not. Not till it's signed.'

'But you can't wait.'

'No.' Sam found the firmness he felt. 'I can't wait. I could build it up. I could make a go of it. I know I could.'

'So I'll have to give up the canteen?'

He did not reply.

'We were doing so well here, Sam. We were. It was working out, wasn't it? Wasn't it working out?'

'I know.' The discomfort he felt at her ill-disguised plea was physical. 'But it could work out again. And you'll be back in the middle of the town.'

Sam had rather calculatingly thought of that as a clincher. She seemed utterly unimpressed.

'It'll be no good for Joe,' she said, quietly.

247

'Why's that?'

She could not find the answer.

'He'll enjoy it. Plenty to do.'

'I have to say yes this time, haven't I, Sam?'

He had calculated and, uneasily, banked on this too. Following her opposition to his going to Australia after he came back from the war, her implacable rootedness and her victory, she could not again pit her will against his.

She got up abruptly and went into the kitchen. He heard the back door open. He followed. She was standing on the apron of grass before the vegetable garden. The sky was crystal, northern stars glittering high in the dark blue-black summer heavens.

'We had to learn the names of some of the stars when we were in the Guides,' she said. 'I remember the Great Bear – there it is – because the last two stars on the pan-handle point to the North Star. The North Star always seemed a friendly one, as if it was our own. Then there was a W over the other side, what they called the Warrior, three stars for his belt, two stars at the shoulders . . . those two I think at the bottom of his legs. I used to look for that when you were away,' she added, very quietly, 'and keep my fingers crossed. I'll go.' She glanced around, taken by a rush of fondness for this place, her small territory of grass, Sam's well drilled vegetable garden. She breathed very deeply through her nose and let out the breath carefully through her mouth. 'But there's no garden at the Blackamoor, is there, Sam? There's no garden there.'

She turned away because she did not want him to see the quick tears which had come to her eyes, but he had heard them in her voice and he let her go in and be alone for a while.

'I'm sure you understand that it wasn't easy in the war for her either.' Mr Kneale, anxious to help, was very careful. Sam had never confided in him before. Neither he nor Sam quite realised how it had happened but they were in Grace's kitchen the day before the move into the pub and Sam had intimated disquiet about Ellen despite the brave face put on it. 'She probably felt very calm in Greenacres. And a pub's no haven of calm, Sam.'

Sam listened hard.

'I think she's worrying over whether she can cope.' They had no cups of tea between them to give the conversation a little help. Sam felt that he was being taught. Yet in this instance he did not mind it.

'The women took a lot on in the war, you know,' Mr Kneale went on. 'So did the kiddies. They must have wondered whether you were dead or alive every other minute. In some way. Not to talk about but those things go deep, Sam. We know that. I often looked at the children at school and I could see it on their faces. Will my dad be shot? Will he come back? Worry's a destructive thing, Sam.' The schoolteacher was moved by his own recollection. 'I can see Ellen here, in this room, night after night, listening to the news. What she was listening for, Sam, was to find out about you. Night after night. And the boy. He had to be told that you were alive. Just that, you see. But it was a fundamental matter, Sam, and a matter that she had to cope with every day, wondering whether you were alive and keeping the boy reassured when she had nothing at all in the way of evidence. It's a funny way for a young woman to manage, year in, year out. We know the horrors of war, we know something about the men – but the women and children waiting and listening out, Sam, helpless and just listening out, with no power to act, none at all, that's another story. When you go through these events they can come back at you in unexpected ways. But she'll be fine, Sam, she'll be fine. You'll see.'

—⟋⟍—

Mrs Hewson held a silver threepence just out of reach and Joe had to wait until she was ready.

'They call it the Blackamoor,' she said, 'because of a little black lad – about your age he would be when they brought him over. They called all little black slave lads blackamoors in those days. They brought him over to be a potboy. In those days children had to work,' she said, regretfully, 'and they used to catch them abroad because they could get such a lot of work out of them. This was a long time ago. You listen. And there was some of the Wigton men – weavers – that just tormented that lad. They wouldn't let him alone. However willing he was never quick enough for them. They made the poor lad's life a misery. He was far from home as it was. Bad enough.' She paused between each sentence now. 'Anyway, those stables kept horses in those days, Joe, they did when Mr Hewson came in, but I wanted no horses – and one wet night, a bad night, a fella came on a black stallion, a terrible size and temper on it, and what those men did was lock that little black lad in the stable with that stallion. Well, he was scared out of his wits. He screamed and he shouted but they just laughed and he must have agitated that stallion because there was a great kicking and squealing from the horse and more and more screams from the boy and it had kicked him dead. There was quite a fuss about it at the time.' The longest pause. 'Mr Hewson always said the little blackamoor won't leave this place. He says he used to hear him running about up under the roof at night.' A final pause. 'This threepence is for you, Joe. Don't spend it all at once.'

250

As she told the story, Joe felt himself going numb. Mrs Hewson's face was large, and so white. Her layers of heavy clothing were drenched in the perfumes of ale. She was a small woman but she bore down on the boy and emphasised the terrible story with significant nods, a hammer driving in a nail.

Poor little boy, Joe thought. Poor little boy. In the dark on his own with that black horse. Poor little boy.

He could hear his screams.

She had frightened the boy, she could see that. Mrs Hewson felt a glow of satisfaction. She enjoyed frightening children.

They had to take possession the same day as Mrs Hewson left. Sam opened up the pub. Tommy Miller with his horse and cart did the moving for them, helped by Ellen.

After two big loads there was a last trip, late in the afternoon. Ellen had biked to and fro to speed things up but this time she walked down to Greenacres. Joe had asked to play on her bike as he did increasingly in preparation for the great ninth birthday bike of his own.

She walked the town gauntlet – 'Moving in, Ellen, eh?', 'I'll be down there', and worst, most stigmatising of all, 'One of the toffs now, Ellen, eh?', 'Going up in the world, eh?' – everyone, intolerably, knowing, everyone, intolerably, noticing, free to comment, to single out, transformed into an exception however much she could protest that they would stand to earn less than their combined wage and for many more hours' work, and what work! Skivvying, constant serving, perpetual clearing up. She would not complain and smiled at the sometimes innocent taunts but 'going up in the world' – did people really believe that?

The only good thing so far was that Colin had mucked in to help Sam and she could see that there would be plenty of jobs for him to do, just across the road from Grace's house. She could keep an eye on him.

As she came down to Greenacres on the fine September day she tried to block out the feelings she had for their council house. It was curious. It was not so much what the place had been for the three of them, as what it could have been. But how could she regret, and so acutely, what had not happened? It was tiring. The only thing was to do the next thing.

They took the mirror, this time, and the wireless, the two little rugs and the side table and the few small ornaments. Tommy Miller had advised that these best things make up a load of their own. 'Have a lift back, Ellen.'

Tommy sat on the edge of the cart, in the old fashion. Ellen would have to sit on the cart itself or take the other front corner, legs dangling, hands gripping the rim of the cart to steady herself.

'We'll look like a pair of tinkers, Tommy.'

'Nothing wrong with tinkers, Ellen.'

His response was serious. Tommy met up with tinkers in one of his other manifestations as a horse-dealer. He knew their language and enjoyed their peculiarities as much as they enjoyed engaging with a teetotal Salvation Army bandsman which was another of Tommy's lives. He and Ellen had been in the same class at school together, right through.

'Get up,' he said. 'Save your legs.'

It was a kind invitation, which forbade refusal.

Tommy clicked his tongue and the piebald mare trotted smoothly down the West Road, passing the fine houses in their own wooded gardens with a flick of its mane, and Ellen half listening to Tommy's observations.

So this was it.

The horse slowed down to a walk up the hill and Tommy kept it to a walk even when they were back on the flat, passing Wigton Hall. Ellen had schemed to get off the cart before the Fountain but when the time came she could think of no good excuse so she went back into the old town as so many women must have done over the centuries, perched on a cart, accompanied by a few possessions, not a little afraid of what they might find, powerless before an unwanted life decided for them by their men.

CHAPTER TWENTY-FIVE

Ellen took him for his eye-test the day after Bella's funeral, upset and somehow hurt at the meagre turnout in the Primitive Methodist chapel. She had decided against taking Joe with her. Apart from anything else, one morning off school was enough.

They had to go to Carlisle. Joe could not shake off the conviction that the test was directly connected with the stone fight and neither could Ellen. Mr Brown, a new maths teacher at the school that autumn term, had noticed Joe's difficulty at not being able to see the numbers on the blackboard clearly and he said the problem must have been there for a while.

The waiting-room was so cram-full that they had to stand for the first hour. The only speech in the claustrophobic silence was the occasional 'When can we go home?' of a child or the hushed whisper of a parent. Everyone wore bulky coats. The weather had turned savage.

Joe's eyes were soused in a gooey liquid and swam in semi-blindness. Their weakness was not in question. Wear in the classroom and when reading but not absolutely essential when playing. Joe grasped at that.

Specs would not only alter the way he would see. They would – and more importantly – alter the way he would be seen. Though only nine he had no doubts on that. Specs meant that you could be called 'Speccy' or 'Four Eyes' or 'Goggles'. Specs meant that you were one of those – like the over-fat, the over-spotty, the incontinent nose dripper, the dwarfish – someone to be picked on. Specs meant that you would certainly be taunted, most days, especially by those older boys who liked an easy fight. Specs meant that you got nasty little welts on either side of the top of your nose and behind your ears – he had seen them, he would inherit them, they marked you out even when you took your specs off. Specs meant girls laughed at you, the pretty girls, the girls you wanted to go with. Specs meant that all sorts of ambitions were snuffed out. Could you imagine Tarzan in specs, or Denis Compton in specs, or Stanley Matthews or Wilson of the *Wizard*, or Joe Louis in specs – how could he be world champion now? – or Freddie Mills, or Captain Marvel? His intimations of a spectacled future were furious and dark. Specs shut you out. And you were always frightened to break them.

'It'll not be so bad,' Ellen said, rather distantly, to cheer him up as the bus came back into Wigton.

But it would. He knew it would. It would be worse than bad.

'You'll get used to them.'

Specs just ruined the whole of your life. Did nobody understand? What was the point of that?

Poor Bella, Ellen thought, as the bus pulled up the hill into the town. The girl had preyed on her mind since the cold funeral. Poor Bella, so few to mourn her.

—⟋⟍—

Sam felt that he had come into his own. He could do this job. He would never break the law so he could never be fired. The business would be as good as he was, no better, no worse, and that suited him. Everything needed cleaning up. Dirt had become institutionalised in gluey patches of leaking grime under unmoved benches. Stains looked like tattoos. Curtains were heavier with dust than material. The rubbish in the cellar had to be waded through. Lino curled and frayed and ripped.

The brewery sent a cellarman to teach Sam about tapping barrels, keeping the beer cool and settling the ale, cleaning the pumps and drawing a pint. Speaking as a connoisseur he said that he had never come across cellars in such a bad state.

After he had sorted out the mess, Sam enjoyed the cellar work. He would go down every morning after he had carried up the crates of bottled beer and done his other jobs. He transformed the place. He drew clear water through the pipes, which he had severed from the barrels and settled in buckets of water, until it came translucent through the pumps. Pull after pull. And if the cloudy water did not quite hit the peak of translucence, Sam went down to the cellar and refilled the buckets with clear water. The improvement in the beer was noticed within days.

There was a bonus in the sense of leisure about the hours. He did not have to clock on. Ever again. In theory he need not get up until after eight, even after nine o'clock, and once or twice he lay in bed that long just for the hell of it. There were the two or three hours clear in the afternoon, especially on weekdays, when midday trade was light, and in those afternoons he could stroll around the town, or read a little, put on a couple of bets personally, drop into the Legion for a few frames of snooker, feel as free as a man of means. The evening work was no bother, not only because the place got busier but because company found him, conversation came to the pub, the pub was its refuge and much of the talk was of sport. Men who followed it in detail talked about it at length, examined it ruminatively, took serious issue, exercised hypotheses, used it as the infinitely flexible currency of communication.

Sam soon knew what he wanted the pub to be distinguished for. There would be darts teams – which Mrs Hewson had let go – and the dominoes would go on. But all the top pubs had an extra dimension. The Vaults was the pub for the pigeon men. The King's Arms was where the football lads met since they had once played in the field behind the pub. The Lion and Lamb was famous for its Sunday quiz and its connection with Carlisle United Supporters Club. The Rugby lads went to the Kildare. Since motorbike scrambling had come in, the Vic had taken that following. The farmers favoured both the Crown and the Crown and Mitre, especially on market days. The Black-amoor, Sam decided, would be the pub for hound-dogs.

These were a craze in a town always dog mad. Hound-dogs – derived from foxhounds but bred for speed – competed for prize money on roughly circular courses through the countryside, generally about eight miles in all, following a strong trail of paraffin and aniseed. It was called the poor man's horse-racing. The dogs were not expensive to keep. The difficulty lay in getting to the meetings, which were held usually in the fells all over the county, sometimes two or three nights a week, as well as on Saturdays. What was needed was a supporters' club, Sam thought, and a regular supply of private buses. He set himself to sort that out. And he might start a Sunday quiz – the town could surely support two.

Through the pub, he found a much darker side of the town. There were the frugal and the unsettled and the rejected, coming in for warmth, often literally, and as time went on, offering confidences, confessing failures, revealing unfulfilled ambitions, and the more Sam and Ellen were trusted, the more lives were uncovered before them. They became secular confessors.

For Sam the pub would serve. It could be a world. It was world enough. It would take care of Ellen and Joe. It would make sure that his father got a regular free drink. Colin had shown willing: for Ellen's sake there might be a chance for him. He could master it, make the work work for him. He had felt the glove fitted from that first encounter with Mrs Hewson and every day confirmed it.

Only Ellen could undermine it and he watched her carefully. He knew that she would not set out to thwart him but there was no doubt that her dislike of the idea of a pub was real. He was asking a lot.

Ellen saw that this was his deal. In years not old, just entering his fourth decade, she knew, she could see it in every move he made, that this was his destination. This was the man she had married before the war but it was also someone else, forever that distance apart, forever following his own drum not so much unwilling as unable to share everything as once they had so long ago, in another life.

The pub depressed her. She was young. She wanted the normal things – dances, evenings, the same rhythm as others. But now she was a landlady. The word made her cringe. Every association of the word made her cringe despite her respect for at least three of the landladies in the town. But they were on a bigger scale than she was, she thought, and older, more capable of standing up to the job. For the first time in her life she feared she might not be up to a task and the feeling was a clammy morning sickness, a burden.

But it had to be borne. Sam had called on her loyalty. The best had to be made of a bad job. Private reservations had to be excised. They were a luxury. At times she thought she would weep all day but she stayed dry-eyed and the tears only stained her mind. It taxed her, though, this doing against her will, and Joe was sidelined, left to shift for himself, given the odd treat where there had been attention. Sam too withdrew from the boy, locked into a new and demanding life.

Ellen found that work helped numb feeling. Cleaning was imperative, cleaning downstairs, on the stairs, in the flat, wanting but having to wait for new wallpaper, new lino, new paint, cleaning a grease-coated stove, a brown-stained sink, opening hours, midday, then tidy up, shop for tea, opening hours again, she had to learn to do the bar while Sam went out to see to the buses for the hounds or take a break, learn the prices, pull a pint. Men were different in a pub: a pub was the extension of their house yet it was her home, especially the kitchen, where they could be having supper, her and Joe, and people would just come in with a drink, for the fire and the company. All the settlement of family at Greenacres blown away, blown far away, never to be lived again. The pub, her home, known as the House. Sam kept a good House.

She paid Sadie to help with the cleaning every morning and that was a blessing. Sadie loved the excitement of the newness. Sadie found Jack Ackerman, Jack Ack, to play the accordion on Friday night and Saturday night. Jack could accompany anything. Never had a lesson. All the old songs. And the new – 'Galway Bay', of course, and 'Woody Woodpecker', 'I'm Looking Over a Four Leaf Clover'; give Jack Ack a couple of lines and he could vamp his way through. Sadie herself was better than the wireless, Ellen thought. Scarcely a film star moved or an American singer sang a note without a salty report from Sadie. 'Air freshener,' she cried in those first few days, 'give us bags of air freshener and we'll make this pub into a holiday camp, Ellen – just you wait and see, like Mr Asquith said.'

Colin was found jobs. Sam paid him a few bob even though he could have done the jobs himself. Ellen saw that as an act of love for her. Colin felt that at last Sam respected him. He bloomed, Ellen reported to Grace, who pleased Ellen by agreeing that she could see it. It would be the making of him. He got himself a crew-cut, which Ellen said did not suit him at all but it was part of a new start, and she could understand that.

The first months were dirty, tiring daily drudgery and the only way to get through was to chatter to Sadie and think about something else all the time. Sam took on the cleaning of the outside lavatories, for which Ellen was grateful. He would try to avoid asking her to serve in the pub at midday through the week – except for the ten minutes he took for his dinner. He tried as best he could to ease the bruise of the disappointment she tried to conceal and ignore.

The curious thing was that Ellen became as big an attraction as Sam. Her admonishments to young men that they were wasting their money on a second pint and should save up instead; her warm welcoming of the Salvation Army selling *War Cry* and the *Tower* on Saturday nights; the pleasant women friends she asked in to help serve in the Singing Room and the Darts Room at weekends; above all, the deep and deepening knowledge she held, and the quiet passion she had for all the doings of the town, brought in its own number who would say not, 'I'm off to Sam's House,' or even 'the Blackamoor', but 'off to talk to Ellen'. And as time went on, these conversations, this court of contact, become a balm.

—⁂—

Sam and Ellen flared up with each other still, but now there was the distorting pressure of others. A confrontation had to be instantly defused when a customer called and the anger of personal passion was immediately masked by a necessary politeness, an imperative sense of privacy, which exacerbated the anger, shovelled insult on it by demeaning it.

There were glimpses. There were moments. Ellen would see Sam, standing at an empty bar in the first opening hour of many a weekday. He would be studying form in the paper or doing his books, smoking a cigarette, the hair still deep copper, something about the confidence of the posture that still moved her, the completion of his appearance by the spirally smoke from the cigarette curling around the motes of dust, the sureness of the man, the man who had gone away and come back half known. And Sam found that in the busy evenings towards closing time when the orders showered in, he would be on the lookout for a smile – not directed towards him, just a real smile that would open up to him the girl he had met when she was very young, the young woman he had craved throughout the war. It gave him a chime of pleasure – that there could be happiness for her here, and in that happiness he could see what he loved.

They were never out of each other's lives. Morning, noon, night. Times of retreat were rare. Such intense cohabitation made demands they had not bargained for. Every hour was intertwined. Love was stretched too thin to cope. Disagreement had a multitude of opportunities. And yet, in that intensity, a new reliance slowly accreted, a proven sense of the two of them. Where nothing could be long disguised or ever hidden, they knew each other as deeply as any other knowing. Empathy became necessity. Tolerance had to find new limits. No mood could be consumed in secret, no slight concealed. The intensity of consistent partnership in all things on all days grafted new roles on to the boy-girl, lovers, man-wife, parents' roles they already had.

Joe ran between the two of them in a suppressed panic in those first raw, effortful, tiring weeks. The newness, the liberties, the privileges teased him into small pleasures and vanities alike. He had the run of a man's world, the secret world of men, men who exchanged a word with him now. Yet outside – in the choir, the Cubs, the baths – he looked for more than he had ever done, the last to leave, organising any game to linger on.

For a while at school he could not keep a straight line on the page. Unless he concentrated flat out, his handwriting would start at the top of the page by abutting the margin on the left-hand side of the paper and then leave it, each line starting further and further away from the margin, each line shorter, a wasted blank space revealed, shaming him. He could not seem to help himself.

Half the time, Mr Brown said, he wasn't there. Mr Brown said this in a kindly manner, but the boy felt guilty because it was true. He was drugged by fantasies of escape.

CHAPTER TWENTY-SIX

Joe came in past bedtime. He had been at the swimming gala in the under tens squadron team. They had only come third, which was a better way of saying they had come last. He did not want his father to ask him the result so he slipped past the side door of the bar. The kitchen was already full. Ellen came out of the bar and went into the galley while Joe sat on a stool in front of the fire. A lady who had begun to come regularly, a wealthy lady, his mother said, who wore strong makeup and glittering jewellery, asked him easy questions about school. The lady told him the fire would dry his hair and took his soggy towel to give it a quick rub and he felt calmer.

One or two goodnights accompanied Ellen and himself as she emerged with the warmed-up pie and a cup of cocoa and they went upstairs.

She watched as he stripped and stepped into the striped pyjamas.

'Clean your teeth, say your prayers, sleep tight.' Ellen laid the lightest of kisses on his forehead. There was no time for anything else.

He was allowed to have the wireless to himself on Saturdays. It was tuned to the Light Programme. He stuffed up the pillow and sat in bed with the pie and the cocoa and a copy of the *Wizard* as the noise of the pub swelled beneath him. He read rapidly and gobbled the pie.

He knelt by the bed. Our Father. God Bless Mammy and Daddy and Colin and Uncle Leonard and Aunty Grace. Please make me better. For Jesus Christ's sake. Amen.

Bed. Dark. The noise growing. A funny sound? The little black boy. Say it often enough and he will go away, his daddy had told him when he had winkled out of him the root of his fear of the loft. But he was there, the little blackamoor. Joe had heard him call out. He had heard him cry.

He woke up to a sound that combined the loud scrape and crash of furniture, the high fearful yelling of women and the jabber of oaths, warnings, threats full-throated from men. For moments he did not know what was happening. An intensifying of the noise, his father's voice? His mother's? Zipped out of bed on to the landing, leaning over the banisters, saw a mêlée crammed in the narrow passage that separated the Darts Room and the Singing Room from the bar and the kitchen, men, jammed together, a sudden gap when a scuffle became a blow and cleared space for the fight.

His daddy not fighting. His daddy doing what? Smiling! Putting his back to the fighting men and pushing, others pushing, with their backs, the fighters shoved towards the front door, women looking out of the kitchen, not his mother, two men helping his daddy to push, 'Heave!' his daddy said, 'heave!' and smiling when there was this fight and Joe's stomach churning, his mind dizzy, sick. Why was his daddy not fighting?

Then the pack of men were outside, quite suddenly, and his daddy slammed the bolt in the door and slapped men on the back and said very loudly, 'It's all over, ladies and gentlemen. It's all over. As you were.' He went to the Singing Room and right away Jack Ack squeezed out 'Rose of Tralee'. 'As you were.'

Joe raced back into his room to look out of the window and into the street where four men were fighting. Right across the street, seen clearly by the light at the bottom of Market Hill. Other men formed a circle, which elasticated around the fighting. One of them was down. The other kicked him! Joe gasped. Another was just hitting his opponent again and again. 'It's over! Break it up!' someone cried out. 'It's over! Break it up!' But the man kicking and the man hitting did not stop until they all ran away, over Market Hill, down Burnfoot, into Tenters, and Joe saw the policeman and pulled back from the window.

He was beside himself. His arms tingled, his whole body flinched and struck, was in the fight, winner, loser, in the fight. Feelings boiled in him. He boxed and bashed and bashed the pillow.

'Time, gentlemen, please. Time, please.'

Joe darted back on to the landing, excited, full of dread, but no more fights. He had watched them leave the pub before on noisy nights when he could not sleep and this appeared to be no different. Yet it must be. There had been a fight! He peered over the banisters weighing up the departing customers: who would cause trouble next? Why had his daddy not fought?

Then they were all gone and he saw his mother at last. Safe! She did not look up. She was busy, emptying ashtrays, collecting glasses, washing up, tidying the chairs, sorting out the main things while Sam counted the takings and entered them in the book, and the helpers with Colin and Jack Ack went into the kitchen where they were allowed by law to be given a drink by the landlord.

Jack Ack told them how it had started, in the Singing Room, when one of the Milburn brothers had sworn at Freddie Johnston, which began the fight, and the other Milburn had joined in and Freddie's mate, Arthur, so fast, said Jack Ack, chairs picked up, women screaming, glasses knocked off the tables, at each other like fighting cocks.

In the corridor, Sadie said, the Milburns had ganged up against Freddie, which was not fair. But the Milburns, they had been up at court three weeks before for fighting each other at the dance! Each other!

I was at the door seeing they got out, said Colin. Arthur had a swing at me but I just ducked and I didn't retaliate. You want them out when they start trouble, he said, best for me to keep out of it with my temper!

Yes, said Patricia, who served in the Darts Room and was shaken though a touch thrilled. You can't afford trouble. It puts everybody in the wrong mood.

The fight went round and round again and Alec, who helped out with the clearing afterwards for the free drink, reported what he had seen through the bar window, the man on the ground, the kicking, the policeman coming, round and round it went, reshaped, touched up, packaged for future use.

Sam knew it was a big test. He took his time with the money. Pennies in neat piles of twelve. Bobs in twenties. Half-crowns in eights. Halfpennies, sixpences, threepenny bits, two-bob bits, even the few farthings still knocking about, all carefully stacked, little chimneys of cash.

Trouble bred trouble. Fighting pubs drew in fighting men. He had been lucky tonight. It had not spread. One bad customer drove out half a dozen good men. And a landlord who fought back was penalised. It was unfair but there it was. His licence would be taken away by the police. He had heard that from all the landlords who had been helpful to him.

He would ban the four men for two months. That would be seen as harsh. The men would want to come back, they might plead, they might threaten, they would blame each other, they would swear it would never happen again, they could turn nasty, they could turn on Sam when they came, as they would, as they did, the two Milburns together, the others singly, at a quiet time to make their case, but he had to stick to his word. Two months. And not be drawn in himself. Much as they might like that. Much as he might feel goaded to. Not to join in. That was another test.

It would not be the end of the fights. Some men in drink, too much drink the one night of the week, too much erupting out of poor diet and the abrupt escalation of expectation and power in alcohol, some men in drink in the town would always be on the lookout for a fight. But not in the Blackamoor. Whatever it cost him to clear it out.

Because he had seen Ellen's face. This was not what he had promised her. This was not a life for her.

Sam knew where she was now. He had spotted the boy wide-eyed at the top of the stairs, shimmering with excitement and fright. Ellen would be up there now, in that dour little parlour most likely, pretending to tidy something, or in the bathroom, listening out for him and feeling, Sam knew, in her heart, at war with him for bringing them down to this.

—~m~—

PART THREE
THE BLACKAMOOR:
1952

—~m~—

CHAPTER TWENTY-SEVEN

Joe finished some minutes after the whistle was blown and all the others had left the pool. The superintendent, the team trainer, had suggested he build up his stamina and so he allowed him to complete the eighty-eight lengths in the twenty yard pool. The boy hauled himself out of the shallow end steeped in glowing weariness. It was always good to swim a mile.

He ambled to his cubicle and locked the door carefully before he took off his trunks and wrung them out. He hated being seen naked. Then he dried himself, not too effectively, and pulled on clothes damp already from the moisture in the baths, further dampened by his water-filmed body. By the time he was ready the last cubicle door had long banged shut and the lights were going out. He walked to the reception area vaguely scrubbing his sodden hair with the thin sodden towel. The cocoa machine was broken.

A penny bought a bright white squirt of Brylcreem, which he kneaded into his soaking head before taking out the tooth-gapped comb. He could linger for a few minutes. The superintendent would be checking the boiler and the slipper baths. Joe knew the routine well. He was a regular. The winter season ticket, which had been bought for his birthday, was already near earning its keep after just two weeks.

The boy stepped back through the swing doors and looked at the pool, now almost still, a mysterious blue-green translucence under the single remaining light, empty of bounced shouts and splash. He shivered. He had raced its lengths, illicitly gone up to the balcony and swung across one of the rafters to drop into the deep end, played endless games of tiggy on long holiday mornings with the pool in possession of no more than half a dozen of them. He loved the sense of speed from the crawl, the thrash of the blind backstroke, the swanning neck of the breaststroke. But more than anything he loved long solitary swimming, length after length, the water cradling him, bearing him up, helping him through, the buoyancy allowing him to sink into something like a trance, self-hypnotised by the lap and stroke and watery ease. He would come out of those aimless reveries as slowly as if he were coming out of an anaesthetic.

His bike was propped around the corner of the small neat sandstone building given to the people of Wigton by its greatest benefactor Mr Banks, whom his uncle Leonard always said had been bankrupted and driven to an early death by the greedy tradespeople. He had to decide which way to go home. Past mid-September, not full dark even though it was almost eight o'clock, but dark enough for the lights to be on along the low track that led past Vinegar Hill. The shorter way, the high road up an unlit hill and down past the gasometer had become a challenge: Joe did not know why. Lately he had begun to duck it and he did so again.

Even on the lit track he was glad when he got to Vinegar Hill and saw people. He knew them. The men came in the pub.

When he got to the Blackamoor he lifted the bike, which was rather too big for him, and carried it up the steps, through the inner door with its stained-glass picture of the little black boy, through the passage and into the back yard where he parked it under the open shed. There was a small outhouse, which used to serve but was now being converted into a ladies'. Way overdue, his mother had said, never reconciled to the flock of female bladders bursting up the stairs and into her bathroom. Joe no less pleased. There was no knowing when they would turn up. When he was having a bath he had not to lock the door. They would come right in, some of them, and just whip up their dresses, tug down their knickers, do their business, chat away, sometimes smoke a full cigarette.

The pub was filling up. Joe was now an expert on the tides of its trade. Friday night had become more popular. Jack Ack filled the Singing Room.

Ellen came out of the bar to get his supper. The boy said he would take it upstairs. Sometimes there was no one in the kitchen who wanted to talk to him. Potato pie, slice of apple cake, cup of cocoa. She would come up later if she could manage it. There was an air about her, a lightness, the smile: it was the dance later that night, Joe remembered, the big dance. They walked from the larder through the kitchen together and somebody said he could be her boyfriend. She laughed at that. He was as tall as Ellen now. He tried to put the dance out of his mind.

The narrow bedroom was cold. He put on his specs and wrapped the heavy dressing-gown over his pyjamas. He puffed up the pillow to make a back rest. Diddler had traded in a maroon and cream plastic battery wireless, which Sam had handed on to him and he found Radio Luxembourg to catch Ma and Pa Kettle and with luck his latest favourite singers: Johnny Ray, Mario Lanza and Frankie Laine, Guy Mitchell, Jo Stafford, Doris Day. He was halfway through 'The Fifth Form At St Dominic's' but he did not want to rush it. He had missed the library earlier in the evening and he had nothing to go on to.

His mother managed to find time to come up to say goodnight

but she did not tell him to turn off the light. He was allowed to be later on a Friday. She did tell him that a mixed group had come in from Carlisle – 'a bit boozy' – and she warned him that if he had not been to the bathroom and brushed his teeth then the sooner the better. She still had that excited look, which made him jealous. He had nosed into their bedroom. Her long red dance dress was hanging up behind the door and on the bed were her long gloves and the shiny little black bag. The dresses of the two women who helped in the pub were hanging behind the bathroom door.

Joe read and listened to the wireless and alerted himself more deeply to downstairs. As the ten o'clock curfew began to speed towards the drinkers, the noise thickened, to cram it all in, let loose the hound of alcohol, crush the flying moments into a fist of pleasure. Joe had seen the Milburns in the Darts Room. They had not caused trouble for more than a year, since they had last been banned and given a final chance. But who could tell? Sam had barred only five men permanently – too lenient, some thought: some of the others barred for a limited period had sulked off to other pubs; the dog-men kept their trouble elsewhere, needing the buses to the trails.

Joe was worried about the Carlisle party. It was always a gamble when people came from another town. He went out and stood on the small landing when Joseph Gilbert, who really could sing, started his Frankie Laine routine with 'Jezebel'. The boy looked down at the milling in the narrow corridor, the flitting from room to room, and tried to work out patterns of eruption depending on who went where, what expressions Margaret and Alfreida, the waitresses, were wearing, whether a voice was raised raw and sudden and unmissable in its baying violence. Everybody said his dad had cleaned up the place, fine pub now, but that had made it much busier and then you never knew, Colin said.

'Time, gentlemen, please. Time, please. Time, ladies and gentle-men, please.'

With remarkable dispatch, the pub's customers decanted into the dark chill street and Joe went down. Sometimes he was allowed to help with the checking up. Ellen, generous through her own impending treat, nodded Joe through the gate at the bottom of the stairs and he went behind the bar where Sam was at the till. The others were skimming away the worst and most obvious damage – the full clean-up was in the mornings – with extra speed, full focused on the dance.

How could he tell them? Could he say he was ill? That was not true. There was no other excuse that would do.

Sam let him pile up the pennies in little towers of twelve, the halfpennies also – twenty-four was too unstable. Shillings and six-pences and florins in tens, threepences and half-crowns in eights. It was a good bet at weekends that you would find a silver farthing palmed off as a sixpence or an Irish two-bob bit. Joe got much satisfaction from this counting up. He liked to see the towers grow, many and orderly. He liked the feel of importance, all this money, this wealth of coins, commanded into numbers and additions by his fingers. He liked the praise for the speed and accuracy he brought to it.

Sam did the notes, checked the cigarettes and tobacco, and when all was counted and bagged up, he did the books. He entered the takings every night, and every night compared them with previous weeks and months and years. It was a story of getting better. Joe looked on, earnestly impressed at these columns of pounds, shillings and pence, and was warmed by his father's satisfaction that the pub was thriving.

'You can come to the bank with me tomorrow morning,' Sam said, 'before the matinée.'

Joe nodded, needing the favour.

'I'd better put my glad rags on or your mother'll be on the warpath.'

This time the smile was conspiratorial. He put the blue accounts book into the drawer beside the till. For a few moments Joe was alone in the bar, behind the counter where the men, only men, stood. Even though he was in the over-large dressing-gown his aunt Grace had bought for him through the club, he felt goose-pimply. The excitement of the preparations for the dance agitated him. The poster was on the wall, next to the poster advertising the films at the Wigton Palace. 'Don't Miss the Grand BATTLE OF BRITAIN DANCE', it read, 'in the Market Hall, Wigton on Friday 19 September. Dancing 9 p.m. to 1 a.m. to the Penrith Melody Makers. Tickets 3/6 each (Strictly Limited).' He knew about the Battle of Britain: the new history teacher had been a pilot in the war.

He went upstairs where the women were transforming themselves. The traffic on the little landing, between the bathroom and his mammy's bedroom, was urgent and he was called on – zips to be slashed shut, stockings judged straight for seams, perfume dabbed, sniffed, dabbed more, fasten the buckle on my shoe, where's my purse, we'll miss the buffet, off we go, off we go, and then there was only his mammy and how could he tell her?

'How do I look, then?'

She sensed he wanted something but her own preoccupation could give him only this gesture – a mark of equals, even collaborators. Joe saw his mother: long black hair, long red sheath dress, long gloves, lips red, eyes shining dark, smiling, smiling so radiantly . . .

'Like a film star.'

'Don't be silly, Joe.' Her tone was firm, even chiding.

But she was. And how could he even begin to understand what he wanted to say? Stay, he wanted to say. Why, though? Why that? Stay, he ached to say. How could a thirteen-year-old boy say that? Please don't leave me alone, he wanted to say. Please. He shivered.

'Bed for you,' she said, and shouted downstairs that she would just be a minute and took him into the bedroom. But her appetite for this grand dance – very few she could get to since the pub – was so keen that she could not stay through his prayers and after a quick hug she floated down the stairs. He switched off the light and went to his window, which looked out over Market Hill. As they tippled out on to the pavement they shouted, 'Bye, Joe,' 'Night, Joe,' but the shouts went into the pub. They did not look up. He watched until they were well out of sight and then he went across the dark room and put on the light.

Next to his bedroom was an equal room to which entry could be gained only by going through Joe's room. Colin had taken that, but after a few weeks Ellen had yielded to Sam's sullen objection and levered him back across the hill to a fatalistic Grace, an openly disgruntled Leonard. Colin's consolation had been the run of the upper half of the old stables in which he bred budgerigars. Now and then in the early days they had experimented with a paying lodger, but although the money had been welcome, Ellen had never settled to it and Sam's jealousy, never well concealed, had aborted that. So, like the parlour, it was clean and neat and unoccupied.

Joe had a compulsion to look in. He tried to resist. He knew it was silly. Nobody could have slipped in unnoticed. But the instant the compulsion reared, he knew he had to follow.

He opened the door quietly and felt around the corner to put on the light before he walked in. Narrow bed like his own. Small wardrobe. Rug on lino red and yellow squares. Bare chair next to bed. A big cardboard box in which there were the old curtains that might come in handy. He stared carefully and then, as if sleepwalking, went across and looked under the bed.

He went through the same procedure in the parlour, in his parents' bedroom and finally the bathroom. He stood on the landing and listened hard but no sound came from the pub below nor any from the yard. He stood until the silence and the cold together penetrated him and then he went to kneel beside the bed and say his prayers.

'Our Father' always began them, the words deep grooved in his mind, the clench of the prayer which Our Saviour Christ had taught us was used to comfort, but this time the sound interfered. His speaking aloud of the words disturbed the meaning of it. Perhaps he might forget them. 'For ever and ever, Amen' was gasped. 'Lighten our darkness we beseech thee O Lord and by Thy great mercy defend us from all the perils and dangers . . .' The words were bruised by the silence. The silence rejected them. The silence closed in. 'Please bless . . .' The list was galloped in a whisper. Light off. Bed. Burrowed. Eyes tight shut. Knees up like in gym: 'Make yourself as small as possible.' Sleep would rescue.

If parallel lines met only in infinity, where was that? He saw the black universe, small stars set like miniature peep-holes, those two tracks, white railway lines speeding past the indifferent stars, on and on and on. But where was infinity? If he kept watching them travel through the pinprick-flecked blackness he would fall asleep. It had helped before.

God had infinite mercy. God had infinite patience. God had infinite love for all men. Even sinners. Even fibbers like him. God had infinite wisdom. The lines sped through the darkness but they would not converge.

He tried the fortress. It was in a desert in a Western. He built it three walls deep. There were no rocks so the walls had to be wood. There was a wide ditch ringing the outer wall, full of sharpened stakes, razored to slice off limbs. Between the outer stockade and the middle stockade was an even wider, deeper ditch crossed only by planks easily hoisted up like so many slices of a drawbridge. The final wall was the highest, the strongest, impossible to scale. Fire arrows were one of the big dangers. A well had been sunk in the middle of the fort. The fort had been built around the well. From there, a system of buckets on a ceaselessly moving chain would carry the saving water to wherever it was needed. Sufficient ammunition was another problem . . . It was not working. The details were in place but there was that agitation in his mind, which did not allow him to believe in them.

He began to do multiplication tables beyond twelve.

There was dread.

He heard his breath and was alarmed by it.

They would be dancing now. He had won a competition with his mother in the Market Hall. In a Dance For All The Family on the early evening before the carnival. They had won the quickstep and been runners-up in the valeta. Ellen had not entered for any more. She would have liked him to learn to play popular tunes and dance music, but Miss Snaith was strict and pointed out that dance music did not get you through exams.

Colin would be dancing with Sadie. He whirled her about the floor, he swung her and rhythmed her. Ellen half proud, half fearful that Colin and Sadie might get themselves talked about. Sometimes Colin would get Joe in the back yard and teach him his own fancy steps, which he said he had patented.

Joe had seen Sam and Ellen dancing in the kitchen at Christmas when, instead of Christmas dinner with just the three of them, people had stayed on after two thirty closing time and it had ended up with dancing. His daddy was not as good as Colin but at the same time he was better, Joe thought.

They would be dancing now. He concentrated. He could see them. They would be doing a slow foxtrot. Being close together. What was a slow foxtrot tune? Didn't matter. He could see them clearly. He pushed his legs down the bed. It was cold. He folded them back into his chest. They were clapping the band. The dance had finished. They were walking to the chairs along the wall. Everybody was leaving the dance floor. Everybody was leaving. Seventeen times seventeen. Parallel. Fire arrows. Everybody was leaving and, and, he heard a whisper, maybe his: and, and . . .

There was nothing.

Was he breathing?

In the corner at the far edge of the window he saw a small dim blotch of light, somewhere between white and grey, trembling just a little, hovering, waiting? It was him, the light was him. He knew it for truth and his mind ebbed all away. Everything left it. There was no him in the bed. The light looked on what remained and saw just a thing. The light was him. If it went away he would be, no, he would not be, be no more, be left a thing. He looked at it. His mouth opened. Short, quiet, most quiet, sighs of air came into his mouth and soundlessly, secretively, he pushed them back out.

He had to get the light back into himself. He just had to. But it stayed there and he, transfixed by it, lay there. Such a terror clouded over him but he held his look at it. It had to come back into him. He was only fear. Where would the light go?

What happened he did not know. He could not cry out. He waited. He just waited as the terror froze him. He was a silent terrified scream in the dark.

He found that he had rolled out of bed and dropped on to the floor. He crawled to the door; a hand reached up and opened it.

On the landing, his mouth wide open. Down the first flight of seven steps he crawled, a hundred-and-eighty-degree turn. Eleven steps to the gate. He pulled his body up and like a very old and ailing man he worked his way down them and into the pub, the floor cold on his feet, some light in the bar and the Darts Room from the street-light on Market Hill. He stood beside the inner door. There was the picture of the little black boy. He heard his screams but could not join in.

In the Darts Room he knelt on a chair and looked through the window at Market Hill, so much of the territory of his short life. He saw nothing but the blackness beyond the weak yellow single street-light glow and no one went by. He was cold now. His head felt so strange, so unlike him, unlike anything, only fear, nothing else, fear, fear, but he could not cry.

When he heard them coming home, he moved, though sluggishly, up the stairs, stayed on the landing.

The door opened, bringing back life, and the boy slumped. He wanted to run down but what could he say? What could he tell them? Their voices were unafraid. He dare not lean forward in case they saw him but their voices were so warm that he wanted to cry but you didn't.

When he heard his mammy say that she was going straight to bed he turned and made himself go back into his bedroom. He did not look in the corner. He waited for her to come in, and when she did, he pretended that he was fast asleep. She looked at him for a moment or two. He was too old to kiss.

CHAPTER TWENTY-EIGHT

'I feel bad about it now,' she said.

'No need.'

But he kept his back to her. They were alone in the bar mid-morning pre-opening time. Sam was at the sink rinsing some newly washed spirit measures. Ellen stood beside the pumps, like a plaintiff.

'I didn't really take in that it was a Saturday.'

'Why should that bother you?'

Ellen knew very well that he needed her to wash the glasses on Saturday of all nights yet she found not sarcasm in Sam's reply but a scrupulous attempt to let her believe her life was just as normal as that of everyone else who could take a Saturday afternoon and evening off.

'Joe's looking forward to it.'

'There you are, then.'

He turned round and any residual resentment dissolved at the sight of her. She could still move him to the heart of himself, at unlikely times these days – now, flushed in her anxiety at letting him down and yet holding on to this small proof of normality that the pub had taken from her.

'We'll manage fine. Alfreida'll help in the bar, Joyce is coming to do the Singing Room.'

'I never thought,' she said, but in the saying there was the nod, the acknowledgement that he understood the reason behind it all, and through that understanding truly understood her.

'Bad enough we take shifts for holidays.'

Ellen for a week to Ayr Butlin's with Joe, Sam unsuccessfully attempting a three-day break at Morecambe: back after two, Joe bribed into agreement with a yellow polo-necked sweater. Their first and last attempt.

He was wearing the sweater when he came into the bar.

'Did you tidy up all the crates in the back cellar?'

'Yes.'

'Here, then.'

Sam fished out two half-crowns and watched with interest as his son's face brimmed full of gratitude, lined with an innocent lust for the heavy coins.

'Thanks, Dad. Thanks.'

Dad now. Quite suddenly. Dad. Long trousers now. And, in public, Mam – Sam enjoyed the boy's pleasure and thought, How simple it is sometimes.

'Away, then. They'll go without you.'

The bus would leave from outside the church at eleven sharp to allow for a full afternoon, even though the trip to Blackpool was targeted on the evening, for the Illuminations.

'Look after your mam, now,' Sam said, as he stood on the steps.

Joe linked arms with his mother by way of an answer. Ellen felt good. Joe on her arm in that terrible yellow polo-neck but so pleased with it she said nothing.

Pleased with Sam most of all. She had seen him harden. In the first years the battle to make it a friendly house had put Sam at odds with some of the tougher men in the town and there had been times when she herself had felt the echo of it, when a walk upstreet was a small demonstration of courage and a Saturday night could be nothing but watching the fuse burn towards the explosive. It was worse, she thought, that he had bound himself never to fight. She had hated it when he had been in those few fights before the war and she would hate it again but the effort to bottle up his temper took a lot out of him, she thought, and then his anger turned on her, on Joe, on himself. But the pub meant independence and for that he would endure what came. Yet it had hardened him so his gentleness just now was not only warming in itself but a reminder of what had been, or what always would be, perhaps, a break in the clouds.

'All aboard the *Skylark*! Roll or bowl a ball!' Colin had nominated himself the life and soul of the bus. 'Joe'll sit next to me,' he announced.

Ellen was relieved to see him in such form. He had found himself a blazer – he was good at winkling out bargains, doing swaps – and this, together with his new cleanly parted, smartly Brylcreemed, unquiffed hair-cut, helped him cut something of a dash, especially among the older ladies. He helped them clamber into the coach, raincoated, scarfed, hatted, gloved, slung with sandwiches and cake and flasks, hard-saved money in the pocket marked for presents, which would be rock mostly, pink-sheathed pure white centre with BLACKPOOL stamped through in red.

Before the engine had turned the singing began.

Colin made Joe laugh with his imitation of the Goons. The boy had not met any other adult as addicted as everybody at school. Colin specialised in Eccles.

First they drove along the Front, a flourish to set the tone. Past the great music halls and theatres housing the stars that packed in thousands every day.

'This is where all the big nobs hang out,' Colin shouted, and in the general excitement no one offered an objection, though Ellen winced and felt the restrained cringe of others.

The bus was parked with military instructions. It would remain at this spot and no other, open from nine o'clock and no sooner, depart at ten o'clock and no later.

Ellen had persuaded Ruth to come on the trip. She was still very shaky after being jilted, even though it was almost a year ago. Ellen knew how devoted and loyal Ruth had been to him, how she had put up with evasions and prevarications that she herself could not have tolerated for five minutes, how love had conjured this dear middling-aged stable responsible woman into a young girl. Sometimes she could scarcely bear to look at Ruth's expression, the hurt of it, the sense of loss, not 'last chance' – Ruth would not think like that – but 'What did I do wrong? Does this make me worthless?' She would stick with Ruth for the day.

They decided to make for the Golden Sands. The day was cold and overcast but it was not raining – that counted as a blessing and they were well wrapped up. Others made for the gigantic funfairs. A select number strolled up the Front, taking in the good sea air, making for the genteel village of St Anne's, which stood demure and cottage-tasteful outside the gut release, the panic scream of pleasure and the Gothic lust for numbing sensation that was Blackpool at its most seductive.

Colin and Sadie were mad to go to the Tower Ballroom, the tea-time dance to the music of Reginald Dixon who was on the wireless every week. The dance floor was the finest in the world, Colin said, big as a football pitch so that at tea-time, not as crowded as the evenings, you could really show off your paces. But the doors did not open until three thirty and they joined Ruth and Ellen and Joe down on the sands to fill in time.

There was a group of Wigton Labour Party people and one of them had brought some stumps, a bat and a ball. They set up for beach cricket on the hard high sands. Colin and Joe joined in and Sadie, when she saw that some of the Labour women were game, took off her unsuitable shoes and stockings and coat and joined in.

Ellen and Ruth sat it out. Ruth was too burdened to be able to lift her spirits. They sat apart, guarding the picnics, their glances and their conversation roving over the piers, the donkey rides, the few bold bathers in the pewter sea, blue-skinned children absorbed in sandcastles.

Colin's voice dominated but Ellen had long decided to force herself to ignore it. He was managing. Sam paid him well enough for the little he did. There were usually a couple of other bit-jobs on the go. Grace gave him roof and board. Ellen found that she was keeping an eye on Colin every bit as much as Joe.

She liked the Labour Party people. When they had asked if they could use the kitchen for their weekly committee meeting, Sam had refused. No politics, no religion. But one of the women who had got the Party going during the war was someone Ellen had worked with at the factory. She had challenged Sam. What was he scared of? They were nice people. They did not drink – so he could not be said to be after profit. They just wanted a convenient place for an early hour on Mondays to talk matters over – no speeches, no propaganda. He was supposed to be independent. She would take care of it, make them tea, they would be no trouble.

Sam agreed despite his better judgement – not just to please Ellen but to prove that indeed he was independent.

Joe sometimes had his supper while the meetings were going on. They never seemed to mind. Now she saw them easy with him and he responding like an eager puppy darting after the ball across the sands in his yellow polo-neck, always at full tilt.

'He's getting more like Sam,' said Ruth.

Ellen turned away from Joe, not wanting to be thought possessive.

'I'm sorry the colouring's going,' Ellen said, as a compliment.

Joe's hair, once deep copper like that of Ruth and Sam, had dwindled to sandy.

'I'm not!' Ruth grimaced as she pushed both hands into the biblical bounty of dark coppery hair. Ellen merely smiled. Ruth had always and sincerely disliked her best feature. Loosened, glossy, it fell fully halfway down her back. And her white, lightly freckled face was framed, its beauty revealed. But it was scarcely ever released from the rather old-fashioned pinioned pouch that locked it away. How could the man – whom Ellen had met twice, briefly, and tried very hard to like – any man, turn away from someone like Ruth whose modesty-bound outer loveliness was matched by such a clear inner spirit?

As always when they were alone, Ruth ran from what she feared might be imminent sympathy. 'He'll be taller than Sam.'

'Not as broad.'

'I don't know.' Ruth considered, carefully. 'Sam was thinner than that at Joe's age. We weren't spoiled for food. Dad got Sam hired with Mr Dixon after he left school which was a shame anyway. He was well known to be a very mean old man, Dixon. Dad shouldn't have put Sam there. I remember we got word once – about a year in – that Sam wasn't well and I went to see him. They'd put him up in the dirty loft over the horses. He shared it with an old labourer who was half deaf. Dixon was feeding him on not much more than bread and water twice a day. That's true. Maybe a bit of raw turnip. He thought Sam was faking. He was near starvation. You couldn't have nipped a pinch of flesh between your finger and thumb. After that I used to save up bits and sneak away after school. Just to feed him. Dixon was a bad man.'

'He's never gone into that.'

'Some things are too hard to talk about,' said Ruth innocently. 'You know Dad was always hardest on Sam.'

He's not easy on you, Ellen did not say. 'Why?'

'Because, I think, Sam was the only one Dad could take it out on after he came back from the war,' said Ruth. 'Sam would be about five. Then all of us coming in a rush and Mam never well. When I got old enough to see it, it would break my heart. Sam idolised him. He was desperate. He tried so hard to please Father. But nothing he could do was right.' Her voice sounded as lonely as the cries of the gulls and suddenly, vividly, Ellen saw her husband as that desperate boy.

A few weak and beggarly chutes of sun slanted through the clouds and the cricketers pulled stumps to walk down to the sea.

They joined forces for the picnic. Joe's gluttony – Ellen's word – devoured nine quartered sandwiches. Unchastened, Colin boasted twelve. At three fifteen, Sadie threw an excited fit and hauled him away to the Tower Ballroom.

'He'll be too fat to bop.'

'Shut your cake-hole, woman,' he said cheerfully, stuffing his own.

'Save a quickstep for me,' said Ellen.

'I'll dance with Joe,' Ruth said, which made Joe grin at Colin.

'He thinks he's won the pools.' Colin's riposte was a challenge.

'He's my dancing partner!' Sadie declared, and smiled all her teeth. 'Lovely sandwiches, thank you all,' she said. 'Come on, Colin! We'll miss something!'

The two of them hurried along the uncrowded beach, up the stairs and on to the front where Sadie's shoes and stockings were rapidly restored. Then they ran, like children, Ellen thought, ran towards Blackpool's high imitation of the Eiffel Tower where a middle-aged man on an organ that rose from beneath the floor would – with his back to his acolytes – draw Sadie and Colin and hundreds like them into the drilled elegancies of ballroom dances still kin to those that had swept the Strausses to success in Vienna. Ellen found that she was looking until they disappeared into the distance and into the crowd, maternal in her feelings both for her old, rough, fast friend, who made so much out of the bare pickings, and her half-brother, who preyed on her and always would, wishing them luck on the dance floor, that it might transform them into the fantasies of themselves they loved.

Ellen and Ruth and Joe missed the ballroom, sidelined by the rowing boats in a small lagoon high on the beach. 'We can dance any time,' Ellen said.

But not, Joe thought, in the best ballroom in the world.

'What do you think?'

Joe was unaccustomed to being asked his opinion. It took him no time to divine that Ellen and Ruth were attracted to the larky novelty of the dumpy little boats.

'The boats,' he surrendered. Once installed, especially when given a chance to row, he did not entirely regret the decision although the vision of the ballroom clung on. Colin would boast about it.

The Illuminations came on at six o'clock and everyone cheered. A number of them had arranged to meet under the Tower, which was suddenly shot with lights, electrified into ten thousand coloured bulbs fitting its long and slender form like a spangled sheath dress. The length of the Golden Mile the lights came on, yellow, blue, red, orange, green, white, indigo, violet, with one throw of the switch, SHAZAM, Joe thought, it was all a marvel. They practically rushed from the foot of the Tower to rake their eyes up and down its illuminated splendour then spread their gaze down the promenade, the strings of bulbs, loop after loop of multi-coloured lights, magical pathways that made the sunset seem ordinary.

Behind the promenade, in the funfairs, Switch and Switch Again and the Big Dipper (Biggest in Britain) and the Big Wheel (Biggest in Britain) and the Rollercoaster (Second Biggest in the World) suddenly flashed from dusk into glamour as the enchantment and sorcery of thousands of simple coloured lights clustered in mass formations turned into wheels and waterfalls, outlined horses, picked out signs, neckerchiefed lamp-posts, ran across spindly bridges built for the occasion, modelled giant swans, elephants, flamingos, leopards. Bulbs so dull by day possessed form and beauty in the night.

Finally the trams were all lit up and the drab workaday became jewel-encrusted, floating along the promenade as if bidden from the other side of the moon. A world so strange to the bleak fall-out of war, a world of colour and light delight, lightening the heart, lightening the northern darkness, illuminating lives long starved of innocent cause for wonder.

Joe followed Ellen in wonder. She had no filters, no scepticism, no envies or doubts or defences. That which was wonderful opened her heart. Joe had seen, though only remotely registered, when she had been transfixed by the magnificence of a sunset over the sea at Silloth, or the way the birds sat like crotchets on the telegraph wire as she looked out of the window of the Darts Room on a dead afternoon, or at the gallantry of someone coping with adversity, or the quality of a voice heard singing on the wireless. From scores of everyday things Ellen could pluck out wonder which only lately had she begun to share with her son. It was like a stream re-emerging way down the track after being forced underground, in Ellen's case by the war which had capped elation and threatened delight. But the growing peace had allowed it to surface and although it would never catch up that waste of life, of years, and somehow be shy as if it were too trivial a thing it had found its way back and at Blackpool Illuminations it sprang to new life.

No illuminated site was considered too simple to pass by without receiving its due. These were hours of high appreciation. Joe was in a daze of the marvellous, which anointed him with the glories of pleasure manufactured to perfection. Blackpool was a glittering beacon in the darkness of the battered island, a dazzle of technicolour and warmth, privileging those who came from the black and white fastnesses of an exhausted land.

Colin claimed him once again for the bus, hinting that he would reward Joe with a surreptitious puff. He raced through cigarettes. Joe had not yet got the hang of them, but he knew he ought to try.

There was a cheer as the bus set off and necks were twisted and craned for the last look at the lights, which too soon fell away into a mere cluster, a diminished spectacle, finally no more than a glow, already thought of with nostalgia as they followed the weak twin yellow beams of headlights cutting a route through night to the north. For a while there was only talk.

'Did you see the boxing booth?' Colin was pleased when Joe shook his head. He looked around and offered the boy a drag. Joe took it, fumbled it, coughed violently.

'Too much sea air!' Colin announced. 'He'll be all right, Ellen. Leave him to me.'

Joe subsided, his face wet with tears which he wiped on his yellow sleeve.

'That's your first and last drag,' Colin whispered. 'You'll get me roasted alive.' He took a deep pull on the cigarette and attempted smoke rings with some success. 'Five pounds if you went three rounds. Two if you went two. I fancied my chances I can tell you.

Even with this.' He banged his chest. 'I could've taken one or two of them to five rounds. Not the two big fellas. A good big 'un can always lick a good little 'un, but never been beat at my own weight . . .' He glanced at Joe and assumed a hard-man stare borrowed from cowboy films. 'You've got to be able to stand up for yourself,' he said. 'I'm a bit worried about your dad sometimes. He never raises a fist. I can see his point, Joe. But it wouldn't do me. I'd be in there. Left, left, jab, right, bang, out!'

The blow at his father jarred the boy but he held his tongue. Plenty of men had told him that they admired Sam for the way he dealt with trouble, the only way, they said, the best way. But something in Joe still wanted to see him fight, to clear the place, just as Colin always said he would if he had been the landlord. He tried not to think on it because it was inconceivable that his dad could be scared. Joe scarcely used the boxing gloves these days although in the gym at school, when there was a bit of boxing, he could still shine, a performance that maintained his reputation as a fighter despite his own spectacled apprehension.

'He's a git!' Colin nodded to indicate the Labour Party man who had walked past them in the aisle. His voice was quiet but vicious.

'Why?'

'Never mind. He's a git! He's on the list.'

'Come on!' said Sadie. 'I'll sit next to my dancing partner.'

'You just want the fags.'

'Take no notice of him, Joe.'

'Didn't we fly on that floor?'

'That floor . . .' Sadie took her time. 'Was. Perfection. That's what that floor was.'

'We had a great time in the boats,' said Joe sturdily.

'Boats!'

'All change, Joe. And I will have a fag seeing you ask so politely.'

Sadie had been sitting next to the Labour man dubbed 'git'. He offered Joe a toffee, a creamy whirl, a luxury item.

The singing began and the old simple counting songs were first up. That was always the order. 'One Man Went to Mow', 'This Old Man', 'Ten Green Bottles'. Then the jolly war songs – 'Pack Up Your Troubles', 'Tipperary', 'Goodbye Dolly', 'You Are My Sunshine' – and on to the present with 'I'll Take You Home Again Kathleen', 'Rose of Tralee', and of course 'Galway Bay'. There were always Scottish airs – 'Loch Lomond', 'Speed Bonny Boat', 'By Yon Bonny Banks' – all word perfect, in precise unison, full-throated. On to the very latest with 'There's Always Room At Our House', 'I'm Yours', 'Walking My Baby Back Home' (Colin's voice rose to a howl here), 'Auf Wiedersehen, Sweetheart', 'Sugarbush' (Sadie in the lead), and Guy Mitchell, Frankie Laine, Doris Day . . . Then back to the old; to marching songs, ballads, lullabies, hymns, comic songs, dancing songs, love songs by the score and always enough who knew all the words.

Ellen felt herself being carried away on the tide of it, and once she had checked Joe and seen him as immersed as anyone, she let herself go into this ocean of sound and song. There was nothing in the world but these notes and words as if the bus fell away and they were gliding independently on the stream of singing. Ellen felt that she disappeared in the voices and she wanted to, finding a curious joy in being indissolubly part of the sound, which overwhelmed all thought and was the only sensation. She was ringed with clarity. A source of joy was tapped by this unison of voices. It was a time suspended as if it were above the rest of life, life as it could be, in common, simple, undivided, thrilling. And when it petered out and finally trickled to an end, she was sad, though that sadness itself was a heightened sadness, a sweet sadness, a sadness superior to most of life.

People began to doze, voices were dropped and the drone of the engine was heard.

The collection for the driver had been taken in Blackpool. Presents were clutched. Out of the bus outside the church on to the empty streets.

Sam was waiting. Joe wanted to stay up for a while but Ellen sent him straight to bed so that he would be able to get to Sung Eucharist in the morning. Sam wandered upstairs with him while Ellen put on the kettle.

The game of cricket. The boat. And the Illuminations! The elephants. The trams. The Tower . . . Joe pulled off his clothes anyhow, but slowly, glad that his dad had come into his bed-room.

'Colin saw a boxing booth.'

'That's where some of the best lads get their training.'

'He said he would knock people out in here,' Joe was yawning now, 'if he was you.'

'Did he now?'

'When there was trouble. Was there trouble tonight?'

'No.'

Joe calculated that if he could get into bed while his dad was still there, then he would be safe. But what about his prayers? He would say them in bed. Just this time. But his dad had not to go until he was in his pyjamas and best of all in the bed itself.

'Do you think he could beat you?'

'What do you think?'

'He's got this chest.' Joe banged his own pyjama-buttoned chest. 'Otherwise I suppose he could.'

Sam smiled. 'So it was a good day.'

'It was great.'

He got into bed. Sam was smiling down on him. Joe did not understand why but he felt calmed by it. 'Mind the bugs . . .'

'Don't bite.'

'Night, old son.'

'Night, Dad.'

The light clicked off. Joe waited and then put the door ajar to let in the light from the landing. Then he started his prayers. It had only come back once in the last week. He prayed.

—⁂—

'Was it all right?'

'Just over a pound down on last week. Absence of star attraction,' Sam said.

'Drink your tea.' But she was pleased.

'He seems to have enjoyed it.'

'He did.' Ellen paused. 'Sometimes you can see them growing away from you.'

'I don't think that'll be his problem.'

'I wish Colin wouldn't egg him on to smoke.'

Sam's amiable, sleepy, affectionate mood changed, but he tried to conceal it. He was convinced beyond doubt now that Colin was pinching cigarettes. But he knew the stakes. Ellen had put so much into the pub despite herself. He owed her a debt.

'Bedtime,' he said. 'No rest for the wicked.'

—⁂—

He would be safe tonight, Joe thought. The relief of security surged through his mind. He would be safe. No need for a fortress. He strove to keep awake just a touch longer to enjoy the victory. It was warm inside his bed now. They were coming upstairs. The coloured lights danced.

CHAPTER TWENTY-NINE

'You'll go to 3L,' said the headmaster. 'Tomorrow. For the day.'

The Latin mistress who was also his form teacher looked a little disappointed. She had hoped for a caning. Richardson's chatter, his coarse accent – no worse than others but it grated on her – his seemingly constant attempts to make what she considered vulgar jokes had unsettled her for long enough. None of her punishments worked. This, she conceded, when the boy, his face smarting, had left the room, might just pull him up short.

'They lost out on discipline in the war,' said the headmaster. 'Stroppy little beggars. We'll try 3L for a start. See how he survives there.'

At which point he waved a bored hand and the self-consciously over-plump Latin mistress immediately retreated, trailing with her the brilliant classics First from Manchester and wondering how she had landed up at this undistinguished school in the back of beyond.

Joe walked the rest of the day inside a strait jacket of humiliation. He was certain that everyone knew, every smile a jeering smile or a pitying smile, every turn away a cut, his public hauling into the Head's office regarded with voyeuristic glee, the wounds plain.

He felt dishonoured. No matter that he summoned up his own

furious dislike of the Latin teacher, her snobbery which he could not fathom but felt like a lash of disapproval, and her sarcasm before which he was helpless, even her pronunciation of his name. 'Richard-son,' she said, separating the syllables, breaking it up, 'Rich-ard-son,' destroying it in front of everyone as if his very name was a mockery and he tried to grin and bear it, trapped in a rage that he dare not release.

Joe considered faking an illness, manufacturing an accident, or, for a few minutes, simple truancy, but on the next day he went to school as usual – looking unconcerned or so he hoped – but after assembly his face burned as 3A filed off in one direction and he tagged after the file of 3L boys.

He had no friends in 3L. On the whole 3L kept to itself. People repeated a year in 3L. The two girls in the school who were known for absolute certainty to be prepared to go all the way were in 3L. 3L boys were caned in morning assembly. There were some very big lads in that class, several of them farmers' sons, whose fathers resented their absence – especially in haytime and harvest – colluded with their truancy and forbade them to play sports which would waste Satur-days. 3L stuck together and stood apart from the grammar school's public-school aspirations. 3L was hard.

Yet Joe's first impression was of comforting similarity. Boys on one side of the room. Girls on the other. Parallel rows of desks and yet the demarcation as clear and straight as the parting in a man's hair. All green-blazered. Girls green-skirted. Boys grey-flannelled. No short trousers and Joe felt a pang of gratitude that he had grown into his just in time. All wearing the green, navy and white school tie. Reassured, took out his glasses, still a little ashamed. Silence when the history teacher, Mr Braddock, walked in. One of Joe's favourite lessons. Perhaps even a sympathetic glance from Mr Braddock who could, at the end of a week, be persuaded to tell you about the RAF in the war. Joe had already done the lessons in 3A so he cruised. The same with maths in the next lesson where, unfortunately, he knew too many answers.

Playtime was miserable. Avoiding his class. Avoiding anybody who might comment. Unable to bring himself to join the mafia of 3L who as usual hung around the lavatories.

In geography he became cocky. There was no doubt that Annie Fleming, one of those who went all the way, was giving him some sort of look that made him uneasily excited. When Mr Williams in physics said he was a 'bit of a boffin', she leered a smile of such invitation that Joe's head turned.

The chief dunce was a boy nicknamed Og. He was picked on by Mr Williams, and however the boy tried to swat away the hornet, it stung and stung again and poisoned him in murderous embarrassment. It was all the worse, somehow, because Og was big. Tall as Mr Williams. It was all the worse because he looked like a man.

When Mr Williams left, a little early as usual, anxious to beat everyone to the staffroom before they ambled across the playing-fields to the canteen, Joe used the slack time to secure Annie's attention by making chimpanzee noises and scratching his armpits with his hands, grunting 'Og, Og, Ug, Og, Ug, Ug.'

They were waiting for him at the end of the corridor.

'After dinner,' said William, Og's friend. 'At the lavatories.'

Joe squared himself up to show courage but he walked alone to the canteen increasingly oppressed. Og was well known as a fighter.

In the canteen he went to his 3A table and was unusually silent. Nor did he have a great appetite. The other boys ignored him until they caught a whiff of the fight.

Then he was plagued by their questions, by their warnings, by their advice, most of all by their advice.

They followed him back across the two rugby pitches and went behind the old Victorian sandstone school to the boys' lavatories.

3L was already in place. Og had taken off his jacket.

Joe did the same although the effort nearly exhausted him. The walk across from the canteen had exhausted him. The prospect of what would inevitably happen exhausted him. He felt weak from his guts to his fists. He was frightened. It was not a new sensation. He had been frightened in the other, few, fights he had had over the last three or four years but somehow there had been enough skill and nous and he had just about escaped shame and concealed his fear. Not this time. He knew that. Og had fists knuckled and boned to hurt as he had been hurt, not just by Mr Williams and other teachers who dumped on him but by all the others, a history. Fighting was getting his own back. Joe was markedly smaller and lighter but so what? He had a bit of a reputation. They were the same age. Fists up. A sort of ring was formed by the boys.

It started slowly. Og was surprised by Joe's form. The straight left, the stepping in, stepping out. The looking like a real boxer. And when Og swung and Joe backed off, dodged, ducked even, and appreciative murmurs grew from 3A, there were moments when there was strength in the fists and he could look Og in the eye and think he could land a real one until Og caught him on the side of the eye, so hard that Joe almost toppled over. He got back his balance and straight left, step aside, straight left again, but his head felt numb. And suddenly he didn't want to hit Og at all. That heavy angry face, the expression of assassin was not to be hit. Was he caving in? Some such cowardice. Or the loss of all lust for this. Og caught him again and again Joe stumbled but did not fall. Now his nose was bleeding. He began to back off. The squiring circle of schoolboys went into many shapes to keep the two enclosed, funnelling them towards the main school building as Joe retreated, his fists now putty, his mind a daze, backing off, anything to avoid another bone-knuckled blow, this time on his forehead, and another which caught his shoulder and knocked him down. He had to get up. Og was not finished. He began a two-fisted pummelling.

It was Mr Braddock who stopped it.

He made them shake hands.

He took Joe into the lavatories and watched while he splashed hand scoops of cold water over his face, soaking his shirt, blood-wet already. He used his own handkerchief to staunch the nosebleed. He took Joe back to 3L and waited until the French teacher turned up and had a word with her.

Joe tried to look at nobody.

In the afternoon playtime, Og came across to him and said, 'Don't think it's over, pal. I'm after you.'

Joe nodded. He understood.

Colin was flattered that Sam had come up to the loft. He took the proffered cigarette with a certain swagger. He knew how impressive his budgerigars were.

He had turned the big loft space into three large floor to roof cages, wire-meshed doors connecting them, a job well done so that he could walk among the brilliantly coloured birds with ease and they had space. He had manufactured perches out of cadged scraps of wood, water trays out of cut-down tins. He had cuttlefish bone wedged in the wire so that they could keep their beaks sharp. There were almost sixty birds now, the biggest collection in Wigton, and the care of them, breeding from them, watching over them, was his principal occupation.

Sam took a good look. They were very beautiful. Blues and yellows – bright, fast, subtle variations in the colours, quick nervous hop, flight from perch to perch. A dash and dazzle in the dark loft. Travellers used to sleep here, their horses stabled below, rough floorboards, untreated bare stone walls, the roof gloomily exposed. Now a dazzle and display of these pretty creatures flitting, chirruping, such brilliance in the colours. Colin picked one up, plucked it from the perch firmly but so that it nested in his slack fist, showed it off to Sam.

'Lovely little things.' Sam took the pulsing little bird, slashed gaudy yellow and white, a feathered quivering life in his strong hand making the hand itself alive. 'Lovely little things. You've done well here, Colin.'

Colin preened himself. 'I'll be the biggest breeder in Wigton this time round,' he said. 'And the best, Sam. See them?' He pointed to a smaller cage at the back of the loft where two blues were isolated. 'They'll come up with winners. Champions. Best of breed. Dead certainties.'

He let his eyes travel across to the rosettes pinned on the inner door of the loft, the door once used to fork out the hay. Rosettes and certificates were brass drawing-pinned, a proud collage, but without as yet the centrepiece of 'First' or 'Champion'.

Sam let him rabbit on, partly because he so rarely saw this aspect of Colin. True enthusiasm based on real achievement. There was a naïveté about him in this context which reminded Sam of young soldiers when first they came into his section in Burma, found their experience fell far short of that of the men who had been marinated so

306

long in intense and savage conflict, and were exposed as innocents where previously they had felt worldly-wise. Something of that in Colin here; a touching lack of those idle boasts which – in Sam's reckoning – disfigured so much of his daily behaviour. And the vulnerability linked him with Ellen – not because she was in any comparable way vulnerable, Sam thought, but because he saw a deeper kinship between the two in the unaffected passion of this half-brother.

But even so he would not be diverted from his purpose.

'I seem to have none left,' he said, as he opened again the pre-prepared packet of Capstan Full Strength.

'Have one of mine.' Colin dived eagerly into his pocket and pulled out an identical packet.

'Thanks.'

Sam lit up and held out the flame for Colin who came close, his hands cupped.

Both men drew deeply.

'That's why I always have time for the Sally Army.' Sam smiled. 'They would always have a cup of tea and a fag. I've seen a man die happy with a fag.'

Colin nodded and drew deeply once more although the direct gaze of Sam was beginning to disconcert him.

'A friend of mine – he was a schoolteacher – was once arguing with somebody who said that fags were a terrible drug and so on, and he said back, "Nothing you enjoy can do you harm."' One of Alex's best, he thought.

'I couldn't care less, me,' Colin said, alert now, trapped in the headlights. 'If I enjoy a thing, that's it . . .'

Sam said nothing for a while. He nicked his cigarette and put the stump in his pocket.

Colin waited, his anxiety unconcealed.

'Well, I'll be off. Lovely little things, Colin. You do well with them.' He looked once more at this aerial garden of lightness, dash, little splashes of harmless pleasure.

Then he went to the corner where the ladder led down to the stable. He put his foot on the rung and then spoke as if to no one. 'Funny thing about Capstan Full Strength, Colin,' he said. 'They seem to fly off the shelves of their own free will these days.' He smiled. 'Sometimes I think it must be those budgies of yours.'

He held the younger man's fearful look for a few moments, in breath-drawn silence, and then, quietly, he climbed down the ladder.

Sam turned up at Grace's house just before eleven on the Saturday morning as had become routine. Earlier he had carried the wooden crates of beer up from the cellar – with Joe's help – cleaned the pumps, swilled out the men's lavatory and set the bar before going upstreet to Martin's Bank with the Monday to Friday takings. A few street conversations, a feeling of leisure, and down to the big house on Market Hill for the quiz questions.

Mr Kneale did the history and the general knowledge. Leonard did local. Sam himself tackled sport. The three men met over a pot of tea and Ellen used the meeting to encourage Joe to go over and do his half-hour piano practice before or after his usual stint at the baths. It had become a good time.

The Sunday quiz was a success. It started at twelve thirty and took up about three-quarters of an hour. Leonard was the quizmaster, which was a rather sly manoeuvre on Sam's part because Leonard had not been suited that the Labour Party was allowed its meetings in the Blackamoor kitchen. He was strictly no politics no religion in pubs and he wanted no Big Brother around, he said, when he was taking a drink. For a while he had withdrawn his custom, which had upset Ellen. However, the ousting of the Labour Party in the recent election had sweetened his temper and the loss of the previous quizmaster had given Sam a genuine opening. Leonard had taken the olive branch with some relief, not least for Ellen's sake, and perhaps a little pleased that Grace could not condemn him as he was going into a pub for the purpose of education.

They went through the questions as always with the intention of weeding out the really hard ones, but they rarely did. Mr Kneale believed that, in principle, there had to be questions that might not find an answer. He said it kept up standards. The others let him prevail. Mr Kneale never came to the quiz, much as he longed to; but it would never do, he said, for a Wigton schoolteacher to go into a Wigton pub.

On this Saturday, he was unusually agitated and hurried them through the questions.

'All done?'

'More stinkers than usual,' Leonard said. He looked at Sam but Sam preferred to keep the peace. Besides, part of his mind was locked into the piano upstairs, now being played with a verve that made him smile.

'Did you see this?' Mr Kneale, unable to contain himself any longer, spread out the *Cumberland News*. '*This.*' He pointed. It read:

Wigton Corporal

He saved a bridge in Korea

One of the United Nations' Forces' most important supply bridges over the Imjin River in Korea might have been destroyed by floods recently but for the efforts of a 22-

309

year-old Wigton corporal of the Royal Engineers. The corporal, Frank Hollick, of Cross Keys, High Street, Wigton, spent a hectic forty-eight hours in torrential rain with his mates in a successful bid to save the bridge . . . Frank and his men had been ordered to keep the bridge intact. Often during the two days and nights that followed, Frank was lowered to within a few feet of the raging torrent precariously balanced on 'shear-water' and placed explosive charges amongst the debris which jammed the supports.

Scrambling to the top of the bridge for safety he waited for the time-fuse to detonate the charge and then clambered down after each explosion to dislodge the smaller debris by hand. Almost without sleep Frank and his men did great work. Had the debris been allowed to accumulate, the terrific pressure would almost certainly have snapped the concrete supports. Frank is a builder by trade, serving his time with his stepfather (Mr Robert Pattinson) before being called up for National Service. His stepfather commented, 'It's just the sort of thing he would enjoy.'

'Didn't he get a county trial?' said Sam. 'Good prop-forward.' 'The sort of thing he would enjoy' – Sam liked that.

'I know them well,' said Leonard. 'Nice family.'

'I think it's a considerable achievement.' Mr Kneale was disappointed: he had hoped for more excitement. 'A considerable achievement,' he re-emphasised in the schoolmasterly manner he tried to put off outside hours, 'both for that young man and for Wigton. And moreover,' he took a sip of tea, hoping that such an emphatic break in the sentence would intensify interest, 'it gave me an idea.'

He paused and looked at the two men who, outside his days in the grammar school and apart from the few fellow enthusiasts for photography, were becoming his firmest acquaintances, men in whom he could confide. He let the pause lengthen. The phrase 'immortal longings' was not one he could offer up, but in his solitary hours under the roof of the high house with a view so regularly photographed, he had slowly concluded that his life must be marked out in some way. No children. No wife. No true intimacy. But a powerful adoptive love of the little plain town into which he had meandered and stuck in his teaching career. His projected book on the veterans of Burma had failed when he finally realised that there would never be enough material. His fascination with war – from which his age had excluded him – had battened on to A-bombs and now H-bombs until even Leonard was beginning to shrink away – Mr Kneale saw that – from this dogged cherubim, personification of the Apocalypse.

' "Wigton Men at war",' he announced. 'That would be the title. There's plenty from the First World War, a considerable proportion with medals for their bravery. We know something about the Second from Sam and his friends and that was just Burma – there's the whole European and African dimension. And now we have our young men on National Service, still in the wars. My guess is that I would find Wigton men at war for centuries. That could be the prologue. And then with National Service, of course, they will be at war – whatever that turns out to be – for centuries to come. That's the epilogue. And the idea,' he smiled, 'the idea,' he repeated, 'the thesis which may come as a shock is that war is what makes this country what it is and always has been, it puts the Great into it. We are a country made for war and made by war, however hard that is on some, and that is always what we will depend on. Wigton men at war. The Ordinary Man. Heroism. Duty. Patriotism. All the great things that will never fade.'

311

'Now then,' Leonard sucked in his cheeks, 'there's plenty to go at there all right.'

'Sam?'

'Good idea.' Sam hoped his tone was convincing. Then 'Very good,' he added, more loudly.

It was nearing half eleven opening time, and the excuse released Sam. He would not stand up, he thought, to any cross-questioning by Mr Kneale. As he came into the cool early autumn air and made for the pub, standing so solid before him in sandstone, the deep front like a stage on which it was set, he felt relief in heading for this homely business, this place of arrival, a base far from war.

But when he opened the pub and stood behind the newly polished mahogany bar, Mr Kneale's heavy words evaporated as he thought of the young lad swinging down from the bridge thousands of miles away in a fight not of his making but one he would see through. He had seen the angry swollen seething of an eastern river and he could imagine the dark, the thin safety rope threatening to catch on the uprights, and the undeterred obedience to this order that the bridge remain intact. As it did. He hoped Joe would do something like that one day. And that it would be 'the sort of thing he would enjoy'.

The bar door opened and Sam turned, took a bright sheer pint glass and began to pull the dark mix of ale and porter.

'There's been worse days, Sam,' Diddler said.

'Plenty.'

Diddler's first sup half emptied the glass, and, as always, 'A good pint, Sam,' he said. 'Sign of a good house, so it is.'

—ɯ—

At the Anglican Young People's Association they had done Four Men In A Balloon. Who should be thrown out? Who was most important? The doctor, the teacher, the scientist or the vicar. Joe had been given the vicar the week before. The responsibility had weighed on him.

He was intimidated by his real vicar because the man did not like him. He never said so but Joe could tell and it bothered him. He would chuck a kind remark to other choirboys or give them a hello by name or even a compliment now and then but Joe might not have existed. Yet he worshipped God and Jesus Christ through this man whose authority was not lightly worn, whose sermons could be threatening and always freighted with names Joe did not know or complex sentences he could not comprehend. The vicar had such a graceful voice, as good as the wireless, and when he spoke the communion 'Take, eat, in remembrance of me,' Joe bred goose-bumps. When the AYPA decided on a balloon debate, he had volunteered eagerly, but drawing the vicar had spoiled it.

The vicar might not turn up. Most times he did not. That would be a big help. And yet the boy wanted the vicar to hear what he had to say – that without the vicar nobody would be able to get to know God and be saved so there would be no eternal life for anyone, and compared with eternal life what was the use of a doctor, a teacher or a scientist? Vicars healed the soul and taught the word of God and knew everything, so they were all the other three wrapped up in one. Without vicars, life was useless. You were allowed three minutes. The vicar came.

Joe stumbled as he stood in the middle of the circle of chairs, but he kept his head enough to make his points although he all but ran out of breath at the end. The vicar was asked to judge and gave it to the scientist but along the way he said that Joe had tried hard and gave him a smile. The boy was well pleased.

313

The sense of pleasure buoyed him up to the fish-and-chip shop where he bought his supper, sixpenn'orth with scrams, and took his time wandering down the High Street savouring the long soft chips speckled with the hard chippings of batter. It was a good moment.

Street lights were on. McQueen stood under the light at the corner of High Street and Market Hill, staring across at the Black-amoor from which he had been barred for life. He took up this position at least once a week.

McQueen was not right in the head. He had been up in court more than once for beating his mother. In drink he went from silent sullen to yelling violent without warning. He had no friends, not even a dog. He was very thick set, deep black hair heavily oiled, rarely without his old navy blue coat. His face was swollen, the cheeks, the lips, usually a glaze of red on the skin.

'Sam Richardson's a bastard!'

Joe, who had crossed the road, stopped and faced McQueen.

'Tell him I said he's a right bastard.'

McQueen began to move towards him and Joe turned away.

'Tell him I'll get him! Tell him I'm waiting for him.'

Joe moved quickly and went through the door of the pub as if seeking sanctuary.

It was quiet.

Sam saw the boy a touch flustered and strolled out of the bar. 'How did it go?'

'I didn't win. The scientist won.'

'As long as you did your best.'

'McQueen's outside.' Joe dropped his voice and looked at the floor. 'He said – he called you names. He said he would get you.'

'He's best ignored, Joe. Just ignore him.'

'But he called you names, Dad.' He hesitated. 'I should have had a go at him, shouldn't I?'

'He's best ignored.'

'But you would, wouldn't you? If you'd been me. If he'd said that about Grandad. You'd have had a go at him, wouldn't you?'

'These things are hard to call, Joe.'

'But you would.'

'Maybe.'

'I know you would.'

Suddenly feeling quite hopeless, Joe went upstairs without first going into the kitchen. He was a coward. He was overwhelmed with grief at the realisation. He was sure his dad could tell. His predominant concern at school now was to avoid Og. He would excuse himself for the lavatory in lessons rather than risk it at playtimes. He would scan the school playing-fields for Og and the sauntering, predatory pack of 3L and tack his way far from them, trying to kid himself that he wanted to play way over there, but knowing, sick to his stomach with it, that his sole purpose was to avoid Og. Even those who thought it had taken guts to fight in the first place could bring no comfort. He knew he was a coward. He was even afraid to be alone in his own house.

He knelt by his bed and read. It had become his preferred position. That his knees hurt helped somehow. He was reading *The Grapes of Wrath* and the story almost blotted out everything from his mind save for the small cold certain feeling that he was a permanent coward now, even scared of getting into bed and turning out the light.

CHAPTER THIRTY

McQueen got on to the bus outside the library in Castle Street. Joe had spotted him from his prime position in the front seat on the upper deck and his stomach had melted at the sight. McQueen had been drinking in Carlisle, the boy could see that – no one could miss the glazed face, the stagger on to the bus and then, to Joe's alarm, the uneven clump of drunken steps announced his ascent to the upper deck. Joe froze. McQueen must have taken the back seat. Joe forced himself to try to disappear through immobility. Though the bus was quite full he felt that there was nothing and no one between McQueen and himself.

He should not have gone to the game. Sam had said he would go and watch Carlisle United with Joe and the boy had given up the chance to go up to Highmoor where some of them had made a dirt track for bikes. Then Sam had pulled out at the last minute – something to do with the dog-bus going wrong – and Joe had climbed on to the crowded Carlisle bus before he could reorganise his forces. He had not found anyone to latch on to. It was a cold feeling going through the children's turnstile knowing that you would meet up with no one you knew on the other side. Somehow he had not been able to lose himself in the game. He had hurried back from the ground, taking the back-alley short-cut his dad had shown him to try to beat the big crowds to the buses. Packed buses, stiff with smoke, stoked up sick. Sick now with McQueen to face as he got off because McQueen would stay on beyond Joe's stop – he knew that – he lived in the direction of the next town.

When the conductor came for McQueen's ticket, he claimed he had lost his return. The conductor was not convinced. McQueen swore he had lost his ticket and when the best he could get was 'Bad luck' he swore at the conductor, who said any more of that and he would stop the bus and put McQueen off. All this clearly audible. Many of the men turning round to look on, enjoying it. The fare was handed over with obscure menaces.

Joe prayed the conductor was not a customer at the Blackamoor, did not know his mam and dad, would not use his name. He handed over the ticket with his face pressed against the side window and escaped with a 'Thank you.'

Wigton tugged the bus in faster than Joe wished. He looked out on the darkening fields, counting the horses, envying the security emanating from the electric twinkle of distant farms safe in the deepening twilight.

The bus stopped on Howrigg Bank and Joe, from his prime position, took in the tight-packed huddle of the town, scanned it, but without the usual lift: the next stop would be Market Hill.

He could stay on. Go past McQueen's stop. Say he had fallen asleep. Walk back. He had no money left over. But he was not sure where McQueen did stop, and would the conductor report him for travelling on without a ticket? Or lying?

Market Hill, into King Street, stop.

Joe's body got up and turned and headed down the bus towards McQueen, knowing that however low he hung his head, McQueen

318

would spot him and, with scarcely any effort, bar him from going down the twisting little staircase. He tried to walk steadily and wished now that he had not been at the front, which made him last in the thin queue and easier to pick off.

'Richardson!'

The boy looked up. McQueen's face was strained with such violence, the boy felt winded at the mere look of him. He stopped.

But McQueen said no more. And Joe's body started again, took him down the twisting little staircase, off the bus, into the blessed air of safety impaled once more on his cowardice, not knowing and not to know for many years, that his father had sought out McQueen and explained that the quarrel was between the two of them, the boy was not part of it and if McQueen ever made the boy part of it again he would come looking for him.

His mother was behind the public bar – slightly uncomfortable, Joe could tell, confronted by the men-only space. The men in the bar were waiting for Sam to return, to talk of dogs and sport and pick up news from the hound trails.

Joe would have enjoyed talking his dad through the game. He had concentrated enough to be able to describe it. Sport was how he and his father talked mostly. In sport they talked about heroes, about skills, about groups, about grace and generosity, about greatness, about weakness, about the miraculous, about the mundane, about the ecstasy of triumph and the deep hole of defeat, about being a man, and about their feelings and care and concern and realisation of each other in a way that had no other means to express itself, no other subject as wide and free and democratic and relaxed. Because all they were talking about was sport.

He took his bike from the back yard and went up to Highmoor to see if they were still on the track. It was beside the big house, in the shadow of the Italianate tower, cleverly engineered out of a dumping place long grassed over, more of a scramble course than the rumoured dirt track. Joe took his half-racer boneshaker around the course a couple of times in the failing light but it was limited fun on your own. He pedalled around the big house – now flats – and up and down the avenue but it was as if all boys had been exorcised from the land.

So he let the bike take over. Took his hands off. It went left. Straight on. Left again. Right. Into a dead end. Start again. Where did it want to go now? Straight on. Right . . .

It was freewheeling down Southend into the town, his hands in his pockets, luxuriously carried down the hill, no effort of his, no sweat, magic, the bike perfectly steady, his charge.

He had six friends at school – Alan, Paul, Edward, George, Malcolm and John. Three of them lived in the old town. His best friend was Alan, who also intertwined through close proximity – Alan's father had a paper shop just up from the Blackamoor – and at weekends Joe would deliver papers sometimes just to be with Alan who was worked hard.

Yet he went to knock on Alan's door with no great confidence. Alan's parents did not like him. That was clear. He was the boy from the pub who could not be redeemed by however many freely donated paper rounds. The commonness of it, the smell of the bar degraded him just as surely as in the eyes of Diddler and others it enhanced him. And he would answer back.

He climbed up the grimy back stairs to the flat above the shop with no great confidence.

Is Alan in? No.

That would have done. But Alan's mother took the trouble to tell him that with Paul and Edward he had been invited out to Malcolm's for some sort of do in the afternoon and they were still there. She thought one or two others might be there too. Joe was certain that she was pleased he had not been invited and her triumph and his jealousy stabbed him, but he said thank you and turned and walked steadily down the stairs.

That left John who lived just out of the town in a farm cottage down a long rutted lane. He set off at high speed as if he were delivering an emergency telegram.

John had gone to set snares with his father. He could come in and wait if he wanted. But they would be late back.

The boy had fought to avoid this but he had to go to Malcolm's house. Paul was there with Malcolm, and Edward, and most of all Alan – how could Alan have gone without telling him?

Malcolm had the biggest house. It stood alone in its own grounds just before Greenacres. It was the sort of house in which you felt you had to keep hushed. It overwhelmed Joe. Everything seemed valuable and not to be touched. It made him feel inferior in a way he obscurely resented and it filled him with envy, which was even harder to cope with. He had to repress himself and consequently it was in Malcolm's house that he tended to knock things over.

He propped his bike against the low wall of a neighbour's house and went cautiously to the open wrought-iron gates. The bay-window curtains were drawn but they glowed from the bright inner lights. He knew that room. The big chairs, the big settee, the sideboard, other things he had not registered in school. Things, impressive things, furniture not necessary but important, pictures on the wall, a grand-father clock. They would be playing Monopoly or ludo or pontoon for matches or maybe blow football. He could picture them – Malcolm had a lot of games. There was a big table, his mother put a velvety green cloth on it. They would all be gathered around the table.

He was utterly incapable of walking along the short drive,

knocking on the door and finding a way of asking to be included. He stood there and soaked up what by now he felt deliberately excluded from. He had a terrible anger against Alan. The curtains were a deep wine and the glow was so warm, friends, family, security.

Now in a racked turbulence of rejection, Joe rejoined his bike and made for Water Street.

Dan and his sister lived in Water Street. They had come as squatters. They were always in on Saturday nights because that was the night their mother came.

Joe knew about them in fragments. Information offered by Dan, who was a little younger than he was and, more occasionally, usually as a correction, Marjorie, who was two years adrift. Their father had been in the navy. He had sunk U-boats. He had come back and – then it became even more blurred. But the upshot was – and his mother, who knew, would not help him on this though he had asked her – that Dan and Marjorie now lived in Water Street with their grandmother, and their mother came from another town, nearby, on Saturdays to help with the baking, washing and ironing and to see them because what their grandmother contemptuously referred to as 'the new fancy man' had children of his own and did not want them to mix. They were poor.

They played snakes and ladders. The grandmother sat by the fire, staring, a woman they had to beware of. It was a bare room. The ironing board dominated the place. Dan's mother, a full woman, ironed with fury, her loose blouse unbuttoned from throat to bra, her breasts swaying as she sped the burning instrument, Joe's guilty eyes flitting there, once catching the glance of the grandmother, and burying himself back in the game.

Dan was not greatly enthusiastic about games. Marjorie was tired, she was usually tired, pale, skin tight on her face, always wandering over to her mother, hovering around her – 'getting under my feet,' her mother said – and Marjorie would retreat, cowed, hoping nobody had noticed.

Joe could help, he thought. He wanted to. In the subdued, ill-lit room, he always felt sorry for Dan and Marjorie and he wanted to help them. He did not have to work to impress them like he did with some of the gang. He was never tripped up by feeling inferior: on the contrary, although he could not recognise this, the opposite was the case, the ease of superiority. They would always let him in to play, and when he invited them over to the pub-kitchen they were on holiday. In the cramped space, snakes and ladders, disturbing breasts, a look on Marjorie's face that moved the boy, Dan pliable, some of the bruises were salved.

While the water was being boiled for cocoa, he rushed out, slung himself on to the bike, burst into the barrage of noises in the pub, stood at the hatch in the barging corridor and bought three packets of crisps. The rule was he got one free on Saturdays, but he saved that for later. His mother took his money reluctantly. It represented three-tenths of his week's pocket money, he calculated, and he arrived back with them like a proud hunter with a kill. When his father served him and knew he was visiting Water Street he would sometimes give Joe a bottle of Mackeson milk stout for Dan's grandmother. She was plainly put out when he reappeared without it and her evident disappointment took the wind out of his pleasure in the gift of crisps.

By the time he returned home the kitchen in the pub was packed, and much as he wanted to it was impossible for him to have his supper there. He went upstairs fearfully, the potato pie, the crisps, the cup of cocoa, made with milk this time. He knew it would happen again. He tried not to glance towards the loft where the spirit of the blackamoor still roved. He ought to have got over that by now.

He did not put on the lights in his bedroom because he wanted to keep the curtains open and look out over Market Hill, beyond, to the baths, beyond, to the Tower invisible now but plain in his mind. All these sights were comforts. He ate standing up. Beneath his feet the growl and pulse of the Saturday night came to print its message on his soles and he sought to orchestrate the voices and the noises. But the food came to an end and nothing happened on Market Hill and he had to make for bed, even though the effort was heavy.

In his prayers his silent voice called on the love of God and feared that he was not good enough to be answered. On his knees he felt that nothing but the fear and love of God possessed him: he was the willing, helpless patient of God, begging for the touch that healed. This abstract but totally fevered passion of terror was primed by Joe's apprehension about the next morning. The vicar had asked him to train as a server at the altar. This meant going into the Holy of Holies with the vicar, aiding him with the communion wafers and with the water and the wine and learning the responses.

Much as Joe had longed for this position, when it arrived he knew from the first instant that he was not up to it. There was that schism of certain alarm which told him he would not be able to cope. No matter he could memorise the responses and had observed the movements of the server several hundred times from the choir stalls, no matter he wanted to serve God and impress the vicar and be there beside the altar where Jesus Christ was most completely present, where the wafer turned into bread, the wine into blood, where every true brave Christian should be – he could not do it. Just as he could never have beaten Og. But how could he refuse?

At his first rehearsal three weeks before he had forgotten to bring the water with the wine and stumbled over a response he had known

324

by heart, but after the blessing and final prayers in the vicar's vestry he knew he had been forgiven.

Not again, though. He could not be forgiven twice. And Joe was absolutely certain that although he could perform the service in his mind without an inch of error, he would surely, certainly, get it wrong for the eight o'clock communion.

Perhaps it was too much. Too close to the presence, to the burning sun, melting the boy's confidence, plummeting him to fated failure. For did this not mean he was unworthy, letting God down? As he finished his prayers he saw himself walking up the chancel steps behind the vicar, the few in the cold church kneeling in expectation of their Saviour's body and blood, his own cold hands numbing on the chalice, his mind suddenly swept of all the forms and words he was commanded to remember.

'Amen,' he said, loudly, getting off him knees reluctantly after the whispered prayers. Bed could no longer be avoided.

The fortress did not work. Nor did the multiplications. He went through the week. That could help. Not the school – that took him to Og and his cowardice – but the week of evenings. The baths on Monday – a good night for training, two lengths in 26.5 seconds, coming on – but then the cowardly loitering to make sure he came back with others even though it was the long way round. The Scouts Tuesday in the school hall, a new troop, reviving the old Wigton Scouts, which had collapsed when Mr Barwise had moved out of the town. The new chemistry teacher had set them up. Sometimes they met in his large house where there was a magnificent train-set running all around one room. You sat at the side and worked all the systems. Too busy for sleep. And Alan refusing to stay late to play with the train-set.

The AYPA on Wednesday. Nothing he could hold on to: a talk about tenors by Malcolm's father who said that Gigli was much better than Joe's proposed champion, Mario Lanza – an opinion that had angered Joe and upset him as if he had been personally insulted. Many of the others had laughed, of course, and they nodded as the man said that Gigli (whom neither Joe nor the others had ever heard of) was so much purer, immeasurably finer, infinitely greater than the rough peasant overstrained voice of the former Neapolitan waiter. Joe felt stabbed and now in the bed, as the customers were turned out into the street, he blushed again but this time in fury for there was in him that which recognised the attack on Mario Lanza as a slapdown of himself. Mario Lanza belonged to him. He even thought he could do a fair imitation of 'Be My Love'. Reedy Gigli weedy Gigli! But that got him nowhere.

Choir practice, piano lesson – increasingly resented now, the relentless preparation for exams, Miss Snaith annoyed with his lessening of interest, his obvious lack of practice, his withdrawal.

Nothing there. The pub was empty of customers.

He could go down and help his father at the till but there was a real hint of drowsiness and maybe if he stayed . . . He tried the fortress again but saw the swaying breasts of Dan's mother and the betrayal by Alan started up again. What did John Cobb feel like when his speedboat disintegrated on Loch Ness and he was dragged down and down into that fearful bottomless loch? Joe was proud of John Cobb, his world land-speed record, being British and best at everything, trying for the world water-speed record as well, but what was it like? The water would be terribly cold, the history master had said, and most likely he was dead before he drowned but what if he drowned? Joe tried to imagine drowning; he aped it sometimes in the baths – or would the H-bomb be worse? They had meant to leave him out. Malcolm's father had just laughed at him about Mario Lanza. He was not supposed to look hotly at those breasts.

Jack Ack went out of the front door – the others would go soon: his mam and dad would be upstairs, soon; he would be safe then, he would sleep then. It never happened then.

But it came. What was him vanished into the light. Only that faint, small light kept him alive. There was nothing inside him. He could not even pray. The fear was terrible.

CHAPTER THIRTY-ONE

It was difficult to get anyone to come out and play on a Sunday. His friends, his gang, whatever their church, were locked into the rule of a joyless, house-bound Sabbath. Shops were tight shut, games forbidden, communal pleasure confined to special zones – Silloth in summer – even the pubs were different, better-behaved, careful not to antagonise the gods of the day.

Joe had been at the altar for Holy Communion, made two mistakes, and later much more happily sung in the comfort of the choir for the Eucharist. Ellen had made his dinner before she went down to the pub. The quiz occupied Sam and she was needed to run the other rooms. Joe ate alone and quickly, got out his bike, stuffed his yellow polo-neck in the saddle-bag and set off the eight miles west for the mining town of Aspatria.

Annie Fleming lived there.

After that day in 3L she had been friendly to him, she had even sought him out once or twice and lolled against the railings while he tried to unnumb his tongue. And earlier in the week, in a mixed swimming lesson, she had let herself be life-saved by him when they were practising and his hands had slithered across the bubbled bathing costume on to breasts, real breasts, his first, so strangely soft, stirring excitement in a body otherwise jellified with the sin and the giddiness of the encounter. It had made him feel bold for the first time for months and he towed her backwards and forwards across the pool until he could no longer disobey the whistle. He climbed out quivering from the contact and amok with further expectation as Annie gave him a sly complicit knee-trembling smile.

He wanted more.

It was a bleak northern early-autumn day and the wind was in his face on the way there. He counted seven cars, all black. There were two cyclists, together, going in the opposite direction. The best bit was the swoop down the hill beyond Waverton and the hard pedal up the hill that faced it. The worst was the stretch alongside Brayton woods in which a man had recently been found hanged. He had used his army belt. He went past it as fast as he could, in third gear, mouthing 'Be My Love' to keep up his spirits.

She had told him she lived in a village a mile or so from the main town and he soon spotted the sign. On the way he took off his green school jersey and arrayed himself in the yellow polo-neck.

He had not told her, not even hinted, that he was coming.

The village was eight short terraces of small houses built for miners. It stood beside an extinct pit. Joe circled it like a lone Indian scout warily spying on an encampment of covered wagons. There were some boys playing on a slag heap but they were too young to approach.

He knew neither the street nor the number.

If he willed it enough, she would appear. That was his conviction. He did not pray. Prayer helped elsewhere, but not for this, which was a bad feeling. But he let loose his longing for Annie, particularly her soft as snow breasts underneath the bubbled costume. She would pick up his signal, he thought. She would stroll out, just as he was passing her house, just like that.

330

He entered the settlement and cycled up and down the bare, narrow streets. Occasionally a small boy raced from house to house. Twice he saw women walking, huddled around folded arms, heads bent.

It took some time before hopelessness set in. He circled and then swung into the streets, wove patterns between the terraces, slowed down to peer into windows, became convinced that next time, next time, if he sped up or went around three times quickly without looking into windows, or shut his eyes while free-wheeling down a street then – she would appear.

A boy in black drainpipe trousers walked in front of him forcing him to stop. The boy was some years older than Joe. His hair was well greased in a wave of a quiff. Despite the chill day he wore an open-necked shirt, sleeves rolled up, right forearm tattooed with an anchor. He nodded to Joe but the nod was not friendly. 'Can I help you, pal?'

Joe shook his head. He was straddled over the cross-bar, both feet on the ground. He felt that he had been captured for a crime.

'What you after?'

'I'm looking for somebody.'

'I'll do.'

The boy was clearly encouraged by Joe's confusion and in no doubt of his physical superiority. He enjoyed the silence.

'You could get off that bike for a start, pal.'

Joe gripped the handlebars tightly. Why was this happening?

'I came to meet somebody,' he said. 'But they don't seem to be here.'

This time it was the older boy who nodded, unwillingly convinced. 'I don't know you, do I?'

'I'm from Wigton.'

'You'd better set off back there, then, hadn't you, pal?' He gave a

331

last hard look and gestured a dismissal. Joe felt grateful. 'Canary!' the boy yelled, and the word bulleted after him.

Joe did not look back until he was well away and when he did the previously seductive settlement of terraced cottages seemed a hostile encampment stuck sullenly on the bare landscape hugged into its own.

Thoughts of Annie Fleming had gone: fear had driven out the pricklings of juvenile lust.

There was no song in his head as he pedalled with the wind behind him, heavy rainclouds coming in from the sea to the west, the road past the hanged man's wood entirely forsaken. The clouds seemed to be pursuing him.

The swoop down the hill and the impetus up the matching hill lifted him a little bit but the pressure on his spirits was growing heavy.

He got a puncture on the back wheel. He took out his kit and turned the bike upside down then realised he needed a spoon to lever off the tyre. And a bowl of water. The clouds darkened the fields all around him.

Wigton was about four miles away. He got on the bike and began to pedal but the grind of the back wheel told him that he was doing damage. You did not ride on a flat tyre, it ruined the bike. He dismounted and began to push it, standing on the pedal now and then in his urgency, using it like a scooter.

It was as if the big clouds were closing in, bearing down on him, isolating him. He heard his panting breath and heard the sound of his own fear. The road ahead was flat and straight and empty. He was cold.

He mounted the bike once again and felt relief in the flow of speed but the grind of the back wheel, the damage being done, too much. Once again he dismounted. Once again he used it as a scooter between times of running.

The heavy rainclouds blotted out sound. A silence encircled him. Silence and cold. As if there were no one else alive, anywhere in the world. This cold silence threatened to make him stop stiff still but if he did he did not know what would happen. He heard his breath, that was all, his breath panting in panic panicking him more. One foot on the pedal. Back on to the bike. Never mind. The cold silence wrapped round him so tightly now and what was he? What was this thing that was him, that was solid with fear and the strangeness of this pressure of isolation?

There was a cottage. A yellow light through the curtains. He could stop and ask for a spoon. Even for a basin of water. But what would happen if he stopped? What was this thing? He dare not stop. He wanted to knock on the door. He wanted somebody to break this spell. He dare not stop.

Now he rode the bike.

The wind pushed at his back.

Big spots of rain. He could not cry.

It was so strange. It was so frightening and strange. He would not get back. Even when he entered Wigton it was different. He peered at the houses as if checking they were really there. He got home, he changed, he went to Evensong and in the concord of the choir the fragment of himself was eased, began to grow back but fearful still as he walked the long way, down the lighted main streets, fearful of what he knew could be waiting for him when he went to his bed.

'Is Alan in?'

'What for?'

Joe avoided her eyes. 'I just want to ask him something.'

'We're having our dinner.'

The door was a quarter open. The stairs behind beckoned him to run away.

'I'll wait then.'

'He's got an invitation for this afternoon.'

Joe smarted at the kick. 'I'll wait at the bottom of the stairs.'

Alan's mother shut the door.

Ellen's background, that queer brother of hers, the common pub, the boy's too obvious longing to be with Alan, not right.

He waited.

He sat on the bottom stair, which looked into the narrow twist of the ancient Church Street which fissured the middle of the town they said, proudly, 'like a dog's hind leg'. She could have invited him in. He delivered papers for no pay, most Saturdays now, the pink sports edition, at the end of the afternoon, winging around the town with Alan, bike to bike, seeing how much time they could clip off their record. Joe felt stabbed by her dislike. It was unfair. It was unfathomable to him. He was always on his best behaviour. But Alan's mother could never wait to see the back of him. He sat in a huddle, unjustly unhappy.

But Alan came down and for a moment the misery evaporated. Alan was almost precisely Joe's height, his hair fair to Joe's sandy, his face high cheekboned, defined, to Joe's round endeavour, both of them fit, Alan the runner, Joe the swimmer, Joe doing Alan's homework, close even within the gang.

'I can't come,' Alan said, apology in his tone.

They had agreed to go on a long bike ride together on this first day of half-term.

'You've had an invitation.'

'Who told you?'

'It's Malcolm, isn't it?'

'How do you know?'

'He's asked you to go out with him in his dad's new car.'

'Yes.' Alan gave in, used to Joe divining his moods or plans.

'But you promised.'

Alan nodded. His mother had told him to go with Malcolm. It was a real treat, she said, not given to just anybody.

'You promised.'

The plangency of the repeated word. Joe lashed out, punched Alan hard on the arm, punched him again, turned away, grabbed his bike from the wall, ran with it before slinging himself on to the saddle.

He headed for home, for the loft, to be with the budgerigars.

They were disturbed by his arrival and shifted from perch to perch. The boy stood still, looked intensely on them as if trying to extract the secret of their lightness, their appearance, even in agitation, of joy. They were so free, no guilt. So light. Colin had given him two blues but he could not make out which they were. They could be any of those dapper little coloured pet birds, painted sparrows, ordinary little things made extraordinary through the flash of high soft colour. Joe watched them for some minutes but even that troupe of innocence and colour did not uncramp the tightness in his chest.

In the corner on a stool were the boxing gloves. Colin had declared that he would turn the stables downstairs into a gym and really train up Joe for the job. He would get a heavy punchbag and a speed ball, he would get weights and a skipping rope, he would clear out the two stalls still remaining from the old days for the horses and Wigton's first gym would be set up. You never knew, he could train others besides Joe. Wigton lads could fight as well as anybody else. Better.

His enthusiasm had overcome Joe's deep reservations, seemed to go some way to repairing the fracture in him. The neglected gloves had come out of the bottom of his wardrobe and there they sat, in the corner, on the stool like a boxer waiting for the bell to go.

Joe pulled on a pair. He shadow-boxed but even that made the budgies tremulous so he went down the ladder into the stable, the fusty, aimlessly cluttered place, always cold, the stalls for the long-lost horses littered with empty crates.

The boy began to box. On his own he was full of style. The thorn of Alan pricked him on. His shoulders moved, rolled, easily, he ducked, he threw a couple of jabs with his left and then a right cross, step back, he came nearer the mottled wall, stone protuberant, unyielding. He hit the wall. Once, twice, then again, the old one-two, into the body, work it, work it, beginning to sweat, hearing his breath but not afraid, not with the gloves on, not when he was hitting the wall, hit, hit, hit the wall, stand close, he had the little black boy screaming in his head, in his sights, slip that punch, sidestep, left, left, and then into the stomach, that slowed them down, that took it out of them, his breath sounded harsh and good, bang, bang, bang, screaming from the horse's hoofs, slam, slam against the wall, his feet apart, his eyes feeling the sweat flow from his brow, hitting the wall, hitting it, slamming, frenziedly, the obdurate wall.

When he stopped he was heaving in breath. He looked at the gloves. They were cut and battered from the wall. The surface leather had split in some places and the sponginess beneath was revealed, little nicks, little wounds, you could not fight any more with gloves like this, they would cut, it would not be allowed. He took them back up the ladder and returned them to the stool. He sat and watched the beautiful birds, exhausted, waiting.

—ɯ—

Colin had been told by Ellen never to take Joe on his motorbike so they met down Burnfoot beside the convent. He had found the boy staring at the budgies and had offered him the treat on the spot. Colin had only had the bike for two weeks. It was an ancient Norton, bought, Colin boasted, for 'next to nothing', and he was enraptured by it.

Ellen's fear was susceptible to no entreaty. It was unlike her to be so openly adamant about risk. Joe must not go on the motorbike. He's too young. Promise? Colin had nodded solemnly at the injunction, feeling that he was thus marked out as a daredevil, and yet addressed as a responsible grown-up. He was pleased with that.

He had found a pair of old flying goggles in a rummage sale. His trousers were tucked into black wellingtons. Grace had loaned him a pair of Leonard's black leather gloves. Joe had been instructed to smuggle out his yellow polo neck to wear over his school jumper. Cold, Colin explained, when it met speed, just sliced through you.

'Best to put your arms around me,' Colin said. 'The real pros use those grips but safer if you put your arms round me. And you'll be able to feel my rhythm. This is an open-air jet. Don't give me the jet set! They should try a Norton. Nobody'll ever beat this bike, Joe, best in the world. Ready?'

Joe got on the pillion rather gingerly. His mind was still submerged in the stables: the boy's screaming was still in his head; he could see Alan and Malcolm in the back seat of the new car; he had surely ruined one pair of his gloves.

'Tighter.'

The boy pulled himself closer to the man who twisted around, his face monstered by the goggles, a grin wiping out the lower half of his face.

337

'TT!' he yelled above the explosions of the engine. 'Wall of Death!'

The bike jerked forward, abruptly, clumsily, and Joe almost fell off. His face bumped into the goggle straps and his nose whiffed the larded Brylcreem. Colin drove cautiously, only beginning to open up when well clear of the town.

Carlisle Bridge was in his sights. Carlisle Bridge was a narrow low-walled railway bridge, which went off the Wigton road at a right angle, and immediately threw another right angle into the Carlisle road. Carlisle Bridge collected more accidents than anywhere else in the county. The approach from both sides was calm and open and then before you knew it, this savage Z-bend was on top of you. Lorries, cars, motorbikes, especially motorbikes, had taken the bridge too fast or had a spot of oil on the road, a slither of rain, a sudden fear of an oncoming vehicle on such a narrow bridge – a young local soldier on leave had crashed his motorbike there less than a month before, thrown over the parapet on to the rails. They spoke of a 'mangled body'. They spoke yet again of widening the bridge. This bridge was at the quick of Ellen's anxiety.

Joe knew the bridge from the upstairs of a bus, when sometimes everyone went 'Whoa!' as the bus swayed around, just making it. And he knew it from his bike when he and Alan and some of the others would get up as much speed as they could and swing their bikes to an angle like the motorbike champions in the TT on the Isle of Man, the trick being to make the angle as acute as possible without hitting the deck. He felt Colin open up the throttle as they approached it and a wild mixture of fear and exhilaration whipped through his mind as sharp as the wind in his face.

'Hold tight!'

Colin opened up yet more as the narrow little bridge came into

338

view. The bushes on either side of the road were still in good leaf and thickly green, the cattle and sheep rushed by, standing still, indifferent and calm.

'Lean to the left! Then switch to the right! Blast off!'

They beat into the first turn at some speed and Joe felt all that was inside him swoop to the left as he followed Colin's body and then the near instantaneous switch a little too late, to the right, but they skimmed the far wall, shot across the road into the lush verge, twisted out of that and proceeded at a subdued pace towards Carlisle.

Joe knew how close they had been. Colin did not turn round. He pulled up in Thursby, a village half-way between the town and the city. He parked the bike against the wall of the school, which stood on a village green of a handsome size. He took off his goggles and walked a few paces, finding a spot isolated enough from the road.

'You'll have to practise that leaning business, Joe,' he said. 'Thing is you lean into the bend, see, lean into the bend, but you have to follow my body to perfection otherwise kaput.'

Joe nodded, suddenly weak, glad to sit on solid ground. Colin lit up a cigarette and a dreamy look came into his eyes. 'This has come just too late for me.' The barest gesture indicated the Norton. 'I've a knack for this, Joe, I can feel it, dead certain. I've got the touch. But it's all money. You have to have the money or know the money men. That's my flaw.'

He looked nostalgically at the smoke that came from the cigarette burning between his fingers, as if in that lazy curl of smoke lay the proof of a destiny denied.

'Know what I think?' He looked at Joe intently. 'I think I'm just going to wait for you to grow up. So we can be real pals. Man to man. You and me. I'm picky, see, and I've made up my mind. You and me's not just related, we could be best pals.'

Joe smiled but the smile was forced. What about Alan? And the others. But still he smiled and when they stood up and Colin slung his arm around his shoulder as they sauntered back to the bike – a gesture Joe himself so often made freely with Alan – he repressed the tremor it caused.

On the way back Colin took the bridge steadily, so that Joe could get used to it, he explained when he let him off back at the convent and made him swear not to tell Ellen.

Although still a touch shaky when he walked from the convent, it was the trace of exhilaration that was imprinted more firmly on Joe's mind. He went past the pub, into the town. He might bump into someone he knew. There was still light, the clocks had not gone back.

But the evening town was quiet, even in the yards where gangs collected there was nothing for him. But he did not mind. He went from Church Street to Water Street by way of the pens in the pig market, which supplied a mild frisson of illegality to top up the exhilaration. He ran down the ramp in Harry Moore's garage, which was not quite as chancy but there were stories of boys being caught.

Colin was already in the pub. Sam paid him partly in kind: a pint of bitter a day which Colin took as two halves or saved up for a spree. It was an effective way for Sam to defray the unnecessary expense of Colin. Ellen approved because it meant that she could keep an eye on him most nights. When Joe looked into the bar, Colin's exaggerated 'Joe! Now where have you been?' alerted his mam, he could see that, and he blushed and she saw that and she knew, he knew that.

'Joe and me,' Colin announced to Sam and Ellen, both behind the bar, she ready to take orders for the Darts Room and the kitchen, 'we're going to be best pals when he grows up. That right?'

Joe tried to nod without it being fully confirmed as a nod. This time it was Sam who looked at him. But where Ellen had frowned, his dad only smiled and said, 'Joe won't be lost for pals, will you?' The boy did not know how to receive that: it seemed to mean so much more than the words.

He went into the back yard to get his bike. This would be a good moment.

It was still not dark but the few street lamps were lit. He tacked up King Street, into High Street, past the church in which he was a failure at the altar, down Proctor's Row, and into the narrow lane that wended by the small stream and led to the baths.

He had not come principally to swim.

He went into the chlorinated water and the thought of Annie Fleming being life-saved was more vivid than any race. He forced himself to stay until the whistle called them out. He forced himself to wait until he was the last to leave.

Then he went out and, already feeling a small distant sensation of fear at the back of his throat, he pointed his bike the short way back, the unlit way.

He followed the riverside path and turned into the hill. Fine for the first bit until he caught the sound of his breath and he stood on the pedals, pressing them harder, even speeding up as he reached the crest of the hill and seemed to pause for a second, looking through the darkening twilight at the gasometer, at the few speckled lights of the town, which seemed so distant and yet were but a couple of minutes away as he kicked down the pedals and shot down the hill, hearing his breath louder now though he was trying not to breathe, past the gasometer and the Tenters cottages, the strangeness beginning to clamp on him again, making for the narrow bridge, which switched across another of the rivers threading through Wigton, too fast, overshot, thudded his leg sickeningly into the wall, managed to twist the handlebars and balance and keep upright, a bad knock, lucky to be wearing long trousers.

CHAPTER THIRTY-TWO

Joe walked through the shut-tight Sunday afternoon town trying to conceal his agitation. His mother had pressed his best suit. He wore his school tie. His black shoes glittered as his father had taught him. His hair was straight parted and plastered down with water and Brylcreem. He had washed his face and cleaned his teeth especially. Even his mother had said that he looked presentable. But something could go wrong. He was going to tea at the vicar's.

The other three new servers had been and the word was that the vicar was about to cut the new ones down to two and this was the final test. Joe already feared that he had failed. Tea was unnecessary.

But he plodded heavily up the grey autumn street, enjoying the stiff wind in his face, carrying his school mac neatly folded over his arm because there had been such heavy storms recently, trying to think of anything but himself.

The vicarage was the most handsome house in the town. Large, white, Georgian, set well back from the road, between the auction and the grammar school, supported by outbuildings, approached along a drive of giant rhododendron bushes, a world of its own.

Joe knocked too timidly the first time and had to do it again. Already he had lost points.

343

'Ah, Richardson,' the vicar himself opened the door, glanced at his watch, 'early. Never mind. Come in. Come in.'

He made much of waving Joe aboard as the boy stumbled into the house.

'Follow me.'

The vicar was not in his cassock. He was not even wearing a jacket. He sported green corduroy trousers and a brown pullover with a hole in one elbow. He strode out and Joe saw a wall of books, paintings of hills, drawings children had done, small coloured carpets on bare floors, a telephone, high ceilings, long windows, a big fireplace, logs. 'Follow me,' the vicar said, twice more booming, 'follow me.'

'This is Joe Richardson,' he announced, presenting him.

The three children smiled, it seemed the same smile. Joe knew Alfred, who was almost his age, from the choir which he joined in his holidays from the local boarding-school. The girls were younger, both long-haired, somehow like the illustrations of Alice in Wonderland in the book Mr Scott had given him after he had sung 'When Johnnie Comes Marching Home' – disturbingly pretty in a way foreign to him. In the smiles there were questions – who is this one? Isn't he rather funny? Why is he dressed so smartly when we are happy to be in muddling clothes? Joe blushed.

'Play with him until tea,' said the vicar, and left.

Joe was surprised at how untidy the room was. As if a grown-up had never been in it. A busted sofa and two old chairs. A couple of carpets really worn out. Books scattered any old how. A big enviable rocking-horse in front of an empty fireplace. Snakes and ladders not packed away. Two teddy bears on the mantelpiece.

'We were working out how to play Winnie the Pooh,' Alfred said. 'For Bernadette.' He nodded to the smaller of the two girls. 'Who would you like to be?'

344

'This is a test,' said Sarah, the nearest in age, the one who looked most steadily with questions in her eyes, the one he wanted to impress.

'Who's Winnie the Pooh?'

The vicar's children did their best to react politely but their disbelief was undisguised.

'Everybody knows Winnie the Pooh,' said Bernadette. 'Everybody in the whole world.'

Joe sucked on his top lip and held it tight between his teeth.

'How can you not know?' Sarah's question sought an answer.

There was a heat flush beating about him. He had to reply.

'We could play Biggles,' he said, out of nowhere. 'Save there are no parts for girls.'

'Girls can be boys in games,' Sarah announced, and Joe felt he had heard an oracle.

'I'll be Ginger.' Alfred sided with Joe and, Joe sensed, came to his rescue. 'The sofa can be one aeroplane; the chairs can be two other aeroplanes and the Germans can be on the rocking-horse.'

'I'll be the Germans,' Joe said, quickly.

Tea was in the kitchen and the vicar's wife seemed surprised and, Joe thought, rather dismayed to see him. Her fourth child was just over a year old and restless in a wicker basket affair such as Joe had never seen. The baby looked so sweet that he had wanted to go across and chuck it under the chin but Mrs Elliott had said better to leave her alone and the tone was cold.

The meal was a poor do, Joe thought. Some crumbly bread on which the vicar spread thin margarine and strawberry jam with lumps of strawberry, which Joe knew he would not like. There were no rock buns or scones but there were toasted teacakes. The centrepiece, much commended by the vicar, was a sponge cake that had collapsed in the middle. This, said the vicar, gave it character.

There was something Joe could not grasp. Something he knew he was supposed to admire, even to covet, but he conceded it was out of his reach. The best word he could find was a 'feeling'. A feeling that he was entering a closed order. A feeling that this was the right way to eat tea and the right tea to eat. A feeling that the tea was not important, the talk was important but the talk was family talk, exclusive and teasing. A feeling of plenty even though the table was not groaning, of leisure even though the vicar would have to be getting organised for church quite soon by Joe's reckoning, a feeling of distinction and difference.

'Joe took the part of the vicar the other week in the balloon game. He put up a very creditable performance.'

'Were you thrown out, Pa?' Sarah asked.

'Afraid so.'

'Why was that?' She turned her steady gaze on Joe who braced himself.

'I couldn't win them over,' he said. 'Maybe I didn't do enough homework on it.'

'Maybe I didn't do enough homework on it?'

Sarah took the sentence and the thick local accent and mimicked it perfectly. They all laughed.

'Sarah's a true mimic,' her father said.

'Do it again,' said her mother, with a pleasant smile at Joe.

The girl obliged. For a wild moment Joe felt the urge to mimic her – to his ear – false-posh accent, but he pulled back. He was soft on her.

'Ten out of ten for trying, though,' the vicar said. 'Vicars should probably volunteer to jump out of the balloon.'

'Would you like a slice of this terrible cake?'

'No thank you, missis.'

'Oh dear.'

'Mummy made it specially,' said Sarah, with some heat.

'I'm full,' Joe said, which was true in the sense that he knew he could eat no more.

'Just the teeniest slice?'

Joe shook his head. There was a fractional pause, as if a family intake of breath, brief, not impolite, to Joe a clear accusation – but for what reason?

'I'll have the biggest slice you can cut,' said the vicar. 'Yum-yum.'

'Are you absolutely sure you don't want a slice of this cake?' The vicar's wife smiled with her mouth but her eyes were hard, and Joe looked and looked away quickly at the woman, knife poised over the collapsed sponge.

'No thanks, missis,' he muttered.

The knife came down and slit the cake in two with some force and then the more careful slicing and distributing and noises of major enjoyment, Joe isolated.

'This is the best cake,' Sarah said, smiling at her mother, 'that you have ever made.'

'I suspect Joe is used to more professional baking.'

'Yum-yum,' said Bernadette.

Alfred left half his cake. Joe stared at the plate.

'Alfred's excused because he's unwell,' Sarah announced, rather loudly.

'Sarah,' the vicar's voice was gentle, 'Joe is our guest.'

'What's wrong with you?' Joe asked.

Alfred waved his hands as if making a conjuring pass over the tablecloth. Sarah looked to her mother. 'We don't talk about it,' she said, harshly.

'That's why they let him come home on Saturday nights.' Joe

knew that Sarah was cross with him yet again, but found some comfort in the vicar's admonitory glance which subdued her.

'This is where we – you and I, Joe – go to my study. Thank you for a lovely tea, darling.'

'Thank you, Mummy.' A salute from the children.

To Joe the study felt holier than the church. After all, there were hundreds of churches. Sometimes he and Alan went into them on their bike rides. But this was the only study he had seen. Books on shelves floor to ceiling, books on the floor, books on the big desk full of drawers, books on the green sofa, glowing rugs on a wooden floor, a Bible as big as a shoe box, piles of paper stacked askew scribbled over, several with paperweights, photographs of Mrs Vicar and Alfred, Sarah, Bernadette and older people framed on the desk, a big globe free standing, which the vicar spun with his finger when he came in and Joe watched the pink of the British Empire appear and reappear like the favourite horse on a roundabout, and candle-holders, many. The vicar was 'High Church'.

'Make yourself at home.'

The boy stood, helpless, until a cluttered chair was indicated.

'Just put the magazines on the floor.'

The vicar flung himself into a deep armchair and lit up. 'Alfred's very sensitive,' he said, abruptly. 'His mother likes to keep an eye on him.'

Joe nodded, understandingly.

'We keep it to ourselves.'

Again the complicit nod: secret safe.

The vicar seemed annoyed. Joe perched on the edge of the chair, looking up expectantly, as a dolphin to be fed by its keeper, an acolyte trembling to be initiated, a boy desperate for reassurance. He knew what he would say when – as he had done with the others – the vicar asked him what he wanted to be.

'I'm afraid it isn't working out,' the vicar said. 'Sometimes one has to be cruel to be kind.'

Yet again, Joe nodded. The roof of his mouth quite suddenly dry.

'You've tried hard.' He was looking away, up into the corner of the room. 'You've done your best. But at the altar itself, when the heavenly host descends, when the bread is made flesh and the wine becomes Christ's blood, then I need something special.'

Joe sucked at his teeth to ease his dry throat.

'Mr Mitchinson says he will be glad to have you back full time in the choir.'

The boy found a voice. 'So you don't want me next Sunday early communion? On the roster.'

'I'll ask Malcolm to do it.'

Again the understanding, submissive nod.

He held in his terrible disappointment. He dare not let it go. Where could it go? Who would receive it? He did not want to be a bother to the vicar and knew from the awesome man's obvious impatience that this was threatening.

'Well,' the vicar sprang to his feet, 'not the end of the world, eh? Not even the beginning of the end of the world.' He picked up a book, a battered copy of a Jennings school story. 'I thought you might like this.'

Joe stood and held out his hand. He had read it some time ago. 'Thank you very much.'

'Now. I have my sermon to dust down. Follow me.' He swept out of the study, wrenching Joe from the spot to trot behind him as he had done on several bleak Sunday mornings from vestry to altar and back again.

'Wait here.'

Alone, in the hall, clutching the book.

He heard a claque of giggles and then a stern sentence from the vicar. The words 'kind' and 'guest' were heard down the corridor.

The three children appeared, shepherded by their father only. 'Say goodbye to Joe.'

They did, and Sarah added, 'I liked being Biggles.'

Joe wandered back through the late-afternoon town now beset with gale-force winds that would test the evening devotion of many a church- and chapel-goer. He was dazed from the blow of failure. He would read the book. A missionary, that's what he would have told the vicar. That was impossible now. He was not good enough.

Sarah had been kind at the end, hadn't she?

Sadie sidled in late and silent in a hooded scarf, hiding her face behind her left hand, the right trembling with a cigarette.

Ellen did not need to ask. The women separated about their jobs, Saturday morning, four fires to make up, floors mopped, tables polished, corridor scoured, the small pub spick and span by opening time when Sadie would drop into the kitchen for a cup of tea. Ellen thought she might not on this morning. The bruises were bad. But she did come, and sat in the corner, cowed, out of character, distressed. Ellen handed her the cup of tea and offered a biscuit, refused.

'There's plenty worse off than me,' Sadie spoke quietly. 'He's a gentleman compared to some I know. And you know, Ellen. We both know.' She lit a cigarette, took a deep pull, let out a long jet of smoke. 'There's some in fear of their lives in this town.'

Ellen wanted to say there was some truth, most likely, in what Sadie asserted though it was not as black as she was painting it. But it was impossible to join in. Sadie's grief was not to be touched, not even by such a friend.

She came to the moment and put the undisturbed cup carefully on the table.

'He says I've got to stop doing this job. He says I've got to stop coming here any time, morning, noon or night. He's promised me a terrible hammering if I don't do what he says.'

Colin. Ellen needed no enquiry. Her stomach lurched in fear, fear so regularly battened down, fear she always knew would be released one day.

'It's Colin,' Sadie said. 'He says we're being talked about. He says he gave us the benefit of the doubt for a bit but last night he went on the drink and some of the men got at him.'

Ellen licked her dry lips, trying to do so without being observed. Colin had exposed Sadie to this. Ellen had told him to be careful but he had disclaimed responsibility.

'There's nothing in it!' Sadie's tone intensified, though she fought not to raise her voice in the barely populated Saturday-morning pub. 'Cross my heart, Ellen.' The thin bruised body began to shudder and Ellen went across to her. 'Cross my heart, Ellen, and hope to die. He is just a good dancer.'

'I know. I know.' Sitting side by side now but still not touching.

'And we had a laugh in the pub often enough, so what? I know there's plenty don't like him – sorry, Ellen – but I always thought there was something about him. Something that made you want to look after him even. But there was nothing in it. Nothing. Never. Nothing.'

Her voice tailed off and Ellen's relief was tempered by regret. Sadie would go. They would meet upstreet now and then or at a dance but these would be no more than poor reminders, sad echoes, indications of the rift. For Sadie had no choice.

'I loved this job, Ellen,' she stared straight ahead of her, 'I loved coming here of a morning. And helping out at night. You know, you might think this is daft but I was proud to be part of the Blackamoor, me. I was. Sam and you's made it such a great little place and I would say to myself, well, I helped a bit with that. You know, Ellen, far and away, it's the best job I ever had.'

Already Ellen was missing her, the singing when the spirit took her, all the new songs, all the words, the scraps from the newspapers, the sandpaper comments on the town, but most of all the presence of her, just being there, a friend, always and ever a friend.

'You'll be a big loss,' Ellen said. 'You'll be a big loss for me. You will.'

'There's plenty'll want this job.'

'But nobody like you, Sadie. It was special, you and me doing it,' Ellen said, the most she could manage to say. It was enough to make Sadie turn away.

'It'll break my heart, Ellen, this,' she said. 'It will.'

'Hello, Richardson.' His hand shot out.

'Colonel Oliphant.' They shook.

'So this is the Richardson establishment.' He looked around the small bar with brisk appreciation. 'Just as it should be,' he said.

'I'd heard you were in Korea.'

'They pulled me out. Off to Kenya. Just time for a quick turnaround and I thought why not a spin through to Richardson's place? Not much chance of finding a good pub among the Mau Mau. God save us, another shambles like India. How's the local brew?'

'Bitter?'

Colonel Oliphant nodded and Sam drew a careful half. They were alone in the bar. The military man had arrived on the stroke of opening time. As Sam levered the pump gently, the Colonel took out a Craven A, bounced it on the bar top and flicked it into his mouth. He offered the slim silver case to Sam, who took one. The Colonel lit up both of them with a flame like a blowtorch. 'Joining me?'

'I don't,' said Sam. 'Not here.' He smiled. 'But I will this time.' He drew his own half-pint more briskly.

The Colonel let the beer settle and then held it up towards the window. 'Clear as glass, Richardson.' He took a small sip, paused, then a real pull. 'And very good.' He sighed. 'God! You miss a decent beer in a proper pub.'

Sam remembered the talk of pubs in Jap-filled jungle. 'Good luck,' he said, and held up his glass for a moment before tasting it.

Although he was in mufti – sports jacket, leather pads on the elbows and cuffs, cavalry twill trousers – Oliphant was unmistakably a military man of a recognisable type. Squared shoulders, emphatic movement, clear focus, restless, high-tempered, highly controlled, very fit. The appearance of one of his former officers from Burma spun Sam back seven and more years from the windy autumn of North European Wigton to the sweltering strangeness of the East.

'Do you see any of the chaps?'

'Only now and then,' Sam said. 'Very rare.'

'That's the story everywhere. Curious, though, I find. You'd have thought. Months together. Years together. Some hairy moments. Come through. The sense of camaraderie might have persisted.'

'I would bet it does,' said Sam, 'but you don't have to see each other for that.'

'Very true.' He finished his drink. 'What do I owe you?'

'On me.'

353

'The next one on me.'

'I'll stick with what I've got.'

'Give me a pint this time, Richardson. Ah!'

Diddler came in looking particularly ravaged after a successful day at the horse sales.

'How do you do?' The regimental cufflinks shone. Diddler wiped his hand on his filthy trousers before taking the proffered hand.

'This is Colonel Oliphant,' said Sam. 'I served under him in Burma. This is Diddler.'

'A soldier,' said Diddler, glad to be in the picture. 'Now that's a thing.'

'And you?'

Diddler looked at the ceiling, sucked his gums and said, 'A very clever man, Colonel, once told me that what I did was the "burthen of the mystery". But I sold a good horse today in Wigton sales and I bought a better and I came out with a profit so the drinks are on me.'

The young officer laughed, loudly, happily, infectiously.

'I've just ordered,' he said.

'Put the soldier's drink on my slate,' said Diddler. 'I'll have a glass of porter, a double Bell's and twenty Capstan Full Strength, Sam.'

Although the Blackamoor was the furthest pub from the auction market, there was enough swollen business – gypsies, dealers, tinkers, farmers, trainers, breeders – at the three-day horse sales to trickle down the town, and Sam's reputation from his bookie years and his sporting buses also encouraged a trade much bigger than that of any normal weekday.

He called upstairs for Ellen.

When she came he wanted to introduce her to the Colonel but the spruce, clear-eyed soldier was in deep with Diddler and three Irish tinkers – Diddler called them his cousins. They wanted to know where

354

the regiment bought its horses and how the situation could be improved: by them.

Joe came back from the baths, looking wetter than when he had been in the water, and Sam again wanted to introduce him, but the Colonel, it seemed, was cut off, surrounded. Joe took one of the tea trays and waited on in the Darts Room and the kitchen.

'Must dash.' The Colonel brandished his watch. 'Been here a couple of hours. Could stay all night.'

'This is my wife. Ellen – Colonel Oliphant.'

'Absolutely delighted to meet you.'

'And you,' said Ellen, suddenly sixteen shy as she took the firm hand. He was the cut of man you very rarely saw in Wigton. The black curly hair, the fine handsome confidence.

'I'll see you out.'

Sam stepped out of the bar as the Colonel left to a warm chorus of farewells. Joe was in the corridor. Sam nodded to the boy to follow him.

'And this is the boy. Joe. Colonel Oliphant.'

'Pleased to meet you.' He pumped Joe's hand. 'Your father and I soldiered together in a nasty piece of business in the war. Very pleased indeed.'

The three of them went out on to the front.

'Have you been in Korea?' Joe asked, to Sam's surprise.

'Just got back.'

'Mr Kneale says there'll be a third world war start in Korea.'

'He's a history teacher,' said Sam.

'It's ugly out there, I'll grant him that.'

'He says the Americans will drop the H-bomb. That's twenty times bigger than the A-bomb,' Joe explained, 'that wiped out Hiroshima and Nagasaki.'

355

'Your father and I weren't altogether sorry about the atom bomb, Joe. Saved many more lives than it took. Never a bad tactic.'

'But will there be a third world war?'

The soldier took the question seriously enough to pause; the pause made Joe feel grown-up.

'There could be, yes. And it could be a good thing in its way. The first war left loose ends that went rotten and, to my mind, the second has done the same. The sooner Communism is stopped the better for all of us, over there and over here. What we have now is a war of nerves as well as a real war. What the boffins are calling psychological warfare. There's a mouthful. So: maybe.'

'But who would be left if the H-bomb was dropped?'

'The winners, Joe. Now I really must fly.'

Once more he pumped Joe's hand and Joe reluctantly knew this to be the cue for him to go back in.

A smart red MG stood by the doorsteps, keys left in.

'She's not mine I'm afraid. More's the pity. What's the boy going to do?'

'I don't think he knows.'

'Lucky blighter. I was marked down for the army from the font. Still,' he looked around the gloom of the town, across to the caves of Market Hill and into the darker holes which signified alleyways and yards, 'can't complain. There's always going to be something for us to do. You might put a word in for us, though. Good army stock around here.' Climbed over the door and into the seat. 'Tremendous little pub, Richardson. Tremendous char- acters. Especially . . .'

'Diddler?'

'The same! Got some rather good ideas too.'

He turned the key and revved up the engine.

'Good luck,' Sam said, and added, 'Is it still Colonel?'

'They did decide to give me another pip. Can't think why.'

The soldier waved, revved up as if going for the land-speed record and rocketed towards Carlisle.

Sam watched until he was out of sight. He would have liked an interval, a quiet stroll, a time to reflect. But the pub was beginning to roar and Ellen was on her own.

—m—

'You could have a word with him,' said Ellen, of Sadie's husband.

'It's not what you've said before.'

'I know.'

They were alone in the kitchen. It was well past eleven and the weariness of the unexpectedly busy evening lay upon them. Sometimes it could have a warmth, like a light daze, make them more open to each other.

'It would do no good,' Sam said. 'He has a point.'

'There's no excuse for knocking her about like that.'

'But he has a point.' The quiet voice disguised the insistence. 'Colin and her were blatant.'

'Nothing happened.'

'They were still blatant. He shouldn't have hit her, I agree.'

'Just because they liked dancing together.' Ellen hesitated. Sadie's distress had triggered a distress of her own, a distress compounded by fears for Colin, the continual effort of the pub, and other darker anxieties that stirred out of reach but not out of mind.

'It didn't seem like just dancing, Ellen, and you know it.' He looked closely at her and saw the unhappiness. He wanted to help, yet he also wanted, quite badly, to get back to *The Big Sleep*.

357

Ellen was silent, not yet giving up. Sam gave it a couple of moments then let himself be taken over by the novel.

Joe was tired of waiting for them to come upstairs. They had let him stay up to help with the clearing but after a quick mug of cocoa and a biscuit he had been declared 'out on his feet' and consigned to bed. After changing, he had stood at the top, leaning on the banisters, waiting for one of them to emerge so that he could tackle his bedroom. He had rushed into his pyjamas and forgotten the dressing-gown and slippers so his feet were turning slab cold and he was beginning to shiver but somehow that helped. Try as he might he could decipher nothing from the low murmurs coming from the closed kitchen.

Mr Kneale had said nobody would be left. Except, he said, primitive tribes in remote continents or archipelagos. H-bombs, because there would be more than one, he said, would not just kill millions, they would make everything on the planet radioactive so that nothing could be eaten or drunk so those not blown to smithereens would starve to death. There was no protection against them, said Mr Kneale. They were the ultimate weapon.

Joe had wanted to ask the vicar what God was doing about it. The other servers had reported that they had had a serious talk with the vicar and Joe had looked forward to that bit. Surely God wouldn't let just everybody be killed off. Everybody could not be bad, could they? Maybe they were. Maybe God wanted to start again. What would the vicar have said?

What would it be like if an H-bomb dropped on you? Did you just frizzle to a cinder right away? Did you turn into atoms? And what about the soul? Would you know it was happening? What would the world be like with nobody on it? The Colonel had more or less backed up Mr Kneale. And on the newsreels at the pictures when they showed the Korean war they made it sound like the end of the world. With the Americans and the Russians and the Chinese involved as well as us it was all set for a showdown; the Colonel had said as much. He would tell Mr Kneale.

The kitchen door opened and he scampered lightly into his bedroom. Not lightly enough.

Ellen came in. 'You should be asleep.' The tone was not unkind, but Joe heard something strained. He wanted to ask what was wrong.

'Are you all right?' she asked.

'Yes.'

'Goodnight then. And,' her voice, not at all loud, dropped further, 'stop hanging about at the top of the stairs. Your dad doesn't like it.'

She closed the door quietly and he snuggled down, drawing up the sheet and blankets so high he all but made a tent. He heard his mother in the bathroom. The warming of the bed summoned up sleepiness. She came out of the bathroom and then, he had not anticipated this, she went back down the stairs.

The sleepiness retreated. He wanted to get up again – but his dad, she had said. And the bed was warm. He had already said his prayers.

—⟋⟋⟋—

'You blame Colin, don't you?' Ellen was unusually blunt.

With an audible sigh, Sam wrenched himself from the drug of Raymond Chandler and re-entered the conversation. 'They're two adults, Ellen,' he said.

'Sadie was just being kind. That's what's unfair.'

The pause lengthened until Sam had to speak. Ellen would talk about this, he decided, whether there was anything much to say or not. For Sam, there was a great deal to say but he would not say it. He did not want her more upset.

'You know she was, Ellen, and I accept it, but others see it differently and he shouldn't have hit her but it's understandable he was maddened. What would I think if you gallivanted with a fancy man?'

'He wasn't her fancy man.'

'A good dancer, then.'

'I think you would trust me.'

'It might be hard.'

'What are you saying?'

'I wouldn't like you dancing about all over the place with somebody else, that's what I'm saying, Ellen, what else was I saying?'

'You would trust me.'

'That isn't the point, sometimes.'

'You either do or you don't.' Ellen spoke flatly, harshly.

'What's up?'

'Why can't we find a way to help Sadie?'

'Because it's none of our business.'

'It isn't her fault. That's what's up.'

'Not according to you. Not according to me. But we don't count in all this.'

'You think it's Colin's fault.'

So rarely did she or dared she bring up Colin between them that Sam was almost thrown. But he had to hold steady. Colin was a no-go area.

'Colin carries his share, yes.'

'You think Colin's . . .' Ellen paused, aware now that, quite suddenly, she was ready to do battle, but for what reason? '. . . no good.'

'I never said that.'

'You did. Right at the start. Right at the very beginning. How could I ever forget? When he first came. You said he was no good.'

'That was then, Ellen. That was then.'

'Now isn't any different, though, is it? You'll blame Colin for this, more than Sadie, and more than that terrible husband of hers.'

'I'll see him if you want. It'll do no good. It could make things worse. But, if you want, I'll see him.'

'It won't do any good. Not in that mood.'

'What do you want, Ellen?'

'We can't even manage a holiday together. Not even a couple of days.'

'Who would look after this place?'

'Others manage. You've taken him to Morecambe for two days, I traipse off to Butlin's.'

'You like it. You both like it.'

'Oh, yes. I like it well enough. But that isn't the point, Sam, is it?'

'He's lucky to get a holiday. What set this off?'

'This place doesn't suit a family, Sam.'

'He likes it. He can bring his pals in to play darts when we're closed. They meet up in the kitchen and play around in the stables. It has a lot of interest, a pub.'

'For you maybe. It jars on him.'

'It jars on you, you mean. That hasn't gone away.'

'I haven't complained.'

'You don't need to.'

'We only meet when we're worn out, Sam. We see each other when everybody else has drained off every bit of life there is in us.'

361

'It'll get better. You always have to work hard building up a business.'

'It's built up.'

'You have to watch it all the time.'

'I think,' Ellen spoke with particular care, 'that it's a way to make a living together but not live together. Not really together.'

Sam closed the book.

'What do you think everybody else does? Jack or Alfreida and Frank or Grace and Leonard for that matter or most of them. What do they do?'

'They sit down together across a fire. They listen to the wireless like we used to. They go for walks like we used to. They go to the pictures together not in single file, and holidays, even if it's only a couple of days, and Saturday afternoon and Sundays off.'

'Granted. But what do they really do? Does this all make them more interested in each other? Does this make them more interested in life? I can't see it on their faces. I can't see it in their eyes, Ellen. As often as not I can see boredom, even desperation, but most times just a putting up with it.'

'What's wrong with putting up with it?'

'Because – because you're on a lead, you're on a leash.'

'We're on a leash. Opening hours, getting ready, waiting on, waiting on everybody who turns up, having to be cheerful whatever you feel like, not being able to be quiet or a bit down, we're at everybody's beck and call, aren't we, Sam? Isn't that a leash?'

'Is that the way you see it?'

There was hurt in his question and she did not want to hurt him more but driven, this rare time, and not knowing why.

'Yes it is,' and added, but as an obvious sop, 'mostly.'

362

'It all comes back to Colin, doesn't it?' Bitterness, for the first time, no more than a touch, but marked.

'You're so uneasy with him.'

'I'll tell you something, Ellen. Now listen. Quite simple. I try my level best with Colin. In fact, if there is such a thing, I try better than my best because of you. That's all I want to say about Colin. And as for the rest, I think you're just romantic about other people's lives. We have company on our doorstep. We have talk every night. We have a bit of money to spare now. The work's hard but what work isn't? At least we get the direct benefit. And nobody bosses us about.'

'You used to be romantic. You used to talk about wanting night classes and trying to be a village schoolteacher. You were the romantic one, Sam, not me.'

'Well, that had to pass.'

'Maybe Joe'll do some of that for you.'

'You live your own life.'

'He's a good reader.' And the piano, she wanted to say, but she had said enough.

'He'll have to make a better fist of it than he's doing at the moment,' Sam said.

Ellen experienced a shadow of recognition, a dark presence inside Sam's words, brushing against her awareness of her son, disturbing her. 'What do you mean?'

He's running scared, Sam wanted to say. I can see it plain. The boy is scared. Sam had seen it enough times. And what followed fear was unpredictable save that it was bad, a lessening.

'Has he told you something's wrong?'

'He's said nothing.'

Sam's smile, which was a smile of recognition for the boy's silence, reassured Ellen sufficiently for her thoughts to revert to Colin and Sadie. It had got under her skin. She had relied on Sadie and liked her a very great deal. And Colin? He was skittish about their father but she wanted to know – how dare she ask it? – had their father been like him? Was he their father's son?

CHAPTER THIRTY-THREE

Joe was surprised when Sam said he would like to come to the baths with him on the Saturday afternoon and watch him in the speed trials. They went the short way, past the old jail, over the narrow bridge, by the Tenters cottages, up the small hill and down again to the sandstone baths, a pleasant easy route in daylight made more pleasant by Sam telling him some funny stories about the war, especially about the mules, stories he used to tell years ago to get the boy to sleep.

He did well in the trials. It was good, sprinting up and down the pool, especially the crawl, freestyle, throwing out his arms as far as they would go, stretching it seemed to snapping point, palming the water down to his groin and then a rapid recovery while the other arm machined its way through the water and the legs powered steadily, the ankles slackening to free the feet to a churning paddle, the face half emerged on the right just before the down stroke to snatch a breath hissed out under the surface, the feeling of water rippling over the skin and faster, driving out all thought, all feelings, all imagination, just the will to win, to beat the rest.

For those seconds he was wholly healed. In competition he was freed from the plague of himself. To compete meant you could never feel you were alone. In competition you were in constant company. It meant you always had to look to someone else. Competition gave the outside of you a clear purpose. Nobody could ask questions, not even you, that was the great beauty of it. You were what you did and you did it just as hard as you could which made you stronger. And it could carry over. Especially when you won. The glow of it could warm and light you through hours, even through a day.

His dad had a word or two with the trainer while Joe did the usual business with the Brylcreem. Everybody told him his dad could get on with anybody. His aunty Ruth had told him his dad was a very popular man. Joe rather cringed at that, sorely aware of unpopularity, of a compulsion to be the organiser, otherwise no one, he was convinced, would play with him. This apprehension of his unpopularity had grown since his beating by Og. But his dad just chatted away, scratched the back of his head in that way he had, smoking, as usual.

'He says you have the makings.'

Joe was pleased: that the trainer had said it, that he had said it to his dad and that his dad thought to repeat it to him. He smiled, to himself.

'Your last time was near the club under-fourteen record. Less than a second away.' Sam sounded genuinely impressed.

They were walking back the longer way because Sam wanted to go into the town. The wind was still high as it had been for the past fortnight, there were already pools of flood water in any flat field, and the little beck beside them fumed like a mill race, but Joe felt warm and calm and as steady as he had been for many weeks.

'So everything OK, then?'

The tone was false. Joe's sympathies, which had been reaching out in fullness, withdrew like a threatened snail's horns. 'Yes,' he answered, sad that the good moments had been so few.

'Nothing on your mind, then?' Sam was aware of his clumsiness but he had little finesse with his son in matters tangled by fear, which he saw, and cowardice, which he scented. He laboured on. 'Nobody getting at you?'

Had anybody told him? Joe only committed himself to a shake of the head.

'Nothing bothering you at all?'

Did Colin count? And not confessing he had not made it as a server? 'No,' he muttered, not looking at his father.

So, Sam concluded, he was right. 'Like swimming better than boxing now?'

Had he seen the ruined gloves?

'You gave those gloves what for.'

But he laughed when he said it.

They passed by Vinegar Hill.

'I still like boxing,' said Joe. But he did not specify whether it was doing it or watching it and the latter was certainly true, which absolved his answer from falsehood. 'Swimming's easier than boxing.'

'Always stick at what you find easy,' Sam said. 'If you find it easy the odds are you've got a bit of a talent for it. But, then, I thought you had a bit of a talent for boxing.'

Joe was not up to a response.

They were at the end of Proctor's Row, which ran parallel with the churchyard. At the empty corner of the High Street, Sam stopped. Joe was forced to do the same.

'Joe?'

'Yes.'

'Look at me, Joe.'

The boy, whose eyes had been scanning the ground, levered

up his face slowly as he dared until his eyes met the blue stare of his father, almost a hard look, almost the look that could freeze him.

'So there is nothing bothering you?'

'No.' The word was almost a gasp.

'You're telling the truth?'

What could he say? Oh, what could be say? How could he possibly begin to describe what was happening, how did he know how to describe it, what on earth would it sound like, it made no sense, it was outside answers to questions, so what could he say?

'I am,' he lied.

'You wouldn't lie to me, would you, Joe? Look at me, Joe.'

The boy tried to hold his father's hard look. He was frightened to the marrow. Don't back down had been drummed into him. We don't back down. There was a prickling sensation over his scalp as, for what cannot have been more than mere seconds, he fought to hold the look.

'You wouldn't lie.'

'No, Dad.'

He so much wanted to tell him. Whatever it was. Just something about it. About in bed, that thing in the corner. On the bike on his own when he was in the country and that awful feeling would sheet over him, the boy wanted to let out some of the pressure of the pain, but how could such things be told, they were not to be talked about, they were so deep inside that words could not reach them, and even if they could what authority could they possibly have? In that moment the boy yearned for an understanding beyond both of them but it was not there and the only course open was to lie.

He knew his father saw through it.

'There's never any shame,' Sam said, 'in admitting you're in trouble. It sometimes helps to admit it. I've known that myself, both ways. I've admitted things to a friend and somebody's admitted things to me.'

Only three people passed by. Each was given a cheery greeting by Sam in a tone quite at odds with the urgency of his speech to Joe. Anybody watching the two of them from a window would have thought the man was giving the boy a telling-off.

Joe wanted to run away. Just to run.

'So: last time. Anything up?'

The boy could hold that gaze no longer and his head dropped. But there was no giving in. This time he shook his head, all he could manage. Another lie. It screamed through his head. Three. He waited for the punishment.

'And then there's times,' he heard above him, 'when you have to keep things in. I know about that as well.'

It was meant as comfort but the boy was beyond that.

They walked back through the town, down the High Street, past the Fountain where the men smoked and spat, down King Street towards Market Hill and the Blackamoor, father and son, getting to be as big as you, Sam, see you later on, Sam, could they not all see that he was a liar? Was it not as clear as glass? A liar as well as a coward, afraid even step in step with his father of the dark night, God could see right through him, he was transparent, could see every bad weak part of him, what have we done to deserve this weather, Sam? almost shoulder to shoulder but so far apart.

On the steps of the Blackamoor, as Sam fished out his keys, he said, 'You know what the referee tells the boxers when he pulls them away from each other after clinching for too long?'

Joe shook his head.

369

'Box on.' Sam smiled. 'That's what he says. "Box on." ' And he opened the door.

Joe nodded and attempted a smile. He went into the pub, reluctantly. Box on.

CHAPTER THIRTY-FOUR

He walked to school the most obvious way, up King Street past the shops. On this October morning just before half-term, potato-picking week, which would, he hoped, line his pockets, his mind was a nesting place for *Ivanhoe*. He had seen the film the previous night at the Palace. Alan had gone with him on the two complimentary tickets the Blackamoor received for putting up the weekly poster. Alan had not been as impressed as he was. He was not convinced by the fighting. Joe had been utterly swallowed up, as blessedly often at the pictures.

His satchel was slung over one shoulder. He was in no hurry. The buses bringing the children from outlying towns and villages had not yet swung on to Market Hill where they stopped to let off the public before moving up to the grammar school. It was another grey day but not threatening. That night the full gang were to come round to the Blackamoor and he had worked out which games would be played, which teams, which competitions. His dad had agreed they could use the Singing Room – generally empty on weekdays – if the kitchen became busy. He had bartered six packets of crisps.

He caught sight of himself in Johnston's window, the blind still down, the boot and shoe shop not open until nine a.m.

As if a bolt had been sharply slid back in a door, he went out of himself. That which he saw was without what was him. He was transfixed by this stranded figure for some moments, and then a noise, a greeting, some sound moved him on.

The walking collected him.

He turned left at the Fountain, by Middleham's the butcher, and took care not to glance in the windows. Windows. Windows right up the High Street. Huge windows for Aird's, the ironmonger and plumber, and Redmayne's, the tailor. He averted his eyes. But towards the end of the street, just before the church, approaching the corner sweet shop, some impulse made him decide to turn to the pane of glass. He kept walking, briskly now, and turned to glance, like a salute, as they did in the Scouts almost at the identical spot when the march for Remembrance Sunday swung into St Mary's.

Nothing happened.

There was literally a spring in his step the rest of the way. He felt it and then exaggerated it, making it like the walk of Monsieur Hulot in the film the French teacher had shown them, a walk that mocked fear, a celebratory springing walk, the walk of a victor. He was, once more, Ivanhoe.

It did not take too long for lessons to agitate and depress him. He was beginning to lose his place in the class, losing his confidence. Cheekiness was a desperate remedy. His mimicking of the teachers was another escape. The teachers turned it back on him in humiliation. Expulsion from the classroom or one hundred lines to be done overnight. 'I must not make a nuisance of myself in class.'

After dinner in the canteen he ducked the usual game of touch rugby and went hunting for Annie Fleming. She had waved at him the previous day in the afternoon break, and talked to the two girls arm in arm with her and waved again.

The playing-fields covered a big spread but he knew them

intimately, not only from school but from times of illegal entry with the gang in the holidays. She was around the big old house, part of which was where the headmaster lived. She was with the usual group, which made it easier.

He asked them if they had seen *Ivanhoe*. Nobody had. He started to tell them the story. Annie knew that she alone was the true audience and she played up better than he could have hoped. She was wearing the green mackintosh but the shape of her was still well visible. When she looked rather alarmed he piled on the drama.

Og hit him on the back of the head with a knuckle blow that raised an instant lump.

'Geoffrey!' Annie's voice was strident. 'Don't you dare do that again!'

Joe turned to see Og, smiling rather foolishly at the rare utterance of his Christian name. No great distance away, the squad of 3L loitered under the large beech tree, waiting on events.

'Don't talk to her, pal,' Og said. 'See?'

He brandished his knuckles. Joe swayed but he did not run. In front of Annie he could not run or he could not run for reasons unknown but he stood.

'Don't you dare!' Annie came across to the two of them. 'I'm not having you two fighting over me. He was just telling us about a picture.'

The soapy smile Og offered was damning evidence of his feelings and Annie's glow no less proof of hers.

'His cock would fit in a biro.'

'Geoffrey!' Annie almost screamed – but with something of pleasure, Joe recognised, as the blazing blush swept from his private parts to his forehead.

He tried to hide his little white worm as best he could. When they changed for gym or for games in the dressing room he performed sophisticated physical contortions to hide the disgrace. Showers were avoided unless whipped in by the games master but that was rare, the man liked to wander away as soon as the exercise was done. Others' might be seen to be white worm-like too but no wee-wee, no number one, no cock if he could brave that inappropriate word, was as white or wormy as his. Joe knew that as he knew there was a God. Og's, Geoffrey's, business was always on full display. It paraded up and down between the pegs. It was weighed in his hand. It was embellished with crinkly black hairs. It made a royal progress through the dressing room as an object of awe. It crushed Joe. That it crushed others too he neither knew nor cared. Og's cosh seemed targeted on him alone.

One boy, Davies, undressed and dressed under a mackintosh – whatever the weather – but Joe knew that would be fatal for him. Davies could get away with it. He was weird.

'See?' said Og. 'He can't deny it.'

Og had not hit him again and with Annie between them Joe felt safe. Did this mean that it was Annie who had saved him and he was still a coward?

'I want you two,' said Annie, again out of some remembered scene, 'to be friends.'

'With that canary?'

Joe, whose right hand had obediently begun to curve into the shake position, knew that although it could scarcely be said to have started with Annie Fleming, it was all over.

'You,' said Og, jabbing his right index finger at Joe's face, 'go. Go now.'

He did not rub the back of his head until he got round the corner. By then, he was shaking.

On the way home he took a deep breath passing the end of Water Street and walked towards Johnston's shop as if he were on a tightrope. The blinds were up but the large sheets of glass still gave a good reflection. He forced himself to stop. Among the clogs and boots and the shoes and slippers and wellingtons, there he was, just as he was, intact. He ran the rest of the way.

——〰——

It happened a few mornings later. And then again. Catch sight of himself, the flight, the what he was bolted out. Avoid windows. Avoid long bike rides alone. But there was no avoiding night.

——〰——

'I'm sorry, Miss Snaith.'

The music teacher looked at the wounded palm without pity. 'It doesn't seem much more than a scratch to me.'

He knew he should have had the nerve to make the cut deeper. But he thought rubbing dirt in it might make it go septic and make it swell up like his boils and then there could be no questioning his incapacity.

'It's time we started getting ready for the next exam.'

'I know, Miss Snaith.'

'This is a very important one for you, Joe. It will take you through.'

Joe looked at the sonata he was supposed to have polished and managed an unconvincing sigh.

'Let me have another look at that hand.'

Miss Snaith inspected it once more and then she took out a lace-edged handkerchief from the sleeve of her heavy brown cardigan and rubbed his hand, quite hard. 'It looks nothing when you clean it up,' she said. 'I think you can play.'

It was an order. Miss Snaith was cunning enough to say that he played it creditably, she told him where he ought not to rush, she admitted the difficulty of the piece and demonstrated, as she always did and in such a way that made it easier for him.

'We had a good lesson after all,' she said, as he left. 'Just put a dab of Germolene on that scratch and you'll come to no harm.'

Again he was transparent.

He went down the stairs with the lavender musty smell so particular to the Miss Snaiths and was exultantly goodbyed by the Miss Snaith in the shop, and came on to the lamplit street with a feeling of the music still in his head, but an obstinacy had set in.

The energy had slipped away. Perhaps it had been going for some time – the practice in his aunt Grace's house was more and more of an imposition and Colin there, not always but often enough, to tempt him out on the motorbike or for a walk upstreet when he really needed to get back or see Alan.

Miss Snaith was very nice, underneath, and he wanted to please her by doing this big exam but he knew that he could not and would not.

Telling his mam would be the hard bit. Especially as Miss Snaith had driven classical into him with attitudes like commandments and notes like nails – so that he was nervous and lacked fluency in front of the popular music his mother wanted him to play.

He would tell her he would keep it up by himself, get some sheet music, learn the new songs, perhaps play in the Singing Room, relieve Jack Ack, they could play together, start a small band, make ten bob a time, instead of spending that money on lessons, it would be far better. Miss Snaith would never let him do that.

First off he would learn 'Galway Bay'.

—⟊—

After about a fortnight of the new fear he went into the bathroom, locked the door and stood in front of the mirror over the wash-basin. His plan was just to stand there.

It happened soon. The life went out of him. There was this head. In the mirror. A head of someone. It did not belong to him. What was him was not in the mirror. The head was strange to him. Like stone. If he did not stand absolutely still there was no doubt like the light in the corner that an end would come. You were looking at not you. He stood still. Still as he possibly could. No move. The face in the mirror he did not recognise. How long could he last out?

He was bent over the basin. He turned on both taps, filled the basin and submerged his face in the water and held his breath for as long as he could. Then he pulled out, covered his face with a towel and after he had rubbed it very hard, he threw the towel away, did not look in the mirror, went into his room and turned on the wireless to find songs he could sing to.

—⟊—

'Everybody's getting together for the Coronation,' Ellen read from the local paper.

Sam made a political noise, one which signalled that the communication had been received but pointed out that it was not going to disturb his reading. The last hour of the night on a weekday had become book-time not lightly interrupted.

'Collections are being made house to house of sixpence or a shilling per house. One committee's already raised forty pounds, another's got fifty and it doesn't even happen until next year. It's marvellous, isn't it?'

'They're starting soon enough, I agree,' he said, rather drily Ellen thought.

'There'll be an interdenominational service,' she read out, 'dances, a whist drive, a choral concert and a carnival, free dinners for old people, tea and sports for children, Redmayne's Social Club and the Townswomen's Guild and the Rugby Club have all promised assistance. There'll be six dances and a queen chosen at each and a coronation queen chosen out of the six . . .'

Ellen spoke aloud, but softly. It was a habit she indulged only occasionally and Sam had no trouble coping with it. It was a habit, though, often as not brought on by a wish to talk which was neutralised by a decision of equal force that talking would not help. The edited extracts from the newspaper satisfied both drives.

While reading aloud she was thinking, unhappily, about the masks of Zorro. Joe had awarded himself a day off after four days out potato-picking. None of his pals had joined him in the work and he felt cut off from their half-term games – set-gaps, bike scrambling, hours of football. He had felt like an intruder. Into his own gang. They were not interested in potato-picking adventures however he embroidered them. He told them that his mother had made them all half masks like those worn by Zorro.

He had arrived in the pub in the late afternoon in a frenzy. He demanded that Ellen make him the six black masks. Immediately. Urgently. It was vital. He was whimpering with the fret of it. She could not remember ever seeing him in such a state. There were the blinds, he said, the black blinds they had used in the war, he had seen them in the bottom of a cupboard, surely they could make six masks but it had to be quick. He found the blinds, he got the scissors, he called her upstairs to the barely used parlour. She was alarmed at the state he was in, on his knees, clipping the material clumsily, angrily. She took the scissors and asked him what the Zorro masks looked like exactly and he had begun to shout, as there was knocking at the door, he would not go down, asked her to look out of the window, his friends, she said, his gang, she was pleased at the way they stuck together, all of them, Alan, Paul, Edward, George, Malcolm and John, standing outside, don't go down, he pleaded, please don't open the door, please. They knocked again.

She went down. They left. When she came back upstairs the scissors lay open on the cut black blind and Joe was in his bedroom. 'Don't come in,' when she tried to open his door. 'Please don't come in.' There was that in the tone which anguished her but she retreated.

He had lied. He had lied and been caught out. He had lied and been caught out by them and now by her. He had lied and was now in a thrash of misery, trying to do something about it.

The vehemence of it all had shaken her.

'"An art exhibition will be staged and all schools will be asked to take part,"' she announced. '"Townspeople are also to be asked to lend articles of interest." Well, I think Wigton's doing her proud and so it should.'

Why was he so very upset?

'Another cup of tea?'

Sam moved his head marginally from side to side.

Why such lies for such a thing as masks?

She rustled the paper recklessly but his concentration was rapt.

379

'*The Quiet Man*'s on,' Sam said, without looking up. 'I was thinking of taking Joe, tomorrow afternoon.'

'To Carlisle?'

'It's been known.'

He appeared to be reading just as intently. A page was turned over.

'It's that film about a boxer. Isn't it?'

'That's why I'm taking him. That and Maureen O'Hara.' He looked up and grinned. 'She has a look of you, Maureen O'Hara.'

'Hm!' But vanity had been teased. 'I suppose you might just say that I have a look of her.'

'No.' Sam's smile held and so did his gaze when he had sought out and secured hers. 'She has a look of you.'

Ellen was warmed. Emboldened she said, 'Are you worried about him?'

'Why should I be?'

'Taking him to the pictures.'

'Is that not allowed?'

'It's unusual, Sam, and I can see you're not really reading now.'

He looked up. 'Maybe I should have taken him once or twice before.'

'So you are worried.'

'No, not basically.' Sam frowned. 'He's having a bit of a rough ride at present but if he has anything about him – and he has – he'll get through it on his own and that's far and away the best thing. It's no good interfering, Ellen. Makes them soft.' He tried to keep criticism out of his tone.

'He won't be persuaded to keep on with the piano.'

Something in Sam's attitude made her add, 'You think I kept on at him too much about it, don't you?'

'Sometimes it just sets up a contradiction. Especially as the lad has spirit.'

Ellen was silent, seeing some justice in that.

'Better to stand aside. There's hopes I find myself having for him,' Sam went on, 'but I think they're more about me than him: you can't live somebody else's life. Sometimes I think I want to sit him down and tell him everything I missed that he could have and all the mistakes he needn't make and he would listen. But it's always better to stand aside, Ellen. If he wants anything, he'll shout out. He'll always bruise easy.'

She was glad she had not told him about the masks.

'You think too much is being made about the Coronation, don't you?'

He was back in his book. One hand went up, a policeman stopping traffic. 'I'll not be drawn, Ellen. Good business practice.'

Upstairs she heard the music. She went up. His light was still on. The wireless turned on low. Deep asleep. Unclouded, she thought, looking at the face devoid of animation. Better to let the whole thing pass. Least said, soonest mended. He was looking much more like Sam now, she thought.

He imagined that he was the Man in the Iron Mask. He could feel the cold metal heavy pressed against his face, the nose slits were narrow, the mouth a mere slash; his breathing filled the mask with a constant heavy surge of sound. His head would burst if he did not get out. The metal was melting on to his skin.

He had wanted to sob while he was reading *Jane Eyre*. He was scared to go into his bedroom at night. He was scared to go past the shop windows. He was scared to bike out of the town alone and beyond the comfort of houses. There were days of freedom and times when he thought he might have been absolved, but it was never long before he was pulled back. There were times when a sentimental song seeped through the floorboards from the pub below and he felt that he might cry his heart out.

Christmas was coming. Maybe if he prayed and prayed on Christmas Eve at the mass, maybe he would be let off. He would go carol singing with Alan, who was not much of a singer but liked the money and it was now unthinkable to go alone. The money would give him enough to buy presents for everybody; good presents, boxes of soap, aftershave, boxes of scent, good biros, a pack of cards, take her the bottle of stout, go with his dad who took miniatures to the workhouse, he would surely be let off.

There was a late afternoon, dark already, Christmas week, alone in his narrow bedroom, wrapping the presents, when he came across a strip of metal. It said J. RICHARDSON. WIGTON. He remembered punching it out, at Silloth, and how pleased he was to use up all the twenty-one chances. GAP J GAP RICHARDSON GAP WIGTON GAP. That's how it really read.

He looked at the name as if mesmerised by it. It seemed to peel away. The life fell from him the harder he looked. GAP – GAP – GAP – GAP.

CHAPTER THIRTY-FIVE

His bedroom resembled a cell. You came in, the single bed was jammed against the wall on the left; about as much space again made up the width of the room. Beyond the bed were three items of furniture: a small chest of drawers, a wardrobe and a three-shelved bookcase. The floor was lino – red and yellow squares. The curtains were yellow and flowery. The wallpaper was also ornamented with flowers. Out of the window he saw Market Hill on which there was always, in daytime, some movement. The buses now used it, which was illegal, said Mr Carrick, Market Hill belonged to the people of Wigton. Beyond the hill he could see the fields behind which lay the baths. There was a telephone box directly across from the pub and a street-light.

Somewhere in his mind he realised – in a fragile, intermittent, all but blind manner – that this room was where he had to fight. If he could not brave being here alone without running out to the stairs or being in a locked terror, if he could not hold his ground here, then there was no hope.

He did not realise this in any worked-out way. There was no plan. Sometimes there were days on end when hostilities ceased. Usually, though, over the next eighteen months to two years, he was, in so far as he was able, fighting it through in that room.

It was easy not to go on long solitary bike rides. It was not hard to avoid windows and mirrors, although even the merest accidental reflection could unbolt him now. His name was still so strange to look at but there were few occasions when he had to.

It was the night which was always waiting for him, the night and that time just before sleep when the attack, if it were on, would begin.

He would come up to the room as late as possible, rush his prayers, still dressed, change in the bathroom, come back and be in bed so fast he would beat it. Sometimes it worked. Or go up very early, with his supper on a tray, put on the wireless, find music, have a book, read until he was heavy-headed, read beyond that, let the story become a world that filled his head, with the music, so he could feed on them when the tiredness forced him to turn to sleep. If he could think about the book and replay the music in his head then that was better than a fortress. The light left on. But there would always be a time when it was turned off.

Spring and summer helped, the curtains left partly open, the window open too so that voices from outside, clear voices outside the room, not the seethe of noise below which was part of the room, helped distract him. But as summer nights lengthened his mother and father would go for walks after closing time and he would always be awake for that and, flat on his back, try to walk with them, to be with them down Burnfoot, into Birdcage Walk, past West Cumberland Farmers, alongside Toppin's Field and Toppin's Farm, past the police station, up the long incline of Station Road, round the Blue Bell, back into the High Street towards Market Hill and the Blackamoor, going step by step with them, trying not to rush, trying not to move, untensed only when the key turned in the door and he heard a voice.

As the months went on he made it harder for himself because otherwise he would never win. He said he wanted to do his homework

384

in his room and not in the kitchen where everybody came in and out. Homework was not now the chore that had much taxed him. He would force himself to sit alone and do it and lock himself in. In the room. He did not have the remotest idea why this action would help but he did it.

Testing himself was good. Not just in straight competition like swimming but seeing if he dared go out of the bathroom window and climb up the steep pitch of roof under which the spirit of the blackamoor boy might still be enraged. Get to the peak. Then sling himself over, let himself slide down the steep pitch, which ended in a long drop on to the concrete front of the pub, see how his nerve held, feel the terror, feel welcome sweat to the palms, begin an insect-like back sprawl upwards, his throat choking.

Testing himself. In the Scouts. In school. Though he had blankings and an overgrasping nervousness that could misfire, he wanted the tests, the tests made his head feel occupied. At the church youth club, to debate harder, dance better, show off more; in rugby to rush with the scrum, disguising the fear of tackling under the puff of effort; how long it took him to do this, go that distance, tests. Save for the choir when testing was pointless, but what reward for that pointlessness! A calm in the mind that made him feel safe, normal, in touch with the heart of whatever he was. Something of the same in reading, particularly when the book's characters took him into their skins, the story of the book became his story, he twinned with these invented people whose paths were certain sure compared with the amoeba and sludge of his own.

Envy sprouted everywhere. Everyone he liked had more that he liked than he had. And none of the fears he had. How could they be so certain of everything? He tried to drive the gang to feats of cohesion difficult for a mixed bunch of half a dozen boys not even in the same class, different tastes, talents, but they had to be together so that he could feel the solidity. Jealousies came from that, all signs of independence were proofs of betrayal, it was hopeless and endless, above all, it was endless.

Somewhere inside, to meet this perpetual threat that scooped him out, stripped the skin from inside his head, took his soul from him, abducted all but the thing of body, he had to build a redoubt. His father had told him about the redoubt, the final place. Where you had to fight until you dropped but also where you could build to win. He was seeking to build that, or a shell, but inside himself not outside. A shell to seal in that which left him, a place almost independent of his body as the inner flask of a vacuum. Blindly he stumbled towards that.

There was a terrible violence in his head. When he heard the preliminary murmurings of disruption from downstairs, he wanted to take a sword and slice them open from head to belly, those who threatened. At the boxing matches in Carlisle he liked the blows to land and growled and yelled in the crowd as deep in it as any, losing his singleness as in the choir but finding blood not peace. His feelings even for the gang could be savage, and he held on as if an unbroken horse were trying to buck him and sometimes he could not hold on and the anger uncoiled would be disproportionate, silencing, puzzling to others and leaving Joe himself dazed.

All he really knew was that he had to keep it secret, not a hint, not a sign to anyone at any time no matter what, he had to conceal the shame. And all he also knew was that he could not give in. He was beaten, he could see that when, for all his tactics, he was still prey, still defeated; but somehow being beaten had to be got through.

In this long time, when the wait of a day for the night's battle could seem like a month and despite all the furies on the surface the depths seemed not to stir but hold a sullen grip on him, there were times of escape, vivid release, a bare intensity of seeing whether a wood or a sky, a candle in the church, stones clear on a river-bed or the face of a girl in the street, to be haunted by him, however hopelessly, it was a mercy.

But he deserved no mercy, because he lied. He lied about himself and what he did in any and every way to protect the secret of what he feared. His contempt for his courage grew as the months went by. You were not frightened of such insubstantial things. You were not yellow-bellied in front of what could not even be talked about for fear of laughter. But the attacks continued and the chasm in his life was covered over as best he could with a desperation of energy that could see a whole day's reparation ripped away in moments as what was him left the body, left it petrified, vanishing into the infinite blackness for eternity unless he could be forgiven.

PART FOUR
A FIGHTING
RETREAT: 1954

CHAPTER THIRTY-SIX

There were solitary times in the bar, especially through the week, in the midday just after opening time. Sam looked forward to them.

He liked to lean on the bar, light up, gaze through the window though registering little of the little he saw and drift, no more than that. It was a luxury. Shelves stocked, bottles carried up and wiped, pumps cleaned, long mahogany bar surface and pump handles polished, glasses shining, in autumn and winter a fire. And on his own. Ellen upstairs, cleaning and clearing there as she had done in the pub, she too glad to be alone, working at her own pace, trying to force the flat into a home.

Perhaps it was an indulgence, adolescent daydreaming he had never had time for as an adolescent. He imagined he could feel his mind soften, become as cloudy and wandering as the smoke from the solid little white cigarette.

It was remembering. Moments of peace and even happiness in Burma. Ellen's face when she opened the door to meet him on his return. Joe's smile of stricken gratitude when they had gone to *Snow White* and the boy had mouthed all the songs, caught sight of his father's smile and smiled back that branding smile. Good memories. The final sing-song on a Saturday night, a run of luck at Carlisle Races,

Alex and a cigarette under a calm starry sky in the east. Memories now allowed time to breathe, to give his life credit.

Incidents became moments to be thumbed through, stopping places in an album of a life first memorialised in the slum of Vinegar Hill, wrenched into war, shocked, appalled, riven in Burma, immured once more in the town. But now, his own man, feeling as free and as leisurely as any man in the kingdom these solitary late mornings, cigarette smoke the laurel wreath, these were good times, a settlement made.

As if at last his past could be easy on him; as if at last clearances could be made; as if at last there was an antidote to the unacknowledged nightmares with which his sleep had battled for years; as if peace had finally come.

Sam did not feel the guilt of selfishness. He did not feel embarrassed thinking himself over-fortunate. This often brief solitary state was sufficient to itself.

Out there, he knew, Joe was avoiding him. Almost as tall now, inward, hard to tease out, best left alone, Sam judged, until it was time to talk over which job he would go for. Out there, the deepening strain of Colin and what to do and how much Ellen could accept. Ellen herself he could see trying to plait together the three men, loyalties confused, fears compounded and the only way he could help was to cut through. But that would be too painful for her, he could see the pain in her eyes at the very thought of it. Out there his own confident ambition now the brewery wanted him to move on to a bigger town, a bigger pub, there was a ladder, they said, he could go all the way.

But by some miracle of detachment or facility for compartmentalisation the darker picture was not allowed to threaten the sweetness of these passages of solitude. He was in desired isolation, untouched selfness until the first customer came in and he took the empty glass and pulled the first pint of the day.

—◊—

'Why can't he get a real job? Everybody else does.'

Grace looked away afraid, not of the question, but of the urgent pleading behind it. Ellen's anxiety was disturbing. Still looking away, Grace replied, 'What brought this on?'

Ellen would not answer directly. Grace, at bay, found the question shamed her. Her own anxiety was too acute to be disturbed.

'He's behaving – not himself.'

Grace would not help her out. Although the doctor had declared her free of the stroke she still acted as though she suffered from it. And though still commanding in her presence and appearance, there was a hesitation that could provoke an unhistorical sympathy towards her.

'He seems to have lost himself, the last year or so, since Sadie.'

If the lips of Grace could clamp even more tightly, they did. The affair of Colin and Sadie had distressed her – everything about it, the exposure to tittle-tattle, the commonness of the connection, the legitimate foothold Sadie had taken it to give her in uninvited entrances to her house, Colin's stupidity.

'They were just friends,' Ellen said, 'dancing partners.'

'Joe tells me he loved Butlin's. "I loved it, Aunty Grace," he said.'

'Because you pay up front he thinks it's all free. Swimming, roller-skating, the dances, all the games they make them join in, ping-pong. It's paradise for Joe.'

'It doesn't sound much of a holiday for you.'

'You always meet up with some nice people. There's plenty laid on.'

Grace sensed the conversation was about to return to Colin. 'I'm still sorry about that piano.' She nodded to the lidded instrument, dead many months.

'You can't force it.'

'You can,' Grace said. 'Sometimes you have to. Being too soft never helped anybody.'

'You think I've been too soft on Colin.'

'I think you worry yourself about him too much and he takes advantage.'

'He wouldn't if I didn't worry?'

'I don't know, Ellen.'

The use of her name revealed to Ellen how serious a matter this was for Grace. The older woman was looking directly at her now, a look that managed to give and ask for sympathy.

'Sam can hardly bring himself to talk to him. I can see that. And even Joe seems to pull back. It hurts Colin. But Joe . . .'

Ellen evaded her own line of thought. There was a gap grown between herself and her son, which had begun she knew not when or why and stayed unresponsive to any attempt she made at closing it.

'Joe keeps himself busy,' Grace said approvingly, with relief. 'Always on the go.'

'Uncle Leonard doesn't much care for Colin either, does he?' said Ellen desperately.

'You'll have to ask you uncle Leonard about that.'

'I must go round and see Sadie,' Ellen said, not realising, consciously, that this was a slap in the face. Grace once more turned away.

She paused briefly outside the house. The sun sweltered the little town in unaccustomed high heat that even blistered the roads. Ellen stared at the steep pitch of the roof of the Blackamoor. The tiles shimmered. A week before she had been coming across Market Hill and seen Joe, flat on his back, lying on top of the roof and, she would have sworn, slipping down towards the edge and a dead drop on to concrete. The pain in her chest had come like a blow. No one but her was around. Then she had started to run. The pain hurt too much. Stopped. It was true: he was sliding towards the edge. She had heard herself shout, the single syllable of the name, shouted out, and later Joe said that he had indeed been slipping, that he did not know why he had gone on to the front roof anyway, but his hands had started sweating, and he had padded his way back, up to the ledge, levered himself and then down the other side where there was the next-door supporting wall and the roof of the lavatories and a ledge for safety.

—∭—

'Megaton,' Mr Kneale read. 'Megadeath. Fall Out.'

'You'll frighten them all to death,' said Leonard.

'NATO,' he continued unrepentantly, 'Countdown, Deterrent, Thermonuclear. I just need three more to make the set. They all relate to nuclear warfare, you see.'

'I'm not sure Wigton's quite ready for nuclear warfare.' Leonard tapped the ash off his cigarette.

'They might have to be,' said Mr Kneale grimly. 'These quizzes are a very useful way to get it across to people, Leonard.'

'If you want war, I rather think military equipment that they know about would stand a better chance.'

'I've no doubt.'

'No good having a dud round. Nobody enjoys that.'

'It's because they're less familiar. You don't have to remind me of the past of these men. That list of Wigton men decorated for bravery in the Great War is quite remarkable, Leonard, and – though keep this to yourself, I don't want it out until I publish – the Prince of Wales himself commented on it. When he went up near the Front. He shook hands with a number of Wigton men.'

'I had heard he went to see some of the lads.' Leonard did not always like being tutored by Mr Kneale in the history of his own town.

'We could throw in A-bomb and H-bomb to start with. An easy warm-up.'

Leonard's expression did not flicker. 'That would make nine.' He glanced at his watch.

'I'll give you number ten.' Leonard waited until Mr Kneale's copperplate had filled in questions eight and nine. 'Who'll sort it out?'

'Not a question with any one answer.'

'It should have.'

'That's as maybe.'

'The Old Man would sort it out if they let him.'

'The tide of time has moved on, Leonard. It waits for no man.'

'This country's treatment of Churchill has been a total disgrace. It's been shameful!'

'I fear he is not the power he was.'

'There's nobody else. There's nobody,' Leonard swept out his right arm in an uncharacteristic theatrical gesture, 'with Churchill's command of the situation.'

'Summit meeting,' Mr Kneale said. 'That's another easier one to make up the mix.'

He wrote it down and looked carefully over his work.

'Local history?'

'All present and correct,' said Leonard, tapping the writing-pad in front of him. 'It's surprising how much some of them know. Not so much the history, but the local.'

'The Big Historical Thinkers,' Mr Kneale said, 'Big Minds. I confess I haven't read every word by any means but you can tell a Big Mind – Oswald Spengler, Arnold Toynbee – the problem is they had no knowledge of the atom bomb and the hydrogen bomb. They saw history in phases of rising and falling. I doubt if they ever thought in terms of a full stop.'

'The only thing I'd be inclined to hold against Churchill,' said Leonard, claiming his turn, 'and I'll lay long odds it's more down to his advisers, is that he didn't root out socialism. I would have liked to see him do that.'

'It can never be done,' said Mr Kneale, at his most dogmatic, Leonard thought, and rather pompous with it. 'This is the age of socialism the world over. We will either destroy mankind with the bombs or we'll all become socialists.'

'Photo-finish,' said Leonard.

'Socialism is inevitable. It is the only system of the future.'

'There isn't a horse born can't be beat,' said Leonard.

'These are deep movements in history, Leonard. We may regret them. We cannot fight them.'

'Deep movements can change just like anything else. The tide comes in. The tide goes out . . .'

'This is the time of the Common Man. The world over, Leonard. Nothing is as strong as an idea whose time has come.'

'Save for the next idea.'

They stopped rather reluctantly when Sam arrived.

The lists of questions were examined with the usual care. The new young girl brought them tea and biscuits. The general conversation was much as usual. The men had grown quite close over the quiz.

But there was a feeling of heaviness, even of sadness, and when Sam left, Mr Kneale said, thinking of Joe, 'I fear Sam is a man with a lot on his mind.'

'A man with worries,' Leonard agreed, thinking of Colin.

—⟨⟩—

They were in the pub kitchen. Sam had built up the fire although it was late. He wanted to finish his book. He held it up so that Ellen, as she had requested, could see the title. *Cannery Row* by John Steinbeck.

'Joe thinks the characters here – bums we would call them, laddos, the dregs some would say – are dead ringers for Diddler and Kettler and the others. He can be quite funny about it. He says John Steinbeck must have passed through Wigton at one time or another.'

'He likes reading.' The approving tone in which this evident truth was fondly delivered jarred with Sam. Reading was his territory. 'Better than boxing anyway,' Ellen continued, glancing up from *Woman's Illustrated*, smiling.

'He likes both!'

'He's more of a swimmer than a boxer,' Ellen said.

'And you taught him to swim, I suppose.'

'Just at the start.' Ellen was puzzled. 'What's wrong with that?'

'Nothing.' And of course there was nothing, he told himself, nothing at all, nothing of the least consequence, and yet he was jarred.

'We talk quite a bit about the books he reads,' he said, lungeing in the dark. 'Don Camillo, we follow him; Eric Linklater; John Gals-worthy: he's getting hard to keep up with. We talk about them.' He stopped there, aware that in truth these encounters were far fewer than he desired.

'His eyes can look sore.'

'He handed me *Sons and Lovers* last week.'

'What's that about?'

'A soft boy who can't leave his mam. When I said something of the sort to Joe he just walked away.' Sam laughed.

But he had felt obscurely put down, his view so rejected.

'It was good of Leonard to say he can find him an opening, wasn't it?' Ellen had returned to this more than once, nursing the feeling of security for Joe, and the satisfying prospect of comfortable clerking work in Leonard's office. Suit and tie.

'Better than a garage?' Sam smiled. One of his regulars who owned a small garage had given Joe a few weeks' work in the summer holidays. Joe's hands had been blistered after day one – they had set him to loosen a huge rusted nut off a tractor. The man liked to joke that Joe was a natural and there was an opening for him the moment he left school.

'Not better,' Ellen emphasised. 'Not better.'

The sense of happy relief, completion, sighed off her. Sam could even glimpse the faintest gleam of victory.

'He's too much on his own,' he said, abruptly.

'He's always out doing something or with that gang.'

'I mean in himself.'

'I don't know what that means.'

Sam shrugged and tried to get into the book. But it was his second reading and there was not the hold, not compared with this contest he wanted to pursue.

'Jack Ack said he would teach him the accordion,' said Ellen.

'When did he say that?'

'Last Saturday. I've been saving it up to tell you. He said with Joe's training under Miss Snaith he would pick it up in a few weeks and then he could play in a band.'

'Why should he play in a band?'

'He would enjoy it.'

'How do you know that?'

'I hate to see all Miss Snaith's teaching wasted.'

'Have you asked him if he wants to learn the accordion?'

'Not yet.'

'Well, don't push it on him.'

'That's not very helpful.'

'He was miserable enough doing the piano at the last.'

'If he'd had a bit more encouragement.'

'From me, you mean?'

'From you,' said Ellen, steeling herself to calm as she finally accepted that Sam was battling with his temper. 'He respects you.'

'I always gave him something when he won a certificate.'

'You did.'

'But that wasn't enough.'

'You did what you could.'

'It wasn't enough, though, was it?'

'He would probably have stopped anyway. Miss Snaith said that boys often do at that age. But,' Ellen could not check herself, 'she said she was particularly sorry about Joe and she wondered if all of us had given him enough encouragement. Including herself, she said.'

'He made his own mind up.'

'He did.' Suddenly Ellen's tone was sad. 'What's the matter, Sam?'

To tell her he would have to know himself much better.

'You seem to want to get at me tonight.'

He shook his head denying the truth of it without words.

'I never wanted to lassify him as you said once. I wanted him to have one or two things I didn't have, that's all. I didn't want to push

400

him either. It would take or it wouldn't. But I wanted him to see something else, Sam.' It was declared like a plea. 'That we didn't have. Just to see something else, that's all. There's nothing wrong with that, is there?'

She looked as vulnerable as he had ever seen her. The white face seemed to tremble, the red lips held steady just, the loosened black hair made her face smaller, as if offering it protection. His anger evaporated. He shut the book. 'No,' he said. 'There's nothing wrong with that, Ellen. Nothing at all.'

He felt so keenly in love with her, like long ago, rarer now.

The blues hit the nape of his neck. Whenever Joe heard that sound, that alley sound, swamp sound, sound on the rocks, he felt he had come up for air. And he held the songs in his mind, mimicked the singers, dug southern American black out of his northern English throat, let himself be submerged, so that he could rise again reborn. They told him something nothing else could and in their bleakness he found hope. Big Bill Broonzy, Leadbelly, Memphis Slim, Billie Holiday, there could never be enough; there never was. He collected what he could, every drop, water in a drought. Best luck of all, to find a run of them on the wireless and listen in the night.

That night he and Alan had biked out the three miles to a village social. There had been a girl there, in the year below at school. Joe had never noticed her. She had black hair, perceptible breasts, peach and white skin, a strong nose, dark troubling brown eyes, a challenging grin. She wore a front-buttoned floral dress. When he asked her to dance she said, 'I'm not much good,' and she was not, but it helped because they talked while he spelled out the steps that had been spelled out to him. Alan had also danced with her. Then Joe again. Then Alan. In the interval when they had lemonade and cake Alan said he would rather not share her so they spun. Joe won. He got the last dance at half past nine, and managed to hold her hand while they sang 'God Save the Queen'.

So in bed that night as well as the music there was the smell and re-created sight and feel of the girl, which seemed to feed directly the inner redoubt which he kept from everyone, even the terror, even the thing that was attacking him. The memory of her and the branching and fantasy in that memory, promises to see again, strengthened the redoubt. He felt he would be safe that night.

When the blues stopped, he leaned down in the dark and turned the tuning of the low murmuring wireless to find more music. Although in the choir he sang anthems and plainsong, and at the piano he had played classical music, he would usually hurry past the classical station – an inheritance that was not for him. But this time a few notes held him. He stayed. It was the last sonata he had attempted to play, so stiltedly, Miss Snaith so disappointed. Here, though, fingers of a magician flowed across the keyboard and Beethoven rose up from this flow like nothing on earth and, with the girl in his thoughts, the music instantly seized his mind, his body. It was his bloodstream, like the blues, he was the sound of it, the smell of her, the impact of freedom in those moments, a time of freewheeling, happy, soaring outside himself but without fear.

CHAPTER THIRTY-SEVEN

Sam laid on a bus for the Dalston point-to-point – an evening meeting. He invited Joe along.

As Sam saw people off the bus he asked Colin if he could give him two ten-shilling notes for a pound. When he had looked at the race-card he handed a very surprised Joe one of the brown well-worn ten shilling notes. 'I've marked your card,' he said. 'Six races. Put sixpence each way or a straight bob win as you fancy. Spend five bob.'

'That means I can only bet on five.'

'You can bet on the sixth if you make something from the first five.'

'Why give me ten bob then?'

'You need a reserve. You bring the other five bob back.'

'What if I just keep the five bob and don't bet?'

'That's a wasted opportunity.'

'What if I win a lot to start with and decide to stop and give you the five bob back but don't bet on all the races?'

'Then you're a better man that I am, Gunga Din.'

They went separate ways.

It sluiced down. Stair rods. At times the riders could scarcely be seen for the sheets of rain. People huddled under the big umbrellas of the bookmakers. The refreshment marquee was steaming. Joe won three and sixpence.

'And you?'

'Lost on the night,' Sam admitted, in the bus home.

'Why didn't you bet on what you told me to bet on?'

'Second thoughts.' He smiled. 'As long as one of us is winning we can't complain.'

He took the shovelled change from Joe's ten bob and thrust it in his pocket without counting it, which Joe noted and appreciated.

Colin tried to get a sing-song going with 'Secret Love' but nobody was keen. He tried again with the new Johnny Ray but people were wet through and in no mood for it even though, as Colin loudly pointed out, 'Such A Night' could be thought 'a good signature tune for the job'. Finally he concentrated on his hair, recently restyled in the DA cut – 'Duck's Anatomy,' he announced to everyone, with a fat wink. Joe noticed that his dad would not respond to any of Colin's overtures on the bus.

He was surprised then when Sam beckoned Colin as they left the bus and walked up towards his aunty Grace's house with him. Sam indicated that Joe should go across to the pub as several others were doing, scurrying through the persisting rain, dark figures in the fast deepening night. 'Help out,' Sam said to Joe, 'I'll only be a few minutes.'

There was an archway next to Grace's house. It was black, a tunnel into the gloom of a yard. The yellow dab of street-light from Market Hill offered only weak illumination.

'This'll do.'

Sam stopped just inside the archway. Colin stood with his back to the wall, Sam on the cobbled way within sight of the steps up which he had bounded so expectantly after the war was over.

'What we stopped here for?'

'A talk.'

'I'm wet. I want to go in.'

'It won't take long. Fag?'

Colin took one. Sam lit him up. He took time to light his own, looking all the while at Colin's half-shadowed face, seeing again the eyes that were Ellen's, the slope of the face: seeing more, though, a man now petulantly alert, a face welded to expressions foreign to his half-sister.

'I've taken to marking the ten-bob notes,' Sam said, after a deep draw.

Colin's silence was adamant.

'One of those you gave me tonight was marked. Proves it was nicked today.'

'I had too much change. I wanted to turn it into a note.'

'Who did that for you?'

'I'm not telling.' Colin's tone was virtuous. 'I wouldn't tell you that, Sam.'

Sam took another deep suck on the fag and scratched the back of his head. He had made a resolution to keep his temper. He took his time.

'You're a liar,' he said.

'Nobody calls me a liar.'

'You're a liar.'

Colin stepped forward, feeling impelled to follow through though there was a tremulous undertow to the aggressive gesture. Sam grabbed his shoulder with his left hand and pushed him against the wall. 'I wouldn't try, Colin. I wouldn't even think about it.'

The older man held him hard, gripping the shoulder, battening him against the wall and Colin heard a vibration of the deep fury, caught the killing anger in the eyes, and slumped. 'I'm sorry, Sam. I'll pay you back. I'm sorry, Sam.'

Whether the sobs were real or feigned, Sam could not tell. Reluctantly he let him go. 'You said that last time. And the time before that. And before that.'

'This time I mean it.'

'You're out, Colin.'

'One more chance.' The sobs grew heavier, seeming real. 'Everybody should have one more chance.'

'You've used them up.'

'What'll you tell Ellen?'

The question fired Sam's anger even more strongly so that he stepped back. 'I'll tell her. I'll tell her you're a thief and I'm not having you in that pub one day longer.'

'She won't have it.' The sobbing stopped. Colin's jaw jutted forward. He knew that a crucial point had been made.

'Don't you mention Ellen.' Sam held himself back.

'She's my sister. She won't let me be thrown out. Ellen won't have it. You'll see.'

Sam's hand shot out and this time found the throat and banged Colin hard against the wall. Colin gurgled in terror. Sam slackened his grip. 'You.' Sam shook his head. 'You've used her for years, you've just traded on her good nature.'

'I can't breathe!'

'You've hidden behind her skirts. I would have sorted you out years ago but for her. I stood back because you're such a kid half the time, but you've plagued my bloody life day in day out. You've confused that boy.'

'Me and Joe's pals.' Colin's voice was strangulated but he would be justified.

'You've led him a dance.' Sam's grip tightened as bitter memories

406

exploded in his mind. 'You've taken advantage of the both of them.' He banged Colin's head against the wall. 'You'll leave him alone. Hear that? Leave him alone and stop the bloody stupid promises and lies and all the rest, or by Christ, Colin, I'll do you harm.'

He let go. Colin's hand replaced his. He stroked his throat and made much of gasping. Finally, he said, 'You needn't have done that.'

'I've thought about the budgies,' Sam said. 'You can have the key to the back-yard door and get into the stables that way. But, Colin, you're barred the pub, at any time and there'll be no let-up. Understand? I hope you do. For your own sake. Give me that ten bob.'

Colin handed it over.

Sam went out of the arch, into the rain, walked, almost marched, across to the Blackamoor.

Colin spat and spat again on the ground, then walked slowly up the street ignoring the weather, seeking a friendly bar, still stroking his throat.

Sam told Ellen that night and he had never seen her so upset. He did not know she could be so shaken. But though she pleaded he would not change his mind and though he felt ripped in two when she left him to walk so heavily, so afflictedly, up the stairs, he would not give in. He was wounded. Had she ever been as distraught over him?

'Was he?'

Grace was held by Ellen's agonised eyes.

'Was he?'

The old lady lifted an arm, as if to ward off this attack.

'Was my dad a thief?'

Ellen had scarcely slept. She had come to the house the moment she knew she was most likely to catch Grace alone. There had been no preliminaries, no making of tea, nor any hesitation.

'Is that why he left Wigton?'

Grace could see the agony and was shaken by it.

'Was my dad a thief?' Like Colin. She did not add. She had not revealed what Sam had told her but Grace knew. Like Colin.

'I just want to know. Don't you see? Why he left Mam and me.'

Ellen held back the tears with difficulty. She was aware that her voice had been loud. She lowered it almost to a whisper. 'I just want to know.'

Grace nodded. The tip of her tongue wetted her lips.

'You have to tell me the truth, Aunty Grace. You have to.'

'I will.'

Ellen let out a big sigh of breath. 'At least I'll know the truth.'

She straightened her shoulders a little, sat up, waited, polite, Grace thought, biddable, as she always had been. But now it was she, the girl, who was giving the orders.

'He wasn't a strong man,' Grace said, speaking steadily, aware of the force of her own emotions, 'but he was never a bad man. He was one of those who needed a bit more help maybe than people could afford to give. Leonard was good with him.'

She stopped. Memories began to crowd out her words. Then she collected herself. 'He wasn't what you would call a thief,' she said. 'Not exactly, not in any real sense of that horrible word. So you can be reassured, Ellen.' Her own words gave her confidence. 'He was not a thief,' she asserted.

'So why did he go? Why did he leave us?' Ellen forced herself to patience. Whatever was said now, she thought, whatever it was would be a resolution, would be some sort of answer, would slay the furies that had been released by what Sam had told her about Colin. It scarcely mattered what it was, she told herself, as long as she knew, as long as she could rest on knowing why her father had gone and without her and before she knew him at all.

'Why did he go?' It was a gentle repetition and perhaps it was that which brought silent sobless tears to Grace's eyes, tears which Ellen had never seen, never.

The old lady once more lifted her arm but this time it was to deny all further talk. 'I can't tell you, Ellen. But he was never a bad man. Your dad would have been good to you. He should never have gone, Ellen. But he did.' She made one further effort. 'He thought he had to go, you see. And who knows?'

'I'm going for a walk,' Ellen said, later that afternoon, and was gone before Sam could question her.

She went across the road, past the old jail and Tenters, the short way to the baths, the way still taken by Joe only when he felt the need to test himself. She had thought to take the lonnings through the fields to Kirkland and then on to the small roads that threaded to the old village of Rosewain, but at the last minute she decided to stick closer to the town and went up the hill that had witnessed so many fearful descents by her son, down past the swimming baths, up Stoney Bank towards the Kissing Gate into the Lowmoor Road. Why had he gone?

The wind had subsided but not disappeared. There was drizzle and the low dark clouds were full of storm. Her headscarf was soon soaked, her coat pasted with rain, the unsuitable shoes damped through.

Ellen was scarcely if at all aware that this journey had any purpose. After meeting Grace and finishing her work she had felt a terrible desire to get out, just go, without an admissible reason. It was a flight.

Plunged into a depression by what Grace had told her, the chatter of her past murmured around her through the lanes. Images of herself in the baths, flicking from tentative childhood through her adolescent passion for swimming, the games with Sam and the others, teaching Joe, pram-walks on Lowmoor Road, the bike rides to Forester Falls, berry-picking, hazel-nut culling, trying to stop the boys pinching birds' eggs.

She went up Crozier's field where the bullocks could be worrying and then Highmoor, the Big House, the high bell-tower that over-looked her getting up and her lying down, the clear reminders of the famous deer park, the marches up there with the Guides and the teas and on to the Syke Road where you could branch off to Old Carlisle and the Roman camp, taken there for school trips, walking up in their neat crocodile, on to the Longthwaite Road and into the Show Fields. Why had he left them?

By now she was clammy soaked. None of her clothing could fight off the slashes of rain that alternated with the drizzle. But the wetness was a curious comfort, reminding her of herself as she near sleep-walked through these so familiar fields of walking and courting, of Sam fishing, of Joe sledging, of the games and the circus, the wending sandbanked charm of the river Wiza, which defined all rivers, the place drenching her like the rain.

She thought she might even go across towards the park and see Ruth to whom she could say as much as to anyone, but this uncommon need to walk alone around the town was too strong and she turned west beyond Greenacres, scarcely daring to look at her old house lit so seductively, and into the narrow lane, getting dark now, which rolled out past a couple of farms and led to the cemetery before which she paused.

Where was her father buried? Colin had evaded that in the way he had, not to answer certain questions so that she would have to keep asking them. That was one of the ways he held on, she knew that, she let him do that. But it would be something, wouldn't it? To be able to go to his grave at least?

She went into the cemetery, past the huge war memorial on which the name Richardson was written in gold leaf several times, up and down the neat gravel pathways between the headstones, mostly simple, only a few at all grand. There was light enough for her to make her way and the sound of her wet soles on the ground was a companion. She would get it out of Colin somehow. But Colin had to be looked after.

She did not want to think about Colin now.

Down Station Hill alongside the cliff of wall that held up the railway line and under the bridge towards the factory. If only Sam had stayed there. Lit up, pounding, even at this time of night, a bright spot in the drizzling northern twilight, almost cheerful under such a severe sky.

And now she pushed up into the town, the lanes, the yards, the clothing factory in which she had worked, every place, so much, every corner, she could reach out, remember and be remembered; soaking into her was this bounded town which had fostered her, and a weary equilibrium, a decision, had been reached by the time she went into the pub and managed some sort of smile in response to Sam's worried look.

She would find out where he was buried and go there.

—⚒—

Colin managed to ambush him. He had waited at the end of the low road from the baths. Joe swerved and unsaddled himself in rather an embarrassed manner, Colin observed, which gave him, he thought, the upper hand.

'You've been avoiding me,' he said.

'I haven't.' Joe's denial was stout but clearly false. He had not been told why there had been the rift between his father and Colin but he had been told it was serious and that Colin would no longer be coming to the pub.

'I can see through you.' Colin grinned and sleeked back his hair. 'I have X-ray eyes when it comes to you.'

He had come quite close to Joe and the boy drew back.

'What's the matter?'

'Nothing.'

'Your dad been saying things behind my back?'

'No.'

'Sometimes men have differences of opinion,' Colin said, staring and as he imagined hypnotising – his new passion – the boy, making absolutely certain that his hunch was right and Ellen would not have allowed Sam to mention the stealing. 'Me and your dad didn't see eye to eye. He'll come round in time.'

'Yes.' Joe wanted to get away.

'But,' Colin was suddenly fierce, 'if he says anything against me to you, to my pal you, and I get to hear, then it'll be this.' He jutted forward his clenched right fist. 'Relation or not relation! That's who I am.'

'Right.' The boy was disturbed by the widening-eyed intensity of Colin's stare. 'I'll tell him.'

'No,' said Colin. 'This is you and me. Just you' – he pointed – 'and me.'

'OK.'

'Silence! Omerta! Between pals.'

Joe nodded.

'Swear. You'll say nothing.'

Joe found he was reluctant. But he wanted to go. 'I swear.'

'Now spit.'

How could he spit with a dry throat? And it was kid's stuff. But Colin could still intimidate him.

'Spit!'

Colin came even nearer. Joe sucked hard for saliva and managed a feeble spray of spit, the only discernible bit of which found Colin's shoe.

'Good,' said Colin. 'So we'll keep the lines open.'

'Yes.'

Joe was released now. The stare was turned off. He put his left foot on the pedal, scooted for a while and then swung himself on to the bike.

'Joe!'

He turned.

'Omerta! Between pals.'

Colin waved.

—◊◊◊—

'They've revamped the churchyard very nicely in my view,' Leonard said, 'and there's a couple of seats against the wall that catches the sun about dinner-time. Let's meet up tomorrow – if it's a fine day – and have a bit of a chat there.'

There was sufficient sun.

'It was difficult to find the right place,' Leonard said. 'Our house would have been wrong for the job. So would the Blackamoor. I couldn't walk into any other pub with you – they would make too much of a fuss of you. This isn't too bad. We can be discreet.'

They sat side by side on the wooden bench beside St Mary's, Leonard and Ellen, wholly familiar to anyone who might spot them, taking advantage of the air, looking over the vicar's newly levelled graveyard, headstones serving as paving stones, only the few ornate tombs left upright, lawn and flower borders dominating now, which ruined or remodelled the ancient cemetery – the town was divided.

'Grace told me about your conversation.' Leonard lit up after he had delivered the sentence, letting it sink in.

Ellen felt herself stretch into full attention. That he had said 'Grace' and not 'your aunty Grace' made the choice of this unusual location even more significant.

Leonard launched in. 'Let me say this. Grace has your best interests at heart. I'm sure you've never doubted that. And your father was her brother. They were very close. What happened upset her, for years. It still does. Which is to say that there are certain things she just can't bring herself to say. You can't think less of her for that.' He drew heavily on the cigarette. 'But when she told me about your conversation, I thought, She ought to know. I thought, If she doesn't know it'll work in her mind until it becomes something terrible, far far worse than it was. It'll fester. Anyway, I thought, it's long past. It's just part of the stream of life now.'

So she would be told. She sat very very still.

'There's a hundred and one ways to dress it up, Ellen, but to get to the point he walked out a week or two before you were born. Grace always wanted to say it was after because she thought that was nicer. It was before you were born.' He glanced at her and then quickly glanced away. No one was in sight but he dropped his voice.

'It was never a good match for either of them,' he said, 'one of those moments of madness that happens but then they were stuck with it. Except it worked itself into your father, it worked itself into him to such an extent that he could not bear to look at the poor woman – and she was bonny, nice, she was a very nice woman, your mother – but he just couldn't, well, I won't say he couldn't stand the sight of her, but that's how she must have taken it. He couldn't conceal it. Others do. And he couldn't live with it. Others have to. Whatever I said was listened to but made no odds. I was sorry for both of them. It was a terrible thing. He tried to be guided by Grace, he thought the world of Grace, but, poor fellow – and I did feel sorry for him even though what he did was a bad and a weak thing – he had a weak side, he knew that himself and he couldn't see it through. So he bolted.'

Ellen sucked her upper lip into her mouth and gripped it hard with her teeth and at the same time she nodded, again and again, only it was not only her head but slightly, stiffly even, her body, from the waist, nodding, rocking, easing the stab in her heart. There was a sound, too, a low hum, intermittent, but Leonard caught it and paused.

No one hailed them. No one passed. The sun warmed the worn sandstone church wall.

'He would send me the odd letter. He was too shamed to write to Grace save for the Christmas card. Then they dropped away. He knew he couldn't come back.'

'Could he not?' The words were squeezed out like a gasp.

'No,' said Leonard, as gently as he could. 'He'd burnt his boats.'

'I wish he'd come back,' Ellen whispered. 'I wish he had come back.'

Still she tried to take on the pain. Leonard dared not look at her.

'Well, Ellen. You've been a wonderful daughter to me and Grace. You have.'

'Have I?'

'We both say that.'

'Thank you.' The voice so low, now, the tone so formal.

She tried to straighten up but she could not, not yet, in a minute or so, did not want to embarrass him.

'But you see,' she said, and her voice broke completely, 'he was my father.'

CHAPTER THIRTY-EIGHT

Sam went up to Mr Kneale's quarters at six thirty as arranged. It was only the second time he had been in the comfortable set of rooms the schoolteacher had carved out of the top floor of Grace's house. The place had seemed very grand on the first visit, the widower had moved in fine furniture that had belonged to his wife and there were, everywhere, objects not seen in any other houses Sam knew. The most striking impression was that it was cluttered, pleasantly so, Sam thought, enviably so, the stacks of books and photographs, several cameras, the little tower of notes on the desk. The drink, well remembered, was the same.

'A little sherry?'

'Gladly.'

It was poured with care from a heavy decanter.

'Take a seat, Sam. Please.'

'Thank you.'

'Your very good health.' Mr Kneale.

'And to you.'

Sam quite enjoyed the sherry this time. 'Mind if I smoke?'

'I brought up an ashtray.'

'The photography still going strong then?'

'A good hobby is a friend for life,' said Mr Kneale. 'But I have to confess that this book runs it neck and neck.' He indicated the pile of notes. 'War gets you into everything.'

'I've come for some advice,' Sam said, not wanting war, stubbing the cigarette and waving away the last spiral of smoke.

'Well, I hope I can be of service.'

'It's about Joe.'

Mr Kneale was not wholly surprised. He waited.

'I suppose I'm looking for inside information.' Sam took his time. He had thought it through.

Mr Kneale nodded.

'If he was a horse I would be asking what his form was.' Sam smiled. Mr Kneale found a surer touch of real friendship in that smile than he had felt throughout his often rather wary relationship with the younger man. 'Or maybe looking for a tip.'

'I see,' said Mr Kneale.

'Leonard's found him an opening after this next year and it's very good of him. Ellen's over the moon. Joe seems quite happy. It's a job for life. Clean work.'

'Leonard says he'll take to it.'

'Did he? He should know.' Sam concentrated. What he wanted to say was that over the last months there had beat a stronger and firmer pulse in him about his son. He had begun to sense another possibility of connection.

'I always wanted to stay on at school, you know,' Sam said. He had not planned on saying that. He rushed on. 'Same as thousands. We had to leave. That was that. But when I had time on my hands in the war I thought about it. Quite a bit. Joe isn't placed like me. He could stay on, couldn't he?'

'There's provision,' said Mr Kneale. 'There is now the opportunity if the parents can afford it.'

Sam nodded.

'It's up to him, mind you,' Sam said. 'But it would help to know his form.'

'Well,' said the schoolteacher, 'I've never brought school into what's between us, but since you ask, he's been disappointing over the last year or two on the academic front after a promising start. He's never been altogether steady. I'm going on gossip from the junior staff who know I know him, and I expect they mean he's rather too lively, which can be a fault but only in the short term. Lately, though, it's been a different matter. The way I see it is it's been a bit like a loss of nerve. I expect you've noticed it yourself. Quite marked at times.'

Sam let nothing show.

'Having said all that, Mr Braddock thinks quite well of him in history. He's good at English, I'm told. All that reading – it always pays off. If he were to stay on into the sixth form he'd need another subject, preferably Latin, though French might do.'

'He likes maths.'

'You can't have that mix. It would have to be French or Latin. Geography at a pinch.'

'So?' Sam looked to Mr Kneale as judge and jury.

The older man took a little time, both to formulate his answer and to ensure it carried the weight Sam needed.

'If he could settle in himself, then, in my view, and I've thought the same since he was a little lad, he's certainly sixth-form material. I'd go no further at the moment but I would definitely advise you, if he could settle in himself, it would be no loss to keep him on. I'd go further. I'd say he's a fair bet, Sam. It's in him. If he was mine I'd encourage him.'

Sam felt a skin of tension slough off his mind. 'I'm grateful for that.'

'He might take a bit of persuading. As I understand almost all his friends are leaving next year after their exams. Friends are a critical influence.'

'I understand.'

'Another drop?'

He stood and took up the decanter.

'I will.' Sam looked the schoolteacher square in the eye. 'I am grateful for that,' he repeated. 'Thanks.' He lifted up his glass.

The sherry trickled carefully out of the elegant decanter.

Sam waited, as it turned out, for a few months. He studied Joe without, he was all but sure, the boy noticing the close observation.

He saw that the boy was nervy. Sometimes when they were carrying up the heavy crates of beer from the cellar he would snap in a sudden temper at some mistake and he could see the boy flinch. But he did not sulk. And he did not walk away.

As the autumn deepened, it seemed to Sam that Joe was digging in more at the schoolwork. Once or twice Ellen mentioned that he was pleased with himself for some mark or other. Sam did not ask directly. He could not start enquiring where previously he had been at worst indifferent, at best a respecter of the boy's independence.

It was difficult to get on terms with him. Talk about sport was good and easy as it always had been. Talk about books became more rare as the boy steamed increasingly into a self-contained world. Occasionally they would discuss politics and Sam enjoyed that most of all. But the boy would withdraw: Sam concluded harshly and sadly that his son did not feel easy spending much time alone with him, feared him or felt stifled.

A winter afternoon. Ellen had gone to Carlisle with Sadie, to the pictures. He wanted Ellen gone. They ate the tea she had left for them after Joe came back from school. He had done his homework at school that day, he said, not much of it, some maths and a bit of French. He was going to a birthday party in Bolton, a village three miles away. He did not say that the girl he had met at the social a few months ago had invited him. Her party. Her house. After exhaustive consideration he had bought her two nicely wrapped bars of soap and a bottle of bath salts in a box. It was in his saddle-bag. He was sure it was wrong.

Joe cleared away, washed up. When he came in from the back kitchen, his father had moved to his usual seat in the corner, reading the *News Chronicle*. Joe checked his watch against the clock. His father was proud of that clock, an ornate mahogany wall clock crested by a rearing horse. Diddler had come by it and the price was very reasonable. It was the only possession Joe could remember Sam being taken by.

Too soon to set off. She had told him her mother did not want them to be early.

'Let's have a talk.' Sam folded the paper and nodded to Joe to sit down on the other side of the table.

Joe did as he was told with that air of obedience which declared mild opposition. Sam repressed the smile. There was fight in him. It had been planted. It would be there when needed. To prove this point to himself he leaned forward, closer to his son, in what might have been interpreted as an aggressive way. Joe flinched, visibly, but his eyes held steady; Sam saw that and was pleased.

'This job you're bound for after you finish at school.'

Joe waited. It was the accepted future, wasn't it?

'Is it what you want to do?'

Again the boy was silent. It did not matter whether he wanted to

421

or not. It had been fixed up and his mother said he was very lucky to get it.

'Have you thought about doing anything else?'

'No.' He shook his head for emphasis and also to shake away all the fantasy careers and lives he called up from time to time.

'There'll be your National Service in about three years' time. That'll get you out of the town. That'll be a great experience. If it's experience you're looking for.'

Joe glanced at the clock.

Sam realised that he was the one doing the flinching now.

'You can stay on at school if you like, you know.'

'Everybody else is leaving. Except Malcolm. He's doing science. Everybody else.' Alan was going to work in his father's shop. They had already decided they would start saving up for a motorbike in week one.

'You don't have to do what everybody does.'

Joe did not respond.

In prospect, Sam had moulded and reshaped what he saw as this crucial conversation many times. It had never guttered out like this.

'I'm told you could be sixth-form material.'

'Who said that?'

'Mr Kneale.'

'He would.'

'Why?'

'He likes us.'

'He meant it.'

'I like Mr Kneale.'

'He could be right.'

Joe's nod this time, Sam thought, was indication of something stirring in him.

He was getting the hang of it, the work was drawing him in, helping him to blank out the rest, it was good to see his marks go up, catching up with people who had passed him years before, overtaking some of them, and the teachers were better with you now you were older, it wasn't like childish 'school'. The possibility was beginning to get through to him.

'I would have to do well in O levels.'

'That's right.'

'Would Uncle Leonard's job still be there if I didn't do well enough?'

'I expect so.'

Joe glanced at the clock yet again. It was almost time to go, he calculated, to be there on time, not early, she had emphasised, don't be early.

'How much did you think you were going to hold back for yourself after paying your mam for your keep?'

'Twelve and six of fifteen bob.' Joe's reply was immediate. He had discussed this many times with Alan.

'I'll give you fifteen bob.'

'A week?'

'Yes. You'll have to do more jobs.'

'What?'

Sam ticked them off. 'Sweep the front every morning. Chop kindling for the week on Sunday. Carry up on weekdays as well as weekends. Do the men's lavatories at weekends. Give your mam two hours off behind the bar on Sunday dinner-time. Other bits that come up. You can fit it in.'

'Fifteen bob?'

'Fifteen bob.'

Joe nodded, heavily. He was being made a fair offer. 'OK then,' he said, 'depending on the results. I've got to go now.'

He was out of the room, his bike ready in the corridor, through the ornate door, into the street, soon urgently pressing the pedals.

Sam took a minute or two and then checked the fires and went into the bar. He had a few minutes yet before opening time.

He leaned against the bar and thought of Joe on the bike cutting through the night, feeling and thinking little if anything, he guessed, of what had passed between them. That was how it was, he thought: that was fine.

Sam saw the boy go. Go where he could not follow. The boy was out there on his own now.

The man took out a cigarette. Tapped it on the counter. Lit up. Let drift.

He did not let his fear of the return spoil his time at the party but it was not easy. The prospect of it made him nervous and over-mad and now and then he saw disapproval. But it was a good party. The farmhouse sitting room had two doors, which was great for some of the games. She let him kiss her.

They all left together. Two or three were picked up by car. The others walked to their homes in the village.

Joe set off at speed. Once out of the village it was black. The thin beam from his front light was only a little comfort. He swung around the corner and down the first hill and then there was nothing, no dwelling, no light but his. I believe in God the Father Almighty, Maker of Heaven and Earth. He held the party in his mind for as long as he could. And of all things visible and invisible. He thought of what his father had said. When to tell Alan. Staying on. God help me to go faster, please. He had told her. He tried to remember kissing her and up the first hill, a long stretch now with a line of dense tall firs on his left, black on black, a cliff of trees and it was here, as before when he had come back in the dark from her, though he tried to hold, tried, tried to hold out, that the being of him was pulled off, ripped away, vanished, and he was just this thing, not even able to scream.

A tightening weight about his head. The bike scythed between the hedges as he flung it into top gear and stood on the pedals, lashing them on, he had to go through it, just to come through it, speeding, the left swerve past the water tower and up the long final hill, where his own breath was fear, it had been getting better, not now – he had to come through it. On the top of the hill he saw the yellow glow from the factory. A few score yards on, at the old hill point, known as Standing Stone, Wigton emerged into view, grew out of the earth, it seemed, and by the distant safety-net of its street-lights he saw that he was there, still there.

There was still the bedroom to face, and he would always be afraid, but he had come back to himself. He had got through. He was there. He freewheeled down into the town.

It was dark in the bedroom but through a slit in the curtains a slender shaft of moonlight picked out the shapes. She had been awake for some time now.

Sam was turned away from her, sleeping heavily, breathing deeply, not for some time the nightmares, now and then the light gravel of a snore.

Ellen had gone around the town, street by street, alley, lane and yard, even house by house, the reliable way to introduce the easy drowsiness which could tip her back into sleep but not tonight. She was too preoccupied.

She had found out where her father was buried. Colin had collapsed before her resolution and she had all the details. When she had been in Carlisle with Sadie she had gone to the information office at the bus station and copied down the connections. If she started early enough she could be there and back in a day, comfortably, and give herself good time at his grave. She would go the following Wednesday.

There was a feeling akin to excitement, an agitation, a desire to be under way. There would be a flower shop near the cemetery. She would borrow some shears. She would tell only Sam and he would keep it just between them.

One day she would take Joe.